Steve Martini, a former trial attorney, has worked as a journalist and capital correspondent in the California State House in Sacramento. He has been engaged in both public and private practice of law. He lives on the US West Coast with his wife and daughter. Steve Martini is the author of the best-selling thrillers *The Simeon Chamber*, *Compelling Evidence*, *Prime Witness*, *Undue Influence*, *The Judge*, *The List*, *Critical Mass*, *The Attorney*, *The Jury* and *The Arraignment*, also available from Headline.

Praise for Steve Martini's electrifying bestsellers:

'Sensationally good' *Los Angeles Times*

'An extremely well written courtroom drama. Madriani is a sprightly and ingenious sleuth . . . the story provides a lot of twists and is distinctly cheerful and engaging' *Scotsman*

'A legal thriller of above average quality, well written with good pace' *Bookseller*

'Positively exhilarating' *York Evening Press*

'The compelling plot builds to a conclusion that should surprise even longtime fans' *Publishers Weekly*

'A fine courtroom drama . . . with a believable plot, a sympathetic hero . . . and a little bit of downbeat humour stirred into the pot' *Irish News Belfast*

'A dazzling climax . . . Martini has written the court-room novel of the year' *Kirkus Reviews*

DOUBLE TAP

STEVE MARTINI

headline

First published in Great Britain in 2006
by HEADLINE BOOK PUBLISHING

First published in this paperback edition in 2006
by HEADLINE BOOK PUBLISHING

1

ISBN 0 7553 3128 1

Typeset in Century Schoolbook by Avon DataSet Ltd,
Bidford-on-Avon, Warwickshire

Printed and bound in Great Britain by
Mackays of Chatham plc, Chatham, Kent

Headline's policy is to use papers that are natural, renewable
and recyclable products and made from wood grown in
sustainable forests. The logging and manufacturing processes
are expected to conform to the environmental regulations of
the country of origin.

HEADLINE BOOK PUBLISHING
A division of Hodder Headline
338 Euston Road
London NW1 3BH

www.headline.co.uk
www.hodderheadline.com

In Memory of Evo

ACKNOWLEDGMENTS

I am indebted to all at G. P. Putnam's Sons for their patience in waiting for this book and in particular to David Highfill for his kindness, the keen insights of his editor's eye, and his encouragement. To Esther Newberg, my agent at ICM, and my New York lawyer, Mike Rudell, I owe thanks for their encouragement, for being my eyes and ears in a distant city, and for their sage advice in times of difficulty. To my wife, Leah, and my daughter, Meg, I owe everything, for without them I would never have put pen to paper. I apologize to them for the endless hours I spent huddled over the keyboard when they deserved more. To their love and loyalty, their endless hours of listening, I owe this story of family devotion. To Marianne Dargitz, who read the early drafts of this manuscript and lent me her encouragement, I am indebted. To David Calof, who helped me navigate the troubled waters that made writing this story so difficult and who revealed hope when all looked bleak, I am thankful. And finally, last but never least, to a God whose presence was palpable during long, dark days of doubt, when seemingly all that was left was the promise of prayer, I owe my existence, the creative energy that is in me, and every word that has ever flowed through me.

SPM
March 2005

This is the generation of that great LEVIATHAN ... to which we owe ... our peace and defence. For by this authority, given him by every particular man in the Commonwealth, he hath the use of so much power and strength conferred on him, that by terror thereof, he is enabled to form the wills of them all, to peace at home, and mutual aid against their enemies abroad.

THOMAS HOBBES, *LEVIATHAN* (1651)

l the click of hard heels on concrete
him. Out of the corner of one eye
n old gent in white boating slacks
zer. He thought he saw a straw hat
g cane, but he couldn't be sure.
s was ambling at a good clip along
wenty feet away and slightly above

the canvas jacket didn't turn or
of experience told him to avoid eye
n sensory perception is less likely
rthing in the brain's memory cells
see is inanimate. People who stay
st another motionless object, like a
sh out of bloom, something the
d fails to record. He'd done enough
veillance and walked into enough
aces to know this. Only another
vould notice anything about him,
it.

ionless figure, he stood facing the
back to the sidewalk until the sound
was well past. Then he took a quick
left and watched as the old man
p the street and finally disappeared
nd a curve.

leep breath, then let it out. If the
ed and asked for the time, or even if
ne down the steps and stopped for a
nce at him on his way to the beach,
been over. He couldn't take the
ald have had to leave, back to square
of careful planning down the drain.
sure how much time he had before
She was busy, a million projects at
might get distracted. Then again,

PROLOGUE

M ist off the ocean was already beginning to drift over the pavement as he cruised along the beach in the rented Chevy. The house stood out like a gem, the last piece of private real estate, before the public steps leading down to the beach. With chocolate-brown siding and white trim, the house sported rustic gables going in every direction beneath a river rock chimney.

He kept driving as he looked back in the mirror and caught a glimpse of the sandstone shelf behind the houses and the narrow beach now partially covered by the tide. White-frothed waves rolled up on the sand. In a few hours the incoming tide would devour what was left of the beach and waves would crash on the sandstone, sending spray onto the seawall that protected the estate's rear patio.

The neighborhood was dominated by modern upscale apartment buildings and small, stylish condos overlooking the Pacific. Ocean-front property was becoming far too valuable for private homes. The only single-family dwellings with ocean access appeared to be the two large homes at the end of the street just adjacent to the small public beach.

He was already familiar with the neighborhood, the daily routine, people walking their dogs, and surfers on the beach.

The house itself was larger than it looked. Set back from the street behind a set of double iron gates, the scale was made to appear diminutive by the use of small shingle siding and undersized dormered gables on the street façade. What looked like a story and a half in front became a full two stories on the ocean side. There, large windows on the second story maximized the ocean views. Beneath these, about fifty feet back, was the stone-and-concrete seawall with two arched wooden doors leading up to an elevated patio overlooking the blue Pacific.

The house had a security system, but it was never used unless the occupant was leaving town for an extended period.

He rounded the block for the second time and checked for signs that might restrict parking. He saw none. The last thing he needed was a parking ticket that would document his presence in the neighborhood. Cops would check for this: an indication of any strange cars parked in the neighborhood. Once they had the license number, they would trace the vehicle to the rental agency and from there they would find his name. It was why he didn't use his own car. The plates made it too recognizable.

He parked two blocks to the north, grabbed a light canvas jacket off the backseat, locked the car, and walked back toward the house on the beach. He stopped on the sidewalk near the steps as if to admire the ocean view while he slipped the jacket

on and rolled the [...] and the side of his [...]

Below he could s[...] beach. From this a[...] south along the sa[...] It was deserted for[...] checked for securit[...] of the new models[...] to see unless you k[...] so that there was li[...] company could sh[...] between two board[...] you'd never know [...] porch, but nothing[...] knew about. His e[...] one last time. The[...] appeared to be bu[...] occasional light sta[...] but these contair[...] lamps for street li[...] police security can[...] confined it to the [...] this neighborhood[...]

He walked part[...] beach, then step[...] that separated th[...] strolled out onto t[...] buffeted his ligh[...] turned up for th[...] profile from the [...] might pass by a [...] the prying eyes [...] the neighborho[...] nothing better to[...] every time a car[...]

As he stood [...]

house, he[...] coming to[...] he glimps[...] and a blu[...] and a w[...] Whoever [...] the sidew[...] him.

The ma[...] look up. Y[...] contact. H[...] to register[...] if what th[...] still becom[...] rock or a[...] untrained [...] recon and[...] dangerous[...] professiona[...] and remem[...]

A lone n[...] ocean with[...] of the footst[...] glimpse to[...] continued o[...] from view a[...]

He took [...] man had sto[...] he had only[...] moment to g[...] it would ha[...] chance. He v[...] one, two wee[...] He couldn't [...] she would a[...] the office. S[...]

she might pull it from a pile on her desk tomorrow and go to work on it. He had set certain parameters of safety before he even started. It was why so many people got nailed. They were careless.

His heart pounded as he watched the ocean. A half-dozen surfers sat astride their boards two hundred yards out, riding over the crest of approaching waves and into the trailing troughs. He was confident that they were too far away to make out human features or to identify a lone figure walking on the rocks behind the houses. The beach was not popular with swimmers. The water was too rough. The waves on an incoming tide would grind a swimmer against the solid sandstone that formed sharp ledges along the shore.

The late-afternoon light had reached that visual netherworld between shadows and vapor. Soon the streetlights would flicker on. He strolled over the rocks, at one point leaping across a craggy divide where foaming surf washed seaweed into a swale on the beach below. He strolled along the uneven surface, hands in his pants pockets, until he reached a point over the water where the rocks became slick with moisture from the fractured waves. Then slowly he turned until his back was to the ocean. He glanced up at the stone seawall topped by its white picket fence and the looming brown walls and large windows behind it.

The house looked deserted. There was no longer any live-in security – that he knew. It was made-to-order.

The only thing left was to figure some way to get rid of the maid, and so he did. Early one afternoon he called the house, knowing that the owner would be at the office. Only the maid would be there. He identified himself, using a false name, and said he was calling from the Isotenics security department. He explained that since security was no longer providing protection at the residence, they had been ordered to obtain information regarding any employees who worked there or who had keys to the house. He then proceeded to ask a number of questions regarding references, where the maid had worked previously, where she had been born, a list of residences where she had lived or worked for the five years immediately preceding her employment in the house. The poor woman tripped over a number of these, hemming and hawing, making it clear by her vague responses that she couldn't answer many of them, at least not truthfully.

He finally administered the coup de grâce. He asked for her Social Security number and date of birth and told her it was just for their records so they could run a background check for security. He couldn't be sure from the silence on the other end of the phone but he figured she must have shit a brick, knowing that if they ran this information through a government computer they would discover that she was in the country illegally. Knock on any dozen doors in posh areas of Southern California and chances are that if a maid answers she will be speaking English, if at all, with a southern accent, and it won't be from Georgia.

Two days later, in the middle of the night, Madelyn Chapman's Mexican maid grabbed her few belongings, stuffed them into a small suitcase and disappeared. She didn't even bother to ask for her final paycheck. The new replacement worked for a large domestic-services firm and worked a normal shift, eight hours. She always left the house by four-thirty. He had watched her today as she went out the front door, turning her key in the dead bolt to lock it from the outside.

He turned and looked out toward the ocean again. The surfers had taken no notice. Their attention was riveted on the burgeoning set of cresting combers rolling in behind them.

He reached into his jacket pocket, plucked out the brown leather driving gloves, and slipped them on his hands as he walked. He glanced quickly up at the windows of the two adjacent buildings. The house on the left was dark. The larger apartment building to the right was angled back from the beach and followed the natural curve of shore so that once he'd gone ten paces, no one looking from the apartment's upper windows could see him.

Within seconds he reached the cover of the seawall and one of the arched doors leading up to the patio above. The door itself was made with heavy planks of wood with a garden latch on the inside for a lock. He slipped the thin blade of a Swiss army knife into the crack between the door and its frame and lifted the latch. In three seconds he was inside with the garden door closed behind him.

He had a set of picks for the lock on the back door but preferred not to use them because they would leave scratch marks, tool impressions, one more piece of evidence that he didn't need to leave behind. It took less than a minute to find what he was looking for: a ground-floor window that wasn't latched. It was not a high-crime neighborhood, as the lackadaisical habits of many of the residents showed.

Within seconds he popped the screen, slid the

lower half of the window up, and nimbly slipped inside the house. He closed the window but left the screen propped against a small bush outside. There was still enough light from outside so that he didn't need to use the penlight in his pocket. He found himself in one of the lower level guest bedrooms. In the corner on one wall, near the ceiling, was a small white sphere of plastic. It looked like an oversized egg with a flat side against the wall. On the side facing out was a recessed area, curved and white, perhaps an inch in length, aimed out at the room. It was a motion detector. His eyes were riveted on the tiny light under the recessed area as he froze stone still and counted silently in his head. When he reached thirty, the light still hadn't flashed. The system was off.

He took a deep breath and started looking around the room. It had three doors, one leading to the closet, another to a bathroom. This was open. He could see the claw-foot tub inside.

He moved to the third door, which was closed, pressed his ear against the wood, and listened for a moment. Then he turned the knob and let it open just a crack as he peered into the hallway. He listened for sounds of movement upstairs, the creaking of floorboards, footfalls, the sounds of a television. He heard nothing except the hiss of conditioned air flowing from the register high on the wall behind him.

He slipped his shoes off and held them in one hand, then stepped silently into the hallway. Walking on the tile floor in stocking feet, he made no sound as he moved past two closed doors and entered the kitchen.

The place looked like the inside of a spaceship: curving stainless-steel appliances, a refrigerator, a freezer, and a sleek square commercial cooker with a gleaming copper hood. He allowed the gloved finger of one hand to brush over the maker's name on the front of the stove as he passed by: the label read *Morice*.

A short hallway led past the pantry to the three-car garage. There was only one car inside, a late-model Mercedes.

He went back into the house. In the other direction was the living room and a large formal dining area. An equally spacious elliptical entry was graced by an intricately carved oval table of dark hardwood, something from the primordial rain forests of Africa or South America. It was laid over with a thick piece of glass, smooth and clear, not a single fingerprint or smudge on it. A staircase curved around the walls of the entry leading up to the second story. Under the stairs was a curving arc of display cases, each with a glass-framed door and a cylinder lock, the kind you would find in a public museum housing rare artifacts. He assumed that just such pricey items were inside: shelves filled with art glass reached from floor to ceiling, ending as the stairs dropped down below head height. The shelves, though built-in, had the look of something that was added – not part of the architect's original vision but functional for the owner.

He set his shoes down on the carpeted floor by the foot of the stairs. He couldn't be sure if there were sections of hardwood or tile upstairs, and until he was certain the house was empty, it was best not to make a sound.

As he passed through the entry, he took care not to allow himself to be captured by the lens of the security camera outside. It was mounted on the ceiling of the porch and aimed back at the double front doors, each of which had a fan-shaped window at the top.

He hugged the doors, stooping slightly to stay under the windows, and slipped through the entry. He found himself in another large entertaining area with a conversation pit and fireplace. There were more items of glass art here, on tables and adorning shelves. Beyond this was still a larger room, this one with mirrors on two walls. It was filled with exercise equipment: two stationary bikes, a treadmill, a weight machine, two different types of ellipticals, a StairMaster and one of those multistations for working every muscle group in the body. These were devices that until now he'd seen only in commercial fitness clubs. Taped to the mirror on the wall was a business card with the phone number and name of a professional trainer. He began to worry. This was something new, unexpected. What other changes might have been made? What if the owner or some later hired help had gone through the drawers upstairs and cleaned them out?

He checked his watch, then moved quickly back toward the entry. Something caught his attention: a noise from the garage. He stood still and listened. It was the hum of an electric motor. His heart skipped a beat. Could it be the garage door going up? He listened, his eyes quickly scanning the room for the nearest register. It was hissing air again. The noise continued. He counted silently in his head. It didn't stop. The noise was the motor from the forced-air system, the air conditioner.

He took a deep breath, then quickly headed up the curving staircase two steps at a time to the second floor. At the top was a sizable landing maybe thirty feet square. It was enclosed on two sides by large lighted display cases showcasing art glass that, by their shapes and colors, made it clear these were not functional objects.

He thought he heard something and glanced over the balcony to the formal entry and the big black table downstairs. He listened for a second. He was getting jumpy. His ears were playing tricks. The landing was carpeted in a sea of deep wool pile that continued down the wide hallway in both directions off the landing.

He headed toward the guest suite at the end of the hall on his left. When he got there he listened at the closed door for a moment, then quietly opened it. A large fireplace with a decorative convex mirror over the mantel gave him a fish-eye view of the entire room, the king-size bed with its neatly made-up comforter, bed skirt, and sham of heavy tapestry. The room had its own bath. Through its open door, light streamed in through an outside window.

He stepped into the room and closed the door. It was spacious, decorated with a masculine touch, all clean lines and dark colors.

He proceeded to the tall dresser at the far side of the room, opened the second drawer, and swept his gloved right hand under a heavy quilt blanket until he felt something hard and heavy. Grasping the handle, he pulled it from under the bulkier cloth: it was a sand-camouflage canvas bag about twenty inches square, zippered on three sides.

Closing the drawer, he put the bag on top of the dresser, unzipped it, and flipped back the top before feeling its weight. A flash of blue metal clattered across the polished wooden surface, hit the wall behind the dresser, and caromed onto the carpeted floor with a muffled thud.

11

He stood motionless, sucking air, looking idly at the long scratch in the dark mahogany surface of the dresser and the nicked wall behind it.

He listened for any sound of movement in the house, waiting for what seemed an eternity. Sweat ran down his forehead and along the bridge of his nose. It burned in his right eye as he tuned every auditory nerve in his head to troll the distant reaches of the house, sending out waves of anxiety like sonar, listening for any sound that might bounce back.

Nothing! Even the air conditioner with its telltale hiss from the room's louvered registers seemed to have cycled off.

Finally he moved, stooped, and picked up the pistol's loaded metal clip from the floor, one of two fitted into pockets in the flipped-open top of the gun case. The loaded clip weighed nearly a pound.

He slapped the metal against the open palm of his other hand, seating the loaded rounds properly against the magazine's rear wall. Then he turned his attention back to the bag on top of the dresser. Held in place in the bottom by a thick Velcro strap was a heavy-framed blue metal semiautomatic pistol.

The letters on the side of the slide read: USSOCOM. The gun was made in Germany by Heckler & Koch and came in only one caliber, .45 auto.

He had brought his own rounds, just six loose ones in the pocket of his jacket, in case he needed them. Store-bought, a common manufacture, so that it would be virtually impossible to trace. As it turned out, he wouldn't need them, not with the two fully loaded clips included in the bag.

Inside he also found the dark metal tube.

He pulled the Velcro tab open and carefully

picked up the pistol. It was accurized, a threaded muzzle on the barrel – special bushings, adjustable trigger, precision springs, a rail slide for the special sight also in the bag, and a chromed barrel, the whole enchilada in a package you could slip into a small backpack.

He slid the gun's sight along the rail until it was seated in the proper position, then locked it in place using the small Allen wrench included in the bag to tighten the set screw. He threaded the silencer over the exposed tip of the barrel, then checked the loaded clip that had fallen on the floor one more time.

It was then that he noticed the strange shape and tint of the bullet tip of the top round. It wasn't lead or copper but something else. He tried to scratch it first with his fingernail, then with the sharp edge of the Allen wrench, but neither made an impression. A highly sophisticated handgun with a railed sight and a silencer. He thought for a moment. Then instinctively he knew what the space-age bullet was and what it was designed to do. Smiling to himself at the brainteaser he would be delivering to the cops, he ejected the top round from the clip and replaced it with one of his own soft lead-tipped bullets from the loose rounds he'd brought with him in his pocket.

He was about to slide the loaded clip into the handle when he looked down and suddenly realized he'd forgotten something. The disquieting thought didn't have time to even settle in his brain when he heard the noise, a kind of metal clang followed by the hum of an electric motor, this time not in the house but outside. The mechanized iron gates at the driveway out in front were opening.

CHAPTER ONE

It was a little after five on a Friday afternoon and the traffic on Prospect was already bumpered up like a train wreck: the start of your average summer weekend in La Jolla.

The pathfinders – those who left the office early – and a few day-trippers were already out in strength, reconnoitering the boutiques so that by Saturday morning the Village would be under full siege.

Male heads turned like an orchard of radar dishes homing in on the growl of the Enzo's V-12 overhead cam engine as Madelyn Chapman cruised by. The sleek red Ferrari was an item of curiosity even here in this parish of plenty. At slow speeds it purred like a panther on the prowl.

Usually chained to her desk until late into the evening, this afternoon she left the office before five to run an errand. She was anxious to complete it and get home before the out-of-towners froze the roads in gridlock.

Madelyn's eyes scanned for a parking space. She wasn't about to start circling the block. Nor was she going to leave the new car in a public garage where some bozo could carve obscenities into the paint job as a manifesto against affluence.

Instead she steered the racy red sports car into a vacant white-curbed space in front of the La Valencia, one of the trendy boutique hotels on the main drag. The sign out front read: *Valet Only*. Behind it stood the hotel's pink-flamingo walls and the Spanish-tile-covered portico leading to the garden entrance.

Two young men in white dress shirts and dark slacks stood near the entrance looking at the Ferrari. They were probably wondering which of them would get to play Mario Andretti in the tight garage under the hotel. One of them grabbed the initiative and sprinted to the driver's door, opening it before Chapman had a chance to unbuckle her seat belt.

'Welcome to the La Valenc– Oh, Ms Chapman. Didn't recognize you.'

'Jimmy.'

Madelyn made a practice of pouncing on the valet spaces whenever the Village was busy. Never one for walking half a mile in heels, she treated the hotel as if she had a lifetime lease on valet space out front.

'Nice wheels!' The kid was taking it all in. He noticed the paper license plate taped to the rear window. 'I take it you just picked it up from the dealer.'

'Actually they delivered it yesterday.'

He glanced at the silver stallion, Ferrari's trademark, on the hood. 'What do they call it? The model, I mean.'

'It's called the Enzo,' said Madelyn. 'After the company's founder. The salesman's pitch was that the car has the spirit of Enzo Ferrari.'

The car was one of a limited edition with the pedigree of a formula racer, the toy of oil sheiks and a few Hollywood stars who could balance California's state budget with one of their movies. Its price hovered in the range of the national debt.

Stepping out of the low-slung racer in a tight skirt and heels was like doing the limbo. Still, Madelyn managed it with agility and grace. At forty-three she looked ten years younger, with a body that didn't destroy the illusion, something she worked hard to keep. Young men still looked at her with a gleam in their eyes.

She fished some green from her purse as the kid watched and then took one of his hands in both of hers.

'Now, Jimmy, I want you to keep the car here at the curb. Understand?'

'Well, I don't know. My manager . . .' He felt the tickle of the papers' edges as she moved the crisp folded currency against his open palm.

When she let go of his hand, the valet looked down and spotted Franklin's portrait, not once, but twice. He smiled and came to commercial attention. 'Thank *you*, Ms Chapman.'

'And my car?'

'Stays at the curb,' said the kid.

'Good.' She offered a confident smile. It had become a common expression for Madelyn, who over the last decade had grown accustomed to getting her way.

'Do you have any idea how long you'll be?' he asked.

She looked at the money still in his hand.

'Not that it matters,' he added.

'I don't know. Twenty minutes, maybe half an hour.'

'No problem.'

He gently closed the driver's-side door. She started moving toward the sidewalk, her arm on his shoulder. 'And if your manager comes out and tells you to move it, what are you going to say?'

'I'm going to tell him a hot car in front of the hotel on a Friday night is good advertising. I'll tell him it's one of a kind.'

'What else?'

The kid looked at her, fresh out of ideas.

'You tell him the car belongs to me, that I kept the keys' – she dropped them in her purse – 'and that if he even thinks of having it towed, I'll buy the hotel before morning and fire his ass.'

The kid smiled at the thought. 'Yes, ma'am!'

She wasn't about to turn over a $700,000 sports car so that two valets could flip a coin to see which of them got to do wheelies around concrete pilings in the basement.

She started to turn to go, then turned back. 'And, Jimmy, I don't want any dings or dents or dimples in the doors or anywhere else when I get back.'

He was already shaking his head.

She smiled. 'The only dimples allowed here are yours.' The kid blushed again, then looked up at his colleague, who was already beginning to show signs of a sneering smile.

Jimmy pushed the money into his pocket.

She mouthed the words *watch the car* as she blew him a kiss and walked away, passing under the Whaling Bar and Grill sign on the pink awning overhead.

The other valet broke into a full smile and started laughing under his breath until finally she

was out of earshot. 'Hey, Jimmy, come over here.
Lemme do your dimples.'

'Yeah, right. Kiss my ass.'

The other kid puckered up his lips and puffed a
few kisses at him, blowing them off the palm of
one hand before offering up a donkey laugh.

'You know what you can do with that,' said
Jimmy.

'Maybe if you got dimples back there, she'll do
those for you, too,' said his friend.

Jimmy didn't say anything. He just smiled,
reached into his pocket, and pulled out the two
crisp bills she'd just given him. He held them up
high, stretched between the fingers of both hands,
shifting them back and forth so that the other kid's
smile faded.

'She gave you two hundred bucks?'

'No shit,' said Jimmy. And it wasn't even dark
yet. Friday night in La Jolla.

Madelyn walked under brightly colored awnings
past shimmering display windows with their exotic
wares. She couldn't help but smile to herself. Two
hundred dollars for a few minutes of parking.
Twenty years ago that would have been half a
week's salary. She had come a long way, so far and
so fast that at times she couldn't remember all of
the critical waypoints in her career or, for that
matter, some of the people who had offered
directions. Looking back was not something
Madelyn was good at. It took all of her vision,
energy, and focus just to keep moving forward.

Several of the shop owners looked up and took
notice as she passed. Chapman's face had become
high-profile, a celebrity of sorts among the regulars
in the Village, especially those in the commercial

community. Her name and picture had been in the business and society sections of the local papers and magazines on a regular basis for at least four years now. Her company, Isotenics, Inc., of which Chapman was CEO and chairman of the board, had gone public less than a year after she moved it from Virginia to California. Madelyn held a block of shares that gave her the controlling interest. This was the cornerstone of her empire, though she had diversified into real estate and other investments.

She owned a total of six houses in different states, including a horse property in Virginia, a condo in Alexandria near the Pentagon, and a town house in New York. But La Jolla was home.

Eight years ago she had decided that her company would lease land out by the university, near one of the technology parks that sprouted during the euphoric days of the dot com binge. It was a time when the words *high tech* were all you needed on a business card for banks to lavish loans and investors to queue up and buy your stock.

When the storm came, most of her competitors went down like paper boats in a typhoon, but not Chapman. Madelyn had taken her company into the safe harbor of government contracts. As with her taste in clothing and cars, Madelyn's sense of timing was flawless. In a time of terrorism, her computer programs had been tailored to the needs of national security.

Her company was now one of the largest employers in the state, with its stock still on an upward arc. The value had tripled in the last year alone. It is said that timing is nature's way of telling us we are in rhythm with the seasons. If so, Madelyn Chapman was in sync not only with the moon but with the planets, the stars, and even the black holes in the dark and distant vacuum of space.

In an age when information was everything, Chapman's company possessed the keys to the defense-software kingdom. She controlled Primis.

Two blocks down, Madelyn reached her destination. She stopped in front of the gallery's main window to study a few of the new pieces on display. Like liquid crystal, the glass flowed in every form imaginable. Translucent colors fused with brilliance in all the hues visible in the human light spectrum. There were large, cavernous oyster shells of glimmering violet and swirling amber, and tubular tulip blossoms in shades of purple running to blue and green, freeformed glass in shapes that could only be matched by the rich variations of nature. Some of the labels carried names of artists now familiar to her, while others were still earning their spurs.

It had been several weeks since her last visit to the gallery. The owner, a man named Ibram Asani, had been making inquiries on her behalf. He had become her agent of sorts in Madelyn's latest addiction, the acquisition of fine art glass. She had developed a collector's eye, and Asani was helping her to refine it.

Iranian by birth, having immigrated with his family to the United States when the Shah fell in the seventies, he had arrived in this country with nothing. He now owned his own gallery in one of the most exclusive shopping locations in Southern California.

As Madelyn walked through the door, a mellow electronic tone announced her entrance, and Ibram turned to look.

Asani's eyes lit up. He put his hands together as if in prayer to the deity whose authority was over all things mercantile. 'Ah, my good friend, Ms Chapman. So good to see you. I assume you received my message.'

'Indeed I did.'

'One moment. I will be right with you.' Asani turned toward two women who were examining a smaller object under glass in one of the cases.

A shop owner who missed his calling in diplomacy, he excused himself and left the women to peruse on their own as he walked briskly toward Madelyn and the scent of money.

'Ms Chapman, how are you?'

'Fine, Ibram. And you?'

He wrinkled up his face, an expression some-where between the Middle East and Europe. 'No complaints. Business has been good.'

'My secretary told me that you called. Something about a new piece by Yadl Heulich?'

'Shh.' He held his finger to his lips, and looked toward the two women, neither of whom paid any attention. 'Yes, it came in yesterday. A truly unique piece. It is one of his early private commissions.' Asani cupped one hand to his lips and leaned in to her ear. 'It is from an estate.' The way he said it – in a whisper – made it sound as if he had stolen the item in question. 'I don't think they knew the value.' He smiled and shrugged. 'At least, the executor did not.' Something that Asani would no doubt quickly rectify. 'A friend alerted me and I was able to purchase it. I want you to understand, there is no obligation. I did not intend to purchase it on commission.'

'I understand.'

'I would have bought it for the gallery even if I did not think you would be interested.'

'Can I see it?'

'Of course. It is incredible.'

He went to the phone on the counter and used the intercom to call to the storage area at the back of the gallery. A few moments later Asani's son pushed a small cart through the doorway and into the gallery's main room as his father stepped around a display case and quickly walked over to provide direction. The cart was specially designed, its top recessed like a deep bowl with deep foam rubber lining the sides so that the object on it was cradled and cushioned like an embryo in a womb.

As they reached the counter, Asani, with a quick, efficient motion, whipped a rubber pad from a shelf under the cart and laid it out on the counter. He shooed the boy away and alone he lifted the shimmering blue sphere from its foam cradle and placed it carefully on the rubber pad.

Madelyn looked at it, moving closer. She had never seen anything like it in her life. Her gaze was fixed on the glass as it glittered in the light. As she moved, the glass took on subtle changes of texture and color. Its form was a near-perfect sphere, its gossamer swirls of blue and white suffusing with light, turning to brilliant indigo just inside the surface of the orb as you looked at it straight on. In its purest form the colors reminded Madelyn of photos taken by astronauts that captured the curvature of the earth from space at dawn.

Asani looked at Madelyn, who appeared to be in a trance as she studied the object. The shop owner smiled, wondering whether his calculator possessed enough digits to cipher the sale and its consequent tax.

Madelyn came to, just long enough to ask a question: 'Does it have a name?'

'Ahh, yes. The original owner, the man who commissioned it – he and the artist agreed that it would be called *Orb at the Edge*.'

He escorted her to the inner sanctum at the rear of the gallery, a small office where he opened negotiations for the purchase. After haggling over the price for several minutes, Asani tried to excuse himself from the room for a moment. A call of nature, he told her. Madelyn looked at her watch and told him she was late for an appointment and would have to leave. While she had a dinner engagement at eight, there was nothing pressing, neither was she left behind the door when the brains were dispensed. If Asani left the room at that point, her offer would be withdrawn and she would walk. Madelyn had no intention of getting into a bidding war via long distance with some acquisitions director for a museum her company was probably sustaining through its program of corporate contribution to the arts.

Finally they agreed on a price and Madelyn cut a check. Asani wanted to deliver it personally the next day, but Madelyn would have none of it. The shop owner and his son went to work packaging the piece.

Madelyn was much more content with the boxed blue sphere on the seat next to her as she maneuvered through traffic. It occupied her attention sufficiently that she missed the change when the traffic light went green. The driver in the car behind her tapped his horn. She could see him gesticulating in her rearview mirror: *Rich bitch in the Formula One can't drive.*

'Relax.' Madelyn looked at him through narrow little slits from behind her dark glasses. 'Keep your shirt on.' She touched the gas with her foot and the Ferrari inched forward, slowly gaining speed. For the first time since getting the car, she regretted not having automatic transmission. That way she would have had one hand free to protect the box if it lurched forward at a stop. Instead she kept one eye on the cardboard container, the other on the road, her right hand alternating between the shift lever and the box on the seat next to her.

The sleek racer never got past thirty or out of second gear. Finally she turned into her driveway and pressed the button on the remote. The double iron gates began to swing open.

A few seconds later she was in the garage, the overhead door closed behind her. She left the briefcase with her laptop along with a stack of important mail from the office in the car. Then, with the strap of her purse over one shoulder, she wrestled the large box through the passenger-side door. She slammed the door closed with one hip to get it out of the way and caught the strap of her purse in the crook of her arm as it slid off her shoulder. In four-inch heels she maneuvered around the Ferrari. The box containing *Orb at the Edge* wasn't as heavy as it was awkward, too big for her to get her arms around. Another woman might have waited for help, but not Madelyn. Ever since she was a kid she resented women who employed their feminine wiles to get some man to do what they should be able to do for themselves. Given the tools and a book of directions, she would be as good at repairing cars as she was at crafting software.

She made it to a small potting table at the end of the garage near the door to the backyard. She carefully set the box on the table, then slid the purse off her shoulder, dropping it on the floor. She hiked the waistband of her skirt up a couple of inches. It had slipped down as she was grappling with the box.

Madelyn was puffing a bit, studying the door leading to the kitchen twenty feet away. She looked around for something she could use.

Six minutes later she stood in the kitchen, in the middle of a small sea of litter, packing tape, and bubble wrap strewn across the floor and over the countertop. A smile formed on her lips, the joy of owning such beauty as she took in the *Orb at the Edge*. Gingerly she picked it up and walked through the kitchen and down the hall. Madelyn made her way to the large oval ebony table in the entryway. The moment she had seen the piece in Asani's gallery, she knew where she wanted to put it. It would be the first thing anyone saw when entering the grand hall.

She set it in the center of the table, shimmering glass over the gloss of ebony. She looked at it, then stepped back a few feet to gain perspective. As she moved backward her heel caught on something. She nearly tripped. Recovering just enough to catch herself, she turned and looked down.

Who the hell would leave a pair of running shoes lying on the floor in her entry hall? They weren't hers. They were too big. The maid, she thought. What was she going to have to do to find good help?

Before she could utter a word in anger, her attention was drawn back to the glass sphere on the table by a beam of reflected light. The *Orb* was now emitting a streak of red from the cobalt blue. The color was so intense as it left the glass and entered her eyes that the pain was severe. She closed her eyes, turned her head, and brought one hand up toward her face.

Before the neural path into her brain could be traversed, the kinetic force translated into the violent snap of her neck. Her raised arm dropped, propelled downward by forces greater than gravity as the discharge of energy exploded through her head to her hand. Instantly the pain in the optic nerve vanished, replaced by a brief burning sensation in one finger, and then nothing. Her head dropped onto one shoulder, a quizzical expression on her face. The second impact buckled her knees and Madelyn's body flooded to the floor like a boneless sack of flesh.

CHAPTER TWO

I had an uncle named Evo. He was a big man, nearly six-foot-four, and though he carried a paunch above his belt and spare tires over each hip, I never thought of him as fat. From my recollection he filled the frame of every doorway he passed through, from top to bottom and both sides, shoulders like a stevedore and an angular head like a bronze bust, bald and shiny as polished stone. The only hair you would have noticed were the unkempt bushes over his brows and several days' layer of stubble on his face. For most of my life, as a child and later, my uncle in physical appearance was the spitting image of Luca Brasi, the notorious assassin of *Godfather* fame.

Evo's enduring expression was a kind of passive, simpering smile, what you might take for the face of a wiseass until he opened his mouth to talk, which he seldom did. Then you would have noticed the missing teeth up front like broken pickets in a fence and the childish thoughts and worries that spilled from his mind.

Caught up in events, just a few years out of high school, I was told that Evo had always been a happy kid, full of life, smiles, and laughter. But as Christmas 1950 approached he found himself perched behind the sights of an M1 Garand on a snow-covered slope, peering out at what must have looked like the edge of the earth. His Army unit had pushed out into the mountains north of the Marine battalion encamped along the western side of a reservoir, an ominous place of ice-covered rivers and barren mountains.

The North Korean forces had evaporated under the massive air assault and pounding from UN artillery. US forces, Army units and Marines, along with their allies, had driven the North Koreans up the peninsula to within a few miles of the Chinese border. MacArthur had broken their backs at Inchon. Victory was at hand. By Christmas the troops would be home. It was late November and temperatures at night dipped to sixty below, driven by icy winds off the steppes of Manchuria, temperatures so cold that at times it froze the actions on machine guns so that they would often fire only a single shot and had to be cycled by hand. Having outflanked the North Koreans by landing far behind enemy lines, the UN forces had moved north so fast that most units had been issued little or no winter weather gear.

Though he didn't know it at the time, from all accounts Evo's unit and those on the line with him had gone as far north as any UN forces would ever get. As Thanksgiving approached, these troops were just a few ridge lines south of the Yalu River, the border between North Korea and the People's Republic of China.

Much of what I know of these events I have garnered over the years from books and articles and from conversations with my father, who was

Evo's older brother. My uncle seldom talked of his experiences in the war. In fact, in the decades after his return to civilian life, I can recall him having only a few conversations, and most of those with my father.

Even with all of this, what drew my attention to him as a child were the gravitational black holes where my uncle's eyes should have been. I often wondered what was going on beyond the vacant depths of those twin dark pits. According to the shrinks at the VA hospital, it was most likely visions of hell.

It is possible that these childhood memories of my uncle have softened my brain and impaired my judgment sufficiently that last week I returned a phone call from a complete stranger, one Colonel James Safford, US Army retired. Colonel Safford, who in civilian life is a lawyer in Idaho specializing in estate planning, wills, trusts, and the like, in his spare time volunteers his services as part of a small veterans' advocacy group known as the GI Defense Fund. The organization was formed in the 1970s in the waning days of the Vietnam War when a growing number of returning veterans found themselves in trouble with the law, oftentimes the result of seemingly senseless and unprovoked acts of horrific violence; this from men who had no prior criminal history or problems with the law before their military service.

Safford had been given my name, along with the names of several other local lawyers from the office of the base commander at North Island Naval Air Station on Coronado Island in San Diego. It seems the Navy keeps in touch with a handful of local lawyer-veterans who from time to time have drawn attention to themselves by defending members of the armed services who have gotten sideways with civilian legal authorities. These attorneys have on more than one occasion given up on collecting their fees. Some might call this pro bono work. But as a practical matter it is difficult to collect from soldiers and sailors whose spouses and children sometimes have to line up at the county welfare office for food stamps just so that they can eat through the end of the month.

What Safford was looking for was some help with a case. It seemed that a retired Army sergeant had gone a little beyond the usual military brush with the law, your typical bar brawl or flashing incident involving a general mooning of society brought on by unbridled hostility, a domestic dispute, or a few too many beers.

It's the reason we are here today, my partner Harry Hinds and I, heading for the elevator at the county jail to interview a prospective client. His name is Emiliano Ruiz. We have never met.

He is thirty-eight years old and until two years ago was an Army staff sergeant, what some would call a lifer. He spent twenty years in uniform. And according to what little I know of him, he saw action in Panama and the first Gulf War. He retired and took a job with a security firm in San Diego about two years ago, one of those companies that offer high-end protective services for corporate executives here and abroad. For the last four months Sergeant Ruiz has been behind bars on a charge of first-degree murder with special circumstances. If he is convicted, considering the profile of the case – involving a victim of prominence in this community – and the cold and calculating nature of the crime, Ruiz is a likely candidate for San Quentin's death row.

* * *

As Harry and I turn the corner for our two o'clock conference, somebody over by one of the satellite trucks hollers, 'There they are,' and within a few seconds they are on us like locusts.

We are engulfed in a sea of bodies hoisting microphones and pushing camera lenses in our faces. Bright lights and a million questions, most of them unintelligible, drowned out by more shouted questions from behind.

There is no telling how many are here. I can't see far enough into the crowd, but the camera crews are jostling each other for position. There are satellite trucks from as far north as LA, all three network affiliates, their dishes already arrayed and aimed skyward, generators running. They are parked at the curb in front of the entrance to the county jail, blocking the sidewalk so that we have to move around them to get there.

'Mr Madriani' – some guy sticks his microphone in Harry's face – 'can you tell us, have you spoken to your client yet?'

With that, everybody jumps on Harry. He is awash in questions, everybody figuring the reporter must know him.

'When are you going to see Ruiz?'

'Why did the defendant fire Dale Kendal? Was he unhappy with Kendal's representation?'

It is my chance to slip the crowd, but I don't do it.

'What about the preliminary hearing? If he's innocent, how come the judge bound him over?'

'What does Ruiz know about the Information for Security Program?'

'Was he working for the government?'

'Do you think Chapman was killed because of

IFS? Has anybody in the administration talked to you?'

Harry keeps trudging forward, wading into them, briefcase up in front of his face; he finally looks over at me, half smiles, then says, 'He's Madriani, not me.'

'Thanks.'

'Don't mention it.'

Like quills on a mad porcupine, a hundred microphones – some hoisted on six-foot booms – are suddenly pointed in my direction.

Even in the afternoon San Diego sun the camera lights are blinding, portable banks of them arrayed on bars held high on stanchions moving with the crowd as we approach the entrance to the jail in lockstep, half an inch at a time.

'We have nothing to say right now. Maybe later, after I've spoken to Mr Ruiz.'

This tentative offering doesn't appease them. Some character sticks me in the ass from behind, trying to lift his microphone boom over my head. I make a mental note to find another way out of the jail.

Using his briefcase like a shield fending off swords, Harry pushes on into the crowd, Don Quixote tilting at micbooms and cameras. We run this gauntlet for half a block, the press mob now a wide circle of bodies around us, shutting down traffic as we cross the street. A photographer with a wide-angle lens tries to get a shot from down low. Somebody jostles him from behind, and by the time he snaps the shutter he is close enough to my face that I can read the f-stops off the barrel of his lens. 'Extra! Extra! See hair up the lawyer's nose!' And some people see this as glamorous.

The murder of a prominent socialite, one of the

state's leading software magnates – a major local employer and a woman who made it to 220 of the Fortune 500 – is a good story, but nonetheless it is one that likely would have had only local legs. This morning a front-page piece in a Washington newspaper changed all that. The story, which has now been regurgitated coast-to-coast on all of the morning network news shows, has linked the victim, Madelyn Chapman, and her company to the controversial Information for Security Program, known to the press and the public as IFS.

IFS has been leading news in the national press for weeks now, ever since it became the largest bone in a tug of war between the White House and Congress, the President saying he needs the program to safeguard national security, and civil libertarians claiming it's an invasion of privacy.

Until this morning Harry and I had agreed to become involved in a nice, quiet little murder trial, with perhaps a few local reporters invited. Now that Chapman has been linked to the IFS program, her murder has been ginned into national headlines, and Harry and I are up to our ass in a sea of questions.

Fifty yards away I can see a small band of uniformed guards. They have crowded up against the inside of the glass doors at the main entrance to the jail. Looking out and laughing, one of them has a cupped hand to his mouth and is talking. They seem to be enjoying the entertainment; two lawyers being engulfed and digested by the news amoeba out front. Want some publicity? Help yourself.

We grind to a halt, unable to move forward or back. I'm beginning to feel like Custer surrounded by the Indians. This kind of stuff can get out of hand. Somebody pokes Harry with his mic and gets a faceful of leather with a handle attached. The guy starts to push back and I stop him before we have a news riot. If this continues, I know that my partner will be packing an anvil in the bottom of his briefcase the next time he comes for a jail visit.

'They're taking their time,' says Harry.

We are cooling our heels in one of the concrete cubicles they call conference rooms at the jail. Harry is standing with a foot up on the steel bench to one side of the table, his left elbow resting on his knee, his hand propped up under his chin as he drums the metal tabletop with the fingers of his other hand.

Harry has had enough for one day. Courtrooms are one thing, crowds are another. Harry is a gentleman of the old school. He has a short temper when it comes to anarchy.

'Why didn't Kendal want the case?' asks Harry.

'Said he was too busy.'

'Look at all the face time he could get on the tube,' says Harry. 'He wants it back, my advice is give it to him. Life's too short for this crap.'

Dale Kendal is one of the brand-name criminal defense lawyers in Southern California. He forages for cases in LA, Orange, and San Diego counties. Kendal handled the preliminary hearing with the result that Emiliano Ruiz was bound over for trial in the superior court. Given the low threshold of evidence required, no one really expected Ruiz to beat the indictment. Still, after the prelim, Kendal made arrangements to withdraw from the case, and the court allowed him to do it.

Harry looks at his watch. 'Suppose you can't expect the jail to operate on the same commercial concept as fast food.'

He looks at me but I don't bite.

'What, you don't think it could happen – that a corporation could take this place over and run it right?'

'Did I say anything?'

'Think of the advantages. A private correctional facility. The county could save a zillion bucks a year in safety retirement with the sheriffs' union alone.'

Harry glances over out of the corner of one eye. By now I'm a cipher, giving him nothing with which to argue.

'They could put a couple of kiosks around back,' he says. 'You drive up and talk into the little speaker, you order a felony and two misdemeanors. Sort of supersize the order. Give 'em the clients' names. "Oh, yeah, and order me up a deputy DA – you know, one of those new ones, fresh right outta law school. The one you gave me last week was kind of tough, an old bastard who knew what he was doing." You have them repeat it to make sure they got the order straight. After all,' says Harry, 'you gotta remember, this is a private business now. And in a private business, the customer is always right.'

He glances at me to make sure that he is getting my easy assent on all of this.

'If it's a private business, what makes you the customer? Why not the inmates?' I ask.

'No. No,' says Harry. 'They're the commodity being bought and sold.'

'I thought justice was the commodity.'

'No, that's just an occasional by-product,' says Harry.

'You're the one with the golden arches.' I'm smiling. 'So where do you go from there?'

'You pull around to the side of the building, reserved parking spaces facing this way. You roll down your window and you pick up the phone. A shade goes up on a window at the side of the building and your client's sitting there with a phone in his hand on the other end just waiting to talk. None of this crap where you have to sit around and wait.' Harry checks his watch again. 'Then a shade goes up on another window and you got the DA sitting there waiting on the other line.'

'You better keep those two lines straight.'

'That goes without saying.'

'What about the judge?' I ask.

'What judge?'

'You're going to need a judge, otherwise you're going to have to walk all the way to the courthouse at some point.'

'Okay, fine,' he says. 'We'll put the judge in a window upstairs so he can look down on us. Make him feel good.'

'What do you mean, "him"?'

'Him, her, whatever. The thing wearing black robes, we put it in a window upstairs, give it a hammer so it can pound on a piece of wood to work out its aggression and a bullhorn so it can be heard. In the meantime we're outside in the car with the air running, checking our calendar, making sure we're not getting behind for our ten o'clock back at the office. I mean, look at the advantages: Don't have to hoof it into the building. Do your business, slip into drive, and you're outta here. Save us a lotta time and money,' says Harry.

'I guess I'm out of touch, but I don't remember the county standing with any particular zeal on that scale, the one that measures savings in our time and money.'

'It's still a good idea,' he says.

'Oh, I think it's a hell of an idea. Just think of the retired set. They can come over every morning, set up their folding lawn chairs out in the parking lot, and take up lessons lip-reading with binoculars while you get the story fresh from your client in the little window – or is it the other way around?' I start to laugh.

Harry gives me a dim look.

'Either way, the audience gets it right from the horse's mouth, so to speak. They can see the whole system at work, right out there in the parking lot. Civics on asphalt.'

'So it has a few problems. Nothing that can't be fixed,' he counters.

'You could just blind everybody over sixty-five,' I say.

'There's a thought.' Harry thinks a moment. 'Maybe I'll write it up. The idea, I mean.'

'Good. Just do me a favor.'

'What's that?'

'Don't do it on the firm's stationery.'

'There you go,' he gripes, 'running a good idea into the ground again.' Within a few seconds Harry's back to tapping cadence with his fingers on the table.

Harry and I have been together for nearly fifteen years, through a marriage – mine – that ended with cancer for my wife, Nikki. He is uncle and godfather to my daughter, Sarah, who is now seventeen going on thirty. A straight-A student, she won't give me a glimmer as to which college or university she wants to attend until she waxes her snowboard and checks out the slopes in each area. This could take a while, as she seems in no hurry. Nor am I anxious to push her out the door. There are times when Sarah seems to be the last contact I have with life as I knew it in happier days.

Harry takes his foot off the bench and glances out through the louvered blinds in the window. 'Here they come.'

Outside, I can hear the jangle of chains and the shuffle of feet coming this way. Two guards, one of them I recognize, a brute who once tried out at summer camp with the 49ers. Between them is a smaller guy, seemingly dwarfed by the two giants on either side.

'What's this about?' Harry is talking about the security.

'I don't know.' I begin to wonder if Ruiz has been trouble in the jail. The jangling metal procession stops outside the door.

By now most clients under indictment for murder, after having been handed off from one lawyer to another, would be a jittery bag of nerves, on edge and itching for answers. But as I watch him standing outside the door, one of the guards working on the waist chain, disconnecting it from the manacles that bind the prisoner's hands behind his back, Ruiz appears to be none of these.

He appears calm, collected, his skin dusky, his face angular and thin, framed by short closely cropped dark hair. In a crowd he would not stand out: the anonymous man. He is of average height – I would say five ten – well proportioned, with a wiry physique that seems more sinew than muscle. Good-looking, but not enough to be noticeable in a lineup. He appears fit, his arms showing well-veined and -toned biceps and broad shoulders. He is dressed in a jail-issue tanktop T-shirt, baggy cotton sweatpants, and a pair of low-top canvas slip-on shoes with rubber soles.

The only visible blemishes are a couple of tiny pockmarks on his forehead and chin, and a small scar over the bridge of his nose at the point where it deviates just slightly to the left, leading me to suspect that his nose might have been broken at one time. There is a tattoo on the bicep of his left arm, what looks like the head of an eagle in profile, its beak sharp and open as if ready to take a bite.

Behind bars for more than four months now, even with the restraint of the chains, Ruiz still bears himself with a certain confidence. It's not the slick, false bravado, the cock-of-the-walk pimp roll of the jailhouse crowd, but something different. I'm just about to turn and say something to Harry when Ruiz does something so fast that, had I blinked, I would have missed it. With one of the guards still holding his left arm at the elbow, Ruiz lifts both feet off the ground, knees to his chest, his upper body stationary as if it's suspended in air, and in a single fluid motion he jumps the manacles so that his hands are now in front of him, feet on the floor again.

'Did you see that?' Harry cranes his neck as he stares through the window in the door. 'You ever see anybody do that before?'

'No.'

'I've never seen anybody do that.'

Neither have the guards, from the look on their faces.

'Guy must be double-jointed,' says Harry. 'I tried that, I'd end up with both shoulders out of their sockets and a hernia from the handcuffs wedged in my crotch.'

Ruiz is not your usual inmate.

'Maybe that explains the security,' Harry muses.

'Could be.'

'Let's hope he's not one of those guys needs to be rolled into court strapped to a furniture dolly, wearing a hockey mask to keep him from sinking his fangs into you.'

'You've been watching too many movies,' I tell him.

'Fine. You get to roll the dolly in and outta court,' says Harry. 'They're not doing all this shit out there' – he gestures loosely toward the window, turning away just before he finishes his thought in case Ruiz can read lips – 'for their health. I take that back. They probably *are* doing it for their health. So what do we know about this guy?'

'What are you looking for – references? The man's charged with murder.'

'I'm just looking to make sure he's not gonna eat us both before the guards come back.'

'He looks normal to me.'

'Looks can be deceiving.' Harry is a good lawyer. A bit of a worrier at times, but that goes with the trade. He is also very practical. He's been jumped twice by clients in the courtroom and once during a jail conference when Harry refused to put a psychotic client's cooked-up alibi witness on the stand.

Call it an occupational hazard. Get a bad result in a criminal case and an uncollected fee may be the least of your problems. One of Harry's old law-school profs once told him, 'When you practice on the criminal side, you want to represent your clients vigorously, but you don't bring them home to meet Mom.' Harry calls it keeping a proper social distance. Like he says, 'Most of these people have been arrested for a reason.'

'Actually, he's clean. No prior criminal record, at least not in civilian life. Military record is a little more clouded.'

'What, as in My Lai Massacre?' Harry's looking at me.

'Nothing like that; just a few blank spots we need to fill in. Some of his unit assignments are a little sketchy. According to Kendal, we just need to get copies of the records.'

When I got the first call in Ruiz's case, I received a file with some materials. Inside, along with documents was a photograph, an eight-by-ten glossy, black and white, a shot of Ruiz in his uniform, garrison cap in hand, standing somewhere on a street, cobblestones and old buildings in the background. He stands there staring directly into the camera lens as if looking right through it. It was as if the figure in that photograph could peer right through me, and could see my soul.

Standing outside the door, as one of the guards now works to remove the manacles from his hands, what strikes me besides Ruiz's composure – his apparent self-possessed lack of fear in the face of a capital charge – is the brooding fix of his lifeless eyes. I could be wrong. The hollow gaze I see staring back at me through the glass could be the look of a cold killer. Anything is possible. But that's not what I see. What I see is the thousand-yard stare, what I have always remembered as Evo's eyes.

CHAPTER
THREE

I introduce myself.

Ruiz smiles, a little sheepishly, and shakes my hand. But it is his first stated concern that would endear him to most lawyers.

'One question,' he says. 'How the hell am I supposed to pay you guys? You do understand I'm out of a job right now?'

Except for his Army pension, which isn't much at present, Ruiz has no means of support.

'For the moment somebody else is picking up the tab,' I tell him.

'Who?'

'An organization of retired military men. People like yourself. Some of them started businesses and have been quite successful. They set up a trust fund some years ago. Our firm has handled criminal cases for them in the past. We got the call on your case.'

'Kendal told me you would be coming by. You come well recommended.'

'I appreciate that.'

'So, you've done cases like this before?'

'You mean paid for out of the fund?'

'I mean a murder case.'

Though he doesn't say it, what he means is a death case, a trial in which capital punishment could be the ultimate result.

'Yes, I have.'

'I hope you won them all.'

I smile. 'I have never had a client executed, except once.'

He looks at me with a somewhat stark expression.

'I prosecuted the man years ago, in another city, when I was a deputy DA. I never took much pleasure in the result.' I change the subject. 'This is my partner, Harry Hinds.'

He shakes Harry's hand. 'Mind if we sit? Ankle chains start to wear on me if I stand too long.'

'Please.'

Ruiz half steps, dragging the chains on the concrete floor toward the stainless-steel table with its welded benches on each side like a metal picnic table. It is bolted to the floor against one wall in the small conference room on the third floor of the jail.

As Ruiz angles himself onto one of the benches, Harry taps on the thick acrylic window in the door. The guard opens it and looks at him through the crack.

'Maybe you could take the ankle chains off our client,' Harry tells him.

The guard shakes his head. 'Sorry. Can't do it.'

'Why not?'

'Orders.'

'We see clients here all the time. This is the first time—'

'First time for everything.' The guard closes the door in Harry's face.

Ruiz laughs. 'That's good, you talk to them. Kendal didn't have any more luck than you just did. Only time they take the chains off is in court. And then there's six of 'em in uniform hanging over me like a dark cloud.'

'I'll talk to the sheriff. If I have to, I'll get a writ.' Harry makes a note.

'You're hired.' Ruiz looks at me and smiles. 'You wouldn't have a cigarette, would you?'

I don't, but Harry does. My partner's fallen off the smokeless wagon again. He offers one to Ruiz, then lights it for him.

Ruiz takes a long drag, sucking the noxious vapor deep into his lungs, then settles back onto the bench seat and blows a smoke ring toward the ceiling. 'Startin' to like you guys already,' he says. 'Now, if you could just get me a good-lookin' woman . . .' He takes another drag, holds the smoke for a few seconds, then expels it through his nose. 'Good-lookin', hell,' he says. ' 'Bout now anything would look good. Four months in this hole. It's not that I haven't been in worse places, you understand. It's just that in those other places, they did things every once in a while to keep you entertained – break the monotony, so to speak.'

'Where was this?'

'Different places. Other countries. You know what they say: "Join the Army, see the world." Or is that the Navy?'

'What exactly did they do to entertain you? In these other places?' Harry wants to know.

'Oh. Sometimes they might use your tongue for an ashtray, put out their cigarettes on it. Other times they'd clean your fingernails with a knife.' He holds up his right hand and waves the fingers as if to show us a ring. 'Drive it right up in there,' says Ruiz. The nails from the middle two fingers are gone. Just a little cuticle and wrinkled skin remaining. 'Then, for a little variation on the theme, they'd wake you in the morning with a good beating, either truncheons or a cane, depending whether they wanted to work on the bottom of your feet or your back and legs. But these assholes' – Ruiz gestures with a slight nod of the head toward the guard outside – 'they just leave you in your cell twenty-three hours a day.'

'Some of my other clients claim they beat the crap out of them over here all the time,' says Harry. 'If you like, I can talk to the guards, see what I can do.'

Ruiz laughs. 'No, thanks. But maybe you can see if you can get me out of here. What are the chances of bail?'

This is not likely. A capital case involving a high-profile victim, a defendant with few contacts in the community, and a penchant for travel ... If Ruiz were to disappear, the judge who sprung him would have a lot of questions to answer. We put the issue of bail on the back burner for now.

He takes another drag, removes the cigarette from his mouth, and looks at it as he inhales the smoke deep into his lungs. 'Kendal's people, none of 'em smoke,' he says. 'Health nuts every one. Gonna live forever, I suppose. Fucking humorless bunch to boot. Don't know why I miss 'em so. Bit of a mystery, though.'

'What's that?' says Harry.

'Why did Kendal quit the case?' he asks. 'He pitched it in right after the preliminary hearing. I thought he did a pretty fair job. I mean, he couldn't have expected to win there, what with all the evidence they had stacked up against us like that.'

'You think they're out to get you?'

Ruiz is looking at the guard outside the door as I ask the question.

'What, him? No. He's just doing his job. Working stiff like me. He's gonna do whatever they tell him. But Kendal pisses me off. No excuse to cut and run. And I thought we hit it off pretty well. Then he ups and quits on me. I wasn't mad at him for losing the prelim. Hell, anybody could have done that.'

'I trust you'll cut us the same slack if we lose at trial,' says Harry.

'Your partner's got a good sense of humor,' he tells me. 'You I'm still trying to figure out.'

'According to what I understand, Mr Kendal had a conflicted calendar. Two other trials coming up,' I tell him.

'Yeah, that was the story he told me, too.' Ruiz is busy bending over, sitting on the bench, adjusting the chains on one ankle, cigarette dangling from his lip as he glances up at me from under hooded lids. 'Still, it would be nice to know exactly how they got to him.'

'Who's "they"?' Harry wants to know.

'Who's "they"?' says Ruiz. 'Who do you think? The government, that's who.'

'Why do you think the DA—'

'I'm not talking about the DA. I said the government. There's only one government counts in this country, and that's the federal government, as in US.'

Harry dances his pupils in my direction, the kind of look he normally reserves for clients relegated to a padded cell.

'Yeah, I know. But if you want to analyze me, at least let me lay on the table.' Ruiz sniffs Harry's judgment from the ether in the room without even looking up. 'We'll see how long it takes them to reach you.'

'What makes you think the federal government is on your case?' I ask.

'That's not it at all. They're not out to get me. Not in the way you think. The fact is, I happen to be convenient. In the right place at the wrong time, so to speak. What they want is this thing with Chapman to go away and with as little fuss as possible. A quick conviction and a closed case, and right now I'm what you might call handy. Like a Kleenex. It's nothing personal. Just another interchangeable unit to be used by people in high places.' He lets the ankle chains drop down over the tops of his canvas slip-on sneakers again and looks up at me to see if I'm following.

'You have to understand, I've been doing this for a long time, watching people get killed and killing people.'

'You *what*?' says Harry.

'In the military,' he says. 'It's called combat.'

'Oh. Right.'

'I didn't kill Chapman, if that's what you're thinking. I would never do anything like that. I know it's hard for some people to believe. They think somebody's trained to kill and it's like a switch they can't turn off. They get out of the military and they have to satisfy some itch to kill. It's not like that at all. Most soldiers I know could live very contented and happy lives if they never saw another drop of blood as long as they lived. But it's a funny thing: You pull a trigger in combat and they give you a medal. Do it in civilian life and they put you behind bars, or worse. But in this one it wasn't me on their radar screen; it was her.'

'Who?'

'The victim. The murderee. Who else? Madelyn. Excuse me – Miss Chapman. It won't do for me to be too familiar with the victim, her being dead and all, and me being the one supposed to have killed her.' He suddenly stops and looks at me. 'She is still dead?'

'Oh. She's dead all right,' I tell him.

'You had me going there for a moment. Thought maybe the people at Spook Central had come up with a new program to raise the dead. At least they haven't changed that part of the script.' He takes a drag and exhales some smoke. 'Of course they start swapping out bodies on us, no tellin' where we'll end up. Get me for doin' JFK from the grassy knoll before they're done. The fact I wasn't born till years after the deed is only a minor setback for these people. Blink and they'll change reality for you.'

'You're telling us the government had a hand in this?' I ask.

'Who knows? Anything's possible.'

'How well did you know the victim?' says Harry.

'Not well enough. Otherwise I'd probably have a better idea who killed her. As for the list of her toy boys, if you want that, you're gonna want to call in a stenographer to keep from getting writer's cramp.'

'Sounds like you knew her pretty well,' I say.

'We had our moments. I provided security. She provided the surprises. There was a fleeting period she fit me into her schedule between her morning massage and her eleven o'clock staff meeting. She liked to be on top. In control. That was Madelyn, always on top and always in control. She'd be up there, jumping up and down like she was breaking some bronco, gripping the hair on my chest with

49

one hand while she waved her little digital dictator in the air with the other. In between groans of ecstasy and elation, she'd lift the pause button and spout a quick memo on some new project or government contract so her secretary could type it up between bouts.'

'So you *did* have an affair with her?' There was some brief testimony at the preliminary regarding allegations, but since the defense never put on a case in this regard, it was unclear from the transcript what the line to be taken at trial would be.

'I don't know that I'd go so far as to call it an affair,' says Ruiz. 'Fact is, I probably wouldn't have even mentioned it, except they have it on tape.'

'Let me get this straight,' says Harry. 'You had a sexual relationship with the victim and the prosecution has a videotape of this?'

Ruiz makes a face, weighing and evaluating the terms used in the question, then shrugs his shoulders. 'Yeah. That pretty much sums it up. It was one of those little cameras: you know, the kind about the size of an eraser on a pencil. Apparently one of our own people installed the thing in her office without checking. Caught the whole thing on tape. Unfortunately for me, the cops now have the tape.'

I can already tell what Harry is thinking. If the judge allows the DA to play that tape in front of the jury, moving pictures in living color of the defendant – who is now charged with murder – screwing the victim – who is now dead – chances of the state getting a conviction will go up about a thousand percent. And it won't really matter who was on top.

'I take it this wasn't part of the security contract,' says Harry.

Ruiz laughs. 'No. It just sort of happened. Call it an after-hours thing. Off the books, you might say. Fact of the matter is, as I remember it, I was on my back, counting ceiling tiles, before I knew what she was doing.'

'She raped you,' Harry says. 'There we go. We have a defense. The murder was a crime of revenge.' Harry looks at me and smiles.

'You'll have to excuse my partner. He believes if you can't defend a good murder case and have some fun in the process, you shouldn't be doing it.'

'I see his point. The fact of the matter is, while I don't exactly remember how it happened, I don't remember saying no as I was laying there, either. And it's not a case of repressed memory.' He says it before Harry can say anything.

'Oh, well,' says Harry.

'Not that it bothered me much. Consenting adults and all.'

'Still, you have to assume your employer might take a dim view,' I tell him.

'You, I suspect, must have a knack for business' – Ruiz points at me with the smoking cigarette, holding it between two fingers – 'because that's exactly the point Madelyn made when she came back for seconds a few days later and I said no.'

'She threatened you?'

'Not in so many words. She just wondered out loud what the people at Karr, Rufus would say if they heard I wasn't servicing the contract to her satisfaction.'

'She said that to you?'

'In so many words, yes.'

'And what did you do?'

'We both laughed, and then she got on top.'

'I had an uncle who was a night watchman,'

51

says Harry. 'He was always complaining it was such a boring job.'

'He didn't work executive protection at Isotenics,' says Ruiz.

'So the prosecution is going to say that you had an affair with her and probably try to build on it from there.'

'How is that?' he asks.

'The usual scenario,' I say. 'She tried to break it off. You refused. The jilted lover. A woman with lots of money. Fill in the blanks.'

'It was nothing like that.'

'Well, we'll have our chance to tell the jury. But that's likely to be their theory. That is, unless they have some other motive that's better. Is there any other reason you might have wanted to kill her?'

'I didn't kill her.'

'That's not the point. The question is, did you have a motive?'

'No.' He shakes his head. 'I liked her. Why would I want to kill her?'

'We could try a stipulation,' says Harry. 'Admit that they had sexual relations. Specify the number of times this occurred. Try to sanitize it. Make it sound like an accountant's audit report and hope we can glaze over the eyes of the jury. Try to keep the tape out of evidence.'

'I haven't seen the tape, but I can't imagine it's all that bad,' says Ruiz.

'Fancy yourself a porn star, do you?' Harry quips.

'No, no. It's nothing like that. I guarantee you, there's nothing kinky on the tape unless somebody dubbed it in.'

'You're thinking the federal government again?' Harry asks. 'Do they have a federal office that does that kind of thing?'

'Come on, gimme a break,' says Ruiz. 'We had a fling. A romp in the hay. I didn't love her. She didn't love me. Two adults, we enjoyed the moment. She went her way, I went mine. That's all there was to it.'

'The problem is, she's dead,' I say, 'and somebody killed her.'

'But I didn't do it.'

'Yeah, well, put that aside for the moment,' says Harry. 'The more immediate problem is that videotape no doubt captures only a brief period in time when, as you say, the two of you were enjoying the moment. When passion was at its height, shall we say. That's what the jury is going to see, and what they're going to remember, not the rational attitude of two sober and mature adults after all the hedonism was over.' Harry pauses. 'That leaves a lot of room for imagination. And therein lies a lot of room for mischief on the part of the wily prosecutor. Ordinarily I'd say they might not get the tape in being as it's so prejudicial. But in this case,' Harry reasons, 'I might make an exception, because it may be the best evidence. In fact, it may be the only evidence to substantiate their theory that you had an affair with the victim.'

'Ordinarily I'd say you'd be right,' Ruiz says, 'but in this case . . .'

'What?' Harry sits up straight. 'You're not gonna tell us you had an audience!'

'Not in so many words. But somebody did see us.'

'Who?'

'Chapman's executive assistant. Gal by the name of Karen. I suspect that's how the cops got the tape. I don't know, but I suspect she probably gave it to them after the murder. She might have thought I had something to do with it.'

'Can't imagine that,' says Harry. 'Your gun being used, your holding over in the house with her, doing security.'

'You don't think it's looking too good,' says Ruiz.

'Let's just put it this way: I don't think anybody would have to threaten me to get me to drop out of the case.'

'You think Kendal took a hike because he didn't believe he could win?'

Harry gives him a look that concedes the point.

Ruiz takes a deep breath and sighs.

'Let's change gears for a moment. What is your marital status?' I ask.

'Why?'

'Are you married?' In the eyes of many jurors, cheating on his wife would compound the problem.

'Divorced,' he says.

'How long?'

'Almost six years.'

'Children?'

'Two. A boy and girl. My son is twelve, my daughter is seven. I don't want them involved in this.'

'Children sitting in the courtroom can be a big plus,' says Harry. 'They don't have to be there every day.'

'You heard me: the answer is no. Besides, their mother is not gonna let you or anybody else put them through that.'

'What about your wife?'

'Ex-wife. Tracy is remarried. She was young when we got hitched. Military life did us in. I was always gone. Not that she wasn't faithful, but you know how it is: she got lonely. I was away from home for months at a time. After a while it seemed like we didn't even know each other anymore. She's not gonna come sit in a courtroom, I can tell you that. And she's not gonna let the kids do it. It'll be hard enough what they see on television. If I know Tracy, she'll be pulling the plug on the set and canceling the newspaper subscription to keep them from seeing it.'

'Well, at least you didn't have any ties at the time keeping you away from Chapman,' says Harry. 'That's something.' Harry makes the best of little favors.

'I have to admit, Madelyn wasn't what you would call discreet,' says Ruiz. 'I mean, she didn't tell the world or wear a sandwich board with pictures. But she didn't lock her office door, either. I guess her attitude was she owned the place, so if people didn't like it they could quit.

'The secretary walked in on us.' Ruiz is talking about Chapman's executive assistant. 'What can I say? We both moved pretty quickly to cover up, but the secretary has to have seen what was happening. She walked in, looked, turned, and walked out. She seemed to look right through me like I was part of the furniture. Maybe she was just stunned. I don't know.'

'So it was the secretary who must have told the cops about the tape?' I say.

'I don't know,' says Ruiz. 'My guess is word would have gotten around pretty fast. I didn't know the camera was there. If it was being monitored we had a live audience. If not, somebody would probably have seen it sooner or later. Like I say, it was only the two times. The first time she came on strong and I backed away. Nothing really happened. Not that anyone is going to believe me.

Then the tape. After I got burned, I started to keep my distance. Not that Madelyn wasn't trying, mind you. I made a point to put another guy on the detail with me at the house at night, so he and I shared the room down the hall. That seemed to slow her down. A couple of months later she canceled the personal security detail, my assignment changed, and the problem went away. Or at least I thought it did.'

'Why did she cancel security?' I ask.

'Beats the hell out of me. Maybe she was frustrated.'

'As far as you know, did she have affairs with anyone else?'

'She had guys over, if that's what you mean. I mean, she wasn't trying to hide the fact. Whether they were friends, business acquaintances, whatever. Don't know their names. But several times they spent the night bouncing off the walls down the hall. I heard 'em. So did the guy on the detail with me.'

'Problem is, that cuts both ways,' says Harry. 'If you knew she was having affairs with other men, it could have fueled jealousy. It feeds right into their theory.'

Harry is right. But it also provides other suspects, other men who might have had a reason to kill her if they saw something they wanted bad enough slipping away.

'A couple of times she had us escort her to parties. You know, business things. On the way home she'd want to stop at this club downtown. We'd sit at one table, she'd sit at another. Guys would come up and talk to her. If she wasn't interested she'd nod toward us and tell the guy that the bulge under our armpits wasn't swollen lymph nodes and the fucker would vanish like vapor. When she got the one she wanted we'd all head home, my partner or I driving while she and her new friend did warm-ups in the backseat.'

'Sounds like the security detail didn't cramp her sense of privacy,' I say.

Ruiz laughs. 'The fact she had an audience probably added a whole new dimension as far as Madelyn was concerned.'

'And, of course, you didn't mind?' I ask. 'I mean, you didn't feel in any way jilted?'

'What? That I wasn't being used like a mechanical bull anymore? No. I grant you she was a good-looking woman, but as far as emotions were concerned, anything with Madelyn had all the depth of a kiddy pool. She could have gotten the same thing from a mannequin.'

We change the subject. 'What do you know about the Information for Security Program?' I ask.

'You know I signed a piece of paper when I went to work at Isotenics. It was given to me by my supervisor at Karr, Rufus. It said I wouldn't discuss any of what they call "proprietary information" that I might have overheard when I was on duty. So I don't know if I'm supposed to tell you.'

'They fired your ass and you're facing a murder charge,' Harry points out. 'I wouldn't worry about it.'

'Yeah. You're right.'

'So what did you hear?' says Harry.

'About IFS? That's all they talked about. Information for Security. From what I gather, it was huge. Biggest project they had. Every time something broke in the press, some committee in Congress started cryin' over privacy rights and people at Isotenics would all start filling sandbags and barricading the doors. They were busy stiffing two congressional investigating committees. I mean, you could hear them talking about it on the phones.'

'So you knew they were writing the software?'

He nods. 'Sure. You hear things. Little bits here and there. You're driving a car and they're in the back on the cell phone, you can't help but hear.'

'Do you know what the software is, how it works?'

He shakes his head. 'Seen the stuff in the newspaper, that's all. I'd read the stories 'cuz I knew there was a connection. But other than that, when it comes to computers, I'm a man from Mars.'

'Did you ever meet any of the people involved in the program from the government side?' I ask.

'It's possible. They had us pick up people at the airport from time to time. A few times we went out to the base at Miramar and picked up some uniforms coming in on military flights. Drove them out to Software City for meetings. But all you got was a name. They never told us what they were working on. There was one guy, though. I do remember him and his name did pop up on the program you're talking about.'

'Who was that?'

'Retired general. Name of Gerald Satz. I'd seen his name in the papers. According to the articles, he was in charge of this IFS thing. From what I read he was hired as a civilian consultant. Thought it was sort of a strange selection myself. You know who the guy is?'

I nod. Gerald Satz, aka 'Poster Boy for Perjury,' according to liberals in Congress; a stand-up warrior and top-notch soldier, according to his fans.

'I knew the name,' says Ruiz, ''cuz I remembered hearing about him when I was in the Army and reading about it in the paper. According to what I heard, he had a long history working with spooks, intel agencies, black-bag shit. Satz had contacts buried in the bowels of governments on every continent. A man knows where the bodies are buried because he put half of them there. And he knows how to dig them up whenever it serves his purposes, or maybe the purposes of his prince. Satz is what some people might call a true believer.

'Some years back – I was a kid, so I don't know the details – Congress got caught screwing with Satz's constitutional rights.' Ruiz continues, 'A committee took his testimony under oath. When they couldn't get him on perjury, they tried to use his own testimony to indict him. The courts said they couldn't do it.'

'It's called use immunity,' I tell him. 'You looked this up and read about it?'

He nods. 'When one of our people was assigned to go pick him up at the airport. The man was coming to a meeting at Isotenics. I got curious and checked his history on-line. Sounds like maybe he beat the charges on technical grounds.'

'Suppose you could call that technical,' says Harry. 'But from where I'm usually sitting, I'd call it a good result.' My partner has a problem with a political system that gives members of Congress a monopoly on lying.

'Still, it ruined his career. Forced him out of the military and still he's hanging around. That's what I call survival. Man sounds like a tough nut to crack. But what I found interesting is the fact that Satz and Chapman went back a long way.'

Harry raises an eyebrow and looks up from his notepad.

'Back fifteen years ago, Madelyn came out of nowhere. Graduated from a small school in the Midwest with a degree in computer engineering and software design. She took a job working as a GS-3 for the government in Washington and three years later she was a technical adviser on the White House staff.' Ruiz looks at me and winks.

'Where I come from, they call that upward mobility,' says Harry.

'Where I come from, that kind of upward mobility usually requires connections,' I say.

'Bingo,' says Ruiz. 'General Gerald Satz. From the little bit I heard and saw, he was the key.'

'Did you ever meet him? Satz, I mean.'

'Heard about him a lot. He was what you might call a legend. Had a reputation for loyalty, not that that's a vice. But in his case it bordered on fanatical. People convicted of crimes, if they were doing something everybody knew was illegal, but to Satz and others it was necessary, he'd stand up for them. Do it publicly. All the rest of the brass would be ducking for cover. Satz would be right there. It made him popular among the enlisted men, the NCOs. I was impressed when I first heard Madelyn mention his name.'

'How old is this guy?' says Harry.

'Satz? I don't know. Probably early sixties. Don't get the wrong idea: I don't think there was anything physical going on between them. From what I know, it was more in the nature of what you would call paternal guidance. She worked for him. Did whatever he asked, long hours, never complained. In return he introduced her around. Madelyn did the rest.

'If you knew her, which of course you didn't, you'd come to understand that with Madelyn, all it took was an opening, a crack in the door, and she was in. She had a natural talent for self-promotion. If you had a vital project, lives depending on it, and you were looking for somebody to put in a forty-hour workday to get it done before men died, Madelyn was your cookie. She could be efficient to the point of obsession.'

'Sounds like you knew her pretty well,' says Harry.

'Nobody knew Madelyn. Not really. Not if you mean the heaving, heaping boiler-stoked-with-white-hot-coals, engine-of-ambition Madelyn. And that's what she was ninety-eight percent of the time.'

'And the other two percent?' I ask.

He looks at me but doesn't respond.

'Where did you get all this information, the history on her and Satz?' I ask.

'Part of it came from Madelyn. Partly, bits and pieces, from what I heard.'

'Go on.'

'The rest,' he explains, 'requires a bit of faith. I don't have any solid information. You sort of have to piece things together. Toward the end, Madelyn was scared. Not all the time, mind you, but at times. Something was happening. I don't know the details. But I do know that she and Satz had some kind of a falling-out. A serious disagreement. I don't know what it was about, but it's not a long leap to assume that it had something to do with this IFS thing, Information for Security. She was angry, she was pissed, but most of all she was scared. Madelyn was used to getting her way. But something had gone wrong.'

61

'What?'

'I don't know. But from what I saw and heard, she was in a box and was having trouble finding her way out. Satz asked her to do him a personal favor. She told him she couldn't do it.'

'She told you this?'

'Not in so many words. But I'm fairly certain.'

'What kind of favor?' Harry presses.

'I'm not sure. It had something to do with business. I assumed it had to do with IFS. The newspapers were full of it at the time. The news out of Washington was that Congress was going to kill the program unless they could find some fix for privacy issues. They don't care if a few hundred soldiers get killed hunting. From what I heard, whatever it was that Satz wanted her to do, there were risks – more than she wanted to take – and their relationship, Chapman's and Satz's, had changed. She wasn't some young staffer at the Pentagon anymore. Madelyn was big business, with a multi-billion-dollar stake, and if I had to guess, given the sweat she was in, whatever Satz was asking her to do was threatening to put all that in jeopardy.'

'But you don't know what it was that he was asking?' I persist.

Ruiz shakes his head.

'The last I heard, she was about to tell him she couldn't do it. That was the last time I saw her.'

'When was that?'

'About a week before she was killed.' He looks at me as he says it, reading the expression on my face, which is one of surprise. This information is not in the file. Nor was it in any of Kendal's notes that he passed to me. If Ruiz told any of his other lawyers about this, they knew better than to reduce it to writing.

Suddenly a deafening sound, loud enough that it feels as if someone has driven a spike through my eardrums. Ruiz's lips move but I can't hear a word. I look at Harry and he has both hands over his ears. The klaxon, a buzzer in a box high on the wall behind us, has erupted, drowning out everything else in the room.

The guard comes in waving his arms. He makes a motion, one finger across his throat. The interview is over.

Harry cups a hand over his mouth and then to my ear and, loud enough that I can just hear him, says: 'Lockdown.'

Something has happened. Another guard comes into the room and we are quickly ushered toward the door. The last thing I see over my shoulder is Ruiz shaking his head, muffling his ears with his hands as the two guards pull them down and cuff them behind his back; he looks at me, wondering, I am sure, if and when he will see us again. Harry and I, my briefcase half open with papers sticking out, are hustled down the hall to the elevator.

CHAPTER FOUR

'Q uestion is, how did the killer know where to find the gun?'

I'm looking at Harry over the conference table in our office. The contents of two cardboard file boxes, documents and photographs, evidence reports and copies of investigative notes obtained by a notice for discovery served on the cops, are spread out in front of us.

Our office has expanded so that we now occupy an entire wing of low-slung buildings under the jungle canopy of banana trees and palms in the courtyard behind Miguel's Cantina just off of Orange Grove, across from the Del Coronado.

'It is possible,' says Harry, 'the killer just stumbled onto the gun. Could happen.'

'I don't think so. Look at the photos of the house, the floor plan produced by the cops.' We have several eight-by-tens, interior shots of the victim's home as well as an overhead aerial shot probably taken from a police helicopter.

'The place is over seven thousand square feet. Nooks and crannies everywhere, drawers galore, to say nothing of all those display cases housing Chapman's glass menagerie.'

'Your point is?' says Harry.

'My point is nothing else was touched. According to the police report, nothing tossed, no open drawers except for the one where the gun was stored, nothing dropped on the floor, no latent prints, nothing. The place was cleaner than your average autoclave. Only the gun and this . . . this one piece of art – what was it called?'

Harry thumbs through his notes.

We have each gone through the materials, Harry taking the time for notes. I have scanned the high points, leaving Harry to fill me in on details.

'Here it is: glass artwork, blue in color, called the *Orb at the Edge*. Got a picture out of a catalog here someplace.'

'It's all right. I saw it going through the photos. It's the only item known to be missing from the victim's house. Is that right?'

'At least according to the cops,' says Harry. 'Could be whoever did it just panicked. Think about it: You just get in the place, getting ready to do your burglary. She walks in. You freak out. You pop her. It's happened before.'

'Hell of a shooter for a panicky burglar.' I am talking about the two shots to the head. 'Less than an inch apart.'

'Could just be luck,' says Harry.

According to the state's ballistics expert, all this fine shooting took place at a distance of at least thirty feet, standing on a balcony above the main entrance to the victim's home.

'So maybe it cooks the theory of a teenage burglary gone awry,' says Harry.

'Unless she's fifteen and her name is Annie

Oakley. And it still doesn't explain how the killer found the gun.'

Chapman's house was large, with six bedrooms spread out on two floors, each one with its own adjoining bath.

'Unless you knew your way around, you would need a map,' I tell him.

'Yeah.' Harry is stumped.

'Do they say how the killer got in?'

'According to the cops, he popped a downstairs screen and came in through a window. One of the bedrooms on the bottom floor on the ocean side.'

'Makes sense. Nobody could see him. Was there a security system?'

'Oh, yeah. Top end. All the bells and whistles, window sensors, doors, motion detectors, glass-break sensors, twenty-four-seven monitoring, eye in the sky, cameras front and back, everything wired up the ass. Chapman paid sixty grand for the system. Only problem was, she never turned it on. According to Chapman's secretary, the hired help was always setting it off, the gardeners, the maid, the Fed-Ex man, the hummingbird that ate out of the feeder on her front porch. Apparently during the first two weeks after they installed it, Chapman got called away from work four times, three of 'em to bail her gardener out of the back of a squad car where they had him cuffed and once to vouch for the hummingbird, which they were unable to catch. Finally she said screw it and turned the system off.'

'You said there were cameras?'

'Front one scanned the entry door and picked up nothing. One in the back somebody took the tape out of it. Could have been the killer. Could have been Chapman or somebody else. Nobody seems to know. All they know is that there was no tape in the recorder on the day of the murder.'

'Great. A sixty-thousand-dollar security system whose only efficient application is to condition the owner not to turn it on.'

'About the size of it,' says Harry.

'Were there security stickers on the windows?' I ask.

Harry looks at me with a blank expression.

'You know the little decals that say "This property is protected by Wile E. Coyote," whatever.'

'I don't know.'

'Better find out. They don't usually put a system in unless they sticker the strategic openings. If that's the case it's bad for us.'

What I am thinking is that the state's going to say anybody who wasn't familiar with the house wouldn't take the chance that popping a screen and opening a downstairs window would set off the alarm and send a signal to some monitoring station somewhere.

Harry makes a note. Who besides Chapman's own bodyguard would know that the security system was seldom, if ever, on?

'And of course the best candidate for the kind of shooting we're talking about here is our own client,' says Harry.

'You mean his military background?'

'I wish that's all it was. It turns out that among his other gifts, like jumping backwards out of handcuffs, is the fact that he qualified three years running for the US Army Pistol Team,' says Harry.

'Wonderful.'

'Yeah, the cops went to great pains to provide us with all the details. Seems Ruiz and his teammates won two of the national shoots back at Fort

Benning. Of course, this was a few years ago now, so he might be a little rusty.'

'Great, we can put him on the stand and have him perform a shooting exhibition with the murder weapon for the jury. Keep our fingers crossed he misses. That should be persuasive. Next you're going to tell me that the pistol of choice he fired during the competition was the same one used to kill Chapman.'

'Fortunately, no. It was, however, a forty-five auto, same caliber,' says Harry, 'but it wasn't an HK. It was the old Colt 1911 Model.'

'So if we draw a jury composed of gun nuts and armorers, we can make the point. Correct me if I'm wrong, but didn't the military go to the nine millimeter for sidearms some years ago?'

Harry nods. 'Yeah, Beretta 92F is the piece they use now. But for some reason Ruiz and his team shot with the old Colt.'

'And yet, the gun used to kill Chapman, a forty-five auto, was issued to Ruiz and belonged to the military. See if you can find out why.'

Harry makes a note.

'How about the state's theory of a love interest: murder by jealousy. Anything in their notes on that?'

Harry shakes his head. 'You have to figure they aren't gonna put that in their notes. Theory of their case. If they have witnesses, you can be sure they'll be well concealed on their list.'

What Harry means is lost in a forest of other names.

What is in the file is the lurid videotape showing Ruiz and Chapman on the couch in her office at Isotenics. While the production values, color, and lighting leave a little to be desired, the action –

punctuated as it is by heavy breathing and some audible moans – leaves nothing to the imagination.

'How would you read it?' Harry is talking about the tape. 'You think she was the aggressor?'

'If I had to call it on points, I'd say it was a draw.'

Harry nods. 'We're gonna need a good wind at our back if we're going to sell the jury on the notion that she seduced him.'

'Anything else?' I ask.

'That's about it. Some details here and there. We have the original pathology report, but the medical examiner is still working on some details they haven't released yet.'

'What kind of details?'

'They aren't saying. They say they're just about done. They'll ship it over as soon as they're finished. As soon as it comes I'll get it to you.'

Harry starts to package up some of the papers on the table. 'One thing is clear,' he says. 'The cops and the DA are putting all their eggs in Ruiz's basket. From everything I've seen and read, he's been their only theory of the case from the get-go. Never even looked at the possibility of a burglary. Ruiz is right about one thing.'

'What's that?'

'He is very convenient,' says Harry. 'The man touches every base. Who would have known where the gun was except him? Who else knew the security system was off? He was familiar with the house and the layout. Only thing they might be a little weak on is motive.'

'Give them a few more days and I'm sure they'll shore that up.'

'You heard him at the jail. He could just be good at covering his emotions, but it sure didn't sound like he was infatuated with her to me. I suppose the DA can try to make out a case of twisted lust, given the tape,' he says.

'If they show it more than once, the judge is going to have to call a break so the jury can take a cold shower,' I tell him.

'That does not a murder make,' says Harry.

'Let's hope not.' For the moment I am worried about the tight group to the head, one of the most damaging pieces of evidence, particularly since it came from Ruiz's gun and given his background in the military as a shooter. 'What about the gun?'

'What about it?'

'According to the police report, the firearm was taken from a drawer in a dresser upstairs, off the main floor, a guest room previously used by Ruiz when he was providing security. With all that glass behind glass, with expensive electronics in open view in the living room, why stop to run upstairs and rifle through the drawers of a dresser if your purpose is burglary? Unless of course you already know that what you're looking for is in that particular drawer.'

'You're saying that the killer knew where the gun was?'

'I'm saying that the purpose wasn't burglary or robbery or any other crime involving property. The purpose was murder. And, based on the evidence, that's what the prosecution is going to say: that gun was the first thing the killer went for.'

'And of course who knew where the gun was kept?'

Harry and I harmonize on this one: 'Ruiz.'

'We need to find out who else knew about the firearm. That's the key. The wider the knowledge, the better off for us. If Ruiz showed it to anyone. If he told anyone where it was. If anyone else in the house knew about it. Put that at the top of your list: things to check out,' I tell him.

He makes a note starting with Ruiz as soon as we can get to him at the jail. They are now in their second day of lockdown. From what we are reading in the paper and hearing at the courthouse, all of this is the result of a stabbing. They are now scouring cells looking for shivs, turning the bedding upside down and tapping the walls, looking for hollowed-out places carved in the concrete, pasted over with watered oatmeal, and colored with acrylic paints used by inmates in art classes: a favored hiding place because it is neutral, not tied to an inmate's bunk or belongings. Life and death in the lock-up.

'Ruiz did tell us he made sure another employee was assigned whenever he slept over at Chapman's house,' says Harry.

If this is true, it cuts against the theory that he was trying to make time chasing after the victim. It augurs well for the defense that he was trying to keep his distance.

'If we can prove it,' I tell him.

'And maybe,' says Harry, 'that other employee knew about the gun, where it was kept.'

'Check it out. Put it on the list.'

'I'm gonna need help if I'm gonna run all this down.' Harry has cases, some dogs barking back in his office. He will have to clear the decks.

'We'll bring somebody in.'

'Who?'

'Let me work on it,' I tell him.

'One other thing,' he adds. 'We need to find out why Ruiz left the gun at her house when the security assignment ended. That's a pretty expensive firearm to just leave behind when you change jobs.'

'The cops asked him that.'

'I didn't see it,' says Harry.

'Said he just forgot it was there. According to Ruiz, he never carried it concealed. It was too big. He carried a small, compact Glock, a nine-millimeter, when he needed to be armed.'

'So why was it at the house?' Harry wonders aloud.

I shake my head. 'Let's find out.'

Harry makes a note to talk to Ruiz about it just as soon as we can corner him at the jail.

'Anything else?' I ask.

He looks down his list. 'Just this *Orb* thing. I don't know about you, but I get the sense it was worth a bundle.'

'She had an extensive collection of art glass, according to the reports. I doubt, given her position, her income, that she bought junk.'

'It's more than that. The cops are playing hide-the-receipt. They won't say what she paid for it. By now they've gotta know. They talked to the owner of the shop where Chapman bought it. They would have seized any bill of sale. Probably found the corresponding copy in her purse or in her car after they found her body.'

Harry is right. It was purchased the afternoon she was murdered.

'So why hide it?' says Harry.

'Motive?'

Harry nods. 'That's what I'm thinking. If somebody saw her buy it, knew what she paid for it . . .'

'Let's find out. Subpoena her bank and credit card statements. All of them. If we have to, get an order for discovery. Force them to cough up the bill of sale. While you're at it, see if we can get some background on this thing. What was it called?'

'*Orb at the Edge*,' says Harry.

'This *Orb*. If she wanted it as part of her collection, it probably has a history. Find out who owned it, where it came from, who might have wanted to own it, when it was made, everything you can regarding its pedigree.'

The building is well past its prime. If I had to guess I would say something from the late forties, put up during the postwar building boom when materials were at a premium. It is a universe away from the opulent government palaces built by dollar-a-day WPA artisans during the Depression: post office buildings with soaring Doric columns of granite and Tennessee marble lining the walls and floors. Today the best of these have all been squatted on by the federal courts and refurbished to within an inch of their original splendor.

What I am looking at from across the street, isn't even a distant relative. Five stories high, it stands ten blocks to the south of the trendy Gaslamp Quarter and maybe a decade from the grasping clutches and wrecking ball of urban renewal.

I skip across the street midblock, dodging cars, and climb the two cement steps leading to the main entrance. Inside is a directory, names and office numbers behind smudged glass with a hodgepodge of block letters of varying sizes and colors, some metal, some plastic. I find the one I'm looking for and take the elevator to the third floor.

The office is on the back side of the building.

The lights are on inside, enough illumination for me to see the hulking shadow of a figure, its outline skipping across the dappled glass every few seconds as it moves. No voices, so I assume he is not on the phone.

As I turn the knob and swing the door open without knocking, I see Herman Diggs, his massive shoulders hunched, neck bowed like a Brahma bull, his eyes trained on a piece of paper. Several piles of papers are neatly stacked across the top of his desk. As Herman looks up, it takes a second before he makes the leap from written word to familiar face, then he smiles. His missing front tooth looking like a gap in a fence.

'Whoa. Look what the wind blew in. Is that Paul Madriani I see?'

'In the flesh,' I tell him.

'Didn't expect to see *you*.' Herman pushes his chair back from the desk. It takes him a second to get to his feet. 'How you been?'

'I'm fine. But you should learn to keep your door locked if you're going to do dangerous work.'

'What you talkin' 'bout, "dangerous work"?' He's smiling, moving around the desk to greet me.

'I've been told you're doing divorce cases. It doesn't get any more dangerous than that.'

'Hell, only dangerous work I ever did was workin' for you.' Herman's laughing, hobbling a little on a stiff leg, one hand on the furniture to steady himself, evidence of the truth in his last statement. He offers me his hand, big and beefy, the size of a baseball glove.

'I hope I didn't catch you at a bad time.'

'Be a sad day when I don't have time for friends,' says Herman.

'I should have called first, but I was in the area.'

'Hey, don't be foolish. Actually I'm busy as hell. You know how it is. When you're good at what you do, your services are always in demand. But I can always make time for a friend. My next appointment's not till' – he looks at his watch – 'let's see, next Wednesday.' Herman laughs, full of his own version of blarney and bluster. 'How 'bout a cup of coffee so's we can sit and bullshit a little longer? Keep me from that pile of papers over on my desk there.'

'Not for me. Just had lunch downtown. A meeting with a client.'

I take a seat in one of his client chairs. The chairs, like Herman's desk, are scarred with someone's carved initials, grooved and tattooed in assorted colors of ink. 'So how's business?'

'It's growin', comin' along,' he says. 'Picking up a few cases here, a few there. It takes time. You know what I mean?'

'I do. I almost didn't stop in. I thought you might be out working the shoe leather.'

'Fact is, you saved me from a fate worse than death.' He gestures toward the stacks on his desk. 'Don't have a secretary as yet, so I gots to do my own filing. Hate that shit.' Herman moves to a little table by one of the filing cabinets against the wall, a coffeemaker and some cups on top of it. He pours himself a cup.

'How's the leg?'

'Oh, that. It's no problem.' He moves his right leg a little, heel and toe tapping – Fred Astaire on one leg – as he rests all his weight on the other foot, a demonstration to show me that the leg still works. 'It's nothin'. Just tends to stiffen up when I sit too long.'

Herman is like the soldier shot in both lungs

who told the medic he was okay since it only hurt when he breathed.

'Be fine,' he says. 'All I need is to pick up a few more clients so I can get out an' about. This sittin' behind a desk is not good. Puttin' on weight, too.'

'Yeah, I noticed that right off.' Herman is a brick, solid muscle, well over six feet. He probably tips the scale at 250 pounds and claps his hands between his hundred push-ups every morning.

He settles his behind on the edge of his desk, cup in hand as he sips and smiles down at me. I met Herman two years ago while trying to tie up loose ends on a case down in Mexico, the Yucatán Peninsula. Herman had been brought in as part of a security team. At the time he was working for a large firm out of Chicago. He ended up taking two bullets; an act that would have ended my life if he hadn't. I've not forgotten it.

'Harry said he heard you were in town. Said he saw an ad in one of the community throwaways. Little yellow tabloid.'

Herman thinks for a second then slaps his good leg. *'Triple Nickel,'* he says. 'Little gold mine. As I recall, I picked up three clients from that one. Divorcées out in the east county. You know, cowboy country. Good ad. Know, 'cuz I wrote it myself. How'd it go?' He closes his eyes and traces the words with a finger through air as he recites. ' "Put a tail behind your husband. Put your mind at ease. Make sure he's got no tail on the side. Discreet Investigations. Herman Diggs & Associates." ' He opens his eyes, gives me a smile. 'Not bad for a guy never finished college, huh? What the man said: "You gotta keep 'em entertained – you gonna put your hand in their pocket." '

'So how long have you been here?'

'What? This place?'

'In town, I mean.'

'Oh, I dunno. Three, four months.'

'And you didn't stop by?'

'Been busy,' he says. 'All kindsa things to do when you open a business. You know how it is. Gotta get furniture and phones in. Name and number in the Yellow Pages. My license over there . . .' Herman gestures with an offhand nod and a dip of his shoulder toward a lonely certificate under glass in a black frame hanging high on the wall behind his desk chair. This is as casual as it gets for a man who tips the scales at eighteen stone and was once viewed as budding lineback material by the NFL. Herman went south to work in Mexico after his college scholarship did the same, the result of an early knee injury.

'Been in this office, what, maybe a month. Course, this is just a watering spot, you understand, a kinda way station like they say. Be workin' my way toward greener pastures shortly.' What Herman means is when he actually catches up with all of those associates he currently has employed only in his ads and on his business cards, one of which he plucks from a plastic holder on his desk and hands to me.

Herman is hardworking, energetic, what you would call a natural self-starter. His enthusiasm is such that trying to chill any plan he has ever hatched is doomed to fail, like throwing cold water on a red-hot stove. With Herman, words of caution usually serve only to make steam. In any endeavor Herman is likely to make a fortune – that is, if he isn't arrested first.

'I needed three years' experience workin' in the field before I could even apply for my PI license,' he tells me. 'But I got lucky. Just so happened my old employer – you remember them?'

'How could I forget. They owned all those big SUVs we wrecked down on the Yucatán.'

Herman laughs. 'That's the one. They was so nice after I got shot. It's like I told them: I coulda been on disability the rest of my life. Know what I'm sayin'? You never know what a doctor's going to say.' He winks at me.

Herman should have been a lawyer.

'Them's almost my exact words to my employer,' he says. 'You never know what a doctor's gonna say.' Especially if he's a surgeon and Herman is threatening to shake his hand.

'They heard that and, well, they really got on top of things. That's why they're the big company they are.' Herman says this as if he has aspirations. 'They're into the details, know what I mean? Anyway, make a long story short, wouldn't ya know, one of their personnel people found them employment records. And that's all I needed. Did the trick.'

'Which records would those be?'

'The ones they forgot to withhold any taxes on,' replies Herman. 'Seems I worked for 'em during summers before college and during the school year.' He puts one finger to the side of his nose and winks at me. 'I forgot all about it,' he says. 'Why, they even went and paid the back taxes and penalties. Then they gimme the stubs showing everything, so's I could give the information to the state and get my PI license. Saved me a whole year working for somebody else just so's I could apply,' he concludes. 'Now how lucky is that?'

Luck to Herman is an eternal exercise in self-help.

'Comes from living a clean life,' I tell him.

'Ain't that the truth.' He takes a sip of coffee, looking over the edge of his cup at me. 'So what kinda sinnin' you up to these days?'

'Actually, I'm up to my ass. Buried in cases, mired in court, investigations I don't have time for.'

Herman's eyebrows arch with the scent of opportunity.

'Which is part of the reason I came by,' I tell him.

'What? You mean to tell me you didn't come by just to say hello?'

'Actually I did, but . . .'

'Never mind, I'll get over it,' he says. 'Just tell Uncle Herman what kinda work you got for him. And please don't go tellin' me it's a divorce. Without worker's comp, I don't need to be shaggin' any more bullets right now.'

CHAPTER FIVE

The county has finally sorted out the problem at the jail and eased up on the lockdown. Harry and I are back, closeted with Ruiz in the cement cubicle for another conference.

According to the transcript of the preliminary hearing, the cops are operating on the theory that Chapman jilted Ruiz and that he smoldered for six months or so before he confronted her at her home and killed her. There is speculation in the press that he may have stalked her, but if the cops have evidence of this, they have yet to produce it.

'You said you left the assignment six months before she was murdered?' I ask.

'Right. I did. But she called. Said she had to talk to me. I told her I was busy, no longer on the assignment. But she said it regarded a matter of personal security. She was scared. She said she couldn't discuss it on the phone but she had to talk to me.'

'So you went to see her?'

He nods.

'Where?'

'A small restaurant in San Diego, on the edge of

the Gaslamp Quarter. She was careful. Didn't want anybody to see us talking. She said it was far enough from La Jolla that people would be less likely to recognize her there. It was mid-morning between breakfast and noon, so the place was empty. We talked about twenty minutes. She wanted to know if I could help her.'

'What did she want you to do?'

He looks at me, then offers up a healthy sigh. 'She . . . she said she had some security concerns. She wanted to know if I could follow her just for a few days. Keep an eye on her from a distance. She said it wouldn't last long and that there was probably nothing to it.'

'Why didn't she just call the security detail back in?' I ask.

'I don't know. She said it was complicated. There were some issues she couldn't discuss. There was some corporate infighting at Isotenics. Nothing unusual. Madelyn was always afraid she was losing ground on issues of control ever since the corporation had gone public a few years earlier. It was an obsession with her. With Madelyn you were either an ally – in which case she thought she owned you – or an enemy. There was nothing in between. Seems there was a minority faction on the board wanted to wrest control from her. She was sure she'd win in the end.'

'I don't understand,' says Harry. 'What did that have to do with her personal security?'

'Some members of the board had made an issue over some of the perks she was getting: the two corporate jets, the fleet of stretch limos, the entourage of security wherever she went. They said it was extravagant. And there had been some bad press. One of the national business magazines did a story, CEOs who live like rajas. Madelyn got her own picture. Half-page spread. She was fit to be tied, spitting vinegar. She suspected enemies on the board had fed the reporter information and then used the story against her.'

'She told you this?'

'Not in so many words. But I know that that's why she canceled the personal security detail. She also unloaded the limos and ordered the red Ferrari so she could start driving herself around. If she went back to the board and told them she wanted the executive security detail brought back, she'd have to give them a reason. What she told me was that she couldn't tell them why she needed it. She also refused to tell me.'

'So whatever it was that frightened her, she didn't want her own board to know about it?'

'All I can tell you is what she told me. Whatever was going on, she didn't want the board to know about it.'

'You think she was violating directions that they'd given her?'

'I don't know. She was willing to pay me on the side for some informal security. I told her it was not a good idea. Whatever I did alone in my spare time was likely to have holes in it – that if there was a real threat, it wouldn't do much good if I was a hundred yards away watching through binoculars. Also I wasn't available all the time. I had other assignments, clients with Karr, Rufus I had to attend. She said she'd find somebody to spell me when I wasn't available, that we could work out a schedule. She said it would only last for a week or ten days.'

'And you agreed?' Harry asks.

'Yeah.' He doesn't seem happy about this. 'I

know I shouldn't have done it. I'm thinking it probably did more harm than good. Probably gave her a false sense of security. It was a big mistake.'

'Go on.'

'Whoever it was who scared her, I think he killed her,' says Ruiz. 'And I wasn't there to stop it.'

'Where were you that afternoon?'

'At home. In my apartment, asleep. I was working the graveyard on another detail later that night. And of course there was nobody there with me. So I have no alibi.'

'Did she hire anybody else, to back you up?'

He shakes his head. 'Not that I know of. She never got around to it. I'd watch the house two or three nights a week. I figured she'd be okay at the office. Besides, I couldn't get on the Isotenics campus anyway. Not without explaining what I was doing there. And they had ample security on the grounds.'

'Unless whoever threatened her was working there,' says Harry.

'What else could I do?'

'You think she might have been afraid of Satz?' I ask. 'You said they had a falling-out.'

'I don't know. It's possible. One thing she did tell me and it's all I know. She said she'd promised something to someone and then she was unable to deliver. They were angry. Whoever it was was threatening her. Nothing in writing, 'cuz I asked her about it. I figured if there was some evidence, she could take it to the cops. She said there wasn't any evidence, but even if there was she couldn't go to the police. One thing is sure: whoever it was had her on the spot.'

'If she couldn't tell her board and couldn't tell

the cops,' says Harry, 'could be that whatever she was involved in was illegal.'

Ruiz shrugs, shakes his head. He doesn't know. 'There was one other thing.'

'What's that?' I ask.

'I thought she mentioned a name . . . No, it can't be.'

'What?'

'Nothing,' he says. 'I think I must have misunderstood her.'

I give him a look, a stern question mark.

'It's just she was talking so fast, and I wasn't taking notes. She was excited, said she didn't have much time, had to get back to the office. I thought she said something about Walt Eagan. But that can't be right.'

'Who's Walt Eagan?' says Harry.

'He was one of her assistants. Eagan headed up R and D for Isotenics. He'd been with Madelyn from the beginning. Sort of her man Friday. Her first hire when she started out. From what I gather, the guy was a software wizard. Real heavyset, wore jeans to work, didn't quite fit into the corporate culture at the place. But Chapman kept him on 'cuz she trusted him. Any important jobs got handed off to Walt. And he reported directly to her. But I think I must have just gotten confused, heard something that I didn't.'

'Why is that?'

'Because by the time of the conversation with Madelyn at the restaurant in San Diego, Eagan was already dead.'

I look at Harry. 'How did he die?' I ask.

'Nothing sinister,' says Ruiz. 'He died of cancer, a little over a year after I went to work there. I remember because Madelyn took it hard. She was also up to her ass trying to handle everything on his desk and find a replacement. I don't think she ever did. But whatever it was that scared her, I don't see how it could have had anything to do with Eagan. Like I say, the man was dead at least six months by the time she called me to meet her at the restaurant.'

'You said Madelyn had a bad temper,' says Harry. 'Did she ever get angry with you?'

Ruiz looks at him. 'What is this about?'

'The cops are operating on the theory that you killed her following a lovers' quarrel,' says Harry. 'Would be good to test out their theory before we get to trial.'

'We weren't lovers – not in the way you're suggesting. And I didn't kill her. And no, she never displayed any anger toward me.'

'But according to you, she had a temper and she could get physical.'

'Yeah. At times.'

We probe his employment with Karr, Rufus. Ruiz said he had worked for the security firm just a shade under two years. The executive protection assignment at Isotenics was one of his first jobs. He'd been on board with Chapman for sixteen months when she pulled the plug and told her board she didn't need security any longer.

'And during this period you would be what, twenty-four hours on, twenty-four off?'

'Usually. Sometimes more. Sometimes less, depending on whether we were traveling or at home. I made arrangements for all travel to and from, screened her calendar for any threats or risks. I'd escort her to and from vehicles, travel with her on the corporate jets whenever she went off on business. If we were away for any length of time, there would usually be two or three of us assigned. And of course at the house I always tried to have another guy there. For reasons that sometimes had less to do with security.'

'But you would be in charge of the detail?'

'I was the lead on the assignment, yeah.'

'And when Ms Chapman was at home, where would you be?'

'If I was on duty I would be there, at her house.'

'You had a room there?'

'Yeah.'

'Where was it?'

'Upstairs, second floor.'

'Where was her room?'

'Same floor. Just down the hall.'

'Anybody else live there with her on a regular basis?'

'No. Except for my backup, as I said. She had a maid, a live-in, but it didn't last. Woman quit. Walked out one day and never came back.'

'The security contract. What else did it call for besides executive protection?' I ask.

'Oh, everything: training for drivers, corporate espionage, uniformed armed security for the corporate headquarters. I suppose you've seen their facilities out by the university.'

'You mean Software City?'

Ruiz nods. 'Most of the property out there belongs to Chapman's company.'

'So it was a sizable contract. How did Karr, Rufus land it?'

'You'd have to ask them that.'

'What about Karr, Rufus? Tell us a little bit about the firm.'

'What's to say? They're an employer of opportunity for retired military like myself. They have contracts all over the world, some with our own government, some with other governments, private corporations. That sort of thing. Company's headquarters are here in San Diego. Offices in five other cities, but this is where they do most of their hiring. They draw from Pendleton, the Marine base, and the naval base out on Coronado, North Island. Mostly retired military personnel. Once in a while a law-enforcement type, but not often.'

'But you were in the Army,' says Harry.

'Yeah, I heard they were looking for new hires so I came out and applied. They offered me a job. It pays well, or did until they canned me.'

'I take it you had a boss, a supervisor you reported to.'

'Jerry Comers. Nice guy. Easy to get on with. He was former Navy. Better than some of the sups they had there. A couple of former Marine staff sergeants. You know the type: tight-ass jug heads. Humorless. So I guess I lucked out.'

'Was it Comers who interviewed you for the job? Assigned you to provide security for Madelyn Chapman?'

'He gave me the assignment. But I suspect it came from higher up. As for hiring, only one man does that: Max Rufus, managing partner. You go through a series of screening interviews, panels, like a promotion board in the military for officers. But everybody has to pass muster with Rufus, sit for an interview with the man and pass it before you're hired. Blow that and you can forget it. He personally passes on all the company's employees, has as long as the company's been around.'

'I take it Isotenics, Chapman's company, was one of their larger clients?'

'As private companies go, it would have been a big contract. I'm not sure if it was the largest. You'd have to ask them.'

'Before your job with the firm, what did you do?'

'I was active duty Army.'

'Where?'

'Lotta places. Mostly Georgia. Fort Benning. Fort Bragg in the Carolinas. That was my last duty station.'

'What did you do there?'

'What is this, twenty questions?'

'What was your MOs?' I ask.

'Ground pounder. Infantry. Did some training assignments.'

'What, like a drill sergeant?'

'Not exactly. Training in special weapons, tactics, that sort of thing.'

'You weren't by any chance in one of the Army's elite units?'

'I did some time in the Rangers.'

'How many years?'

'I don't know. Twelve. Maybe a little more.'

'Jump school?'

He nods. This is like pulling teeth. There is something Ruiz isn't telling me. I begin to suspect that perhaps he has done time, either in the brig or maybe at Leavenworth. Still, it doesn't make sense: soldiers who do hard time for serious crimes face a dishonorable discharge, and Ruiz has an honorable discharge and full retirement benefits. I make a mental note to check it out.

'So Karr, Rufus couldn't have been too happy when one of their own was arrested for killing the CEO of a major client.' Harry's tact could use a little polishing, but his statement is to the point.

'They fired me the day after the prelim as soon

as the judge bound me over for trial. I suppose they had to keep me on the books until then. According to Kendal, anything else would have sounded too much like an admission.'

On this score Kendal was probably right. Over the last two weeks there have been stories in the press that Chapman's company has been consulting its own lawyer as to whether it might have a civil claim for money damages again Karr, Rufus, depending on what they knew and when they knew it regarding Ruiz's background. Isotenics will be watching our case closely, as will lawyers for Karr, Rufus, who will be anxious to have their client sidestep anything messy that might splash their way. They will want to know whether Ruiz should have been considered a risky employee when he was hired, whether he'd had scrapes with the law previously, perhaps in the military. All of this becomes grist for the mill.

Harry starts to hone in on one of the critical questions. He wants to know whether there was a specific reason the corporation hired executive protection for Chapman. 'Any names you can give us, people who may have threatened the victim? There must have been a reason you were hired.'

A good lawyer given just one such candidate can take a shot at crafting the honored 'SODDI' defense: some other dude did it. There are silver-tongued artists who, given this opening, wouldn't even have to point a finger, would just nod in the general direction while broadcasting seeds of doubt like a tuberculosis victim coughing on the jury. Feed and cultivate this with care for a few days and it's anybody's guess what noxious weed might spring up out of the jury box to strangle the state's case.

'Threats came with the turf,' says Ruiz. 'I mean, people with Madelyn's kind of money and social status aren't likely to be loved.'

'So there were threats?' Harry asks, a note of surprise in his voice.

'Sure. It ran the gamut,' says Ruiz. 'Nutcases, most of 'em. People who claimed she stole their software. Former employees who took their job termination personally. Then you get the people at Christmastime whose lights aren't all blinking, see her picture on the society page, and send her season's greetings with a PS: "Wish you were dead." '

'These were in writing?' Harry is making notes.

'Some of them. Some were called in, some by e-mail and fax. A couple of times they were hand-delivered to the front counter in envelopes addressed to *Madelyn Chapman, President and CEO, Isotenics Corporation* and marked *Personal* or *Confidential* like she was gonna open them herself. I guess they figured that way whoever delivered it would have time to get away before they were opened upstairs. We were able to nail one of them from pictures on the videotape at the public counter.'

'And the letters: any of them threaten to kill her?'

Ruiz makes a face and nods as if to say this would be in the natural order of things. 'Sure.'

'And the company has these?'

'In their files, I suppose. We always advised them to keep this kind of mail. That was the procedure so we could track past correspondence if anything happened.'

'Good advice.' Harry can't believe his good luck. He wants the name of the custodian or clerk in charge of filing and maintaining executive death threats at Isotenics so he can serve the guy with a subpoena.

'There was one event that pushed 'em to hire security for her,' says Ruiz.

'And what was that?' I ask.

'Some nut nailed her with a cream pie at a shareholders' meeting a couple of years ago. That's what got the company's attention. The board of directors finally woke up and realized it could've just as easily been somebody with a gun. It was shortly after that they called us in and we got the nod to go to work.' Ruiz starts to see the implications for his case. When you're charged with murder it never hurts to have a victim who wasn't loved. Besides the specter of a victimless crime, it increases the universe of possible perpetrators, hopefully to the point of confusion for the jury.

'Hell, if I had a dollar for every one of those letters came in, I could've quit and clipped coupons from a hammock on the beach two years ago,' says Ruiz. He is smiling now, warming to the idea that he is not alone in the universe of possible suspects.

Still, it leaves us to deal with one of the overarching ironies of the state's case against him. A corporation hires executive protection that, according to the cops, ends up murdering the company CEO. It's the kind of paradox that can lead jurors astray, causing them to disregard issues of reasonable doubt and focus instead on just how hard they might want to jump on the scales of justice to compensate for life's inequities.

'Let's talk about the firearm, the gun used to kill her.' I shift to another subject.

With this the smile evaporates from Ruiz's face.

I look at him. 'I understand it was traced to you.'

'Yeah.' Ruiz expels a deep breath as if to say sooner or later he knew we would get around to this. 'What can I say? It was mine.'

'Not according to the federal government,' says Harry.

'I didn't kill her, if that's what you're thinking.'

The only evidence that came in on the firearm during the preliminary hearing came from the police. They were able to trace the handgun, an exotic .45 automatic, back to its last owner, the United States government, more specifically, the Army base at Fort Bragg, North Carolina. The problem for Ruiz is that government records show the firearm by serial number as having been issued to one E. Ruiz, his signature and military ID number on a form six years before the murder. After that there is nothing, no record to show that he ever turned it in or surrendered it upon his discharge from the military.

'Tell us about the gun,' I say. 'How did you get it?'

Ruiz cocks his head a little to one side, shrugs a shoulder. 'I kept it when I left the Army. No big thing,' he says. 'It's not that unusual. A lot of times they don't even check. Hell, half the people I know retired from the Army kept their sidearms. Besides, a piece like that, it's accurized. You know, I mean for your own touch and feel. It's like a pair of boots: once you break 'em in, who else is going to wear them? I spent maybe a hundred hours working on it, stripping it down, changing out bushings, shot out I don't remember how many barrels and replaced them, reworked the action, adjusted the pull on the trigger for my finger. I lived with the thing. By the time I was finished with it, there probably weren't two parts in that firearm that were the same as when it was issued. The action, that's it.'

'Yes, but unfortunately for you, one of them was the frame with the serial number,' Harry counters.

The expression on Ruiz's face concedes the point.

'All of that aside,' Harry continues, 'let's be up front. You stole it, right?'

There is a lot of grousing, grudging expressions from Ruiz on this before finally he says: 'Yeah, I suppose you could say that.'

'You can be sure that's what the cops are going to say when they get on the stand in your trial,' says Harry. 'It's a major point for them, and while it doesn't go to the murder itself, it goes to the murder weapon, the tracing of the firearm. We probably can't keep it out.'

'Let's not jump to conclusions,' I say.

'What?' Harry turns to me. 'Like a jury isn't going to make inferences that a man who steals a gun might use it in a crime? Let's be realistic.'

'Actually, that might be a point for our side,' I tell him. 'After all, Mr Ruiz had to know that the firearm was registered in his name on military records. You did know that, didn't you?' I look at Ruiz.

He nods.

'So if he knew the weapon was going to be traced back to him, why would he use it to kill Madelyn Chapman? It doesn't make any sense.'

'Lovers' quarrel, crime of passion. People don't take time to think under those circumstances,' Harry points out. 'Besides, it's the fact the gun was stolen that puts him in a bad light. You have to admit, it's not something that helps the case.'

'That may depend on whether Mr Ruiz takes the stand. Right now all they can say is that the firearm once owned by the federal government, according to their records, was last known to be in the possession of our client. That was six years ago. Without Mr Ruiz's admission on the stand, they can't say whether it was stolen by him or lost somewhere along the way. Fact is, they don't know *what* happened to it.'

Harry looks at me a little cross-eyed like I'm crazy. Any rational jury can connect the dots. 'What are you saying? That we can sell the jury on the theory that somebody else managed to get a hold of a firearm that was once issued to the defendant? That they held it for God knows how many years and then used it to kill Madelyn Chapman so they could frame him? Why?'

I give him a look like *Who knows?* 'I'd be willing to bet that military records regarding issuance of firearms and ammunition aren't that orderly or neat. You can bet they make mistakes and that somewhere there's a written report or a government audit showing the frequency of such errors: lost or stolen firearms, military weapons used in crimes. It's the one thing you can count on in any government bureaucracy: they keep records on everything, including their own mistakes. All I'm saying is that we can shower a good deal of doubt on who had this gun last.'

'Yeah, but here the defendant kn—' I put up a hand and stop him before Harry can finish the thought: that it's too much of a coincidence that Ruiz knew the victim, had stayed overnight in her house, and that his firearm was used to kill her.

I look at Ruiz. 'Let me ask you: Do you have any sense as to how often the Army might make mistakes in this area? Say somebody checks a gun back in and fails to sign off, or they lose a piece of paper. There are people in the military, I assume, who would know this, if in fact it's a problem. We could put them on the stand.'

What I am telling Ruiz is that there may be a way to put an evidentiary wedge, a slice of reasonable doubt, however slender, between him and the murder weapon, deceptive as this may be.

I stop talking and all eyes are on him. Ruiz looks to Harry, then back at me. Finally he shakes his head. 'I don't get it. What's the point?' he says. 'The gun is mine.'

It's the thing about desperate defendants, especially those laboring under a psychic load of guilty knowledge with no one to share the burden. In such cases it's the rare soul who won't grab any straw in an effort to weave some gold. And I've never known one yet to ask questions about ethics in the process.

'I think you understood it very well, Mr Ruiz. It's simple and it's straightforward. It's called the truth. It's not the answer a lawyer might look for in court, but then, a smart lawyer would never put you on the stand and allow the question to be asked since he already knows, as I did, that any other answer would be a lie and would likely be exposed as one.'

'So you're testing me to see if I'll tell you a lie?'

'You have to excuse him,' says Harry. 'He's a lawyer.'

'And you're telling us that you didn't kill Madelyn Chapman and you don't know who did. Is that right?'

Ruiz looks at me for a second, wondering, I'm sure, what part of the question is a trick. 'Yes, sir, that's exactly what I'm telling you. You don't believe me, I guess I'm just going to have to go look for another—'

'Relax, Sergeant. I believe you.'

CHAPTER
SIX

At first glance the grounds of Isotenics, Inc., aka Software City, look like an Ivy League academy. However, once inside the gate, a closer inspection reveals something more akin to a military base.

The outer-perimeter fence, constructed of ornamental iron for architectural effect, is at least eight feet high and decorated at the top of each picket with a fleur-de-lis, forked and needle sharp like the point of a pike. Anyone trying to climb this would require either the strength and agility of an Olympic gymnast or a ladder on each side. One slip and you would end up like a hot dog on a skewer.

The front gate, with a guardhouse in the center, is manned by uniformed security backed up by surveillance cameras on poles set on high ground as I drive in.

Beyond the gate, the blacktop lane winds through the hills and climbs in elevation toward the top of a ridge in the distance. On the way I pass clustered villages of redbrick buildings, commercial offices designed to approximate colonial New England with names posted on signs for various divisions of the company. The buildings, some with ivy climbing their walls, are erected in a rectangle around a green common, the irrigated and well-manicured lawn contrasting sharply with the dry grass of the California hillside. In places carefully engineered hedgerows covered with oleander and ficus have been used to conceal inner security fences, electrified chain-link topped by tight coils of razor wire. None of this is unusual for a company whose principal client is the United States Defense Department. Marked private patrol units cruise the roads.

The rolling hills, more than a thousand acres of brown grass parched tinder dry by the arid climate of Southern California, are punctuated by occasional groves of stately eucalyptus trees.

As I climb, and look back down from on high, the buildings, their peaked roofs and gabled ends glistening in the morning sunlight, spread out below me, then disappear behind a ridge as I round a curve. It is plain to see how the place acquired the appellation *campus* among the press, its various divisions separated as they are like colleges at Oxford. According to the materials I have read, Madelyn Chapman designed the setting so that corporate divisions could each compete against the other in that elevated entrepreneurial quest, the pursuit of perfection.

Halfway to the top of the hill, I am stopped at a second security kiosk where the pass I was given at the front gate is collected and exchanged for another. My name is checked off a clipboard and I am handed a paper parking permit. Here the surface of the road suddenly transforms from asphalt to cobblestone arranged in an intricate

eliberations in order to secure a seat on
Those who believe it doesn't happen have
reality that borders on the innocent.
econds later I hear a soft voice behind
adriani?'

you follow me, please?'
pretty redhead, fair complexion, dressed
colored skirt and white blouse, a light
looped over her shoulders and tied in a
in front.
iles as we walk but doesn't say a word,
comment on the weather or to inquire
difficulty finding the place. Staring
head, she has an inscrutable expression
sh *Mona Lisa.*
y down the corridor we stop in front of a
evators and head up. The ride, not far
asses in silence sufficiently taut that if
d it with a knife it would snap. As soon
rs open on the second floor, it is clear
ve entered executive row. Here the hum
nd the clattery clicking of keyboards is
whole by the thick Berber that carpets

ce is huge, taking up what I assume is
west wing of the building. In the center
ted partitions offering a modicum of
secretaries and assistants, each in their
ed world, surrounded by a plant or two
es, small snapshots of loved ones and
few heads look up as we pass down the
formed by the partitions on one side
wall punctuated by office doors with
rass plates on the other.
er to the end, where we arrive at a set

herringbone design. The road is lined with
jacaranda trees, their petals in late bloom covering
the ground like a sky-blue shadow under the
spreading branches. I take all of this to be a sign
that I am entering the commercial equivalent of
nirvana, a place set apart, above the mercantile
gnashing of teeth and struggle for survival in the
world below.

As the Jeep's tight suspension rattles over the
surface of the road, I look to my left and see the
endless blue haze of the Pacific as it comes into
view a few miles to the west.

I hook the paper parking pass to my rearview
mirror and press the accelerator up the hill. Two
minutes later the Jeep crests the top. I swing into
the parking area marked Visitors and nose into
the first open space. The parking lot, which takes
up a good part of the eastern edge of the knoll, is
nearly full. In front of me is a large Roman Revival
two-story brick building with expansive stairs
leading to a broad portico out in front. The roof
over this is supported by five large white Doric
columns complete with scrollwork and massive
masonry pedestals. Rising above the roof of the
building like the top layer on a wedding cake is a
gleaming white dome supported by more smaller
columns and sporting round porthole windows
halfway up its curving arc from the base. I am
guessing that this architectural statement is just a
little smaller than the gold dome on the state
capitol. If you had a helicopter with enough lift,
you could pick the building up and plop it down at
the University of Virginia and the entire structure
would feel at home, right down to the simulated
aged brick with its tumbled edges and manufactured chipped corners.

I gather my briefcase and head toward the terrace of stairs leading to the portico and the main entrance. Climbing the stairs, I enter through the main entrance. Inside, the cavernous rotunda echoes with the click of high heels and shuffling shoe leather on the marble floors, the hum of voices punctuated by the occasional cough and sneeze, all bouncing off of hard surfaces and resonating in the lofty dome.

Careful attention has been paid to every detail so that the interior imitates to perfection the traditional architecture of government. This replication of the architecture of power no doubt has a subtle effect on the customers who visit it, mostly military brass and civilian bureaucrats. Operating as it would at the subconscious level, the design is likely to take advantage of the subservient instincts of those in the employ of the political beast to curtsy and bow in such surroundings.

I am left to wonder whether Chapman may have followed through on this theme upstairs, and if the conference rooms where sales are consummated are designed in the form of congressional hearing rooms, the proverbial political woodsheds for the Pentagon.

A circular counter directly under the dome serves as a public information desk peopled by a small army of scurrying attendants answering phones and pushing paper.

I take my turn in a line behind two other people. When I get to the counter I introduce myself: 'Paul Madriani. Here to see Victor Havlitz.'

With the mention of the names I get the distinct impression of being in one of those television commercials where every conversation dies and ears are suddenly tuned in my direction.

'If you'll wait just a mo[ ] doesn't ask for a busines[ ] an appointment. No doub[ ] expect me by a phone call[ ] road.

I have the sensation of[ ] scores of eyes glancing in[ ] of having your face and[ ] the papers and the six o'cl[ ] of the man charged with[ ] tion's founder and chief e[ ]

As the receptionist pi[ ] starts to dial, I look arou[ ] eyes suddenly return to[ ] before I arrived. The dro[ ] up again until I can no lo[ ] said on the phone. What[ ] hangs up.

'Someone will be down[ ] If you'll just wait over th[ ] my left toward a broad c[ ] west wing of the build[ ] direction, briefcase in h[ ] eyes boring holes in my[ ]

Twice this week news[ ] on the street in front of[ ] tumbrel with the medi[ ] pushing lenses in our fa[ ]

Ruiz's impending tria[ ] those who tune in t[ ] entertainment. There is[ ] to cover the trial, somet[ ] to wade in on. I am not[ ] in the courtroom. In the[ ] is nothing more insidio[ ] or two asserting their[ ]

steering [ ]
Nightlin[ ]
a view o[ ]

A few[ ]
me: 'Mr[ ]

I turn[ ]
'Woul[ ]

She is[ ]
in a rus[ ]
silk scar[ ]
loose kn[ ]

She s[ ]
not ever[ ]
if I ha[ ]
straight[ ]
like an [ ]

Halfw[ ]
bank of[ ]
but slow[ ]
you touc[ ]
as the d[ ]
that we [ ]
of voices[ ]
swallowe[ ]
the floor[ ]

The sp[ ]
the entir[ ]
are insu[ ]
privacy fe[ ]
own cubi[ ]
and pictu[ ]
friends. A[ ]
hall that[ ]
and a so[ ]
names on[ ]
I follow[ ]

of double doors, polished mahogany with brass fittings. She taps lightly.

'Come in.' It's a male voice from the other side, almost imperceptible.

As she opens the door I realize I am being ushered into a conference room, mirrored walls and a table, twenty feet of shimmering dark mahogany surrounded by burgundy leather high-back swivel armchairs. All of this is centered under a brass chandelier large enough to accommodate an entire village of monkeys.

I had been led to expect a private meeting with Victor Havlitz, vice president and chief counsel for Isotenics and for the moment Madelyn Chapman's replacement and stand-in as CEO. Instead it looks like a gathering of the Joint Chiefs of Staff. There are five people gathered around the table, six by the time the woman who has led me here takes her seat. The man at the head of the table is standing, tall and dapper, decked out in a blue pin-striped power suit.

'Mr Madriani, welcome, I'm Victor Havlitz.' Spider to the fly. The folded French cuffs of his linen white dress shirt peak out beneath the sleeves of his jacket as if they were measured where he is now standing with a ruler for uniformity. He toys with one of the gold cuff links at his wrist as he smiles at me. His burgundy club tie appears as if it might have been pressed on his body with sizzling steam and color-coordinated to match the leather of the chairs.

'How do you do?' There is nothing I can do but smile back, sandbagged as I am by a group gathering.

He can tell from my expression that I did not expect a crowd. 'I hope you don't mind,' he says. 'I asked a few of my colleagues to join us. They may be in a better position to answer some of your questions.' It seems the price of talking to Havlitz is an audience.

'The more the merrier,' I tell him.

'Please, come in,' he says, about to start the introductions, then stops. He apologizes, then offers me coffee, tea, or a soft drink. I pass.

'If you need anything just ask,' he says, then begins: 'I'd like you to meet Mary Collard.' He indicates a blond woman in her midthirties on the far side of the table, at the end. She bares an obligatory half-smile. 'Ms Collard is the corporation's chief financial officer. Next to her is Jim Beckworth. Jim assists me in legal and oversees most of our dealings with outside hired counsel. Next to Jim is Wayne Sims. Mr Sims is with the law firm of Hayes, Kinsky, Norton, and Cline. I asked Mr Sims to join us here today since no one in our legal department has much experience in criminal law and I thought it best, under the circumstances, to have someone with some knowledge assisting us.'

'I didn't expect it to become adversarial,' I tell him.

'Oh, I'm sure it won't be,' says Havlitz.

I don't know Sims, but I know the firm: three hundred plus lawyers with offices in five states. They are part of the silk-sock set specializing in business law and white-collar crime.

Havlitz works his way around to my side of the table. 'Over here on this side you've already met Ms Rogan.'

My escort on the elevator. 'Actually we haven't been formally introduced,' I tell him.

'Allow me,' says Havlitz. 'Karen Rogan. Ms

Rogan was Ms Chapman's executive assistant and personal secretary.'

This conjures an immediate image of Ruiz half-naked on his back on Chapman's couch. She turns to look at me, a fleeting smile, a few light freckles clustered on the slope of her cheek around her nose, Bambi in the headlights.

In her early thirties, her amber hair is thick, medium length, and worn in the kind of natural wind-tossed style that looks as if she's just stepped off a stormy beach on the Irish Sea. She nods in a kind of awkward gesture and immediately turns back, her eyes downcast toward the table.

If this is the woman Ruiz talked about, the intruder, it is difficult to imagine her not turning several shades of scarlet, given her fair skin and obvious discomfort in the presence of the defendant's lawyer.

'Last but not least is Harold Klepp. Harold is the ... *acting* director of research and development.' For Havlitz, all the emphasis is on the word *acting*, an inflection that is not lost on Klepp if I am any judge of facial expressions. He turns quickly to greet me, a smile and a nod. Klepp is African-American, the only person of color at the table.

Trying to put faces to names, plugging them into my own mental organizational chart of the company, Klepp has the dubious honor of stepping into the shoes of Walt Eagan, his trusted predecessor and Chapman's man Friday. No matter what he says or does, he is not likely to measure up.

'Harold is part of our technical staff. A programmer and design engineer by training.

'Please have a seat,' Havlitz says, gesturing

toward the only empty chair at the table. This has been carefully positioned between himself and Karen Rogan, Chapman's redheaded assistant. It is directly across from the lawyer Sims so that if my questions become too pointed, Havlitz's lawyer can sink his fangs into me without having to coil before striking.

'If I'd known, I would have brought my office staff,' I tell him.

Havlitz laughs. 'Yes, I suppose we could use name tags. But you can relax, we won't test you,' he says.

I sidle in behind the redhead, bumping her chair with my briefcase in the move.

She turns a pained smile my way. We exchange 'Excuse me's' and she tries to wheel her chair a little closer to the table to make room.

The position offers everything but the naked beam of a spotlight directed into my eyes. Though Sims, the lawyer from Hayes, Kinsky, does a fair simulation of this with a probing stare from across the table. He has yet to break a smile.

'Mr Madriani . . . I am pronouncing your name correctly?'

'Yes.'

'Good. Mr Madriani called a few days ago and requested a meeting. As I'm sure you all know, he represents Mr Ruiz, who some of you knew—'

In some cases more intimately than others. I glance at Rogan next to me.

'—and who unfortunately has been arrested in connection with Madelyn Chapman's death.' Havlitz makes her passing sound like an accident.

'I hope we can answer some of your questions. We'll help in any way we can.' He looks at me and takes his seat.

'Well, thank you. That's a generous offer. If I'd known you were going to be that helpful, I would have brought confessions for everyone to sign.' There is nothing but silence and stark expressions from around the table.

'Sorry, a bit of tasteless humor,' I tell them.

There's a twitter of nervous laughter. Everybody smiles except Sims, the man hired to keep the dome from sliding off the building. At this point, given the publicity that is erupting, I imagine that the goal of Isotenics is to have all the issues surrounding Madelyn Chapman's murder go away as quickly and quietly as possible. That way the company can get back to making money from the government.

It is the only reason Havlitz agreed to a meeting. His board of directors would prefer that I ask any embarrassing questions here than in court.

'I take it that with Ms Chapman's passing you've been promoted to CEO of the corporation.' I look at Havlitz.

The proximity of this remark to my bad joke is not lost on him. Who stood to gain? Looking around the table, seeing no one else senior to himself, he says, 'Unfortunately, I guess I am.'

'You make it sound like bad news.'

'What am I supposed to say?'

'I don't know. You tell me.'

'The board of directors has taken no formal action to appoint a permanent successor.'

'But they did pass a resolution asking that you take over temporarily. I think I saw that in the newspaper.'

He nods grudgingly. 'That's correct.'

We talk about the history of the corporation, Chapman's early days with the Pentagon, the fact that the company is heavily involved in defense work. Then I pop the question.

'Can you tell me what programs Ms Chapman was most involved in at the time of her death?'

'She was involved in almost everything,' says Havlitz.

'I understand she was the CEO, that she oversaw everything, but I have to assume that she would have delegated most of these responsibilities to others. Did she retain anything for herself?'

'She was lead on IFS.' The answer comes not from Havlitz but from Harold Klepp at the other end of the table.

'Ah, that would be the Information for Security Program? Read about it in the newspaper,' I say.

'She held that and a couple of other projects,' Klepp adds.

Havlitz cuts us off before I can start a dialog with Klepp: 'I have to say I'm uncomfortable getting into any of this. Specific programs, I mean. We discussed this, Harold, and I thought I made myself clear.'

'I'm sure that Harold was only trying to be helpful.' It's the redhead next to me, Rogan, trying to come to Klepp's defense.

Havlitz cuts her off at the knees. 'I don't care what he thinks he's doing. I laid down the ground rules before we started.' He turns to me, speaking from the heart now. 'I hope you understand there is no effort to conceal anything. But there are proprietary issues here.'

'Also security concerns.' This from the lawyer Sims across the table. 'Information requires clearance from the government on certain programs.' He looks at me and arches an eyebrow.

'Precisely,' says Havlitz. 'We simply cannot

discuss certain matters. I trust you understand.'

'I don't need to know the details or specifics,' I tell him.

'Let's move on.' Just like that, the lawyer Sims decides the issue.

'Fine.' I move to the next item. 'Maybe you could tell me how the decision was made to terminate the personal security detail for Ms Chapman.'

Havlitz is suddenly a faceful of wonder. 'Why is that important?'

'Happening as it did just a few weeks before she was killed, let's just call it a curiosity,' I reply.

'Oh. Oh, well, I suppose,' he says. 'It wasn't a corporate decision. I mean, the decision to terminate security, if you want to call it that, was made by Ms Chapman herself.'

'Can you tell me why she made the decision?'

Havlitz shakes his head, shrugs a shoulder. 'As I understand it, she simply didn't think that the level of security was necessary. I didn't really discuss it with her. She simply made the decision.'

'Had something changed?'

'What do you mean, "changed"?'

'Well, as I understand it, the board of directors decided that executive security was necessary. Correct me if I'm wrong, but I've been told there had been a number of pieces of threatening correspondence – phone calls, crank letters, that sort of thing – as well as an incident involving an assault . . .'

'Assault? I don't remember any assault,' he says.

'An incident at a shareholders' meeting. Somebody tossed a cream pie.'

'Oh, that,' he says. 'Yes. Ah, that was regrettable. Unfortunately, someone got past security at the door. We don't know how it happened. Looking back, I suppose that was the event that led to the issue. Executive protection, I mean. It was brought up by the board after that unfortunate experience. I see how someone could key in on that, I suppose.'

'Yes.'

He looks at me as the conversation dies. 'What was your question again?'

'What had changed to cause the board or Ms Chapman to believe that there was no longer any threat to her security?'

'Oh, I don't know. I suppose you would have to ask her that.'

'That's a little difficult,' I tell him.

'Of course,' he says. 'But I don't know what else to tell you. She made the decision that she no longer needed security. I certainly wasn't in a position to second-guess her. Perhaps she found it to be an invasion of her privacy.'

'Did she say anything to you about it at the time? Explain her reasons?'

He shakes his head.

'Did you have executive security in your position?'

'No. No. I didn't think there was a need.'

'Were there any others: members of the board, other people in management?'

Havlitz looks to Karen Rogan sitting next to me. She thinks for a second, then shakes her head.

'I think the issue was Ms Chapman's public visibility – her name recognition,' says Rogan.

'Of course. She was sort of the embodiment of the corporation. She was Isotenics, Incorporated. Whenever anyone thought of the company, they thought of her. It's probably why most of the threatening letters were directed to her.'

'Was there a lot of this hate mail?'

'What's "a lot"?' he says. 'One letter was too much, as far as I'm concerned. Most of it was the typical. Class hatred. Rambling tirades written in an unintelligible scrawl spouting conspiracy theories. That sort of thing. We turned them over to security. But then, what *do* you do? And as you say, after the incident with the pie, it could just as easily have been a gun.'

'Perhaps Ms Chapman spoke to someone else on staff regarding her reasons for ending the security detail.' I look around the table, my eyes finally settling on Karen Rogan.

The redhead is studying the wood grain in the surface of the table, avoiding my stare.

'Is it possible that Ms Chapman might have prepared a letter or a memo on the subject explaining her reasons at the time?' I ask.

'Umm, Karen?' Havlitz gives her permission to speak.

'Not that I can recall. I'd have to look.'

'Could you do that? And while you're at it' – I lean over and open my briefcase on the floor at the side of my chair, pull out a large manila envelope, and hand it to her – 'You probably want to give that to your lawyer.'

'What's this?' Sims looks at the thick envelope as she slides it across the table to him.

'A subpoena duces tecum, for the production of documents. It's fairly detailed.'

Sims sits up straight in his chair, takes the envelope, and opens it. Time to earn his keep. He pulls the papers out, a generous portion of a ream, and hefts the weight, looking at the pile with an expression as if to say, 'You can't be serious.' Sims knew this had to be coming, but he'll make a show of it anyway, if for no other reason than to impress the client. We are likely to spend the next several weeks trading paper, subpoenas met with motions to quash, the lawyer's version of a ticker-tape parade.

From another section of my briefcase I slide a copy of an article from a magazine, a national business weekly. The stark and unflattering black-and-white picture of Madelyn Chapman glaring out from the front page appears to have been taken with a fish-eye lens up close so that every feature of the woman is distorted. The headline reads:

CEO'S: THE NEW CORPORATE ARISTOCRATS
Shareholders? 'Let Them Eat Cake'

From the picture as well as the content of the article, it is clear that Chapman had been blindsided by the publication, probably led to believe that it would be a corporate puff piece extolling her management of Isotenics. Instead, the six-page feature piece is a sniper attack par excellence. It includes two other pictures, one of them showing Chapman boarding a corporate jet with an entourage of security; the second, another fish-eye exposé, this time of a uniformed chauffeur holding the yawning back door of a stretch limo open as if the camera's lens is about to be swallowed up.

I can almost feel Karen Rogan shudder in the chair next to me as she glances sideways at the pictures. No doubt she has seen them before, probably moments after Chapman went ballistic, raging through the building with a machete on a head-hunting expedition to her own PR department.

'I assume you've seen this before?' I slide the stapled pages along the table toward Havlitz, who takes one look and then clears his throat.

'Umm. Yes.' He flips a page or two and then leaves it untouched on the table.

For the moment Sims abandons the subpoena and its attachments and turns his attention to the article. He grabs it and starts flipping pages, studying the pictures.

'From the date, it would appear that the article was published less than a week before Ms Chapman's personal security detail was withdrawn.'

Havlitz and Sims hover over the piece, studying the date and exchanging glances. Then Havlitz looks at me. 'I don't know. I'd have to check. If you say so.'

'The date of publication speaks for itself,' says Sims.

'It does, and it would appear that the publication of this article and the humiliation visited on Ms Chapman in a national business publication may well have caused her to abandon security,' I continue.

'That's *your* assumption,' says Sims.

'You'll notice on the second page, the article goes into some detail criticizing her "security entourage,"' I tell him.

Sims flips to the page. I have highlighted this with a yellow marker so he can't miss it.

When he's finished, he looks up at me. 'Your point is?'

'The article likened Ms Chapman's security to that of a head of state. And you'll notice the picture.'

One of the shots, the one showing Chapman

boarding the plane, has one of her bodyguards carrying what is obviously a woman's overnight bag up the stairs behind her. If they could have stuffed a toy poodle with a diamond collar under the guy's arm, they would have done it.

'I see it,' says Sims.

'I'm wondering whether anyone here or on the board of directors had an opportunity to talk to the reporter who wrote the piece, or anyone else at the magazine, before it was written.'

'What are you getting at?' Havlitz asks.

'I'm wondering where they got their information, the reason for the story. I have to assume they didn't pick your boss by throwing darts at a list from *Forbes*.'

'Are you suggesting that somebody here put them up to it?' says Havlitz.

'I'm not suggesting anything. I'm asking whether anyone in the company talked to the reporter or anybody at this magazine either before or after the piece was published.'

'We'll have to check on that and get back to you,' he says.

'I'm told that there was a faction on the board that was at odds with Ms Chapman. That this group may have wanted to wrest control of the corporation from her.'

'Who told you that?'

'Is it true?'

'No, it's not true. There's always some dissatisfaction on every corporate board,' says Havlitz. 'That doesn't mean somebody inside the company wanted to push her out the door. She was well liked. Highly regarded. She was the founder of the company. Why would somebody here want to kill her?'

'I said they wanted to wrest control of the corporation from her.'

'Well, yes, but the inference . . .'

'And unless she was shot twice in the head by accident, somebody wanted to kill her. From my reading of that article, there are a number of unidentified sources close to the corporation who fed the reporter information. That kind of detail could only come from people working inside the company. Since the article wasn't terribly flattering, it would be difficult to view them as friends and supporters of the victim. Wouldn't you agree?'

Sims puts a hand on Havlitz's arm before he can get into it with me. His chest shrinks a size or two. He settles back into his chair.

'What is your point?' says Sims.

'I'm simply trying to find out why a woman, the head of a significant corporation, would want to get rid of her own personal security detail just weeks before she is killed.'

'And my clients have told you they don't know.'

'No. Mr Havlitz has told me he doesn't know. I haven't heard from anybody else.' I look toward the far end of the table, hoping to be able to take a poll, maybe open some lines of communication. No one wants to look at me except Harold Klepp.

'I know she wasn't happy about that arti—' he says.

Havlitz cuts him off. 'My answer goes for everybody at the table.' The corporate answer.

Klepp leans back in his chair and shuts his mouth.

'So I guess we have to leave it that whoever engineered the article may have had a hand in effecting the removal of Ms Chapman's personal security, at least indirectly.'

115

'As I said,' says Sims, 'that's *your* assumption.'

Havlitz, squirming in his seat, can't resist any longer. 'From where I sit, we would have been well advised to terminate the security detail much sooner, seeing as your client – one of her bodyguards – is charged with her murder.'

'I thought you said the corporation didn't terminate security – that the victim made that decision.'

'She did,' says Havlitz.

'But you just said "we" should have terminated it sooner.'

'Did I say that?'

'Yeah, you did.' Klepp mumbles it under his breath and gets a look that could kill from his boss.

'Then I misspoke,' says Havlitz. 'Let me be clear: the corporation had nothing to do with ending the security detail for Ms Chapman. That was entirely a personal decision on her part.'

'But you said you didn't talk to her about it.'

'I didn't.'

'Then how do you know that it was a personal decision or, for that matter, what it was based on?'

'You're twisting my words.'

'No, I'm simply asking you a question.'

'We don't have to sit here and listen to this.' The large vein in Havlitz's neck begins to bulge from under the starched collar of his linen shirt. 'This isn't a courtroom,' he says. 'I invited you here as a courtesy.'

'For the purpose of obtaining information,' I tell him.

'Exactly,' he says. 'If you want to know the truth, I'll tell you the truth.' He is working to a fever pitch. 'Your client was stalking Ms Chapman.

That's right.' He smirks. 'Why else do you think they arrested him so fast?'

With the word *stalking*, Sims's head snaps back. He looks at his client wide-eyed. He had been preoccupied scanning the magazine article, skimming it with a finger for details, trying to ferret out the unidentified sources. Now he has a bigger problem, but it's too late.

'Was this before or after Ms Chapman ended the security detail?' I ask.

Havlitz looks at his lawyer, who shakes him off like a pitcher on the mound.

'Forget it,' says Havlitz. 'Just forget I said anything.'

'Did you tell the police this?' I ask.

'I can't remember,' he says. 'I'm not sure.'

But I am. Not only did he tell the cops, they had taken pains to keep it out of their reports. The police made sure not to put it in their notes. They would have the DA put Havlitz or another witness on the stand for some other purpose. Then on cross-examination I would find myself tripping through the tulips in a minefield, working over the witness, only to have him coldcock me with the gratuitous testimony that Ruiz was stalking the victim before she was killed. It's the kind of bombshell that would cave in the sides of an M1 Abrams tank. You can object all day, but if you've asked a question that opens the door, you're dead. Even if the court strikes the testimony from the record and instructs the jury to disregard it, it's going to be there like a screaming penny on top of a cash register when it comes time to tally up in the jury room. Suddenly they have a mental image to go with the state's motive: a jilted lover dogging the victim after she told him to get lost.

'Did Madelyn Chapman tell you she was being stalked by the defendant?'

He doesn't answer but shakes his head. It's not clear if this is a yes or a no, but if I had to guess, she didn't. The little vein on Havlitz's forehead is now pulsing, beading over with sweat. It's clear he either saw something or heard it from someone else.

'I think we're going to have to call it a day.' Sims is on his feet. 'I have an appointment,' he declares. He looks at his watch, an afterthought, the obligatory haphazard glance at the gold chunk on his wrist. It's the only way he is going to get me out the door and he knows it. 'I've got to be somewhere,' he says.

Right. Anywhere but here. I'd love to be a fly on his lapel when he calls the DA to explain how they managed to accidentally detonate one of the state's major roadside bombs a little early.

CHAPTER SEVEN

'That can't be Paul Madriani?' If you can visualize a smiling face, round as a cherub's, Asian and with freckles, it would belong to Nathan Kwan.

I had been walking at a good clip, halfway through the rotunda on the way back to my car, when I saw him.

'Nathan?'

'By God, it *is* you.' He is all smiles, five foot seven and trim as the day I last saw him more than a decade ago. The only change is a little more gray at the temples so that he now looks the part of the seasoned statesman.

'Jeez, where have you been?' he says. 'I haven't seen you in so long, I thought you were dead.' He glides toward me across an acre of marble, hand outstretched. When he reaches me, he grabs my hand and drops his briefcase, his other arm going around my shoulder. 'God, it's been such a long time.'

'It has. What are you doing here?'

'Business. What else?' He is wearing power pinstripes, a three-piece suit, and is carrying a thin leather portfolio that is now propped against his left ankle on the floor. He has always been the dapper dresser with the right accents.

'I'll bet you didn't recognize me. A face from your forgotten past,' he says.

'I wasn't paying attention.'

'How have you been?'

'I'm fine.' He's still shaking my hand, engulfing me with the kind of radiance I remember from our earliest days together. Nathan may be shorter than I am, but he is one of those people who stands tall on the ladder of social dominance. He can overwhelm you in any setting with a kind of affable assault on the senses.

'And you?'

'I can't complain. Actually I could, but it wouldn't do any good,' he laughs. 'What ever happened to you? I turn around and you're gone.' This is how he describes ten years without seeing each other.

'I moved down here. My partner and I opened an office.' I try to bring the conversation down a few hundred decibels.

'You know, somebody told me that a year or so ago. But I didn't believe them. I couldn't believe you'd ever leave Capital City. But then I saw something in the paper on the plane on the way down. You're involved in the case: what's her name . . .' He lowers his voice, suddenly realizing. 'Here . . .'

'Madelyn Chapman.'

'That's the one—' he begins.

'Yeah, I am,' I say, cutting him off before he can get further into it, the fact that we are both standing in her former headquarters where all the walls have ears.

'What brings *you* down here?' I change the subject.

Nathan is a lawyer I once practiced with in the DA's office in Capital City. That was more than twenty years ago. I have not seen or heard from him for more than a decade, though from the familiarity in his voice you would think that I had just stepped out for coffee. I once considered him an intimate, but that was before his rise to office, when all things political consumed him. Nathan is a member of the state legislature: after four terms in the Assembly, he now sits in the Senate, representing the old neighborhood where I once lived in Capital City.

'Actually I get down here quite a bit, at least the last six months or so. Legislative business. I'm surprised they actually let you in here. You are defending the guy—'

'They may not be letting me in again,' I tell him. 'Right now they're probably reading our lips off one of the security cameras. And if my parking pass expired, they probably towed my car.'

He laughs.

'What does the legislature have going on that brings you here?'

'Nothing as exciting as you do – at least, I hope not. Some redistricting stuff. Nothing major. What do you know about the company?' he says. 'Maybe you could give me insights.'

'Just what I hear. The computer gurus to government. What I read in the papers. Defense Department contracts.'

'That's what I heard. I came down last month for my first meeting with them and I'm still trying to catch up. Seems they're the only game in town these days. You put out RFPs, bids for software, and nobody else shows up.' Nathan chairs one of the legislative committees doing business. 'They used to come to us. Now Muhammad has to go to the mountain. Actually I don't mind. Gets me out of the capitol. Place is the dregs these days. Not like you remember it, I'm sure.'

'To tell you the truth, I never spent much time there.'

'The turnover is awful. Friends are mostly gone,' he says. Most of Nathan's friends – liberals from the old school, people who acted with a modest amount of reason before the partisans took over and started rolling live ordnance across the aisles in the capitol – are now gone, tapped out by term limits, unable to run for re-election. Some have migrated into lobbying jobs so that they can stay in Capital City, where they have put down roots. Others have drifted back to their old stomping grounds in the districts they once represented in hopes of cashing in political chits for jobs. Two I know have taken seats as LA County supervisors and now preside over domains that dwarf their old legislative districts. Nathan himself is getting close, probably in his final term. I have seen press reports that he is nibbling around the edges, sniffing for a seat in Congress whose previous occupant passed away a few months ago. The only problem being that Nathan doesn't live in the district.

'Like I say, it's good to get away. The weather down here this time of year has the valley all beat to hell. I usually stay over. Got a place with a suite on the cove in the village. What are you doing tonight? Maybe we can get together for dinner.'

'I'd love to but I can't. Back-to-school night with my daughter.'

We drift toward the door. Nathan seems to be headed in my direction.

'As I remember it you never cared much for the fog up north. Always hot for the sunshine. And your tan is looking better than I remember it.'

'That's not San Diego. That's the Caribbean,' he says.

'Don't tell me you guys still go to Jamaica in the interim! I heard the Rules Committee made you folks clean up that act.' I am talking about the midterm follies when lobbyists take their legislative friends outside the country to violate all the reporting laws, and where bribery can be served straight up without the diluting fizz of campaign contributions.

'Well, at least you haven't lost total contact with the real world.' What Nathan means is Capital City, the center of the western political universe. 'There was really nothing going on. I don't know where the public gets all this misinformation,' he says.

'Probably from the federal grand jury indictments,' I tell him.

'Yeah, well, that was bad,' he says, referring to the shrimp scam, an FBI sting operation that went undercover a few years ago and didn't come up for air until they'd snagged four legislators and a small army of lobbyists. 'I could never understand it,' he remarks, shaking his head.

'What, that bribery was alive and well in the capitol?'

'That they would sell themselves for so little. I like to think I'm worth more than a thousand bucks.' Nathan laughs. 'Not that I condone what they did, you understand.'

'Of course not. You would have asked for more.'

'Absolutely not.' Nathan gives me one of his most imperious looks. 'I would have had my legislative assistant ask for more. And I would have hired nothing but ex-felons. That way if they tried to roll over on me, they would have had no credibility. I may not have your legal skills, but I did learn a few things as a prosecutor.' He smiles.

'You're right. You're smarter than your friends.'

'Those people were the exception, not the rule. Most of the members in the capitol are honest people,' he asserts, climbing on the stump. I have heard it before. How you never sell your vote. How money in the form of donations come election time just assures access. It doesn't buy your vote. This particular line hasn't changed in thirty years. Nathan heard it from the second generation, the people who called money 'the mother's milk of politics' and suckled at the nipple until their lips turned blue. I often wonder which greasy political scientist from which university came up with it. But when some lobbyist has his hand up your rectum and he's pulling all the right levers, it's difficult to tell exactly where this right of entry begins and ends.

I look at my watch. 'Listen, it's good to see you but I've got to run. Stop by the office sometime.' I peel a business card from my wallet and hand it to him.

'You sure you can't do dinner tonight?'

'No. Wish I could.'

He takes the business card and shifts the leather portfolio to his other arm so he can keep his left hand on my shoulder as we walk, like I'm leading the blind. Nathan is one of those people who can never talk to you unless he has at least one hand on you, invading your private space. I used to watch him do this outside of court with opposing counsel. I came to the conclusion that it was an acquired social tool, like LBJ thumping other pols in the chest with his finger when he talked to them. There is something subconscious and discomforting in its effect. I often wonder how many people were forced to cop pleas by their lawyers and ended up in state prison because Nathan hadn't used mouthwash that morning.

He shakes his head as he's holding me back with his hand on my shoulder. 'Jeez, where does all the time go? And I suppose you don't own a telephone to call a friend, tell him that you're picking up sticks and leaving town?' To Nathan all telephones work in only one direction: incoming to Kwan.

'I didn't know I had to ask permission before leaving.'

'You don't have to apologize. Just get your ass back up north.' He laughs. With anyone else you might resent it, but Nathan has a gift, a kind of Asian blarney – Chinese father and Irish mother – that allows him to roll back the clock with impunity.

'How's Nikki and your daughter . . .' He finally drops the hand from my shoulder, snapping his fingers lightly as we walk, struggling for Sarah's name. 'Don't tell me, I'll get it.'

'Sarah,' I say.

'That's right. I remember. A cute little girl,' he says.

'She'll be eighteen in three months.'

'No!'

'And off to college in the fall.'

'I don't believe it. And that gorgeous wife of yours . . .' We keep walking. 'The only woman I knew who took pity on your bachelor friend. I remember,' he says. 'She must have had me over for dinner every Tuesday night for a year.'

'I don't remember that.'

'You weren't there,' he says.

We both laugh.

'I just have to see Nikki. I owe you guys a dinner or two.'

'I don't know how to tell you this, but Nikki passed away.'

He stops in midstride, a half smile on his face like he's waiting for the punch line to a bad joke. Then he realizes that I'm not kidding. Suddenly a dour expression falls over his face. He is flushed all the way to the ears. 'No.'

'I'm afraid so.'

'I'm sorry. I didn't know. When did it happen?'

'Almost nine years ago.'

This seems to stagger him: that Nikki has been dead this long; that he has without guarding himself stepped on this land mine, knocks him off stride. 'I didn't realize. Nobody told me.'

'Cancer. She was sick for quite a while.'

'That explains why I didn't see you. Jeez, I'm sorry. Must have been hard. Difficult on your daughter. On Sarah.'

'It was. They were close.'

'Why didn't you call and let me know?'

'What could I say? There was nothing anyone could do.'

'I could have been there,' he says. 'I'm sorry.' It is one of the few times I have seen Nathan at a loss for words. We walk in silence for a couple of seconds as we move toward the door. 'We have to get together,' he says.

'Yeah.'

'Talk about old times.'

'I'd like that.'

We finally make it to the door.

'Listen, I'll give you a call. Next time I'm in town. We'll do dinner. On me.'

'You got it.'

I shake his hand. He gives me a hug, something I hadn't expected, his portfolio digging in my back. Then I turn and head for my car. Knowing Nathan – and life being what it is – unless he gets arrested on a felony, it is not likely that I will see him again, in this life or the next.

CHAPTER EIGHT

If the experts are to be believed, Madelyn
Chapman and her minions have perfected
software that allows the government to monitor
its people and their activities in ways that would
cause most of us to shudder. The stated purpose,
at least publicly, is to do what geologists cannot do
when it comes to earthquakes: predict with
accuracy the tremors of terrorism.

This morning Harry and I have made arrangements to be briefed by one of the few people outside
of government and Chapman's own company who
has knowledge of the Information for Security
Program – IFS – and how it works. We are huddled
in the conference room of our office in the far
bungalow behind Miguel's Cantina on Coronado
Island.

James Kaprosky is in his sixties, tall, slender,
stoop-shouldered, and from all appearances frail.
Every few minutes he has to pause to cough up a
lung.

If what I have read in news accounts on Nexus
is accurate, a good part of Kaprosky's current
physical state is the result of more than a decade

of litigation against the federal government. During this time Kaprosky, his company, and his family have been ground into dust by a bureaucracy with bottomless pockets and legions of government lawyers. He has been at war with Uncle Sam in a series of civil suits that have worn him to the nub and that two years ago sent his company, a once prosperous software manufacturing firm, reeling into a federal bankruptcy court. From all appearances he is a walking, breathing warning label that litigation will kill you and that legal tangles with the federal government will most likely follow you into your grave.

This morning Kaprosky stands in front of us, a pointer in one hand and the remote control to an overhead projector in the other. He is giving Harry and me chapter and verse on the IFS system while his wife looks on.

Jean Kaprosky has driven her husband to this meeting because he no longer has a license. His doctors have had it revoked because of his failing health. If I am any judge, Mrs Kaprosky is perhaps ten years younger than her husband. If I had to pick the dominant expression readable in her eyes, it would not be weary but worried, as if she long ago realized that the war with the government was over but still cannot steel herself to tell her husband. So she drives him and comes along for moral support.

'The heart of the system,' says Kaprosky, 'is the Primis software. Primis is what makes it all work. Without it you have nothing. I know because I wrote it.'

Kaprosky is here today not because we are paying him but because he is now at the point of desperation where he will talk to anyone willing to listen. Like everyone else, he has read about Ruiz's case in the papers. Unlike everyone else, Kaprosky sees a link between Madelyn Chapman's murder and the IFS program, the government's proposal to monitor everything that is now digitized in American life. He is convinced that Chapman's murder and his own battle against the government are somehow linked.

While Harry and I have to weigh our suspicions that maybe Kaprosky has gone around the bend and finally snapped under the pressure, what is undeniable are his professional credentials. He has been writing software and designing programs – some of them for Fortune 500 companies, and most of it for large mainframes – for more than forty years. Regardless of his faltering finances, he is an icon in the industry.

'Jim . . . You don't mind if I call you Jim?' I say.

'Why should I? It's my name.'

'Why don't you have a seat? Let's just talk.'

For a second he looks bemused, as if without the pointer and slide show he might be lost. Then he breathes a deep sigh, sets the pointer and the controls on the table, and slumps into one of the swivel chairs at the other end of the table.

'Tell us a little bit about Primis. We don't need to know all the technical details.'

'What do you want to know?'

'For starters, how did it come about?'

'I created it seventeen years ago. Of course, back then it had a different name. Probably didn't have all the bells and whistles it does now, though I haven't seen their final take on it, so I really can't say. When I owned it, it was called Paradize. The Defense Department wanted to buy it. They wanted to modify it, use it for their own purposes.' He coughs a short jag, then catches his breath.

'Of course, that was good news for my company, back then. If you could only roll back the calendar . . .' Kaprosky muses. 'I guess I was a little naïve.' He looks at his wife as if to apologize for the rugged ride through life he has given her. 'But I was dealing with the federal government. Who would have thought?'

'Tell us about it.'

'We thought it was a tremendous opportunity,' he recalls. 'We signed a contract, not to sell, but to license the program to the Pentagon. They wanted to use it for random processing of large amounts of data, but they wanted some changes. That was fine . . .' His voice trails off, and for a moment I think he's gone to sleep in the chair. But Kaprosky is just catching his breath.

Jean Kaprosky looks at me with a kind of mournful expression and shakes her head.

'Everything was fine for a while, about a year,' he resumes. 'Then the government claimed that we had somehow violated the contract. They canceled it and refused to return the source codes or stop using them. Except for a small sum that they paid up front, we received nothing. They claimed that we had failed to make required changes they wanted to the software.'

'Did you?' says Harry.

'No. The problem was they failed to provide any specifications. How do you write parameters for a program when you don't know what they are? No: The people running the program never intended to pay us.'

'Why?' says Harry. 'Why would the government want to take your software without paying for it?'

'The government? No. The government is just a concept. Figment of our imagination,' says Kaprosky. 'It took me a long time to figure that out. It's the people who run it who do the Devil's work. Ambitious dogs. We think we're protected because they come and go. But along the way some of them reach out and grab things, things of value. Things that they want for themselves and their friends. I never thought of the government as a friend or benefactor. But I once believed that while they could draft me, tax me, or put me in jail, there were rules they had to follow. Now I know better. You want to know who took the software? His name was Gerald Satz.'

Harry gives me a look. The first possible connection with Ruiz's case.

'What we found out during the lawsuits,' Kaprosky goes on, 'is that the government had already hired another company to come in and make the changes they wanted, using my source codes.'

'What is this thing?' says Harry. 'You've mentioned it a couple of times: The source code.'

'To an operating program, the source code is like DNA. It's written in programming language, what you would call human-readable instructions, like a long list, using logic. For it to be used by a computer, the source code has to be translated into machine language, something the computer can read. What is important about this,' Kaprosky explains, 'is that you can only make changes to the program if you have access to the source code. The changes are written in the original programming language and then converted to machine language.'

'So if you don't have the source code, you don't have anything,' I say.

He nods. 'That's why most software companies only license the finished product. As long as they hold the source code in secret, it's protected. Once they release it out into the public, they've lost any claim to ownership.'

'But you said you gave the source code for Paradize to the federal government,' says Harry.

'Actually, Paradize contained more than a hundred different source codes,' says Kaprosky. 'That's why it took them a year before they cut us off and canceled the contract. We had just delivered the last in the series when they pulled the plug. It was the final piece they needed. And so that you understand, we didn't give the codes to the government. The contract called for licensing of the program for the government's use. It did allow access to the source codes, but only for limited purposes and only if they used it under our license.'

From the breast pocket of his coat, he takes a handkerchief and coughs into it, then wipes his lips. 'Besides, I figured like everybody else it's the government, right? They're not going to steal it. Well, I was wrong.'

'Why would they go to somebody else to rewrite the program?' Harry asks.

'It wasn't a rewrite. They just wanted to tweak it so they could claim it was their own: an original item.'

'But it was based on your source codes,' says Harry.

'Yeah, well. Try telling that to the federal courts. They don't seem to care.'

Kaprosky has employed a generation of lawyers in an effort to get the government to pony up damages, including hundreds of millions of dollars for infringement of copyright. He has gotten within a hairsbreadth of delivering the case to a jury on two occasions, only to have the government raise the specter of national security and refuse to disclose the source code for its program. The code is the critical piece of evidence needed to confirm Kaprosky's claim. Because the software in various forms is currently used by a number of intelligence agencies – the CIA, the NSA, and others – and because in more watered-down forms it has been licensed by the US government to allied foreign intelligence services in other countries, the courts have sustained the national-security defense.

The crowning blow came last year when a federal circuit court in Washington, DC, threw a blanket over the entire case, denying Kaprosky's appeal on national security grounds. Three months later the Supreme Court denied a hearing on appeal. That decision in effect leaves Kaprosky and his company without legal recourse. He cannot prove his claim without the evidence that is in the possession of the government. And the courts will not compel the government to turn over the evidence on grounds of national security.

'And you think General Satz played a major role in all of this,' I say.

'Oh, I know he did. That's not even in question. He was the principal officer in charge of contracts at the time we signed the agreement. Back then he wasn't a general, but he was on his way up the ladder. He was no fool. When he saw the Paradize program and had a chance to examine it with his technical people he knew that what he had was golden.

'If information is power, Satz was holding the keys to the kingdom,' Kaprosky continues. 'I don't want to sound immodest, but Paradize was the genie in the bottle, and Satz knew its value. He knew somebody was going to build a commercial empire on it, and it wasn't going to be me. I don't know if you're aware, but the US military – not the soldiers in the field, but the top brass, the ones who survive long enough to make it into top offices in the Pentagon – if you check it out, you'll discover that they aren't usually buried in a pauper's grave when they die. Knocking around in a courtroom for a dozen years, talking to other people, you learn things.'

Kaprosky pauses, then resumes: 'I could give you the names of ten corporations, most of them funded almost entirely out of the Pentagon budget, the US military being their biggest customer. In some cases their only customer. Check the board of directors of these companies and you'll find they are controlled by former members of the Joint Chiefs of Staff and a good number of their cadre. That's no accident,' Kaprosky notes. 'I can tell you about inventions and innovations with military or intelligence applications, some of them so advanced, you begin to wonder if the government isn't sitting on a time machine in one of its warehouses. Somehow these things always get gobbled up by newly formed corporations. And when you look at the company's organizational chart, it reads like the roster of the Army–Navy Club. So I suppose I shouldn't have been surprised when Satz picked somebody else to write the modifications to my software. But back then I didn't think stuff like that happened.' He smiles wearily. 'I guess you could say I was green.'

'Let me guess who wrote the changes,' I say.

'Madelyn Chapman.' Kaprosky says it before I can. 'So now you know why I called, why I talked to your partner. Back then she hadn't formed her corporation yet. But she was outside the fold. She'd left the Pentagon. She had two or three people plus herself working in a small office in Virginia, spitting distance from the Pentagon.'

'Gerald Satz steered the software to her company. Gave it to her.' This comes from Jean Kaprosky, who until now has sat silently at the other end of the table, across from her husband. She can no longer contain herself.

'What he got in return we don't know,' says Kaprosky.

'You can bet it was plenty,' Jean says.

'They changed the name of the program from Paradize to Primis.'

'They just took it?' says Harry.

'I know: people don't believe me when I tell them,' says Kaprosky. 'They think I'm crazy. But that's what happened.'

'And you sued them?' I ask.

He nods. 'I sued the government. Secretary of Defense. I named Satz and several others.'

'Did you sue Chapman?'

'Once, but it was dismissed,' he replies.

'Why was that?' Jean asks, scratching her head. 'I can't remember anymore.'

'She wasn't a party to the original contract,' Kaprosky says. 'Unless we could prove that the government had done something wrong, we couldn't reach Chapman or her company.'

'Yeah. Now I remember.'

'And you couldn't get traction against the government because of national security,' I say. I have read this travail of tears in the news accounts.

He nods slowly, his shoulders slumping. 'We've been in and out of the courts for twelve years,' he sighs. 'Closest we got was a judgment from the district court telling them to surrender the source codes from Primis so they could compare them to mine. That decision was blocked and overturned by the court of appeal on grounds that the Primis program constituted – how did they put it? – a fundamental national-security asset. My lawyers tell me that politicians have used national security in the past to cover up crimes. That's supposed to make me feel better, since in this case they've only committed civil fraud.'

I could tell him that I know how he feels, but I don't. I don't think anyone could unless they've been through Kaprosky's particular wringer.

'What else do you want to know?' he asks.

'Maybe you could tell a little about how the software works,' I suggest.

'Why not? Paradize, or Primis – whatever you want to call it – is what they call an all-inclusive relational database. The end-user defines parameters and the software searches through massive amounts of digitized information, finding anything that falls within the stated boundaries. It can sort through oceans of information looking for certain predefined transactions. For example, maybe you want to know whether anybody purchasing airline tickets flying to specified destinations purchased certain chemicals, or transferred sums of money between certain banks. Paradize would tell you. The theory is that the software, if properly programmed, can identify patterns of activity that are likely to reveal criminal acts that are being planned or are in progress.'

'Predicting terrorist activities?' asks Harry.

'Not just predicting,' Kaprosky replies, 'but

providing information as to who, when, and possibly where. If you can believe the government, at the moment the program is functioning at a minimal level because they don't have access to all the data. I don't happen to believe them, but then, I suppose I'm jaded.'

'What do you mean?' I ask.

'In order to function at full efficiency, the software requires access to as much data as possible. Mountains of it. An ocean of digitized information. That's what IFS, Information for Security, was supposed to provide. Congress was supposed to pass legislation that required every private, commercial, and government database in the country to hook up to a bank of supercomputers in the Pentagon and to feed everything they had into the Defense Department computers so they could process it with the software.'

Harry is visibly surprised. 'No search warrants?'

'Minor details,' says Kaprosky. 'They wanted everything: medical records, banking and financial transactions, addresses, telephone records, lists of all the property you own, the names of your children and the schools they attend, whether they were in day care and where, their grades, all of your e-mail transactions, including the content of the messages, the sites you visit on the Internet, all of your credit-card purchases. Anything and everything in a computer database anywhere in the country was supposed to be available. If it was digitized, they wanted it.'

'I thought Echelon was bad.' Harry is referring to the feds' party line in the sky. 'If the British prime minister sneezes during a phone call with the French president, Uncle Sam says "Gesundheit."'

138

'I never intended that my software be used in that way,' Kaprosky says, shaking his head. 'In the end it didn't matter, since they had one major problem: Congress refused to pass the legislation forcing everybody to hook up to their system. They couldn't get the data.'

I remember seeing the story in the newspaper, but I hadn't followed the details.

'They did have an interesting pitch to sell the plan politically,' he points out. 'What they proposed was to slap one more Band-Aid over the software so that everything they looked at from the massive data feed would be anonymous. They would have access to all of the information on three hundred and fifty million Americans, but if you believed them, they wouldn't be able to tie any of it to a specific individual unless they got a search warrant.'

'How would they do that?' I ask.

'That was the creative part,' says Kaprosky. 'It was supposed to be guaranteed by a separate system of software that Chapman's company was going to write. I suspect that was one of the reasons they needed my source codes: so they could filter this in. The add-on was called Protector. If the government's computers detected a pattern of activity that raised suspicion – enough to convince a court to give them a search warrant – Protector was supposed to be written in a way that, by keying in the number on the warrant, the filter that masked out the individual's identity would fall and they'd get the name, address, everything.'

'Pretty ingenious when you think about it,' Harry observes. 'It's hard to argue you're invading somebody's privacy or infringing on their Fourth Amendment rights when you don't know who they are. The government could rummage around in everybody's digital trash to their hearts' content. Then if a pattern pops up on the screen, they run to a judge and get a search warrant.'

'But Congress didn't buy it,' I say.

'No.' From the look on his face, this is the only silver lining in Kaprosky's dark cloud. 'And for good reason. I am told that programmers who delve in the dark arts were already at work devising ways to get around the identity filter. Anything devised by man can be circumvented by him. Show me a lock and I'll show you a pick.

'In this case it was called a trapdoor. They'd used it before. I can't prove it, but I'm told by people who would know that Chapman wrote one for them years earlier. According to the information, the federal government had licensed Pentagon-inspired software to some of our allies, early versions of the altered Paradize program. What they didn't tell our foreign friends was that Isotenics had installed a trapdoor in the system allowing the US to monitor the activities of these foreign intelligence services without their knowing it. The US was able to look over their shoulder as they used the software.'

'All's fair in love and war,' says Harry.

'But here's the part that will interest you,' says Kaprosky. 'Apparently there was a major argument brewing between Chapman and the Pentagon at the time she was killed.'

'Over what?' I ask.

'That's the question.' Kaprosky shrugs. 'I don't know. What I do know is that it was getting very ugly. The word is that General Satz was making noises that if she didn't get in line, he might have to go to the Justice Department to have them take the program away from Isotenics. Out of Chapman's hands.'

'Maybe she refused to go along with them on the trapdoor thing?' says Harry.

'No,' Kaprosky says. 'They couldn't very well go to Justice and tell the lawyers that Chapman wasn't playing fair because she refused to allow them to violate the law. Besides, the trapdoor would only be useful if Congress allowed the Pentagon to wire up all the computers in the country to get the raw data. Only then could they mine it for information, and if they found something – say, a pattern of conduct – they could slip through the floor without a search warrant to identify the party involved, to put them under surveillance, arrest them, or do whatever else it is that they do.' It is obvious that Kaprosky has darker thoughts about the government than most people.

'Without some source or raw data, the trapdoor was useless,' he goes on. 'It was premature. If they approached Chapman on it, it's possible she said no, simply because it was too risky. If they got caught, she and her company would have been toast. But Isotenics wasn't the only shop that could engineer something like that. I think it was something else.'

'What then?' I ask.

'According to some of the data junkies in DC – people working for other government agencies, and I know a lot of them – the word is that Defense is already running Primis to mine data. They're getting massive amounts of digitized information somewhere. Maybe it's only beta testing. Maybe they're only working out the wrinkles hoping that Congress will ultimately come along. But what if they're not? What if they found some other way to get inside, to tap into the databases? What if Chapman wasn't involved? What if she found out? She couldn't afford to just sit by and watch.

'The government tapping into private information on three hundred and fifty million Americans in violation of federal law,' Kaprosky continues. 'If that kind of a web started to come unwound, you'd have a scandal that would make Watergate look like child's play. If that's what it was, Isotenics would have been at risk. The company would have been ground into dust by the lawsuits and congressional investigations that would have followed. My battles with the government would have been a virtual paradise compared to what she would have had waiting for her.'

If it is true, Kaprosky is right. Chapman would have been in a bind, caught between loyalty to old friends; Gerald Satz, her protégé; and the continued existence of her own company. If she started making disagreeable noises, it would explain why she was feuding with the Pentagon. And if they suspected that she might go public – or, worse, engage in the favored political pastime by leaking the information to congressional staff or the press – the anxiety that might grip those in high places would provide a mountain of motive for murder.

'How do we prove it?' Harry asks. 'Can you give us names? Your sources inside the data Beltway in Washington: will they testify?'

'Not in this lifetime,' Kaprosky replies. 'Their jobs would vaporize. Trust me. After more than a decade fighting with the government in and out of court, there is one thing I do know with certainty:

whistle-blowing on that level is bureaucratic suicide. Besides, even if you got close – assuming you could find somebody willing to testify under oath – I guarantee you, before you could get them on the stand, the Justice Department would have them bundled up and shipped off to Anchorage in a box marked Top Secret. The old national-security defense,' he says.

We sit around the table in silence. Jean seems to be studying the grain of wood in the shimmering surface, lost in her own thoughts, security in their old age slipping away.

'You look puzzled, my friend.' Kaprosky is looking at me.

'What I don't understand is that if they're cut off from getting the data by Congress, which refuses to compel business to allow them to tap in, how are they getting the information?'

'I don't know,' says Kaprosky. 'But I can tell you one thing. They're running Primis, and they're doing it around the clock.'

CHAPTER
NINE

Of late I find myself reading into the wee hours, reviewing evidence, forensic and police reports from the crime scene at Chapman's house, taking notes and scouring new appellate cases that may have a bearing on Ruiz's trial – everything spread out over the empty half of my king-size bed in stacks.

Usually I am so weary that each morning as the alarm on my nightstand emits its dreaded buzz, I swim toward the headboard and reach for the snooze button. Invariably I sink back into a half hour of deep slumber that is often rich with dreams. Lately it seems that these moments of subconscious thought brim with visions of my uncle.

As a child I had only vague notions of what Evo had been through. The war in which he had suffered was long over before I could harbor any memories. In the little free time that I can steal from the trial, I have turned to a short stack of published journals and military histories to capture in detail just a glimmer of the horror that was Korea those many years ago, the first of two forgotten wars of a century littered with violence on a scale not seen since.

On 22 November 1950, unknown to US intelligence, 250,000 Chinese regulars crossed the Yalu River into North Korea under cover of darkness. According to later reports, an equal number were encamped on the other side, held in reserve in the event that they might be needed.

At night over a period of five days the Chinese infiltrated American lines, isolating and encircling entire units, including Evo's.

The Chinese separated the UN forces from support on their flanks. With quiet efficiency they set up barricades and fire blocks cutting off roads of escape to the south. They played havoc with UN communication lines. Allied forces, unable to reach headquarters units by radio because of the mountainous terrain, were forced to rely on miles of hastily strung field telephone wire. When the field phones failed, officers at the front had to figure it was due to the rapidly deteriorating winter weather. Scouts and repair parties sent out to fix them never returned.

The US soldiers lacked tents, warm footwear, and long winter coats. Nighttime temperatures dropped to sixty below zero, driven by a wind chill off the steppes of Manchuria that froze everything they had, including the saliva in their mouths and the bolts on their weapons.

Just before midnight on 27 November, to the blare of bugles and whistles, under the flare and hiss of colored rockets, tens of thousands of Chinese troops rose up like a tidal wave. US sentries, pickets asleep in their foxholes, were killed before they could reach for their rifles. Waves of Chinese troops washed over isolated American and UN forces. What little I gleaned from my uncle, listening to the accounts he told my father, was this: his unit was attacked from the side when the forces protecting their flank collapsed in chaos. They never knew what hit them.

Hundreds of soldiers were caught: many of them lying out on open ground in sleeping bags were killed in place by Chinese using Thompson submachine guns, part of the lend-lease given to them by the Allies during World War II.

UN forces scattered over hundreds of square miles were suddenly confronted by Chinese regulars in numbers that overwhelmed them. That anyone survived was a miracle.

The Chinese stormed into rear areas, overrunning supply and headquarter units, killing clerks and officers by the score, shooting cooks and GIs on kitchen patrol in mess tents, cutting down anyone wearing an olive-drab uniform.

The Chinese tore up motor pools, shooting mechanics and drivers. They stormed through a tented field hospital, shooting and bayoneting the wounded in their beds, and killed every doctor and nurse on duty. Thousands of American soldiers died in the remote frozen wastes of North Korea that winter, many of them with expressions of shock etched into what would soon become ice-covered, frozen faces.

According to what I was told later by my father, my uncle saw only small slivers of this horror, but it was enough.

In the forward areas, in the chaos and darkness, a few here and there survived. Some made it out of the killing zone before the enemy could close its grip. Others lay wounded or unconscious and were left for dead. They crawled behind snowbanks, scurried into the shadows, and waited for the opportunity to escape when the enemy was busy elsewhere. Some made it. Others were killed or captured in the attempt. Many wandered aimlessly in the mountains, leaderless and alone, where they froze or stumbled into Chinese units and were killed or captured, sometimes within sight or hearing of other American soldiers on the lam.

From everything I have heard or read, it was horror on the scale of the surreal. There are accounts of dazed American soldiers wandering among rampaging Chinese whose bloodlust was momentarily chilled as they scavenged for food, weapons, watches, or clothing. Some of these GIs actually walked within a few feet of scores of armed Chinese soldiers who didn't lift their rifles. The Chinese seemed not to notice as the GIs wandered off into the snow, some of them actually finding their way back to American lines. Others lying on the ground wounded were shot or bayoneted when they groaned in pain. From the written reports, neither logic nor the conventions of humanity seemed to have played any part in this. Years later, historians would conclude that many of the Chinese troops were themselves starving to death.

A few GIs, navigating by the stars at night, hunkering down by day, gradually moved south, found buddies along the way and formed small groups. These survivors stumbled, crawled, and ran for days without rations or water over barren, rock-strewn mountain passes covered by snow, across frozen valleys, and through rivers of icy slush. Largely unarmed, always just ahead of the Chinese, dragging frostbitten limbs through the snow, these half-dead soldiers stumbled toward the first pickets outside the defense perimeter of the Marine compound at Chosin. On their fixed faces the thousand-yard stare that in later years I would come to know as my uncle's undeviating expression, the haunted look that for decades was Evo's death-like gaze.

I spend the morning in the office going over some ancient history. Janice, my secretary, has been culling old news articles from Nexus as well as material off of the Internet, items providing detailed background on General Gerald Satz. She has downloaded them onto the office network and this morning I go over them on the computer in my office.

Like Haldeman and Erlichman, hot dogs and mustard, Gerald Satz and the word *scandal* go together, etched on my mind by the salty tang of southern politicians digging through the national trash on live prime-time television on hot summer evenings a decade ago.

General Gerald Satz's picture had been plastered on every front page in America for more than a month. The old newsprint photographs, digitized and coming alive on the screen of my computer, revive all the memories of what I had watched on television.

It was the kind of fame you might reserve for your most despised enemy. Satz's name had been mentioned by a legion of witnesses, all under oath at the bar of politics, a Senate investigating hearing. By the time Satz got to the green felt table and raised his right hand, the spit was already sharpened, hot and ready for the roasting.

It was one of those scandals, the details of which no one is able to remember a week after it is over, but that invariably enters history with the *-gate* attached as its defining suffix.

As a soldier, Satz had seen combat. Cast by the press in the role of an idiot, burdened by a zealot's wealth of initiative and a fanatic's dearth of judgment, he won that year's Tony as the administration's military court jester in the timeless Washington melodrama *Plausible Deniability*. He became a political bullet magnet, absorbing every shot aimed at his prince, devouring the scenery and stepping out even to grab a few ricochets lest they wing some minor functionary or a janitor in the White House. When it was over, the only group still scribbling notes was the White House Secret Service detail, all taking pointers on how to provide executive body protection.

Of course, all of this left the multiheaded senatorial hydra seated at the committee dais writhing in anger, furious that none of their needle-like teeth had passed through the general's body to nail the President. As a measure of satisfaction they took Satz down for perjury.

Most people of sound judgment have long since concluded that anytime mouths move among the members of Congress, they are either eating or lying, sometimes both simultaneously. Uttering lies from the floor of the Senate is one of those functions processed by the autonomous part of the brain, like breathing. Even when caught in a falsehood, it is thought to be a social lapse no worse than passing gas during a dramatic pause at the opera. But for outsiders who are testifying under oath before a Senate investigating committee to slip up, to say 'Yes' when they meant 'No,' or 'Maybe' when they should have said 'I don't remember,' is viewed as an unforgivable and deadly sin. The fossilized serpents of the Senate went after Satz tooth and tong.

He was convicted on two counts of lying under oath to a committee of practiced and confirmed liars who knew the product well when they saw and heard it. He was sentenced to six years in a federal penitentiary.

When his trial ended, committee staff collared Satz before he was hardly out of the courtroom and tried to roll him, to turn state's evidence against his political handlers. Satz refused. Like a soldier tied to the stake and refusing a blindfold, Satz told them to go screw themselves, and he did it on live TV, replete with images of Senate staffers skulking away from the camera lights into the dim shadows of the courthouse. By then most of the members of the committee who had brought the hammer and nails to this particular crucifixion were disclaiming any responsibility. They had read the tea leaves in the polls, and voters back home weren't particularly happy.

In the end, Satz never served a day. Like most of everything that comes out of a Congress laden with partisan poison, Satz's conviction was flawed, overturned by the court of appeals on what critics called a technicality, the fact that members of the committee couldn't stop talking and fawning for the cameras long enough for their attorney to establish the predicate.

In order to convict for perjury, it is necessary to establish with precision the questions posed to the accused and in response to which he was supposed to have lied. This would seem straightforward to the average person.

The problem with Satz came about as a result

of one of the more august members of the committee, an octogenarian who couldn't move without being carried, and whose mental as well as other bodily functions had last operated in a normal fashion several decades earlier. The man had been propped up at the committee table by staff who took turns kicking the back of his chair with their foot every so often in order to jar him back to reality. This presented some difficulty for a committee in which the live microphone moved around the table. Sooner or later this doyen of the Senate would be expected to produce something beyond a muted snore. As it turned out, he produced a reversal on appeal.

On cue, when his turn came, staff kicked him awake and handed him a list of typed questions carefully prepared by committee counsel and printed out in sixty-four-point type. The man stumbled and stuttered, the single sheet of paper moving like a hummingbird's wing in his palsied grip.

In the end the senator managed to turn each of the two critical questions posed to Satz into a double negative. This left the court of appeals to conclude that while Satz may have said one thing at one time, in answer to the two questions for which he was convicted – though he may not have intended it – on the record transcript of the committee hearing General Satz had actually answered both questions truthfully.

The fact is that in the last three decades, congressional committees in political war paint have ruined enough Justice Department prosecutions to cause one to wonder if this is not intentional. Skulk around Washington too long and you'll find the bones of Diogenes – frustrated in his lamp-lit quest for the last honest man in the

American Athens – piled up somewhere in the
Senate cloakroom.

After the court hammered them in the decision
in Satz's appeal, the Senate investigating
committee stumbled around, bumping into one
another for a while until they decided some other
burning issue from the previous Sunday's *60
Minutes* required their immediate attention.

As for Satz, while his name was indelibly
stamped with scandal, his reputation carried the
Good Housekeeping Seal of Fidelity. The general
was now known to the world as a man who would
keep his mouth shut and do time if he had to.
Whether it's the mob or the White House, friends
in high places usually appreciate this and can often
be counted on to find positions in their regime for
these qualities.

When it was all over, Satz found a dark corner
of government in which he hoped no doubt to
quietly serve out a few more years before merging
his military pension with a fresh one from civil
service and then disappear from the partisan hell
that is the nation's capital.

Satz was given a job overseeing an obscure
computer project at Defense, some pie-in-the-sky
spy-wars project intended to create a massive
computer database: Big Brother's ultimate clearing
house, Information for Security, or IFS, and the
Primis software program.

According to the news articles culled by Janice
and downloaded to my computer, everyone knew
that the IFS proposal was dead on arrival. The
ACLU and opponents in Congress didn't even
bother to center it in their sites, as the project was
already down on its knees, gripping its chest, when
it was first proposed by someone at Central

Intelligence. They would spend federal pocket change – forty or fifty million dollars – on feasibility studies, then the program would go the way of the dodo. General Satz would lose himself on some river in Oregon, where he could spend his retirement perfecting fly-casting techniques. That was the plan.

All of this changed when two airplanes flew into the twin towers of the World Trade Center. Like a wilted dragon who inadvertently squatted over an oil-field fire, Satz suddenly found his project aflame with political vitality. The whacko theory of some intelligence analyst at the CIA all of a sudden looked both politically compelling and technologically feasible.

And Gerald Satz, once a convicted felon, found himself minister, soon to be in charge of the tree of knowledge – not just an opportunity to pluck a little fruit but fee-simple title, ownership, everything, including the roots, trunk, and branches. Even J. Edgar Hoover had been reduced to using three-by-five cards and wooden file drawers in his closet in order to compile dirt on his enemies. Satz, who had a long list of get-even announcements waiting to be printed, was being given a warehouse filled with the latest supercomputers and a portfolio to go forth and ransack the lives of everyone in the country. All Americans, including every member of Congress, the Supreme Court, and the press – their lives were part of his playground now. It was enough to put the fear of God into anything that moved.

Opponents in Congress were suddenly howling that the administration, inadvertently or not, had put the poster boy for perjury in charge of the most sensitive government program in US history.

CHAPTER
TEN

The missing art glass has been a puzzler from the beginning. The district attorney is going to have to deal with it in his case. But how? The real question being what do they know that we don't? It is possible that the cops are as confused as we are by a lonely part that doesn't seem to fit anywhere, as if the picture on a puzzle's box cover is a Currier & Ives print, but the piece in your hand is something from a Picasso.

'You're never gonna believe what Herman found.' Harry is smiling like a Cheshire cat.

I shake my head: no clue. Herman is already inside my office, shifting around on the couch against the wall, trying to get comfortable.

Harry is seated in one of the client chairs on the other side of my desk. He has a stack of papers and files in his lap. We have been meeting each Thursday morning to go through the evidence, new items that have come from discovery, motions to produce delivered to the police and the DA, and subpoenas served on private parties.

'She paid a small fortune for it,' says Harry.

'The *Orb at the Edge*. Guess how much?' Harry wants to play twenty questions.

'How much?'

'Almost six hundred grand,' he says.

I whistle. 'It must be nice to have that kind of pocket change for an afternoon shopping spree.'

'Five hundred ninety thousand and change, assuming you don't wanna put a fine point on it,' says Herman. He's reading from a piece of paper he has pulled from his coat pocket, a pair of reading spectacles pushed down toward the end of his nose. He hands the paper to Harry, who looks at it and hands it to me.

The document is a copy of the bill of sale. From the form, it looks like the kind you might buy by the booklet in any stationery store. In the upper left-hand corner is the name and address of the gallery in La Jolla. This appears to have been impressed on what was probably foolscap on the original form, since the inked stamp seems to have bled a little into the paper.

'Apparently the thing, the *Orb*, had a history,' says Herman. 'Once belonged to the widow of the Shah of Iran. I'm told that type of thing tends to drive the price up. According to an expert we talked to, the highest-end Tiffany lamps, the very tip-top, go for maybe two hundred thousand dollars. That gives you a kind of benchmark of what we're talking about here.'

This doesn't help much, since I doubt that I have ever seen a real Tiffany lamp, much less purchased one.

'Course, I ain't no expert,' Herman goes on, 'but listen to this.' He starts reading from a second sheet of paper he's unfolded from his coat pocket. '"The work christened *Orb at the Edge* is composed of the most expensive sa- . . . sa- . . . safussid . . .'"

Harry looks over his shoulder and reads, 'Suffused.'

'Yeah.. ". . . suffused blue crystal known to man . . ."'

From the ragged edge on the paper, I assume Herman is reading from something he probably ripped from an art catalog in the library when no one was looking.

' "The *Orb* is carved and shaped from a solid block of lead crystal that weighed nearly one hundred pounds before it was reduced. In its original form, the crystal took more than two weeks to cool." Can you imagine that? "The shimmering cobalt-blue *Orb*, with its filigreed threads of twenty-four-karat gold spun through the crystal in a style and using techniques known only to ancient Venetian glassmakers, last sold at auction in New York for 250,000 dollars." That was more than ten years ago,' says Herman. 'Probably before the Shah's wife bought it.'

'No wonder the cops didn't want us to know about it.' Harry is indignant. 'According to the shop owner, Chapman wrote him a check on the spot and took the piece with her when she left the store. The gallery offered to deliver it but she said no. She wanted to take it with her. They packed it up and helped her load it into the front seat of her car.'

'And the cops have no idea what happened to it?' I ask.

'Catch this: we hit 'em with a motion for discovery,' says Harry. 'Demanded everything they had regarding that object of art previously owned and in the possession of the victim Madelyn Chapman and known as the *Orb at the Edge*. We attached a photograph and a written description of the glass from the catalog.' Harry is holding an envelope. He removes a folded piece of paper, a single sheet through which I can see three or four lines typed on the other side. 'Listen to this. This is what we get back. And I quote: "This office is not in possession of any object either identified as the *Orb at the Edge* or resembling the item described in your motion for discovery dated . . ." blah, blah, blah.' Harry looks at me and smiles, teeth bared, like a shark. 'That's it. That's all they say. Can you believe it? An item valued at more than half a million dollars is missing, the owner is dead, shot twice through the head, and they see no motive for murder in any of this.'

'Come trial, they may claim our client took it,' I tell him.

'Then where is it?' Harry asks.

'Your guess is as good as mine. Maybe as good as theirs. Any idea how many other people were in the gallery at the time Chapman showed up to look at the piece?'

'Exactly what I was thinking,' says Harry.

'Problem is,' says Herman, 'according to the shop owner, the only other people in that part of the store that afternoon were two old ladies. He remembers 'cuz he wanted 'em to leave so he and Chapman could talk in private.'

'I'll bet.' I'm looking at the single page from the DA's office that Harry has just handed to me. I spin around in my chair and begin thumbing through a stack of files on the credenza behind me.

'What are you looking for?'

'I'll know when I find it,' I tell him. It takes a minute or so. I locate it about halfway down in the stack that has been growing steadily with each motion for discovery served on the DA and the cops. I pull several stapled pages from the pile along with an envelope containing some photographs. I place the stapled pages on my desk next to the DA's letter. I jot a note to myself on a Post-it and stick it on the letter. Then I paper-clip the entire bundle together, with the DA's letter on top.

'What is it?' says Harry.

'Could be a point for our side – that is, if the sand doesn't shift under our feet between now and trial.'

'Let's just hope the cops don't find this *Orb* thing in a pawnshop somewhere with a ticket under Ruiz's name,' says Herman.

'Now, that's a cheery thought,' says Harry.

'Well, like your partner says, that's the kinda sand you don't want shiftin'. You want lotsa optimism, go into politics,' says Herman.

Herman is right. Happy thoughts of easy endings are fine for those who deal in pixie dust. But a criminal-defense lawyer who skips into court on a bubble of buoyancy is likely to slink out missing a sizable chunk of his ass, to say nothing of his client's. Even when you've crossed all the t's and dotted all the i's, you can still find yourself bouncing objections off the uneven surface of some intellectual gremlin in black robes. Unanswered questions about the *Orb*, why it disappeared and where it went, may be one of our better arguments, but to place all of our hopes in this one basket would not be wise. Ask any defense lawyer and they will tell you. You can usually punch more holes in a prosecutor's case with a shotgun than a rifle.

For the moment we drop it and move on.

'Do we know whether the cops have a time frame for the murder?' I ask.

'If they do, they aren't saying,' says Harry. 'Playing it close to the vest.' According to Harry, they are going to make us pick through everything in their reports to reconstruct the state's best guess as to when the murder occurred. 'According to the police reports, none of the neighbors heard the shots,' he says.

'No mystery to that. Silencer on the rocks.' Herman makes it sound like a posh new drink in some upscale bar.

Besides the murder weapon, the handgun that the police found in a flower bed in the backyard, they also found a six-inch cylindrical silencer, its gun-blue finish not even scratched or dented on the sandstone ledge of rocks behind the victim's house on the other side of the wall near the ocean.

'We do have something from the art shop where she bought the glass,' says Herman. He takes a small notebook from his pocket and starts flipping pages. The cheaters have now slid down his nose so that he is holding the notebook at arm's length and reading long-distance. 'Talked to the owner and his son. Middle Eastern fella. Last name is Asani. Father is Ibram. Boy's first name is Hassan. Best they could figure, the victim left the store a few minutes after five. Kid says five-ten, no later than five-fifteen. The father says it could have been as late as five-thirty. Old man was a little uptight, the kid was spacey. You want my advice, I'd go with the father.'

'Do we know whether she stopped anywhere else before going home?' I look at them, elbows on the desk, hands open, looking for an answer. Herman shrugs his shoulders. 'Last place she was seen alive was the art shop. Far as I know.'

Harry shakes his head. 'Figure it's unlikely she's

gonna stop anywhere else. I wouldn't want to leave something as valuable as the *Orb* inside a vehicle on the street or in a parking lot, would you?'

'Unless, of course, she delivered it someplace else on her way home.' I tap the DA's letter still lying faceup on my desk. 'Of course, if she did that, then what's all this packing material doing all over her kitchen?' I turn the police photograph around and show it to Harry. The victim's kitchen.

Harry peers at the photo. 'Quite a mess.'

'Surpassed only by the blood all over the entrance hall,' I tell him. 'Her purse and some bottles were spilled on the floor out in the garage.'

'You think there was a struggle?' says Harry.

'No. I think we have a lady in a hurry.'

'You think they're playing games with us on the *Orb*?'

'Who knows?'

'It wouldn't be the first time some cagey prosecutor left a tempting piece of evidence out on the end of a limb, hoping some stupid defense lawyer would crawl out there to get it.'

'Let me see the DA's letter again,' says Harry.

I hand it to him.

He reads silently to himself, forefinger of his right hand running over the letters on the page. 'Interesting,' he says. 'They say they don't have it. Doesn't say they don't know where it is.'

'Yeah. I noticed that too.'

'They can do that?' Herman asks.

'That depends. If it's only an educated guess and it can't later be said that they had specific information, maybe.'

'Is it possible she took it back to her office?' Harry offers.

'Five-thirty on Friday night. The traffic in the

area around La Jolla can get thick. We know she had a dinner engagement later that night.'

'Eight o'clock,' says Harry. 'She was meeting friends for dinner.'

'She coulda brought the glass piece to her office instead of the house,' says Herman.

'I don't think so,' says Harry. 'Cops found all the packing material at her house. The box, tape, bubble wrap.'

'I can check with the company, this Isotenics place,' says Herman. 'See if they have any record of the *Orb* bein' there.'

'Check it,' I tell him. 'But I suspect Harry is right.'

'If it's not there at her office, and the cops don't have it, we have to figure whoever killed her grabbed it,' says Harry.

'One would think so. Back to the time of death: what do we have from the state's pathologist?' This is not likely to be of much help. Without witnesses to nail it down – someone who saw the victim alive, and another who discovered the body – this is a guessing game at best.

'He says it could have happened any time between five-fifty and ten-forty that night. They're assuming she left the glass gallery sometime between five-fifteen and five-thirty. The cops found the body just before eleven that night,' says Harry.

'Sounds to me like they're operating on the notion we are: that she went straight home from the art shop,' Herman says.

'How do you figure?' Harry asks.

'She couldn't have gone to her office and made it back home in twenty minutes,' Herman explains. 'Not that time of day – not with the traffic and all.'

'That's if she left at five-thirty,' Harry says.

'What if she left a few minutes earlier? What if the shop owner's son is right?'

'Maybe,' says Herman. 'But I don't think so. Traffic's too heavy to go anywhere else. And, like you say, she ain't gonna park the car someplace and leave the *Orb* sittin' there.'

'If no one heard the shot, why did the cops show up at her house? Who called them?' I wonder.

'She missed a dinner appointment,' says Harry. He is looking through the pile of papers in his lap, finds what he wants, and scans it with his eyes. 'Chapman had a dinner appointment at eight o'clock that evening. A place in San Diego. Restaurant in the Gaslamp Quarter. When she didn't show, people waiting for her called the house, then her cell phone. They left messages both places. The cops confirmed it: messages on voice mail. First one was received at eight twenty-two that evening. She didn't answer.'

'Then the pathologist is off,' I say.

Harry looks at me.

'The time of death. Medical examiner is saying anytime between five-fifty that evening and ten-forty that night when the responding officers showed up. But if she wasn't answering the phone at eight twenty-two, it's a fair assumption that she was already dead.'

'You're right,' says Harry.

We are now down to a time frame for the murder of less than three hours. Unfortunately, Ruiz has no alibi for the evening in question. According to the statement he gave the police, he was at home alone in his apartment, asleep, since he had worked the graveyard shift the day before and was scheduled to go to work at eleven that night.

'Cause of death,' says Harry, 'was bleeding

coupled with massive trauma to the brain.' He is looking at the pathology report.

'Who was it that called the cops?'

'Someone in the dinner party waiting for her. They got worried about her and called the security contractors at Isotenics. When they couldn't reach her and she didn't show up at the restaurant, they called the police. They asked for a drive-by. Cop went to the front door and saw the body on the floor through an opening in the curtain on one of the windows next to the door.'

'Do we have a name, the dinner guest who placed the call?'

Harry looks through the papers. 'Hmm. That's strange.'

'What?'

'No name. The police report lists all the witnesses, neighbors they talked to, people at dinner waiting for her, but it doesn't say who placed the call.'

'It had to be somebody who knew her pretty well if they had her cell phone number,' says Herman.

'See if you can find out,' I tell him. Herman makes a note. 'So let's work the time frame,' I say. 'Figure it took her what, maybe fifteen minutes to drive home from the glass studio depending on traffic.'

'And assuming she didn't stop anywhere else.' Harry is milling through one of the files on his lap as he talks.

'That would have put her in the house maybe five-fifteen, say five-twenty at the latest. So play out the theories. First one to consider is theft.'

'The art glass,' says Harry.

'Right. Let's say someone who saw her in the

shop got a good look at the piece, a sense as to its value. Maybe he overhears the sounds of commerce, a figure mentioned. He'd have to know where she lives.'

'Or follows her home,' says Herman.

'He'd have to have access or find a way in. But most important, he'd have to find the gun before he could shoot her.'

'Figure he followed her,' Harry hypothesizes. 'Waited to break in. Got into the yard, found the window. Even if she's in the house, like you say, it's a big place. She's downstairs. So maybe the killer goes upstairs looking for the *Orb*, doesn't find it immediately, so he starts going through drawers.'

'Why would he be going through drawers? We have pictures of the item. It was too big to fit in a drawer,' I tell him.

'Maybe he figured he'd grab a few other trinkets as long as he was already inside.'

'And he stumbles on the gun?'

'It's possible,' Harry says.

I'm shaking my head.

'Why not? Cops didn't find the body until almost eleven.'

'Yes, but if we're right, she was already dead by the time the call came in from the restaurant. That was what?'

'Eight twenty-two,' Harry answers. 'That means the guy had about three hours.'

'It's not the lack of time: it's *too much* time.'

'What do you mean?' he says.

'Think about it. You break in and you're rattling around in somebody's house, a strange place, going from room to room, going through drawers. If it was that easy to get in, why take the chance on getting caught? Why not just go back to your car, watch the house until she leaves, then go back in and take whatever you want, including the *Orb*?'

Harry mulls this over for a moment, the devil's advocate at work. 'Maybe she was in the shower. Didn't hear the phone when they called her from the restaurant. In which case our guess as to time of death may be wrong.'

'No.'

'How can you be so sure?'

'Because he killed her in the first few minutes after she got home.'

'How do you know that?'

'Where are the crime-scene shots? The ones showing the victim.'

Harry looks at me, then starts pawing through one of the files. He finds a large manila envelope, opens the flap, and turns it upside down so that a half dozen eight-by-ten glossies slip out and slide across the table, stopping only when I slap my hand down on them.

I pick up the photos and finger through them until I find the two I'm looking for. One of them shows Madelyn Chapman lying face-down on the floor. Her left eye, the one I can see, is open, staring at eternity. What is left of her lower jaw is resting in a large dark pool of blood, strings of blond hair matted to the floor. Blood has soaked into her white silk blouse, turning portions of it along her left side into what looks like a mottled, formless shade of black. A shot like this can subvert notions of justice. Mystical abstractions like the burden of proof and reasonable doubt tend to get lost when jurors start having nightmares. If this photo makes its way into the jury box, Harry and I will need the overhead sprinkler system in the courthouse to put out the fire every time Ruiz makes eye contact with a juror.

I turn the picture toward Harry. 'Correct me if I'm wrong, but according to witnesses, her secretary at work and the studio owner, this is the outfit she was wearing that day.'

'Ah. You're right.'

'Yes. She was dead within minutes after she got home. Think about it. She's going out to dinner, has to be there at eight. She's going to want to change, and probably shower first. With most women that's going to take at least an hour, and that's if they're speedy.'

'I wouldn't know,' says Harry.

'Trust me, I'm an expert, having once been married,' I tell him.

'Go on.'

'By the time she selects and lays out her wardrobe, showers, puts on new makeup, fixes her hair, gets dressed, and selects her jewelry, you're looking at a minimum of an hour. If she bathes, figure anywhere from ninety minutes to two hours. It's going to take her at least a half hour to get wherever she's going for dinner. Friday night south on Five to the city. She'd be lucky to get there and park in that time.'

Harry nods in agreement.

'She'd be getting ready by six-fifteen, six-thirty at the latest. But here she is' – I point to the picture – 'still wearing the same outfit she wore to the office that day. She never even had time to get upstairs. Look' – I point at the victim's feet – 'she's still wearing her high heels.'

Actually, one of Madelyn Chapman's shoes came off of her foot as she twisted and went down, part of it still visible in the photo, pointing in the opposite direction as if she'd been walking in it backward. 'No woman I know wears four-inch heels around the house after she gets home from work. She hadn't taken them off yet because she hadn't finished what she was doing when she came in the door.'

I turn the other photograph toward Harry. This one is less graphic, a shot of the kitchen, pieces of plastic bubble wrap and shipping tape strewn across the granite countertop and on the floor. Next to the sink is a small-wheeled cart of some kind. An empty cardboard box sits on the counter; the two corners facing toward the camera are slit from top to bottom, its side facing the lens, laid down like an open drawbridge. The knife is still on the countertop next to the box.

'The pictures tell the tale,' I tell him. 'She came in from the garage and unwrapped it in the kitchen. We know that because her purse was found by Forensics on the floor in the garage where she dropped it while wrestling the box in. Uncrating it couldn't have taken her more than two, maybe three minutes. Where the art glass went from there I can't say. But when she was finished, she walked from the kitchen toward the front of the house, probably headed for the stairs to go up to her bedroom and bath to get ready for dinner. She would have been in a hurry. Her purse. Most women don't go anywhere without it. If they're home, they usually keep it in one place where they can find it. But hers was on the floor in the garage where she dropped it.'

'Maybe they tussled out in the garage,' says Harry. 'Could be that's where he first confronted her. Why she dropped her purse. The cops found some plastic bottles, cleaning fluid spilled on the floor in the garage. Indication is there could have been some kind of a struggle there.'

'If that's the case, why was she shot in the entryway?'

Harry shakes his head. He has no answer for this.

'The answer is the cleaning cart,' I tell him. 'In the photograph of the kitchen.'

Harry looks at the photo.

'I'm guessing she used it to roll the box containing the glass into the kitchen from the garage. It would have been easier than carrying it and safer if she didn't want to drop it. If she was in a hurry, she probably just swept the bottles off the top of the cart in the garage onto the floor. Figured that hired help could clean it up later. The bottles on the floor are not a sign of struggle. It's a woman in a hurry.'

'Which is why she forgot to go back out and get her purse,' Harry adds.

I nod. 'One thing is clear: she never got any further into that house than the front entry. Otherwise her high heels wouldn't be on her feet. Most women would kick them off at the first chance, but she had her hands full, first opening the box and then running upstairs to get ready. Only she never got there.'

Harry mulls this over for a few seconds, looking at the two photos. 'So whoever killed her had to know where the gun was.'

'Yes. And he didn't kill her over a piece of glass,' I tell him. 'Oh, he probably took it, but that's not the reason he went to her house. I could be wrong, but if I had to guess, whoever killed her really wanted to take only one thing: her life.'

CHAPTER
ELEVEN

S ome years ago, I came to the conclusion that of
all my death-house clients, the worst are the
talkers. The unavoidable impulse to chatter is
usually egged on by a little absolution and some
cheering from the cops who have collared the
suspects, who will rattle on, talking with one hand
while signing Miranda waivers with the other,
conversing on every topic imaginable except the
need for a lawyer.

All of this will generally result in enough lurid
details to earn your client a ticket on a gurney
ride to the gas chamber before you ever arrive at
the police station.

There are those who will tell you that such
people are simply stupid. Having seen enough of
them over the years, I can tell you that this is not
the case. Most criminal defendants who hang
themselves do it because they want to, or because
they have to. Call it an irresistible impulse, a
death wish. They do it for the same reason that
some fleeing felons commit suicide by cop. In their
minds, and in the absence of a good exorcism,
they see it as the only avenue of escape for

whatever good remains inside of them.

Fortunately for Harry and me, Ruiz feels no such compulsion. Whether you can equate this to a total absence of guilt or a dark spot on his soul that has swallowed the human emotion of remorse, it is becoming clear that when all is said and done, the only person who will ever know with certainty whether he did the crime or not is likely to be Mr Ruiz. He is tight-lipped, not only with the cops and the jailhouse crowd, but with his own lawyers.

'Let's talk about this gap in your résumé.' Harry presses this issue with some vengeance. We are back at the jail, confronted by what appears to be a seven-year gap in Ruiz's life, an apparent blank in his military records.

'All I can tell you is what I told Kendal. There is no gap. I don't know what to say.'

Harry paws through the papers. 'Says here your last posting was Fort Bragg.'

'That's right.'

'Then there's nothing, no activity until four years ago.' Harry puts the papers down in front of Ruiz and points at the dates and the brief blocks of print with his finger, some orders where Ruiz's name is listed with three or four other military types traveling from one base to another.

'So we have a period of more than seven years where your name doesn't show up anywhere. How is that?'

'I don't know.'

'You were at Fort Bragg that entire period?'

'Correct.'

'Doing what?'

'Like I say, I was training. Mostly weapons and tactics.'

'You never traveled anywhere? Because if you

traveled, they'd have to cut orders. Your name would show up somewhere.'

'Guess I didn't,' he says. 'It was late in my career. Once they post you like that, sometimes they don't move you around much. It wasn't like now. We weren't at war.'

Harry isn't buying it. 'There are no pages missing,' he says. 'They're numbered and dated at the top.'

Ruiz looks at them. Concedes the point. He doesn't have an answer.

'Tell us what you were doing.'

'I told you: training.'

'I assume this involved some shooting?'

'I told you it did. At the range.'

'Pistols, rifles?'

'Both.'

Like pulling teeth.

I enter the fray. 'But you weren't a drill sergeant.'

'No. It was advanced infantry.'

'Rangers?' I have made some phone calls, done a little research.

'Yeah.'

'How many Ranger outfits were at Bragg when you were there?'

'Jeez. I don't remember. I know they had a jump school.'

'Did you do jump training?'

'No.'

'Did you get that at the shooting range?' Ruiz is wearing a loose tank top this morning. As he leans over the table in the little cubicle, there is a deep scar visible an inch or so from his right nipple.

Ruiz glances down and adjusts his top a little to cover this. 'That? That was an accident.'

'Bullet wound, right?' Harry has seen enough of them over the years, mostly on clients, to recognize it.

'Yeah. Standing in the wrong place at the wrong time.'

'A training accident?'

'You could call it that.'

'We've seen the booking report when they brought you in,' Harry tells him. 'You've been shot at least four times. There's enough metal inside of you to set off a magnetometer.'

'Meaning?'

'Meaning that besides the bullet wounds, you're carrying shrapnel from explosive rounds. Steel,' says Harry. 'Fragments from artillery; mortars, maybe?'

'It was a grenade accident.'

'When?'

'I don't remember. It was a long time ago. I was doing some training with a recruit. He had the grenade. He was supposed to pop the pin and throw it over a wall. Heave it as far as he could. He got nervous and dropped it. I tried to kick it into the sump. It would have gone down a chute and exploded harmlessly. I was a little late.'

'That's all there is to it?'

'That's it.'

'This happen at Bragg?' I ask.

Ruiz looks at me, thinks for a half a beat before he answers, then says: 'No.' He knows that if he says yes, it won't square with the military records on the table in front of him.

'The bullet wounds – those are all accidents too?'

'Some of them.'

'What about the rest?' Harry asks.

'What do you mean?'

'Where did you get 'em?'

'Different places. One in Panama. You remember that?'

Harry nods.

'Can't remember the other one.'

'There's three more.'

'You ever been in the military?' Ruiz looks at him.

'Reserves,' says Harry. 'A long time ago.'

'When you been in the infantry for twenty years, you pick up things. You don't always remember where you got 'em.'

'I think I'd remember where I got shot,' says Harry.

Ruiz shrugs his shoulders and takes a drag on the cigarette he started when he came in. 'By the way, I wanted to thank you,' he says.

'For what?'

'For getting them to dispense with the leg shackles when we meet.'

Harry has gone to bat for him with one of the muni court judges. He got an order two days ago directed to the sheriff that Ruiz is not to be shackled when inside the confines of the jail.

'Trust me,' he says. 'None of this, the military stuff, has anything to do with the case.'

'We're just trying to fill in the blanks. You can bet that if we put you on the stand, the DA's gonna ask the same questions.'

'And he's gonna get the same answers,' says Ruiz. 'Trust me,' he repeats. 'You don't want to know.'

That's enough to pique Harry's curiosity. 'Is that why Kendal dropped the case?' says Harry.

'I have no idea. You'd have to ask him.'

'We have. He's not talking.'

I shoot Harry a look. This is a sore point with

my partner, the fact that Dale Kendal test-drove the case through the preliminary hearing, kicked the tires, and put his head under the hood, only to walk away. Whatever it was that scared him off, Kendal isn't telling us.

'You're gonna have to trust me on this.' Ruiz is adamant, so we leave it for the moment and move on to other issues.

Ruiz has had months to meditate on his fate. Alone without family or friends for support, he has had endless opportunities to make his situation worse by talking to the cops immediately after his arrest or by purging his soul in the jailhouse confessional, passing damaging tidbits of information to other inmates in the lockup in return for camaraderie. He has done none of this.

I switch gears. 'Let's talk about the murder weapon. The handgun.'

'What about it?'

'Where did you get it?'

'The military. It's in the records.' He points to the pile of papers in front of Harry on the table.

'They issued it to you at Bragg?'

He nods.

'Was it a training weapon?'

'Yeah.'

'It's not a standard sidearm?'

'No.'

'Did they issue you one of those as well?'

'What do you mean?'

'I mean a Beretta. Nine millimeter. That is the standard sidearm for the Army, isn't it?'

'Yes. They issued me one.'

'And where is that? Did you turn it in when you were discharged?'

'I did.'

'But not the forty-five. Why not?'

'Like I told you. That weapon was heavily modified. We used it at the range all the time for special training. You give it back to them, they're gonna junk it. It's had too much wear. Changed out the barrel at least twice. The trigger was set for my pull. Would have been worthless to anybody else.'

'So you used the forty-five for training all the time, but you didn't use the nine millimeter?'

'I didn't say that.'

'But you didn't wear the nine millimeter out?'

He sucks on the cigarette, expels the smoke through his nose. 'True.'

'One thing I don't understand,' I tell him. 'Why did you bring the gun to her house in the first place if you never carried it for security work?'

'Huh?'

'Why did you bring the gun to Chapman's house?'

'If you wanna know, I brought it there because she asked me to.'

'She *asked* you?' Harry cuts in.

'Yeah. She wanted me to take her to the range, show her how to shoot. She kept pestering me, so finally I agreed. She had a thing for firearms. Handguns. Some women do.'

'Forty-five auto's a pretty heavy piece for a woman,' says Harry.

'That's what I told her. I suggested a twenty-two, something light. She said no. She wanted something challenging, a real firearm. So I brought the HK over.'

'Bag and all?' I say.

He nods. 'I figured she would fire it once and

that would be the end of it. I was wrong. She actually liked it.'

'You let her fire it?'

'It's what she wanted. And Madelyn always got what she wanted. Tell you the truth, she didn't even flinch, not even the first shot. It had a laser sight and a silencer. Course we couldn't bring the silencer to the—'

'What did you say?'

He looks at me a question mark. 'It had a laser sight.'

'Where?'

'In the bag.'

Harry and I look at one another. 'Not when the cops found it.'

'What are you talking about? It was there.'

'They found the gun outside in the backyard in some bushes near the back wall. The silencer they found on the rocks out near the water on the other side. The bag, according to the evidence report, was upstairs in the bedroom, on top of a dresser. They found an extra loaded clip with the bag and that was it.'

Ruiz takes the cigarette out of his mouth and looks at the two of us.

'You're sure the sight was in the bag when you brought the gun to the house?' I ask.

'Positive. I was a little nervous about the silencer.'

Under federal law, possession of a silencer or sound suppressor for a firearm by anyone other than the military or law enforcement is a felony.

'I'd been meaning to crush it, throw it away,' says Ruiz. 'I should have done it.'

I'm making notes as he talks. The silencer explains why none of the neighbors heard the shots that killed Chapman. The laser sight could be critical. Up to this point the cops have been operating on the theory that only a crack marksman could have placed the two shots that killed Chapman. It is one of the key points of their case, that Ruiz owned the gun and in their own words is a 'world-class expert marksman' with a handgun.

'The laser sight. How does it work?'

'Red dot. You put it on the target and pull the trigger. The sight slides in a rail under the barrel. It runs off a nine-volt battery.'

'I assume this would lower the marksmanship threshold for the shooter. Make it easier for someone shooting the gun to hit what they were aiming at.'

'You bet. As long as you can see the laser dot and the sight's aligned properly. You put that dot on your target and that's where the round's gonna go. I used the sight when I took Madelyn to shoot. It was an indoor range, a shop out near Escondido. She shot the shit out of the center ring at twenty-five and thirty yards. Then nothing else would do: she wanted a silhouette target.'

'This was with the laser sight?'

'Yeah. Truth is, she had a kind of natural talent. Steady hand and a good eye. And that's a piece with some recoil. She held it, two-handed the thing, and laid down a pretty fair pattern. Tight, if you know what I mean.'

'What you're telling us is that somebody who was unfamiliar with that particular gun, if they could have figured out how to use the laser sight, could have made the two shots that killed her pretty easily?' Harry asks.

Ruiz makes a face. 'I don't see why not, if your

target isn't moving and it isn't shooting back. Piece of cake,' he says. 'There's no trick to the double tap. The key is hitting the target with the first round. You don't sight-align your second shot. You set up and just pull the trigger twice in quick succession – bang, bang. Like that. They use it to clear close-in targets, make sure of the kill.'

'According to the cops, the shooter was thirty feet away when he killed Chapman,' says Harry.

'It's a little long,' says Ruiz, 'but doable. Especially with the laser sight. Probably froze her in place if the laser got in the eyes. The red beam tends to put you in a daze.'

A client facing capital charges usually leaks more acid than the average battery. Closeted in a cell with only their own dark thoughts for company twenty-two hours a day, even rock-hard cons used to doing long stretches can sometimes lose it. Some exude enough sweat that you would swear every cell wall in their body is collapsing, leaving you to wonder how it is possible to fashion a defense around a formless bag of saline. After a few jailhouse visits, you can usually smell it in the air, fear dripping from them like the psychic odor of warm urine. But Ruiz emits none of this. It causes me to wonder what makes him tick.

'Who else knew that the gun was in that drawer?' says Harry.

'Madelyn, for one.'

'You told her you kept it there?'

'She asked me about it. When she came back for protection, after the security detail was disbanded. Said when she was alone in the house, it made her feel better knowing it was there if she needed it. That's why I didn't take it when I left. I've got half a dozen handguns. That was one I didn't use much.

It was too large for concealed use. I used it at the range with her and that was about it. I figured if it made her feel better, I'd leave it there.'

'According to the police report, you told the cops you forgot the gun at the house,' Harry points out. 'Now you're telling us you left it there because she wanted you to.'

'At first I did forget it. When she called me, after the security detail was ended, I told her I needed to come by and pick it up. That's when she asked me if I could just leave it there a while longer. I figured there was no sense telling the cops: they weren't gonna believe me.'

'What about other people on the security detail? Did they know the gun was there?'

'They may have. Like I said, toward the end I tried to make sure I was never alone with her at the house. It was getting to be bad form.'

'So somebody might have seen the gun in the drawer?'

'It's possible.'

We go over the list of names. This is short: two other employees of Rufus, Karr.

'Did they find any fingerprints on the gun?' asks Ruiz.

'Should they have?' says Harry.

'I assumed that if they found somebody else's, they wouldn't have arrested *me*,' he says. 'Did they find mine?'

'No.'

'I'm not surprised,' Ruiz says. 'I cleaned and oiled it pretty well last time we used it. After we went to the range. Put it away wet: figured I probably wouldn't be using it again for a while so it was best to give it a good oiling. You're not likely to find prints on something like that.'

Ruiz seems to know a lot about this, the forensics of fingerprints on firearms. It is a truism that most people don't realize that good prints are rarely found on a firearm after a crime. One of the reasons is the oil used to clean the gun, along with the shooter's sweaty hands – that is, if he isn't wearing gloves.

'The oil and the recoil usually screws up anything that might be readable,' says Ruiz.

'You sound like you might have worked crimes at one time,' I say.

'No. Just done a lot of shooting. You pick up bits and pieces of information.'

Harry changes the subject. 'Have you ever heard the term, "Primis"?'

Ruiz looks at him as if perhaps he's talking to someone else. 'Excuse me?'

'Primis software?'

He gives Harry a face, a kind of scrunched-up expression, then shakes his head, shrugs. 'Never heard of it.'

'What about "Protector"?'

He shakes his head again. 'No. What is it?'

'You never heard Chapman talk about either of these?'

He thinks for a moment. 'No. Like I told you, she didn't talk about business. At least not with me. What are they?'

'You never overheard her talking to anybody else when she might have mentioned these?'

He shrugs. 'I told you. No.'

We're done for the session. Harry begins to gather his papers, slipping them back into his briefcase.

'Oh, one other thing before I forget: the hand-gun. The forty-five. It has some letters engraved on the side of the frame. Do you know anything about those, what they stand for?'

'I don't think so.'

I pull a slip of paper from my pocket, the yellow Post-it, and read from it. 'The letters read USSOCOM. All capitals cut into the side of the slide.' I look up at Ruiz.

He's standing there, one foot up on the metal chair at the other side of the table, gaze cast down at the flat stainless-steel surface in front of him. He arches his eyebrows, cigarette pressed between his lips, one hand up to cup it. He slowly shakes his head. 'Doesn't ring any bells.'

'I checked it out. Ran a Google search. You know what that is?'

'Internet, right?'

'Yeah. Seems there's actually a site on this particular model handgun.'

'That so?'

'Yes. Heckler & Koch Model Mark Twenty-three. Originally it was made for only one customer, the United States government.'

'Really?'

'They make a civilian model now, but the original, the one you had, that was made only for military use under a special contract. The letters on the side' – I look down at the note in my hand again – 'USSOCOM: it stands for United States Special Operations Command.'

If this sets off galvanic responses in his skin or elevates Ruiz's blood pressure or respiration, you wouldn't know it by looking at him. 'Oh, I have heard of Special Ops command. Didn't recognize the acronym.'

'They're headquartered down in Tampa,' says Harry. 'MacDill Air Force Base.'

Ruiz takes it all in but doesn't say a thing.

'Seems there's a lot of interesting things going on down there,' Harry remarks.

'Really?'

'According to the online site, they have an Army Ranger unit attached. Seventy-fifth Ranger Regiment?'

'Not familiar with them,' says Ruiz.

'And there's something they call Psy Ops,' says Harry. 'Psychological Operations Command. And a special-warfare school.'

Ruiz doesn't say anything, just takes a drag on the cigarette, which is now down to a butt.

'So, have you ever been there?'

'Where?'

'MacDill Air Force Base?' says Harry.

Ruiz smiles. 'I was wondering when you were going to ask. Sorry to disappoint you. The answer is no. Listen, the fact that that sidearm was issued doesn't mean a thing. That particular weapon is probably issued in half the military ranges in the country. For training purposes.'

'So you've never been attached to Special Operations Command?'

'To be honest, I don't think I've ever even driven past MacDill Air Force Base,' says Ruiz.

CHAPTER TWELVE

For the veterans of Korea who were ahead of the psychiatric learning curve, it passed for battle fatigue. Today we have a name for the condition that afflicted my uncle. It is called Post-Traumatic Stress Disorder and it produces symptoms in varying degrees of severity. In my uncle's case it was catatonic. His soul had been possessed by this particular demon in the winter of 1950 somewhere north of a place on the map of Korea called the Chosin Reservoir. Those who survived to tell of it have become known as the 'Chosin Few.'

Through the hell that was the battle at Chosin and the retreat south to the coast, from what I came to learn later, my uncle functioned normally. He drove a truck carrying supplies and the wounded, and used a rifle and fought when he had to. His problems, the mental cloud that descended on him, came later, after he'd had time to think, a kind of delayed reaction.

For the better part of a year after returning from Korea, he seemed fine. With the war winding down, he found himself stationed at Fort Ord, assigned to drive an ambulance. With little to do but dwell on the past, the memories of faces and voices, of dead companions, he passed time waiting for his discharge. It was there, during this period of psychic decompression, that the twin demons of battle trauma – the guilt of survival and depression – began their corrosive affect. Evo began to ask troubling questions. Why was he alive when so many of his friends were dead? Like a man who escapes by a hair the carnage of a catastrophic collision and an hour later succumbs to uncontrollable tremors, my uncle fell into crying jags without any explanation. On leave at home, my grandmother would find him in the morning curled in a fetal position in the corner of his room, soaked in cold sweat and shaking. Within weeks Evo was catapulted into a psychotic pit beyond reach.

By the time they had finished with him at the VA hospital, shooting a zillion volts of electricity through his body – shock therapy, the cutting-edge treatment of the time – Evo was completely catatonic. To a wide-eyed kid of seven, my Uncle Evo was a scary guy.

When he smiled, which wasn't often, there were gaps up front where teeth were missing. On most days, uneven dark stubble, whiskers like a wire brush, covered his expressionless face.

On visits to my grandmother's house where he lived, I would watch him sit in his chair silently, staring at nothing in particular – the wall, the television, whether it was on or not – the expression on his face an impassive mask. At times I could not help but look at him in fascination and fright until my father would gently call my name and shake his head, a message that this was not polite.

For hours Uncle Evo would sit chain-smoking in a stretched out white tank-top undershirt, burning holes in the upholstery with his cigarette while he drilled psychic holes in the wall with his eyes.

Years later I would swear that the paint, the brown nicotine-stained walls of the living room, bore scorch marks from Evo's gaze. He could stare for hours and never blink, lost somewhere in thoughts of past horror, his own private hell. At times his senses were so dulled by the anesthesia of past mental pain that a cigarette held between his fingers would burn down until it singed the flesh between them, filling the room with an unmistakable sickening sweet odor.

On the few occasions when my uncle turned his dead eyes on me, I felt as if I would melt. Once after nearly a year sitting in his chair without uttering a word, getting up only for food or to relieve himself, he did something I will never forget. Visiting with my father, I sat silent in a corner watching the adults talk, when suddenly Evo swung around, looked at me, smiled his toothless grin, and said: 'Paul. How is school?'

You could hear the clock ticking two rooms away in the silence that filled the room. All eyes were on Evo. As I picked myself up off the floor, he laughed just a little, the happier face of times gone by. Then just as suddenly the leaded curtain behind his eyes dropped once more, his unfocused gaze passing through me as if I were transparent.

To my grandmother, who spoke no English, it was a miracle in the order of the fishes and the loaves. To this day I remember it as one of the truly unnerving events of my childhood, seared into my memory as if placed there by a white-hot branding iron.

'The truth is that we would have had to let him go even if they hadn't charged him.' Max Rufus is talking to me from behind a massive antique partners desk, quarter-sawn oak, probably two hundred years old, with brass-pull decorated drawers and leg wells on each side. The top is covered by a blotter of inlaid burgundy leather. Atop this is an antique letter box of darker oak and an ornate gold desktop pen set complete with gold-nib pens and two square crystal ink bottles for dipping, both of them empty.

Everything about Rufus is big, from his desk, to the size of his office, to the man himself. His hair is thinning and gray, his face tanned with creases like the furrows of a field across his forehead and around the corners of his eyes. I would guess he is in his late sixties and that the tan is from sailing. There is a large photograph of a boat under full sail on the wall behind him. This is flanked by framed certificates and licenses. The photograph, obviously taken from the air – the strut of a small plane visible in one corner – is close enough to make out the gray head at the helm, behind the oversized stainless-steel mariner's wheel in the boat's cockpit.

This morning Rufus reclines, almost laid out, in the leather executive chair, rocking back, his hands clasped behind his head as he talks.

'I liked Ruiz. He was a likable guy. He always had a good word and a smile. He would take any assignment you gave him, and for the most part he was good at what he did. I think he's a little wanting in judgment – well, more than a little wanting,' he says. 'Having an affair with a client is about as far as you'd want to go. Except for killing her. But then, I'd like to believe that he didn't do that. I wish him well. I do,' he says. 'I hope you can get him off. God knows, this firm doesn't need the bad publicity that surely will be showered on us if he's convicted. That phone' – he nods toward the one on his desk, a marble and onyx French antique – 'hasn't stopped ringing with calls from the press since the day they arrested him. So you can be sure that we have an interest in the outcome of your trial.'

The main offices of Karr, Rufus are not located in downtown San Diego but situated in the heart of the village in La Jolla. It's a strange place for a large security firm. Rufus tells me that Emmit Karr, his longtime partner, now deceased, came here nearly thirty years earlier when commercial real estate was a relative bargain. Karr managed to buy one of the larger buildings with an ocean view and now has one of the prime locations in downtown La Jolla. Most of the company's equipment and security personnel are housed in cheaper quarters, in an industrial park out near La Mesa.

'But you say you would have had to let Ruiz go even if he hadn't been arrested?'

'Sure. What else am I supposed to do? I'm sure you're aware he was taken off the executive security detail out at Isotenics at the request of Madelyn Chapman herself. After the rather embarrassing situation.' Rufus is talking about the videotaped incident between Ruiz and Chapman on Chapman's office couch.

'I take it Isotenics was one of your bigger clients,' I say.

He gives me an expression as if maybe this is true and maybe it isn't. 'Karr, Rufus has clients all over the world. But Isotenics is a substantial account.'

'So the company hasn't changed security consultants since Ruiz was charged?'

'Oh, no. Why would they? There's no reason,' he says. 'It's nothing *we've* done.' He calls the whole thing 'a difficult situation.'

'When the CEO calls you and tells you that she wants her security detail terminated because she's not comfortable with the agent in charge, that's a problem,' Rufus continues. 'But her death: we had absolutely nothing to do with that. Ruiz had been told – told emphatically – to stay away from Isotenics. He was assigned to other duties, mostly low-security night-watchman functions for other clients, pending an investigation of the events on the videotape. We would have fired him sooner, but that investigation hadn't been concluded when he was arrested for her murder.'

'Madelyn Chapman called you directly to have Ruiz removed from security?'

'Yes, she did.'

'What did she tell you?'

'I expect you've seen the accounts in the police investigative reports,' he says.

'I'd like to hear it from you.'

'What did she say? What *could* she say?' says Rufus. 'She had been captured on video surveillance with the man in a compromising situation. I wasn't in a position to ask her questions. She said Ruiz's conduct was unprofessional, that he took advantage of her in a weak moment.'

'She was on the couch with him, in her office, the head of a large company, Isotenics, and she viewed Mr Ruiz as unprofessional?'

'That's what she said. Or words to that effect.'

'How is it possible that she was caught on a videotape in her own office?'

'What do you mean?'

'I mean, she had to know that the cameras were there.'

'Ah. I see your point,' he says. 'Actually, she didn't know that the camera was there. I mean, it was a small pencil cam, about the diameter of your middle finger. It had a fish-eye lens that allowed it to capture pretty much the entire room. It was connected to a monitor in the security observation area.'

'You mean there were other people watching when Ruiz and Chapman were being taped?'

He smiles. 'Actually, no. In that regard you're lucky,' he says. 'The only other witness was this Ms, ah . . .' He tries to remember the name.

'Karen Rogan?'

'Yeah, that's it. Actually if everything had been up and running, there would have been security on the monitor watching. But as it was, the system was still being installed. You see, it was new. The camera had been installed in a small hole in the back of a bookcase just two or three days before the event. Ms Chapman had been traveling, away on business. The head of security out at Isotenics – who, by the way, was fired shortly afterward – thought it would be wise to install a camera in her office. He was concerned that occasionally she met with people who might not be thoroughly vetted by security. Needless to say, he should have checked with her first.' Rufus has a kind of pained expression as he explains all of this.

'In short,' he concludes, 'it was a major screwup. Of course, that doesn't relieve Ruiz of the responsibility that he violated strict company policy. It's in our operations manual: no fraternizing with clients or employees of client companies, on or off company time. He knew that. When Ms Chapman found out that it was all on tape, well, she was embarrassed to say the least. And angry. She called and read me the riot act. I told her we were merely providing the service the client requested.'

He sees me smiling from the other side of the desk and catches himself. 'I, ah, I didn't use that exact phrase,' he says. His face now red, he sits up, leans forward in the chair. 'I meant that we had only installed the camera at the client's request, and I told her that we were operating in good faith on the belief that the installation of the camera in her own office had been cleared by her through her own security personnel who had requested it. Obviously, if we'd known that the head of Isotenic's security division hadn't checked with her first, we would never have installed it. Goes without saying.'

I can believe that Rufus has a vested interest in the outcome of the trial. There have already been reports in the newspapers that Chapman's survivors, her mother in New York State and a sister in Oregon, have been consulting lawyers with an eye toward suing Karr, Rufus for negligence in assigning Ruiz to the security detail. In the news articles Rufus has been unavailable for comment. No doubt their defense would be that they had no way of knowing that Ruiz might be a risk as an employee. If he can beat the murder charge, the civil liability for Karr, Rufus may disappear with it.

'So you see, we would have been compelled to fire him no matter what,' says Rufus. 'There were other reasons as well. I can't go into everything at this point.'

'Are you talking about reports that Ruiz was stalking Chapman after he was removed from the security detail?'

He is looking down at the top of the desk when I ask this, so that his gaze darts up at me. He seems surprised that I would know about this.

'As I said, there are things I can't discuss. When they arrested him, that cut it. We discharged him. I'm sorry, but we had no choice.'

'I'm not here to get his job back. I'm just trying to find out what happened.'

'I understand,' he says. 'The fact is that you run a business these days and you get sued every time you turn around, at the drop of a hat.'

'What about Ruiz's military record?' I ask.

'What about it?'

'Was it good, bad, indifferent? Your firm hired him. I assume you checked him out?'

'Oh, sure. He had a good record. Exemplary,' he says.

Of course this is what Rufus would tell lawyers if he were on the stand and his company were being sued for wrongful death on grounds that they had negligently hired a dangerous employee and put him in charge of Chapman's security detail.

'What did he do in the military? What was your understanding?'

'You're asking *me*? I assume you've talked to your own client,' he says.

'I have. But what was your understanding as to what he did in the military?'

He makes a face, sits back in his chair again, and looks at me across the distance. Then finally he says: 'I'm sorry, but that's a personnel matter, and I really shouldn't go into personnel matters.'

'If you're called to the stand in his trial, you may have to.'

'Well, I guess I'll have to cross that bridge if and when I come to it. But for now, company policy doesn't permit me to get into personnel matters. I'm sure you understand.'

According to Ruiz, company policy is whatever Rufus says it is. For now, he is trying to tap-dance, to keep all his options open. I can't say I blame him. If he can avoid having to testify on the issue of Ruiz's prior military background during the murder trial, and he is later sued, his lawyers have more latitude to go back and fill in terms of what they knew and when they knew it. For my part, I was hoping that he might shed some light on what appears to be a seven-year hole in my client's life, when, for all intents, Emiliano Ruiz seems to have vanished from the planet.

CHAPTER THIRTEEN

Unless we can produce the laser sight, we are going to have a tough time arguing that an average marksman could have made the double tap, as the media is now calling the two tightly grouped shots that killed Chapman. Without the sight, the best candidate for Shooter of the Year is Ruiz. The cops already have two large glossy photos of him posing with the Army pistol team, a trophy the size of a small car sitting on the ground in front of the group.

There are a raft of evil deeds people can commit and remain under the radar of public attention. Killing the rich in America in the age of cable is not one of them.

As Harry and I cross the street two blocks to the north, I can see a sixty-foot white dual-axel box trailer parked on the street along the side of the courthouse. Block letters printed on the side of it read *MPV*. This is the production mothership leased by the cable stations and the networks in hopes that the judge will allow them to broadcast the trial directly from the courtroom. This has become the portable studio for the media until

Ruiz's trial is over. On days of heavy court activity, after the trial starts in earnest, a small fleet of satellite trucks with their antenna arrays and microwave dishes will nose in and try to dock near the trailer in order to pick up the feed from inside the courthouse.

This morning a small army of photographers, camera crews and reporters, who stand out in their colored blazers, are huddled around the van, its side doors open. Like members of a wagon train waiting to be attacked by Indians, the news crews are all looking the other way, toward Broadway, as Harry and I cross the street behind them.

For more than a month now the press has become a growing problem, haunting our office, slipping through the gate and hanging out at Miguel's, using the tables in the cantina as if they were paying customers. They sit there and organize their notes, load their cameras with film, waiting to catch Harry and me coming and going from the office. We are beginning to appreciate why some celebrities have taken to punching out the paparazzi and spray-painting their camera lenses.

Harry and I have had to lease a hotel suite in one of the downtown high-rises to schedule meetings with witnesses so that the press will not pick up their trail and hound them. My worst nightmare is that this horde finds out where I live. Twice they have tried to follow me on motorcycles until I stopped and called the cops on my cell phone. Both times a patrol car appeared and held the motorcycle and its two riders until I left and was well away. All of the lawyers in the case are now under a court-issued gag order, prohibited from talking to the media about anything involving the trial.

I am beginning to think that Harry is right,
that one day some Renaissance scholar is going to
discover that Dante's Inferno includes a tenth
circle of hell and that it is filled to overflowing
with pricks who once carried microphones and
cameras.

'Sooner or later they're gonna figure it out,'
says Harry. What he means is the fact that we
bought a janitor's pass to the back door. Harry
has slipped one of the custodians fifty bucks. He
calls the man on his cell phone when we are a
block away and the guy comes down and plays
doorman at the rear service entrance near the
loading dock. Courthouse security would frown
on the practice, but what they don't know won't
hurt them.

'What do you think happened to the laser sight?'
says Harry. This has been bothering him for two
days, ever since our last meeting with Ruiz.

'If I had to guess, I'd say the killer probably
dropped it off the rocks into the surf.'

'Behind the house?'

'Probably.'

'Then why didn't he toss the whole package,
pistol and silencer too? Why just get rid of the
sight?' Harry is huffing and puffing, hauling his
brief box full of documents as case authorities and
he trudges along a halfstep behind. He carries this
like a Roman soldier carries a shield and spear.
The brief-case must weigh fifty pounds. This
morning before we left he added an old laptop
computer to the load. This is an ancient clunker
that he never takes out, and if he did, it probably
wouldn't work. When it comes to writing and
research, Harry is low tech. If he could get copies
of documents from monks laboring in a scriptorium

with quills, he would abandon the copying machine.

'I mean, if you're gonna do it, why not get rid of the whole enchilada?' Harry is talking about the gun, Ruiz's .45 auto that belonged to the government.

'Unless I miss my bet, the cops will argue that he tried to get rid of it and failed.'

'I don't get it.'

'Think about it. The killer shoots Chapman, then leaves the house the same way he came in, out the back. He's disassembling the gun as he goes, unthreading the silencer, sliding off the sight. In the yard he tosses everything toward the ocean. He's probably rattled. Maybe something distracts him: a neighbor, voices on the beach. The lighter parts made it over the wall. The laser sight, if there was one, goes into the water; the silencer lands on the rocks. But the gun itself, maybe it hits the wall or maybe he just didn't throw it hard enough. It lands in the flower bed on his side.'

According to the police report, the cops found the .45 in the bushes just this side of the wall near one of the rear gates leading to the sandstone bluffs behind the house.

'Why didn't he go and get it, throw it again?' Harry asks.

'Maybe he didn't see where it landed. Maybe he was afraid some neighbor would see him skulking around in the yard. Maybe he didn't have time. At least, that's what the prosecutor is going to argue.'

'So the cops find the gun in the yard,' says Harry.

'Right. And the silencer out on the rocks.'

'And no laser sight,' says Harry.

'It's all very convenient.'

'In what way?'

'Think about it. If the gun had been left in plain view, we could argue that Ruiz, being linked by ownership to the murder weapon, wouldn't do such a thing. He'd have to be a fool. The very fact that the gun was so obviously left for the cops to find would point to someone else. This way the evidence makes it appear that the killer tried to dispose of the weapon but failed. The fact that the sight is missing prevents us from making a case that almost anybody, except perhaps the blind, could have made the shots that killed her.'

'So you think somebody's trying to set him up?' says Harry.

'It entered my mind.'

'And of course the cops wouldn't spend a lot of time looking for the laser sight in the water,' Harry notes.

'Why go looking when it doesn't help your case?'

'So what do we do, put Ruiz on the stand to verify what was in the bag? The accoutrements that came with the murder weapon?'

'Accoutrements?'

'You know what I mean.'

I smile. 'Accoutrements.'

'Gimme a break.'

'I don't know. Putting Ruiz on to ID the gun or its parts would not be my first choice.'

We hustle up the stairs to the loading dock. The janitor is waiting for us at the door. He uses a mop that he holds up for a second or two in front of the lens of the security camera that is aimed at the door. He blinds it momentarily as Harry and I scurry through and into the stairwell a few feet away.

We head up to the criminal court department. On four we hit the gauntlet, the print press and the electronic set who have gained access by leaving most of their equipment outside. Hobbled like this, they can only act as megaphones for what we say, repeating it and describing what they saw for the cameras when they get outside.

'Mr Madriani, will you oppose the motion for cameras in the courtroom? What is your position on the people's right to know?'

'Let 'em buy a ticket and take a seat,' says Harry.

'Is that your position? Does that mean you'll oppose the motion?' They close in around us. One of them pushes a notebook in Harry's face, making like he's taking notes, trying to herd Harry in another direction. This is a mistake.

'Mr Hinds. Could y—' In midsyllable the guy groans. He turns a shade of scarlet, something close to the color of a cardinal's cap. Then he disappears, bent over, lost somewhere in the crowd.

While the brief box contains useful points and authorities, it's the sharp corners on the container that Harry appreciates. In tight clinches he can deliver these with the underhanded subtlety of a pitcher throwing a high-speed softball. No one would notice except the victim. Dropping the old eight-pound laptop into the box was, for Harry, like loading lead shot in a leather sap.

A couple of the reporters, two of the women, are now distracted, trying to help their colleague, who is doubled over, notebook and pen to his crotch.

'Are you okay?' One of the women is slapping the guy on the back like maybe something is caught in his throat.

This has created an opening. Harry slips through and is behind me again, up close in my ear. 'The man seems to be at a loss for words.' He pushes me from behind. 'Maybe I should get in front.'

'No.' Visions of writhing bodies covering the corridor outside the courtroom, film at five.

We continue to push our way through toward the courtroom. It has been open warfare with most of the press since Harry and I issued subpoenas for certain items, reporters' notes of interviews with the cops and some videotape taken outside of Chapman's house the night of the murder and the following day as crime-scene techs processed the place. The public may have a right to know, but as far as most of the reporters are concerned, the squiggles in their notebooks and the raw file footage captured by their film crews is inviolate. We have noticed that in their coverage they have started taking it out on Ruiz: graphic stories of the murder and reports of rumors as to an affair between the victim and the defendant that may have resulted in stalking.

Harry and I push our way along, doing our best to ignore the questions.

One of the bailiffs outside the courtroom door wades in from the other side. 'Come on, out of the way. Let 'em through. Come on, folks, you're just making it hard on everybody. Keep it up, the judge is gonna chase you out of the courthouse. I'm telling you.' He finally parts the waters, enough for Harry and me to squeeze through. We clear the door and the bailiff closes it behind us.

Inside is hushed silence. The courtroom lights are on but the bench is empty. The clerk is back at her desk in the anteroom just outside the judge's chambers. I can hear her talking, then a deeper, male voice. This is followed by a lot of laughter.

We make our way through the railing at the bar

and toward the sound of the voices. Halfway there, a figure breaks the light in the doorway at the end of the hall. I recognize the profile, the bald head and the bow tie, the perpetual smile and the laughter, as he bounces past the opening like a ball. Peripheral vision being what it is, he notices our movement and an instant later comes back into the doorway for a better look.

'Speak of the devil. Mention Madriani's name and he appears like smoke. Genie out of a bottle,' he says.

'That can't be Larry Templeton!'

'Who else do you know who can substitute for a doorstop?' he asks me.

Bald as a cue ball but sporting a goatee, Templeton's facial features and appearance, if pressed into service, could easily provide a good facsimile of a death mask of Lenin. This would be striking in and of itself if it wasn't for his height, which tips the ruler at four feet six inches. He suffers from a condition known as hypochondroplasia, a form of short-limb dwarfism.

My partner is into it with him before he gets to the door. 'Larry, you shouldn't belittle yourself like that.'

'Is that you, Hinds? What did you say?'

'You know what I mean.'

'I know what you said. What you mean is that I should allow some needy defense lawyer to belittle me.'

'Well, now that you mention it . . .' says Harry. We get to the door and they both laugh.

Millie, the judge's clerk, is sitting behind her desk, smiling at the road show. The judge's door is closed.

'Are we late?' I ask.

She shakes her head.

'Where's Harrigan?'

'Mr Templeton was just telling me,' she says.

Curt Harrigan is the deputy prosecutor who has drawn Ruiz's case file. To this point he has been accommodating, hiding only half of the cards in the deck up his sleeve.

'So you haven't heard?' says Templeton.

'Heard what?'

Larry is always at his best when he has something you don't. This morning he savors it.

'Alas, fair Harrigan is no more. He has been removed from the realm of the living. Lifted into the heavens on the arms of nymphs and the wings of angels.'

'He's dead?' says Harry.

'Not dead but deified, like Caesar's horse. It seems the Governor appointed him to the Superior Court at ten o'clock this morning. He no longer wishes to be seen with mere mortals, fearful that this might taint his appearance of neutrality.'

'Neutrality?' says Harry.

'I said *appearance*.' Templeton is quick.

'Why not just arm him with a needle so he can do lethal injections from the bench?' Harry is no longer kidding: his blood is getting up.

'It's a thought,' says Templeton. 'We'll work on it.'

'Or, better yet, they could sell tickets and let Harrigan cut out the defendant's heart with a stone knife. Right from the bench, like an Aztec priest,' says Harry.

'Can I put that in the suggestion box?' Templeton winks at him.

'Why bother?' says Harry. 'The DA's Association

probably already has it drafted as an initiative for the next election.'

'Down, Harry.' Templeton gestures as if cracking a mythical whip to keep him at bay.

'Screw you,' says Harry. 'Your office is taking over the courts.'

'Who's counting?' says Templeton.

'I am,' says Harry.

'And I understand completely. I would be upset too.' Templeton's hands, small as a child's, are now joined, fingers threaded together, eyes downcast as if in remorse. Because of his size and disproportions, large head, short legs, and a torso that seems to fit neither, his every movement seems exaggerated like the choreography in an old silent movie.

'Yeah, right,' says Harry.

'Still, as black as this funnel cloud may be,' says Templeton, 'there is a little sliver of silver in its slipstream. Even for you.'

'And what's that?'

'Back at the office,' says Templeton, 'the Governor's press release is still smoking, burning a hole through the top of Snider's desk.'

Grudging as it might be, an expression – not quite a smile, but something more like the vacant look on the face of an infant at the instant of relief from passing gas – crosses Harry's face.

Roy Snider is the chief deputy district attorney and Templeton's immediate supervisor. He is not loved, either by those in his own office or others outside of it. For that reason he has been lighting incense and praying daily for more than a year that the Governor might give him a reprieve from the hell of the workaday world by naming him to one of two vacancies on the Superior Court. With

Harrigan's appointment, the last of those slots is now filled.

Somehow this seems to tickle Larry Templeton. He stands in the middle of the room, thumbs of both hands tucked into the belt of his suit pants, the wrinkled legs of which look like sharply tapered Bermuda shorts with cuffs. Along with his red bow tie he wears a starched white shirt and a brown herringbone tweed suit, what has become a virtual uniform. I have never seen him in anything other than brown tweed. His chest comes just to the top of Millie's desk.

Lawrence K. Templeton is a Stanford Law graduate. Editor of the *Law Review*, he graduated second in his class. Based on his academic record, he was recruited by half of the silk-stocking law firms in the country. In each case he ran into a buzz saw as soon as they realized that he carried a large pillow in order to sit up high enough to make it to the conference table at the interview.

He tried a solo practice for a short time, but it didn't take. Clients shied away. Then ten years ago someone told him that the district attorney in San Diego was hiring. Templeton filed an application. Given his academic pedigree and the fact that the prosecutor's office was an equal opportunity employer, they had no choice but to make him an offer. It was either that or face a discrimination suit they couldn't win in federal court.

At first, Templeton was a novelty. All of the secretaries thought he was cute. The local paper did a feature piece on 'The Littlest Law Enforcer in Town.' Templeton got his picture on the front page of section two, just above the fold.

But in a world where convictions are like

notches on the handle of the fastest gun, he didn't get what he wanted most: an opportunity to show what he could do, and respect. The people who mattered, the other prosecutors in the office, figured that Templeton would shuffle misdemeanor files until he got bored and quit. Maybe they could send him over to juvenile, where he could connect with troubled kids, someone their own size to talk to. But it didn't happen. Fate intervened.

Five months after he was hired, one of the worst flu epidemics in decades swept through Southern California. It ravaged the DA's office like the plague, laying low more than half of the felony prosecutors, decimating their senior staff. Supervisors were forced to pull people from every division just to meet trial dates. Hires out of law school, kids whose bar results might still smear if you ran your thumb over the print, were trying homicide cases. With blood in the water, defense attorneys refused to waive time. Deal brokers who specialized in plea bargains, lawyers who had never been in front of a jury in their lives, were falling over one another to demand speedy trials for their clients.

When the DA handed a case file to the last man in line, he found Templeton standing behind him. He looked at Templeton, thought about it, and figured, why not dump a dog?

For almost a year the office had been getting hammered in the matter of *People v. Bernard Russell Chester*. The defendant was a prominent philanthropist, a self-made industrialist accused of killing his wife. Represented by one of the cardinal criminal defense firms in LA and backstopped by an army of experts in forensics,

Chester's lawyers had been picking the DA's office to pieces with motions and demands for discovery. Filed chiefly because the defendant was rich and the newspapers would have castigated the DA if he'd given Chester a pass, the state's case was circumstantial: its knees had been broken and, like most of the people in the office, it was now coughing up a lung. In short, it was a loser, no matter who tried it. Templeton drew the file.

For eleven weeks Templeton rode the case like a cowboy on a bucking bronco. At first his antics in court made for rumors around the courthouse. At one point he set up two plastic recycling bins in front of the jury box and laid two twelve foot boards across the top of them. He then climbed on top and proceeded to pace back and forth like a pirate walking the plank. After the jury stopped laughing, half of them fell in love. Templeton mesmerized them with an opening statement that lasted two days, alternating between a vaudeville act and a Harvard lecture on murder through the dark arts of toxicology. His activities in court drew headlines and feature articles in a dozen major newspapers across the country. When the jury came back with a verdict of guilty on a single count of first-degree murder, it was breaking news on all three networks. Then, in a show-stopping penalty phase, Templeton convinced the jury, eight women and four men, that Bernard Russell Chester should be moved onto San Quentin's death row. Chester would become the wealthiest man ever to be housed there.

With eighteen scalps on his belt, Templeton has yet to lose a capital case. What he has can't be bottled or bought. Most women would like to take him home in the same way that kids want perpetual puppies and kittens. Templeton eats expert witnesses for lunch. He can lecture most of them on nearly any subject, and he bonds with juries like a precocious child while he slays half of your witnesses with humor and microwaves the rest with a million kilowatts of intellect.

We stand for several seconds in silence, pleasantries and smiles all around. We talk about the weather and the family photos on Millie's desk. Finally I gin up enough sand to pop the question: Who brought the pink elephant to the party? 'So tell me, Larry, you just filling in for the day, right?'

Thumbs still planted firmly under his belt, Templeton puffs out his chest a little and gives me a kind of wicked sideways grin. 'And some people will tell you that pigs can fly. But in the real world we believe in facts. And the fact is, I'm afraid you're stuck with me.'

CHAPTER FOURTEEN

'W onderful,' says Harry. 'We have a client who won't tell us where he was or what he was doing for seven years, who is caught on video in the buff doing push-ups on top of the victim on her office couch. We have an exhibition of fine shooting that, in the absence of a critical piece of evidence or Annie Oakley, could only have been done by that same client. And if that wasn't enough,' he says, 'now we have to try the case against the "Death Dwarf."'

We are back at the office. I am going through phone slips as Harry paces in front of my desk. Included in the stack is a message from Herman Diggs, our investigator in waiting.

'Picture it.' Harry holds out both hands like he is framing a shot. 'You're channel surfing and you tune in to see a lawyer the size of a fireplug shooting questions at witnesses on the stand. Now, I ask you, are you going to keep pushing the remote with your thumb, or settle back on the couch and be entertained?'

The judge in Ruiz's case has taken under submission the application by two cable stations to broadcast the trial live from a fixed camera in the back of the courtroom. Harry and I fought it tooth and nail, our worst nightmare, especially with Templeton now in place. Harry has visions of the prosecutor doing backflips across the courtroom between witnesses.

'He did oppose the motion?' I ask him.

'As I recall, Templeton told the judge that his office had "reservations" concerning cameras. That's not exactly storming the barricades,' says Harry. 'You saw the gleam in his eyes. The thought of appearing daily on the small tube, given his track record in front of juries, could spawn a whole new fad in reality television: *Lilliputians in Court*.'

'Okay, he's a problem.'

'A problem?' says Harry. 'A nine-point earthquake is a problem. Getting too close to a star when it goes supernova is a problem. Mud wrestling with a midget in the middle of a murder trial while he moonwalks on boards in the front of the jury is not a problem. I would call that a catastrophe, maybe a cataclysm.'

'If he gets out of control, Gilcrest will rein him.' If Templeton is the dark side of our case, Sam Gilcrest, the trial judge, is the bright seam. He's a former public defender, one of the last survivors, a point for our side. He'll listen politely to Templeton's arguments, but if he has to, he'll sit on him.

'Be easier to disarm a nuclear warhead while you're in the middle of a grand mal seizure,' says Harry. 'Face it: this thing's gonna be tried in the center ring of a circus. And you and I are likely to be outside the tent.'

'I think you're overstating it.'

'That's not possible,' says Harry.

'It is what it is. At this point we don't have a lot of choices.'

'Kendal found one.' Harry means backing out of the case.

'Even if I were inclined – which I am not – the court wouldn't allow it. Not at this stage. Not this late. Not unless the client fired us, and I don't think Ruiz is going to do that.'

'If you let me talk to him alone, I think I can arrange it,' says Harry.

I smile and ignore him. The message from Herman includes a number. According to the note, he'll only be there until four o'clock. I check my watch. After that I'm supposed to join him. He's left the name of the place and an address.

'We end up doing this on live television,' says Harry. 'Twenty or thirty million people watching while every unemployed lawyer in North America vies for face time so they can criticize our every move during each break. When it's over, they'll erect a tombstone out in front of the office. You know what it'll say?'

'No.'

' "Here Lie Madriani and Hinds, Killed by Tom Thumb." '

'I didn't ask for Templeton. And unless you know something I don't, there's no process for removing a prosecutor with an affidavit. So, short of finding a magical shrinking potion, inhaling helium, or learning how to sing "The Lollipop Guild" in falsetto, what is it you would like me to do?'

'For starters, we could have somebody fall on the little fucker,' says Harry.

'Or maybe you could just drop your briefcase on him.'

'Hey. The man pushed me first. There is a limit.'

'There's also something called assault and battery,' I tell him.

'I was defending myself,' says Harry. 'The guy was trying to feed me the spiral end of his notebook.'

I pile the telephone slips in the middle of the blotter on my desk, keeping only the one from Herman. I'm out of my chair and heading for the door. I grab my jacket from the coat tree as I go.

'Where are you going?'

'To get a drink,' I tell him.

'First good idea you've had all day.'

'Alone.'

In the light of dusk you can see it a block away, the words Crash 'N' Burn in purple neon, blazing against the white stucco on the building's façade. The place is set back from the street in a small strip mall about a half mile from the main gate at Isotenics, Inc.

According to Herman, this is the chief watering hole for the programmers, the number crunchers, and a few of the execs at Software City, the principal after-work hangout at rush hour. They come here to down a drink or two while they kill time waiting for the solid stream of red taillights on I–5 to snake south and break up. Herman has been coming here every night for a week. Three days ago he made a contact and has been cultivating it each evening since.

Except for a small Chinese restaurant and a private parcel shop, Crash 'N' Burn takes up nearly the entire retail space along the mall. Its large neon sign spans the length of the building, emitting an eerie violet hue that illuminates the front of the club like a black light.

It takes me a couple of minutes to find a parking space in the lot out in front. The place is packed. I leave my jacket, take my wallet and slip it into my hip pocket, and lose the tie. The object is to look as unbusinesslike as possible, hoping the man with Herman won't recognize me, at least until I have a chance to sit down.

I lock the car and head for the entrance under the art deco canopy spanning the sidewalk in front. The sleeves of my white shirt take on a phosphorescent glow under the hum of the neon tubes overhead. The canopy leads to double doors of smoked glass and very heavy. I can feel vibrations from the bass boom of music inside before I arrive.

I pull one of the doors open. Inside, the crush of bodies, laughter, and loud music from the sound system becomes an exercise in sensory overload. The place is a fire marshal's nightmare. People are forming up and adhering in tight little circles like grease in detergent, some of them turned sideways just in order to move. Standing bodies everywhere, most of them holding cocktail glasses, some of them shimmying to the beat of the music.

The lighting theme from the building's exterior is intensified here. Black light transforms flesh into shades of bronze. Smiles become blinding.

The crowd, mostly in their twenties and early thirties, is an assortment. Business types in suits mingle with the more casually dressed. Some of them have joined me in ditching their suit coats. Two young women, their backs to me, cocktail glasses in hand, block the way. One of them, wearing a short white shirtdress, seems to glow with incandescence as she gyrates in place to the music. She is shouting at the top of her voice in order to be heard by a young guy standing next to her.

Off to my right is a bar that spans the room, all the way to the back. Behind it is a wall of mirrored glass and shelves of bottles. I count at least three bartenders pulling stemmed glasses from the overhead rack and juggling bottles to mix drinks, their hands moving at the speed of light.

To my left, through an occasional parting of bodies, I can see people sitting at a few low tables. These are arranged like toadstools around a dance floor that is covered by humanity, standing room only.

In the distance, on the other side of the dance floor, two terraced areas are set off behind a railing: booths and tables, all of them occupied.

It isn't hard to find Herman. When he stands up from the booth in the far corner to wave, the two people sitting at the table in front of him turn to see if the wall behind them isn't moving. The size of a small house, tonight Herman is wearing a loud Hawaiian shirt, prints of tropical foliage covering enough cloth to outfit the sails on a schooner.

I raise a hand to let him know I've seen him. Then I sidle and slither across the dance floor, slipping through the crowd and up the two steps to the raised area.

The man sitting with Herman is also African-American. He's busy scanning the rest of the crowd as I approach, looking the other way. By now Herman should have had a chance to feed him a couple of drinks and, if I am lucky, to put him in a talkative mood. He turns to look at me just as I reach the table. The light is disorienting. Above the collar of my shirt, my face is probably an orange blob. I don't think he recognizes me.

Herman is waiting for me with an outstretched arm. 'Paul, I want you to meet a friend of mine.' He's shouting into my ear to be heard over the music, then turns away so I can barely make out the rest of it. 'Harold, this is Paul. Paul, Harold.'

Harold Klepp has one hand cupped to his ear trying to pick it all up. Unable to stand, squeezed into the back corner of the booth, he leans over the table as far as he can and shakes my hand.

Herman quickly sits down, blocking one end of the booth. I sit across from him blocking the other.

I figured that if Herman or anyone else showed up at Klepp's house identifying themselves as an investigator in the case, they would get the door slammed in their face.

'How you been? How's tricks?' Herman looks at me and smiles.

'Good. And you?'

'Oh, I'm fine,' he says. 'Have to order you a drink so's you can catch up with us. Harold, how about you? Why don't you have another one?' Herman pushes the drink menu toward me in its clear plastic stand-up display.

'Not for me,' he says.

As I read the menu I can feel Klepp's eyes beginning to bore into me from the side. He's checking me out, assessing, trying not to be obvious. 'What'd you say your name was?'

'Paul.' I say it without looking at him and try to swallow the word. I change the subject. 'What's good here?' The specialty drinks all have high-tech themes: The Memory Leak, The Data Bomb, The Meltdown, The Code Grinder, and The Infinite Loop.

'They're all good,' says Herman. 'Try the Loop. It's my favorite.'

'Loop it is,' I tell him.

Herman almost reaches out to tackle a waitress as she cruises by. 'Loops all around,' he says.

She holds up three fingers and he nods.

'No, no,' says Klepp. 'I've gotta get home.'

'Oh, you have to have one more,' says Herman.

The waitress waits for an answer.

'Bring three,' says Herman.

'Oh, what the hell,' says Klepp. He has one empty glass in front of him. I'm hoping that the waitress policed up at least one more dead soldier before I arrived. If I waited another half hour, Herman might have been able to put Klepp under the table and I could have crawled underneath to question him.

As it is, he is beginning to take a keener interest in me. 'One more time on the name,' he says. He leans over and shouts it into my ear.

'Paul.'

'You know, I think we met once before. Are you a lawyer?'

Bingo. I snap my head toward him like I'm surprised. 'Don't tell me I represented your wife in a divorce?'

'What's your last name?'

'Madriani.'

If he is going to run, it's going to be now. Instead he looks at Herman. 'Do you two work together?'

'Do I look like a lawyer?' Herman laughs without answering the question.

Klepp isn't sure whether to believe him or not, so he comes back to me. 'You're representing Ruiz.'

'You know Mr Ruiz?'

'I work at Isotenics. We met at the office, at the

214

meeting upstairs. Victor Havlitz, Jim Beckworth. In the conference room.'

'You were there?'

He nods.

'What is it you do again?' I ask.

'Acting director, R and D, Research and Development.'

'Oh, yeah. I remember. We didn't have a chance to talk. You were down at the other end of the table.'

He nods. He's wary.

'As I remember ... what was his name? Your boss?'

'Victor Havlitz.'

'Yeah, Havlitz. He kept getting his shorts in a wedgie. Very uptight,' I tell him.

This draws a smile. '*Uptight* isn't the word for it,' says Klepp.

It was clear from the meeting that among the executives at Isotenics, Klepp was feeling like the odd man out. While he may not be at the center of power, I am guessing that if anybody is going to talk openly about what was going on inside the company at the time Chapman was killed, Klepp is the most likely candidate.

I'm moving to the music again as if I have only a passing interest in conversation. A few anxious seconds pass as Klepp sits there, trapped in the middle, looking at the two of us. He's not sure if it would be impolite to leave. The waitress arrives and deposits our drinks on the table.

Herman puts them on the open tab and slides one of the full glasses over to Klepp. Then Herman gets rid of the straw from his own glass as if to say, 'Only sissies use straws.' 'Drink up,' he says.

I'm afraid Klepp is going to get lockjaw. If he

gets up to go to the restroom, I can tell he won't be coming back.

From the look on Herman's face, he knows one of us is going to have to jump into the void.

'You know' – Herman leans across the table toward me and shouts so that Klepp can hear it – 'I got tickets to the Lakers game Tuesday night. Harold and I are goin'. Why don't you come with us?'

I figured this would probably come later, after we broke the ice. But since we are walking on a glacier . . . 'Gee, I don't know.'

'You don't mind, do you, Harold?' Herman looks at him.

'Sure.' Klepp's expression is something less than certain, but what can he say? 'Why not?'

'Sounds like fun,' I say.

I had my secretary buy three tickets online the minute Herman told me he'd connected with Klepp. It wouldn't do to yank on the man's arms and twist for too much information on the first date. A long drive to LA, the three of us in the car talking, drinks over dinner, basketball, followed by a long drive home. If we're lucky, we'll catch Klepp talking in his sleep.

I try to take the edge off with some small talk. I have to repeat myself every once in a while to be heard over the music. It takes me ten minutes, but I learn that Klepp is a graduate of Ohio State, a degree in business, with a master's in software engineering from Pennsylvania. He has a wife and two sons, one in high school, the other in middle school. Once he starts to talk, the anxiety takes over and I learn everything I ever wanted to know about high school soccer. In between I'm taking sips from my drink.

Challenged by Herman, I have to down The Infinite Loop without the straw. He has done his homework. I'm betting it's the most potent thing on the menu. Based on the blast of alcohol that hits me when I first lift the glass, I'm guessing that if you lit a match it would blow the hair off my head like a torch.

The fact that Klepp is working on his second and possibly third, not slurring and still sitting upright, gives me a new sense of respect for the man. As for Herman, I have watched him drink enough tequila in Mexico to know that his insides are clad with copper.

Klepp and I cover the personal points. Then we sit in silence for about a minute with just the music filling the void. Finally he feels compelled to say something. 'How's your case going?' The only thing he can think of that we have in common.

'It's coming along.' What's one more lie?

'I, ah, I didn't know Ruiz very well,' he says. 'Ran into him a few times in the building. He came up and sat with me one day in the lunchroom. We talked for a while. He seemed like a nice enough guy. You know how you get a feeling for somebody?'

'Yes.'

'I just don't think he did it.'

'Is that an opinion? Intuition?'

'If you mean do I know something, the answer is no. Like I say, just a . . . It's probably not worth anything.'

We sit without talking for a few seconds, Klepp looking down at his drink. Then he leans toward me so we don't have to yell. 'Let me ask *YOU* a question. You came here tonight to talk to me, didn't you?' He's no fool.

'Yes.'

'And Herman?'

'My investigator.'

'You're thinking I'm the weak link?' he says.

'I'm thinking you wanted to say some things that day we met at the conference room.'

'You picked the wrong person. I can't help you. I don't know anything. The fact is, I'm outside the loop. If you come back to Isotenics in a month, I probably won't be there.'

Havlitz is pushing him out the door.

'I don't know how long I've got. I've been filling out applications, looking for another job,' he says. 'I don't know if Chapman's death had anything to do with the company. That is what you want to know, isn't it?'

I nod.

I suspect Herman can't hear a word we're saying, but from his expression he can tell we're getting to the nitty-gritty.

'That day in the office, before Havlitz cut you off, you said Chapman kept personal control over the IFS project?'

'Right.'

'She didn't delegate any of it to anybody else?'

He shakes his head. 'She had programmers working on it, of course, a good-sized team, but she was the one who held all the pieces. She was the one who knew how they fit. The final architecture was hers.'

'That sounds like a heavy load if she's running the company,' I say.

'She had a problem with delegation,' says Klepp. 'Whenever there was any problem she grabbed it, tried to fix it herself.'

'So she still wrote software?'

'Sometimes. Not often,' he says. 'It got worse after

Walt Eagan died. My predecessor at R and D. He passed on of cancer last year. Eagan walked on water as far as Chapman was concerned. Part of my problem,' he says. 'How do you fill shoes like that?'

'Did Eagan have any part of IFS?'

He shakes his head again. 'They'd been together since the beginning, the days back in Virginia. Walt oversaw all the other government contracts for software, anything that wasn't defense. We do stuff on education, motor vehicle licensing, elections, mostly special programs for number crunching ordered up by the states or Congress. Walt had been trying to wrap up a package on elections. Some district boundaries for Congress. When he died, there was a lot of chaos. Things started falling through the cracks.

'Chapman was under a lot of pressure, in part because she wouldn't let anybody else help. Toward the end, Walt was in a lot of pain. I know he was on a lot of medications. He was trying to work as long as he could. I don't know why, except that he was devoted to Chapman. But at the end he was making mistakes.

'When he died, I tried to pick up the slack. I told her some of the stuff he'd done, that the numbers didn't add up. The software was out of sync with the raw census data. I told her it wasn't a problem, I'd take care of it. She told me to put the file on her desk, she'd do it. The company was heading downhill because the CEO was getting lost in details. She couldn't let go. It's the way she was.'

'I was told that toward the end she was having a lot of problems with people at the Pentagon over the IFS program,' I say.

'You mean General Satz?'

'Yes. Did you ever meet him?'

He shakes his head. 'She wouldn't let anybody near him. Especially at the end. Like he had the plague. Chapman seemed almost paranoid about it.'

'Do you have any idea what the problem was between them?'

He shakes his head, shrugs. The music is getting louder. 'Shouting matches over the phone, I know. People in the outer office heard little bits. Chapman had a temper and she could lose it. What I was told, Satz coulda heard her yelling in Washington without picking up the phone. It was the morning after one of the networks did a piece on IFS and the threat to personal privacy. They mentioned Isotenics and used some file footage showing Chapman entering the Pentagon for a meeting with some brass. I guess she felt the Defense Department could handle the heat. Nobody was gonna put the Pentagon out of business.

'But a private company like Isotenics, that was another matter. Our stock dropped like a rock after the story. She had her secretary place a call to Satz. I was told he avoided her for two days.' He smiles and takes a drink. 'She finally ran him down, screaming about how they were making her and her company look like they were doing nothing but making spyware, like she didn't know how Satz and Company were gonna use her product. Lady was funny,' he says. 'She didn't care what you did so long as the result was good. But if she got caught in the crosshairs, baby, you better look out.'

'You say there were people in the outer office who overheard—'

'HAROLD!'

The music may be loud, but the tone in the voice causes Herman to jump in his seat. When I turn I see the red hair and the fire in her eyes. Karen Rogan is standing on the level just below us, a few feet away, looking through the railing with an expression that could melt iron.

'What are you doing?' she says.

'Karen.' Klepp knows he's in trouble.

'Have you lost your mind?' she says. 'And you . . .' She looks at me. 'You know something? Harold has a family. If Victor finds out he's sitting here talking to you, he's going to get fired. And you're going to be responsible.'

I can tell by the look on Herman's face, he's wondering who opened the door and let the wildcat in.

'We were just having a drink,' I tell her. 'Would you like to join us?'

She gives me a look to kill.

'I gotta go,' says Klepp. 'Excuse me.' He slides toward Herman, who gets up to let him out.

Karen moves toward the steps and waits for him to come down, then turns to give me one more death stare over her shoulder as they walk away.

'Give me a second.' I leave Herman at the table and head after them. I catch Karen Rogan by the arm as she's sliding through the crowd. She turns toward me, then jerks her arm out of my hand. Klepp doesn't seem to notice. He keeps moving toward the door.

She stands on the dance floor looking at me with an expression that says she'd like to hit me.

'Klepp had no idea I was going to be here,' I tell her. 'I was just getting deep background.'

'Good for you. You know, Havlitz comes in here all the time. Harold's career is hanging by a thread.

If Victor sees him talking with you, he's finished. Harold is a nice guy. I don't want to see him lose his job and, worse, get blackballed in the industry. It's a very small world,' she says. 'Tell me you're not going to call him as a witness!'

'In case you haven't noticed, my client's life is dangling by a thread. I'm afraid I can't make promises I might not be able to keep.'

'What did he tell you?'

'Nothing.'

She doesn't believe me.

'He's having trouble filling Eagan's shoes. Chapman wouldn't let him take over and do the work when his boss died. She was a control freak. I don't think any of this is classified information.' I don't mention the shouting match between Chapman and Satz over the phone. My guess is that Karen Rogan, being Chapman's gatekeeper, probably already knows about it. This may have been where Klepp got the information in the first place. 'I'll tell you what I will do. I won't say anything to anyone about my conversation with him, and if I can avoid it – if I can find the information I'm looking for elsewhere – I won't call him as a witness.'

She softens just a little around the eyes. 'You'll leave him alone?'

'If I can. Is there any chance that we could have a drink sometime, perhaps over dinner? Somewhere private, out of the way?'

'If you're thinking I can tell you anything, you're wrong,' she says.

'You can't blame me for trying to eat my way up the evidentiary food chain.'

She smiles a kind of bewitching and bemused grin. 'If you can spare Harold, I'm sure his family would appreciate it. And so would I.' Then she turns and walks away.

Herman comes up behind me. He has already settled up with the waitress, signed the tab. 'I suppose that means our basketball date with Harold is off?' he says.

CHAPTER
FIFTEEN

By all accounts, General Gerald Satz is an intensely private man, so much so that three efforts to find him in order to serve process, a summons to compel his attendance to testify at Ruiz's trial, have failed. Harry has called the process servers in Washington and told them to try again.

This morning I am on my way to a meeting I have been dreading for two days, putting it off, hoping that we would come up with something hard by way of evidence.

Two weeks have passed since the light show at the bar, my meeting with Harold Klepp, and I have nothing to show but rumors and innuendo that Chapman was having serious disagreements with the Pentagon. A couple of newspaper articles and wire service stories out of DC are nibbling around the edges as if they can smell a scandal in the dark holes of the military-government complex like sulfur from fumaroles, but so far there is no fire, nothing but hot gas.

Everything at Isotenics has been closed to us, battened down tight since my meeting with Klepp.

We have tried to find home phone numbers for several of the key employees at the company to see if they might be able to shed light on what Klepp told me about Chapman's battles with Gerald Satz. All of them were unlisted, including Karen Rogan. Herman tried to find a home address for Rogan and came up dry. Ordinarily he could do a skip trace and find an address in a heartbeat. According to Herman, he has seen this only once before. His guess is that Rogan, Klepp, and the others probably have high-level security clearances from the government. This is no doubt required of most of the software wizards and executives at Isotenics, anybody who might touch documents or see information dealing with IFS.

This morning, alone, in a rare drizzle that fits my mood, I trudge from the parking lot to the jail. Fortunately it is early. There is only one television crew out in front of the entrance. My guess is they have probably been tipped off by one of the guards that I would be coming by to see Ruiz.

As I approach the steps, the camera lights snap on. The reporter sticks a microphone in my face. 'Is it true that there is a deal in the works, that you're trying to negotiate a plea bargain to save Emiliano Ruiz's life?'

I say nothing. Instead I brush past him and into the public area of the jail on the first floor. Here several other reporters are waiting with notepads. The same question. Harry had already heard rumors that Templeton has been leaking information. Now we have the confirmation.

I put my briefcase and overcoat on the conveyer to be X-rayed and searched, then pass into the airlock. A guard sitting at the imaging machine inside the bulletproof booth can see everything on a cathode-ray screen, including my private parts. The electric bolt on the door behind me locks. For a couple of seconds I am trapped inside the small chamber with its inch-deep acrylic windows and doors all set in stainless-steel frames, metal sufficiently thick to outfit the bridge of a battleship. The lock on the door in front of me snaps open and I enter the inner sanctum.

I grab my briefcase and coat and follow one of the guards, who escorts me to the elevator and rides with me to the upper floor, where I am handed off to another uniformed guard.

When I get to the concrete conference room, Emiliano is already waiting for me, sitting at the table inside, looking at me through the window in the door. The waist chain and leg restraints have been removed, but his hands are cuffed as usual.

This morning I have brought cigarettes for him, though I don't smoke. I show the pack and the book of matches to the guard outside the door. He checks the matches, then feels the package of cigarettes, squeezing it in his hand.

'He can smoke inside the room, but take them with you when you go. We'll search him before we take him back. I don't want to find the matches,' he says.

Matches and cheap butane lighters, once common in jails, have been banned. A small plastic lighter in a breast pocket can become a lethal explosive if somebody figures a way to ignite the tiny fuel tank. Ignition sources for cigarettes are now confined to the dayroom of the jail and carefully monitored by staff. They favor small battery-powered electric lighters. In some counties smoking is not allowed anywhere inside the jail.

The guard opens the door and I step inside. I

flip the cigarettes and the matches to Ruiz, who catches them on the fly even with his hands cuffed.

'Thanks.' He smiles.

Emiliano seems to have warmed to us in the months since our first meeting. 'You called the meeting. I hope you have some good news. Any word on when I can see my kids again?'

'Probably next week.'

'Good. I've been missing them – a lot,' he says. 'It's funny.'

'What's that?'

'When you're locked up, you have time to think. All the regrets in life seem to pile up. At the top of the list are my kids. Time was, I was overseas, posted in another state, I didn't see them for months. Guess I was so busy I didn't notice. You could say I'm a lousy father,' he says.

'That's not true. I've seen you with your son.'

'Richie. Yeah.' He smiles as if he were dreaming, transporting himself to a happier time and place. 'He's a good kid. Good baseball player. We used to do a lot of that' – his expression returns to the present – 'when he was little.'

I have seen him with his son. The boy is twelve going on thirteen. Dark hair and large brown eyes, a face that has seen too much personal pain for his tender years. And yet, when they are together, his son's face lights up like a lantern. You can see it in his eyes. The last time they visited, after the boy left, Ruiz, a man who has been shot at least twice, judging from wounds that I can see and count – a man who no doubt has seen friends killed in combat – began to cry. Tears ran down his cheeks until he saw me. Then he turned and rubbed his face with his manacled forearms. When he turned to look at me again, he had the same untouched and dead eyes that I remembered from our first visit.

'Tracy won't come in to see me. Can't say I blame her,' he says. 'But she does bring the kids. Tell her I do appreciate it. Can you do that?'

'Sure.'

'You won't forget?'

'No.'

Tracy is Emiliano's former wife. They have been divorced nearly six years. She has remarried and lives in LA County to the north with her new husband. She called the office two weeks ago to ask how the case was going. I told her I couldn't discuss it. Then she got to the point. She wanted to know, in the event that Emiliano is convicted, if her new husband can adopt the two children. I told her she would have to talk to another lawyer, that I had a conflict of interest. Since that phone call I haven't had the heart to tell Emiliano.

I sit down at the table across from him. 'We have to talk.'

He is all eyes, looking at me as he lights up.

'The prosecutor has made an offer.'

'A deal?' He holds the match an extra beat, burning the end of the cigarette, then shakes the match until it goes out. The cigarette dangles between his lips.

'If you're willing to plead guilty to one count of first-degree murder, they will drop the special circumstances.'

He looks at me, a question mark, a little shake of the head, and takes the lit cigarette from his lips. 'I don't understand.'

'What they're offering is life without possibility of parole. What's known in the trade as an L-WOP.

They would drop the capital charges. You would avoid the death penalty.'

He looks at me, thinks about this for a moment, then takes a drag on the cigarette.

'Sooo, how much time would I have to do?'

'You don't understand. It means what it says. You would stay behind bars for life. There would be no parole. No release date. You would be there until you die.'

This seems to settle on him like a boulder. Ruiz has always seen his fate in terms of black and white, darkness and light. He would either be convicted and executed, or acquitted and set free. He has been left to contemplate death for months now, a slow, choreographed execution, strapped to a gurney, a machine pumping lethal fluids into a vein in his arm while witnesses look on from behind a glass partition. This thought has not seemed to move him. But the concept of life without the possibility of parole is an entirely new matter.

'Why would they do this if they thought I killed her?' he says.

'Because it's a certain result. The state avoids the cost and time it takes for a trial and all of the appeals that would follow if they get a capital conviction. And politically, for them, the stakes are high. If they shoot and miss – if you walk with all of the publicity surrounding the trial – it's the kind of case that's likely to be remembered come election time.'

There are no doubt other reasons for the offer but I don't go into all of them. I don't want to sugarcoat it. They are all longshots. There is the chance that, given Ruiz's background, we will be able to show the defendant in a positive light: his years of military service, injuries and wounds that he suffered – some of them perhaps psychological – what the man has endured while defending his country. These are things that could make the defendant more sympathetic in the eyes of the jury. Beyond this is the fact that the victim was a wealthy woman with all the toys that money could buy. The DA knows we will have no choice but to put the dead on trial, and in Chapman's case there is a universe of unknowns behind that door. Anything and everything that Chapman did over the last ten years, if we can drag it into the ring of relevance, is going to come out. If there is any doubt in the minds of jurors as to whether Emiliano did the crime, juror attitudes toward the victim could steer the state's case into a ditch – *could* being the operative word.

'What do you think I should do?' He looks at me through a blue haze curling toward the ceiling.

You can hurdle the bar exam and sally forth to spend decades in front of the bench. You can deflect thunderbolts tossed by gods in black robes and do battle daily with other lawyers. But in the end it is this question posed by someone in the position of Emiliano Ruiz that is the riddle most feared by every attorney I have ever met.

'We're not talking dollar damages,' I tell him, 'or whether you should do a few years of hard time as opposed to going to trial. We're talking about your life.'

'You haven't answered my question.' There is no fear visible in his eyes as he says it. It's not that Ruiz is cavalier about death. If I had to guess, he has confronted the issue before and more than once, though maybe not on the certain level of capital punishment, which in this state is slow and tortuous at best, taking years to grind out appeals.

But there is no question in my mind that Ruiz is a man who has studied closely the dimensions of his own mortality and done so enough times that, while what lies beyond the veil is a mystery, it is not one that terrifies him.

I'm shaking my head. 'It's the toughest thing for a lawyer. I can't tell you what to do.'

'But you must have an opinion?' he says. 'Forget the death penalty. What I want to know is, what are my chances of beating the case if we go to trial? Of walking free?'

He has already made up his mind. A man like Ruiz would claw the walls inside his cell until his fingers bled the moment he knew he had no chance of ever getting out. A death sentence – and my guess is he might not even appeal it – would be preferable to life without possibility of parole.

I have told Ruiz about my meeting with Harold Klepp and reports of an argument between Chapman and General Satz. According to Emiliano, this squares with Chapman's concerns conveyed to him in the days immediately before her murder that Chapman was scared to death. This, according to Ruiz, was the reason she hired him off the books to provide security at a distance.

'You're entitled to the truth. I won't dress it up,' I tell him.

'It's that bad, is it?'

'Unless we can crack the wall around Isotenics to get at the evidence of what was happening inside the company when Chapman was killed, if we go to trial we'll be throwing dice for your life. And that's a dangerous game. One usually reserved for fools and those who are desperate.'

'You're telling me to take the deal?'

'I'm telling you that, given the evidence as it is

right now, your chances of an acquittal are not good.'

He gets up from the table, cigarette to his lips. The guard outside the door turns to look through the glass to see if perhaps we are finished.

'Can they . . .' Ruiz stops to reorganize his thoughts. 'What happens if they convict me? They go to a penalty phase, right? The jury, I mean.'

'That's right.' I have talked with him about the procedure before.

'What happens if they decide not to give me the death penalty?'

'If it's a conviction for first-degree murder, you'll be sentenced to life without possibility of parole.'

'Promise me one thing. Promise me that you won't let that happen.'

'I can't promise you that.'

'You have to.'

I shake my head, take a deep breath, and look up at him. 'I'm your lawyer, not your executioner. I can't do that.'

'I'd rather be dead than locked up for the rest of my life.'

'I know.' I sit in silence for a moment as he paces a couple of steps, all that the room will allow.

'I'll convey the message to them. Tell them that you've rejected their offer.'

All I can see is his slowly nodding head from behind.

I would like to console him, tell him not to dwell in the dark corners. But anything I say at this moment would sound cheap, condescending. Ruiz is a man who is broken in many ways, has seen too much, and – unless I am wrong – has lived grasping the thin edge of life far too long.

To the average person his attitude at times can

be off-putting, seemingly careless, almost casual in the face of death. I worry about the jury and what they might think if this becomes their perception of him at trial.

Recently in these sessions when we meet, looking at him through the haze of smoke, it is as if I see another aspect, larger, more brooding: memories of the dark visage of my uncle. I get flashes of Evo from my childhood, in the haunted decades of life after his return from Korea. I remember veiled and faded images of what had once been, a hearty and happy soul, a spirit that was buried inside by the violence he had seen and what he had endured. Emiliano may be made of harder stuff, but when I listen to his voice and look into his eyes in times like these, moments of stress, I can see the outline of tiny fissures where the hard emotional veneer is beginning to pull away. I sense that he is starting to crack at the edges.

It is in these moments that the pain for me is real. Looking back, I cannot be sure when it happened, but at some point in the months that have intervened since we met, the trial of Emiliano Ruiz has taken on a frightening dimension that even I do not fully comprehend.

Lately this has been accompanied by dark visitations. They seem always to come at night when I am alone, after my daughter Sarah is asleep in her room. I am left to huddle with the documents that would condemn Emiliano – police reports and the state's forensic details of the crime – and one set of items in particular: a few photos of Ruiz in uniform, battle fatigues, his face haggard and dirty. He is with a small group, other men similarly worn and tired, all huddled in a half semicircle, giving it their all to smile.

The reason is no doubt lost in the dark recesses of my childhood, but looking at these pictures in the solitary hours of the night there is a palpable sense of fear. It emanates from somewhere deep in my core, ominous and cold, as if I am being paralyzed. There is a feeling that I am locked in battle with dark forces, held in a death embrace by the demon, scrapping, tearing, pulling hair at the edge of the pit for the damned who are about to be lost. Somehow this ordeal has become the battle I could never wage as a child. I cannot explain it, but Emiliano has become the proxy, the surrogate, that somehow has me struggling for the redemption of Evo's soul.

CHAPTER
SIXTEEN

This morning Harry and I dodge a projectile the size of a cannonball. Judge Samuel Gilcrest is up on the bench, peering down at the five lawyers assembled at the other counsel table. In flowing black robes, his narrow, crooked nose and hairless dome shining under the beams from the courtroom's overhead canister lights, Gilcrest resembles a wingless bald eagle about to hop down from its perch to eat its prey.

Gilcrest has decided that there will be no cameras in the courtroom for Ruiz's trial.

Harry is leaning back in the chair next to me at the defense table, taking a deep breath, psychically hyperventilating.

Templeton has given up the prosecution table temporarily to the legal brain trust for the media, lawyers representing three of the national television cable franchises. They may be arguing lofty First Amendment issues, but the bottom line is dollars. The trial of Emiliano Ruiz – the man accused of killing Madelyn Chapman in what is now being called the 'Double Tap Murder' – is worth tens of millions in ad revenue if they can get it on live TV. What is driving the story in terms of news value is not only the lurid details that have slipped out – the fact that Chapman was part of the international super-wealthy and is believed to have been having an affair with the defendant – but the fact that her company was up to its eyebrows in IFS and the seething controversy in Congress over government intrusion and individual privacy.

They try to haggle with the judge.

'You've heard my ruling. The answer is no.' Gilcrest's tone climbs a couple of decibels in volume, not quite angry but getting there.

The only thing that didn't come up during more than an hour of pitched argument is the eight-ton elephant, the psychic presence of Larry Templeton. The cute little man has his feet propped up on top of his briefcase, which he has set on the floor in front of his chair to use like a footstool. Templeton has the fingers of both hands laced together and braced behind his head, his elbows spread as he leans back, enjoying the argument. His head is a full four inches below the top of the chair's backrest. It is just this kind of lovable, take-me-home-and-squeeze-me image in front of the jury that has Harry and me worried.

Gilcrest is in his midsixties. With narrow, slumping shoulders, his slender six-foot-four-inch frame drips folds of black polyester as his robe fans out from his skinny neck and disappears behind the top of the bench. Everything about the man is sharp, from the angle of his nose to the high, prominent cheekbones set like boulders under eyes that are sunk so deep in the man's skull that any color from the pupils is lost in shadow.

'Mr Templeton, if you could join us, take your seat so we can move on to the other items.' The judge motions with a hand and a nod toward his bailiff, sign language to clear the courtroom now that the issue of cameras is behind us. Next up are motions on pretrial evidentiary items. These are closed to the public, though ultimate rulings and their significance are sure to seep onto the front pages of the newspapers and the minute-by-minute cable TV accounts of the trial.

Noise and commotion as foot traffic heads for the exit. The mob is out of their seats, milling toward the double doors at the back of the courtroom.

At the other counsel table the lawyers juggle loose papers and grab their briefcases, one of them holding a pen in his teeth, his half-open briefcase in one hand and papers in the other. Templeton lifts his feet off his briefcase and up onto the seat to avoid getting trampled. He arches his eyebrows and smiles at me, a portrait in miniature: *Escaping the Exiting Horde*. Harry is right. Templeton is going to kill us in front of the jury.

'Next item is the videotape?' says Gilcrest.

'I believe so, Your Honor.' Harry fingers through the folder to find our notes.

Templeton lugs his briefcase forward. Lifting it shoulder high, he pushes it up onto the table. He is joined by Mike Argust, one of the lead detectives in Homicide and the man who headed up the investigation of Chapman's murder. He will be state's representative for 'the People,' entitled to sit in the courtroom and listen to all the testimony even though he is a witness and will be called to the stand. Argust's name had been highly visible in the papers before the court issued its gag order

237

silencing both sides on the case. The detective's face and image are still prominent in file footage whenever Chapman's murder pops up on the televised news.

'Your Honor, if we could have some help with the seat assist.'

Gilcrest is reading, trying to get a head start on the next motion. He looks up abstractedly from the file, as if encountering a man from Mars. 'What? Oh, yeah, of course. Jerry!'

He calls to his bailiff, who is just locking up the back doors. Jerry turns toward the bench.

'Chair,' says Gilcrest, who has resumed reading the file. He gestures absently with his hand toward Templeton. More sign language. This is understood in all the criminal courts where Templeton does business.

'Oh, yeah. Sorry.' The bailiff hooks his keys onto his belt and hustles back toward the judge's chambers. A couple of seconds later he emerges carrying a dark square object like a box with rounded corners.

The county has designed a special fixture for the cushioned tilting armchairs used by the lawyers at counsel table. This device, made of wood, padded, and covered with dark fabric, fits inside the arms of the chair and lifts Templeton to a height so that he is seated on a level playing field with everyone else. The bailiff installs the thing and Templeton scrambles up into the chair like a truck driver climbing into the cab of an eighteen-wheeler.

'On this issue I don't know that I'm gonna take a lot of time,' says Gilcrest. 'I have looked at the tape and, except for a case I once heard involving prurient interest and socially redeeming values in the realm of porn, I have to admit it is pretty graphic.' The judge is talking about the videotape from the camera in Chapman's office that caught her and Ruiz in half dress, going at it on the couch. 'Of course, I can't verify that they consummated the act,' says Gilcrest, 'but a jury can come to its own conclusion, I suppose.'

'That's the point, Your Honor.' I'm on my feet, the only advantage I have over Templeton, at least in front of the judge. 'The tape proves only that they engaged in a single indiscreet act,' I say.

'I'm inclined to lean toward Mr Madriani's argument,' says the judge.

'Surprise me, Your Honor.' Templeton is smiling up at him from the other table, still pulling papers from his briefcase, not missing a beat. 'The video speaks for itself. It is the best evidence of the relationship between the defendant and the victim. The state believes that that relationship was at the heart of this crime: that it is the reason the defendant killed the victim. The tape is vital. And it is corroborative of other evidence pointing to this relationship.'

I turn it around on him: 'If they have other evidence, why do they need the tape, Your Honor? The contents of that tape are highly prejudicial.'

'I agree,' says Templeton. 'It shows that he had a reason to kill her. He was in love and she'd cut him off.'

'It shows nothing of the kind, Your Honor.'

'One at a time,' says Gilcrest. 'Mr Madriani, since it's your motion to suppress, you first.'

I cite provisions of the state's evidence code that gives the court discretion, allowing the judge to keep items in evidence out of the hands of the jury in situations where it could poison their view of the defendant to such an extent that he could not get a fair trial. 'Prejudicial effect versus probative value,' I say. 'What is the state trying to prove? That two people had an affair that lasted over a period of time, and that it became so intense that the defendant became infatuated with the victim to the degree that when she told him to go away he killed her. That's their case.'

'That and the murder weapon and some awfully good shooting,' says Templeton.

The judge swats him down. 'Enough, Mr Templeton. You'll get your chance.' Templeton bows his head toward the bench in acquiescence and straightens his bow tie.

'But does the content of that videotape prove the existence of such a long-term and torrid relationship? No. It establishes one incident of what can only be called a moment of lust. Not a motive for murder. And the images on the screen are so likely to offend a jury as to make it impossible for the defendant to redeem himself or have any chance of a fair trial. Your Honor, to show that tape to the jury is to poison their minds so irreversibly against the defendant that the contents of the videotape must be excluded.'

Gilcrest absorbs this without any hint as to whether it sways him. 'Mr Templeton. Now.'

Templeton somehow gets the heels of his shoes on the front part of the seat of the chair so that an instant later he is standing on the seat, the wrinkled knees of his suit pants an inch or so above the level of the table. The image is a gripper.

It is a first for me, never having tried a case against him. My jaw drops. When I turn back toward the bench, it's apparent from the judge's expression that he has caught the astonished look on my face.

'My learned opponent says that the tape fails to establish a long-term and torrid relationship,' says Templeton. 'What does he expect, a four-night miniseries? That tape proves that they had an affair. It is one piece in a sequence of evidence that establishes the duration and the intensity of a relationship between the defendant and the victim that is at the heart of the victim's death. Without that tape, the state's case would be immeasurably weakened,' says Templeton. 'And that relationship is central to our theory of the crime. Take it away and you may as well' – he pauses for effect – 'cut off my legs.'

Still standing at the table, I glance sideways down at Harry who is seated next to me. Harry's face is an expression of *I told you so*.

'That's all fine and good,' says Gilcrest, 'but I'm still concerned about the tape. How do we get the jury to disregard all of that huffing and puffing to say nothing of the sweaty bodies on the screen? Especially since only one of those bodies is going to be present during the trial?'

Gilcrest is the best kind of former defense lawyer, the kind that wears black robes.

'It goes with the turf,' says Templeton. 'It is what it is. What's on the tape is what they did.'

'But what's on the tape isn't an act of murder,' says Gilcrest. 'Not unless he humped her to death.'

'Of course not, and we're not saying that it is, Your Honor,' Templeton laughs. 'But it's an incremental part of our case. Vital evidence,' he says.

'It's also highly prejudicial—'

Gilcrest puts up a hand and stops me as if to say

he's heard enough from my side of the argument. 'So it comes down to whether there is anything that the state might be able to substitute for the contents of that tape. Is that where we are?' asks the judge.

'Your Honor, there's nothing that can substitute for that tape,' says Templeton.

'If my goal was to poison the jury, I'd agree with you,' says Gilcrest. 'As I recall, there was a young woman who entered during part of the tape. Though my eyes were riveted – as yours were, I'm sure – on the action, I believe she was a redhead.'

I supply the name. 'Karen Rogan, Your Honor.'

'Good. For the record Ms Rogan. She'd have to be blind not to have seen what was going on,' says the judge.

'The defense would stipulate that Ms Rogan can testify as to what she saw,' I say.

'I'll bet you would,' says the judge, 'after seeing that tape. She can testify, can't she?' Gilcrest puts it to Templeton like a robber pointing a gun.

'I don't know,' says Templeton. 'We haven't planned to put her on for that purpose.'

'Well, maybe you should,' says the judge.

'Your Honor . . .' Templeton tries to stop him before he can rule.

'Put her under subpoena and find out,' says the judge. 'Next item.'

'Does that mean the tape is out?' says Templeton.

'It does.'

'Your Honor, the state takes exception.'

'I'm sure it does. Let's move on.'

What I had hoped for: Gilcrest is our leveling hand.

The rest of the morning we run through pretrial

motions, mostly minor stuff. We win a few, lose a few, until just before noon, when Templeton announces that he has a witness and outside counsel with an interest in the remaining issues. They won't be available until afternoon.

Gilcrest decides to take the noon break. Harry and I head to lunch.

Mac's is a greasy spoon three blocks from the courthouse, a small sandwich shop, a hole in the wall stuck in the crack between two larger office buildings. Harry and I have made a habit of coming here for lunch whenever we're in trial. There are four tiny tables against one wall, a counter against the other, and a narrow corridor between the two just wide enough for one person to walk. It is one of the few places within shouting distance of the courthouse where the walls don't have ears. While the occasional bailiff or clerk may come in for takeout, there aren't enough tables or space for the courthouse crowd to hang. Whenever the tables are full, Harry and I take sandwiches to one of the benches outside. It's the nice thing about San Diego: you seldom have to worry about rain, and the last time it snowed, people were still hoofing it across the landbridge from Asia.

Today we are a little early and Mac's is empty except for one other guy in a shirt and tie under a dark trench coat who came in just behind us.

The fare here is sandwiches, but for the few regulars who eat in and who know what's available off the menu, Mac can turn a wicked Caesar salad, though it takes a few minutes. Harry orders the barbecue beef along with a towel to keep the sauce off his suit, then heads for the john through the closed door in the back.

I shuffle through a stack of newspapers by the

register, find the front section of the morning edition, and grab a table.

Madelyn Chapman and the 'Double Tap Murder Trial' make it into a double column just below the fold on the front page. Speculation that Isotenics, Inc., one of the largest employers in the county, may be drawn into the trial occupies the lead and several paragraphs following it. Apparently some enterprising reporter has heard the flutter of angst from Havlitz and his cronies over the subpoenas I served on his lawyer that day at the office. The fact that Harry and I are trying to burrow our way into filing cabinets out at Software City has the local economic prophets more than a little edgy. While the nationals may love the idea of dragging IFS into the middle of the trial, the local paper is nervous as to the fallout. If the government project is canceled, a lot of county residents – newspaper subscribers who fertilize the economy and justify full page ads for white sales – could be laid off.

'I'll have a Diet Coke.'

My eyes drift up over the top of the page to the guy in the dark blue trench coat at the counter.

'In the cooler behind ya. In cans.' Mac is busy cracking an egg into a stainless steel mixing bowl, adding lemon juice and beating it all with a metal whisk.

I'm working my way toward the bottom of the inside jump on the story when the bell over the door jingles behind me. I'm beginning to wonder if Harry has fallen in.

The customer at the cooler is looking my way. 'You want a Coke?'

For a second I think he's talking to me, then I realize he's been joined by whoever it is that just entered.

'No. Not for me.'

I flip back to the second page to scan headlines as the footsteps from the door stop at the edge of my table. The guy's stopped, probably to look at the menu on the wall over the counter. Then that feeling that always comes over you, something radiating from the sixth sense. No, he's looking at me.

I look up just as he grabs the chair on the other side and slides it toward the open end of the table in the aisle.

'You don't mind, do you?' He doesn't sit. Instead he turns the back of the chair toward the table and puts his foot on it.

'I'm waiting for a friend. He'll be back in a second.'

'This won't take that long,' he says. 'I just wanted to talk to you, give you a heads-up, before something bad happens. I'm a little worried that some of the stuff you're getting into over at the courthouse is way off base. To tell you the truth, it's not gonna do your client any good. And it's possible that it could cause some real problems for you.'

The guy is big, six-three, maybe six-four, shoulders like a linebacker. His hair is dark, cut short, almost a buzz, but not quite. He is wearing aviator glasses, straight metal frames with a little clear plastic on the tip ends over his ears. I can make out just enough from the pupils behind the gray lenses to know that they are boring holes through me at the moment.

'Exactly what kind of stuff is it over at the courthouse that you're worried about?'

'You know what I'm talking about.'

'No. I'm afraid I don't.'

245

'Well, for starters . . .' He pulls the newspaper out of my hands, leaving little tabs of torn newsprint between my thumbs and forefingers. Leaning with one foot on the chair, he closes the paper to the front page and starts to fold it up into a tight rectangle.

While he is doing this I'm studying his foot, which is almost in my lap. It must be a size thirteen. The rubber sole, heavy tread, covers the seat of the chair front to back. The high top of the tactical boot now exposed by the raised cuff of his gray polyester slacks doesn't quite go with the dark turtleneck and the blue blazer.

When he's finished folding, he leans down into my face, in close, invading my space, so that as he exhales I can smell his breath.

'This is what I'm talking about.' He pushes the folded paper into my chest with two fingers of his right hand. Even through the thick paper he somehow gets under my rib cage and triggers something in my diaphragm. Suddenly I'm struggling, trying to catch my breath. The pain is intense but I can't move. It's as if I'm paralyzed.

'I'm only gonna say this once, so listen.' He is down, right in my face now. 'You're nosing around in places you shouldn't be. Sending out pieces of paper and looking for answers to questions you shouldn't be asking.'

He takes his hand away and puts the folded newspaper on the table in front of me.

I gasp for breath.

The tight little rectangle of newsprint on the table displays only the headline and the story on Ruiz's trial. He thumps the crinkled paper with his finger so that it sounds like metal hitting muffled wood. 'This is what I'm talking about,' he says. 'They say you don't wanna believe everything you read in the newspapers. But this – this I would take to heart.' He lifts his foot off the chair and looks at his friend. 'I think we're done here.' He turns and walks toward the door.

His partner leaves a bill and some change on the counter for the Coke and swaggers toward me, his trench coat brushing the tables. 'You wanna lean over, put your head between your knees. It'll feel a lot better. I just hate it when he does that.' He's smiling as he heads for the door.

Mac has his back to me as he mixes the salad. He's missed the whole thing and doesn't seem to be paying attention to either of them. A few seconds after I hear the jingle of the bell over the front door, Harry emerges from the back.

'Sorry it took so long.' Harry slides the chair out of the aisle to the other side of the table and sits.

I'm breathing again, but sweat is running down my face. 'Some young guy back there with a bad leg got jammed in the john. Says he caught some shrapnel in Iraq. He was trying to get out the back way to his car. Asked me if I could give him a hand. Clean-cut kid. Big guy. What are you gonna do?'

So there were three of them, one to stall Harry, the good Samaritan.

247

CHAPTER
SEVENTEEN

Over lunch I tell Harry about the incident. My ribs are still sore where the guy stuck his fingers, trying to do a cavity search where there is no cavity. After telling Harry, we eat. I pick at my salad in silence and think about the comments made by Ruiz at our first meeting; his theory that Dale Kendal, his original lawyer, had been frightened off the case suddenly doesn't seem so far-fetched.

Sore as I am, we don't have time to dwell on it. Harry wants me to report the incident to the judge, but we have no evidence, not even bruises. The man was an expert with pointed fingers.

In the afternoon Harry and I hit a rough patch in court. It is strewn with rocks and boulders in the form of Victor Havlitz and his lawyer, Wayne Sims. Sims is joined by three other attorneys from his firm. The press and the public remain locked outside, pieces of brown paper taped over the narrow window slots in each door so they can't see in. I have asked that Ruiz be present this afternoon. The issues in dispute involve business matters that Madelyn Chapman was working on at the time of her death. They are key to our case, and Emiliano has a vested interest. I want him to know what is going on firsthand. Harry and I are getting desperate for something that we can get our teeth into.

The door leading from the courtroom to the holding cells opens and the phalanx of guards leads Ruiz like a dog on a leash to our counsel table. He is wearing an orange jail jumpsuit, something that will not be allowed once the trial starts and we are in front of the jury. His hands are manacled in front to a chain around his waist, and he is jingling from his ankles as he walks.

'Your Honor, I would ask that the restraints be removed from our client, at least while he's in the courtroom.'

'Your Honor, may we approach?' Templeton is bounding down from his chair before Gilcrest can respond.

The judge tells him he can do it from there, since there is no one in the courtroom.

'I'd prefer it at the bench, Your Honor.'

'So be it.' The judge motions us forward.

Harry and I join Templeton and Sims in front of the judge.

'Your Honor, the defendant is highly skilled in certain martial arts. He has employed these both in training and in combat.' Templeton seems to know more about my client than I do. Ruiz could probably snap him in half by just looking. Maybe this is the reason Templeton wants to do the argument in hushed voices at the bench. More likely it's because Ruiz knows that Templeton's information, if not false, is at least overstated.

'There is considerable evidence in the file

regarding his aptitude in these areas,' says Templeton. 'The man is highly trained.' In whispered tones Templeton is trying out his argument in front of the judge, my guess is to see just how far Gilcrest will let him wander in the theoretical fields of Ruiz as 'trained killer.' For months now the cops have been setting the stage for this as part of a major theme in their case.

'Your Honor, there is no evidence that Mr Ruiz has been anything but cooperative during his entire period in jail.'

'That's not the point,' Templeton whispers. 'What if he decides to become *un*cooperative? If they take the manacles off, are you prepared to restrain him? If so, I'd like to see your black belt.' Templeton looks up at me, all smiles.

'Give it a rest,' I tell him. 'This is a game, Your Honor. They're trying to paint Mr Ruiz as a natural-born killer. If they're allowed to continue with these antics in front of the jury, the defendant is not going to be able to get a fair trial.' I turn it on Templeton: 'What are you going to do come trial? Dress him in a suit and bring him in manacled with his ankles chained?'

Templeton gins up a smile and tugs on his bow tie. This is exactly what he has in mind. Even if he loses a pitched argument in front of the court, any hint he can make – even the faintest whiff of ether in the air that the jury might pick up on – that Ruiz is dangerous would put us on a steep downhill slope.

'Mr Madriani's got a point,' says Gilcrest. 'I don't want to tell the sheriff how to run his jail, but is there any evidence that the defendant has been a disciplinary problem in the lockup?' Gilcrest has to pull himself toward the front of the bench just to see down far enough to engage Templeton in eye-to-eye contact.

Templeton turns to look at the defendant, an appraising eye followed by an exasperated expression. 'Not in so many words.'

'There either is or there isn't,' says the judge.

'No direct evidence, Your Honor.'

'Then I think in my courtroom we'll have the restraints removed during proceedings. After all, you've got six guards and the doors are locked.'

'They won't be during the trial, Your Honor.' Templeton always tries for the last word.

'Well, if he can scramble over all those reporters, get through the throng out in the hallway, and hurdle the mass of humanity waiting to get in at the front door, and the guards can't tackle him or shoot him,' says Gilcrest, 'maybe we should just find him not guilty by ordeal the way the Indians used to.' The judge looks up. 'Mr Ruiz,' he intones in full voice now, 'you're not going to cause us any problems here in the courtroom, are you?'

Ruiz gives him a mystified look. 'Sir? I don't know what you mean by *problems*.'

'I mean a physical confrontation. You're not gonna try and escape or anything like that?'

'No, sir. I wouldn't do that.'

'Deputy, I think you can take the restraints off of Mr Ruiz while he's in the courtroom. I'm going to take you at your word, son.'

We head back toward the counsel tables. I have known for weeks that Templeton would try to quash most if not all of the subpoenas for documents that I had served on Isotenics. There is no telling what we might find if Harry and I are allowed to root around in the private papers of Madelyn Chapman compiled in the weeks and months before her death. If Kaprosky is right and war was raging between Chapman and the Pentagon over the use of her software – what Harold Klepp referred to as spyware before Karen Rogan shut him down that night in the bar – then anything is possible. What I had not expected was the oblique direction that Templeton's attack would take, the use of Sims and his client corporation as part of a well-orchestrated ambush.

It takes the guards a couple of minutes to find the keys and work the locks as Ruiz stands by the defense table, taking it all in. He has a kind of bemused expression. The judge up on the bench is paternal in his black robes as Templeton climbs back up on top of his box on the chair to look at papers and confer with Sims and the other lawyers. I can tell by the look on Emiliano's face that he is wondering who let the prosecutor in without a jester's cap, bells hanging from the point.

As he takes a seat between Harry and me, he leans my way with a broad grin while looking at Templeton. 'That's the DA?'

Fortunately, at the moment Templeton has his back to him.

I poke him with an elbow and give him a stern look. 'Leave it alone,' I tell him. It wouldn't be wise to give Larry anything more in the form of personal motivation. He has been busy proving himself to the world for forty-three years, and so far he hasn't come up wanting.

Templeton's motion to quash is based on arguments that I am off on a fantasy looking for pixie dust, anything I can find to flip in the air in an effort to distract the jury. Templeton would like to cut my legs out from under me and leave us with nothing for a defense but Ruiz up on the stand making bald denials. He would carve Emiliano into tiny pieces.

By now I had hoped for something solid by way of a footing to start building my SODDI – Some Other Dude Did It – defense. As it is, all I have is hearsay regarding heated arguments between Chapman and the Pentagon, and industry rumors that Satz and Company are running Primis and feeding it information in violation of federal law, neither of which are admissible as evidence.

Harry and I huddle over a stack of papers that were dumped on us by Sims as we entered the courtroom.

Templeton claims he had nothing to do with any of this. Still, he makes the introductions while we're still reading.

'Your Honor, if the court please, there is a motion, not being offered by the state but by private parties seeking to quash the subpoenas duces tecum served by Mr Madriani regarding his request for documents from Isotenics, Incorporated. As I understand it, the motion is grounded on the fact that most of the documents being sought either constitute or include information that falls in the realm of commercial trade secrets.'

'If you're not making the motion, maybe we should hear from the people who are?' says the judge.

'That would be me, Your Honor. Wayne Sims of the firm of Hayes, Kinsky, Norton, and Cline. We represent the petitioner, Isotenics, Incorporated.'

Gilcrest nods. 'How is Charlie Norton? I used to try cases against Charlie when he was with the DA and I was with the public defender's office.'

'He's fine, Your Honor.'

'Give him my regards.'

'I will do that. I apologize for the tardiness in our application, Your Honor.' Sims is skilled. He anticipates the problem in an effort to deflate it. 'You will find our motion along with points and authorities . . .'

Gilcrest looks around but doesn't see anything on the blotter in front of him. The bailiff hands up a folder bound with half an inch of paper between the covers.

'Mr Sims, I take it you are aware that local rules require ten days' notice?' says the judge.

'That's correct, and we object, Your Honor.' Harry puts our two cents into the pot.

'I'm aware of that, Your Honor, but under the circumstances, we found it necessary to obtain an order shortening time. Isotenics, my client, is not a party to these proceedings. We did not receive notice as to the closing date for discovery.'

'It was on the subpoenas,' I tell the judge.

'One lawyer at a time,' says Gilcrest. 'Who's going to argue this, you or Mr Hinds?'

Harry looks at me and shrugs his shoulders. We are on an equal footing, both of us equally ignorant and blinded by the lack of notice or an opportunity to read Sims's papers.

'I will, Your Honor. Mr Sims was notified as to the date to produce the items requested. It was set forth on the subpoenas.'

'What about that?' says Gilcrest.

'We were told that the parties extended the deadline,' says Sims. 'We were told of the extension but we were given no extended date for production.' Sims looks over at me and smiles.

'Your Honor, may I have a moment?' I lean over toward Harry.

'Templeton's secretary told me they'd notify Isotenics,' Harry whispers.

'Did they confirm it in writing?'

Harry shakes his head, shrugs a shoulder. He doesn't know, but if Harry can't remember seeing one, chances are they didn't.

'I'm told, Your Honor, that the people, through Mr Templeton's secretary, assured us that they would notify Isotenics as to the extended date for production of documents.'

Sims turns to look down at Templeton in the chair behind him. Templeton raises two empty hands, open palms up toward the ceiling. 'That's news to me. I don't know anything about it,' he says.

'So apparently nobody notified the company?' says the judge.

'Apparently,' says Templeton.

'I don't remember signing any order shortening time,' says Gilcrest.

'You didn't, Your Honor. You were out of town. We had to go to the presiding judge,' says Sims.

They have sandbagged us. Gilcrest knows it – you can see it in his eyes – but for the moment there is nothing he can do. 'Very well. You may proceed.'

Sims steps up to the wooden rostrum, situated just in front of and between the two counsel tables in the center of the courtroom. 'Your Honor, as you know, the victim in this case was the chief executive officer and chairperson of the board of directors of my client company Isotenics. In those capacities she was privy to extensive amounts of vital information relating to commercial and proprietary trade information belonging to the company. Many of the documents that she prepared and the correspondence that she sent and received included sensitive corporate information. This information, should it fall into the hands of business competitors, would place Isotenics at a serious disadvantage. It is conceivable that disclosure of some of this information would allow competitors not only in this country but abroad to take unfair competitive advantage that might very well destroy the company economically. Because the disclosure of this information would in many cases result in the loss of valuable trade secrets that could be exploited by competitors – which in turn would cause irreparable injury to my client – we are requesting, not only that the items sub-poenaed by the defense and listed on our schedule be quashed, but that the court issue a preliminary injunction precluding the defense or any of its agents or attorneys from making inquiries or conducting investigations that might invade these areas. We are asking that Mr Madriani and his associates be kept away and precluded from contacting employees, officers, or agents of Isotenics, Incorporated.'

'Your Honor' – I am on my feet – 'I've never heard of such a thing. Isotenics is where the victim worked. It is entirely possible, and highly probable, that her interest in the company and her activities at work led to her death.'

'Mr Madriani, you'll have an opportunity. You'll get your chance.' Gilcrest motions me to sit.

Sims then launches into a twenty-minute lecture on the law of business secrets. To listen to him, not since the Medicis ruled Florence has the world of commerce and trade been so threatened by commercial intrigues. According to Sims, it is necessary that virtually every scrap of paper that the victim touched be guarded by an impenetrable wall of secrecy until it can be scrutinized by lawyers and software wizards inside the company. He cites the Uniform Trade Secret Act. Gilcrest sits attentively and listens as Sims tells him about conclaves of lawyers and lawmakers convening in councils like cardinals in the High Middle Ages, not to hammer out religious dogma enshrined in papal bulls, but to lay down laws in the form of treaties to protect the formula for Coca-Cola and the recipe for Hershey's Kisses, sacred processes that form the root and stock of multinational corporate fortunes.

Sims then makes the leap. He hoists the defense of trade secrets to cover Chapman's e-mails, everything sent and received as well as all hard-copy correspondence and internal company memos regarding IFS and the Primis software system. He uses the argument of trade secrets like a shield, trying to push us away, to keep us at bay while Templeton gets at our innards with his short sword from underneath.

'The IFS project and the software that underlies it,' says Sims, 'are the economic cornerstone of Isotenics. Mr Madriani would ransack internal memoranda of the company on a wild-goose chase, the result of which would be to ruin my client's company.' Sims then makes an offer of proof. He tells the court that he has two witnesses.

Gilcrest waves him on.

Sims calls Victor Havlitz to the stand.

Havlitz has been locked out and sitting on a hard bench in the outer corridor. The bailiff has to unlock the door and call his name.

Not being a party to the proceedings, Havlitz has no legal right to be here other than to testify if he is called. He has ended up on both our witness list and the prosecution's. As a result, he will be excluded from the guilt-or-innocence phase of the trial in which the name of his company is likely to figure prominently in daily news accounts. For a guy like Havlitz, whose anxiety level is as taut as goat gut strung on a violin, waiting to hear the news each day is likely to kill him.

Havlitz is sworn and takes the stand.

Sims moves quickly through the preliminaries.

'To your knowledge, has an effort been made,' says Sims, 'to identify and to produce those portions or items of the subpoenaed materials that would not violate the confidentiality requirements of your company or result in the disclosure of trade secrets?'

This has all been well scripted. Havlitz launches into detail, telling the judge that he supervised this process personally. To listen to him talk, Isotenics wore out at least one machine copying pages that were delivered to our office. At one point Havlitz pulls a slip of paper from the pocket of his suit coat and tells the judge that, in all, they copied 1,214 pages that were delivered to our office.

What he doesn't say is that many of these were copied four or five times and that nearly all of them were documents that had previously been published in corporate reports, materials prepared for the unwashed shareholders and mailed to them or handed out at their annual meetings. If the company were in bankruptcy, its assets had fallen through a crack into hell and burned, and if all of the directors were under indictment for fraud, you would never read about any of it in the pages turned over by Havlitz. In the original, most of these would have been four-color and glossy. One of them showed Havlitz's smiling face peering out like a flimflam man when I flipped the first stapled page. In all the copied pages, there was nothing about pissing contests and shouting matches on the phone between Chapman and Gerald Satz, not even in the footnotes.

'With regard to the other items,' says Sims, 'the materials you deemed confidential. Did these items involve information or data of a sensitive commercial nature concerning proprietary trade matters?' Sims recites the magic words as if they were sacred script. If it would do any good to brace his argument, he would shake a bag of freeze-dried bones in front of the witness to complete the hex on our case – lord high legal shaman.

'They did,' says Havlitz.

'And in your opinion, as the chief executive of Isotenics, would public disclosure or the risk of public disclosure of these materials cause damage to your company that would result in irreparable injury?'

'Absolutely, without question,' says Havlitz.

'Your witness,' says Sims.

Templeton is smiling through all of this, the chance to stick a pike through the heart of our case without even moving his lips. He is taking up half a wooden chair from the row behind the prosecution table just inside the railing. This time he is using one of the courtroom's metal waste cans turned upside-down to rest his feet on so they don't dangle in midair from the platform of the chair. Today he has wound Sims up like a coiled spring and turned him loose in court to see what kind of havoc he can wreck in our case.

I stand with a single sheet of paper in my hand. 'Mr Havlitz, you say you read all of the subpoenas.'

'That's right.'

'Do you remember one of the subpoenas that included among the items being sought' – I look down and read from the page – 'any telephone directory or list of that company known as Isotenics, Incorporated, that includes the names, telephone numbers or extensions of employees, officers, or agents of said company?'

'I think I recall it,' he says.

'Do you remember whether you produced such a document?'

'I, ah . . . I don't think we did.'

'Do you consider a company telephone directory to be a trade secret?'

He looks down at the floor, shrugs a shoulder, then looks at Sims.

'Objection: calls for a legal conclusion,' says Sims.

'The witness testified that he supervised the process to determine which documents were produced and which were not. Surely he must have exercised some standard in making that determination?'

'He did so only with the assistance of counsel,' says Sims.

'So is counsel now testifying, Your Honor? If so, I would ask that he be sworn and take the stand.'

Havlitz speaks up before the judge can rule on Sims's objection. 'I had the help of lawyers.'

'Too many people talking at once,' says Gilcrest. 'The witness can answer the question.'

I put the question to the witness: 'So what was the standard that you applied?'

'I . . . I don't remember. It was written down. But we tried to be fair.'

'I'll bet. Was the prosecutor, Mr Templeton,

involved in this process? Did you confer with him?'

'I, ah . . .' He looks at Sims for help. The lawyer would raise attorney-client privilege, but Templeton is outside the umbrella. Instead, Sims pores through a stack of papers in front of him until he finds the stapled sets he wants. 'Your Honor, as a matter of fact, the company's telephone list does qualify for trade-secret protection. Isotenics has guarded the contents of its internal phone directory for proprietary reasons. While the general telephone number of the company is listed, the individual extensions for divisions and specific employees of Isotenics are not. I have a case on point,' says Sims. He hands one copy to the bailiff for the judge and the other to me. 'In this case,' he continues, 'the court held that where the company compiled its internal directory, maintained it in confidence, and where the disclosure of names, phone numbers, and divisions or job descriptions included employees who were in the possession of legally protected trade secrets, the telephone list itself was a protected item. And in answer to Mr Madriani's question, the court lays out in detail the standard to be applied in determining the existence of trade secrets.'

Gilcrest is nodding. 'Yes, I see that in the headnotes,' says the judge.

'Your Honor, we've had no time to look at any of this. The motion by Isotenics and its lawyers has been sprung on us like a trap. The witness has not answered my question. Did he or his lawyers confer with Mr Templeton or anyone else from the prosecution in determining what documents to release and what documents not to release?'

'You can answer the question,' says Gilcrest.

'There were some conversations,' says Havlitz. 'Meetings. I was present only at one of them.'

'But your lawyers met and talked to Mr Templeton, isn't that correct?'

'Objection. Anything conveyed by counsel to the witness as a representative of the client corporation is privileged information,' says Sims. It may be privileged, but he has just admitted to it.

I may have shown Templeton digging this pit with Sims and Isotenics, but the fact remains that we've fallen into it. The company phone directory is not a significant piece of evidence for us, but it is a bad example because of the case in point that Sims is able to put in front of the judge.

'I get the point, Mr Madriani.' Still, Gilcrest is distracted, reading the case. On the eve of the trial, there is no easy way out. He will have to make a decision on whether to open the door on the company's records, and if so, how far. The troubled expression from the bench as he reads says it for him – judge on the horns of a dilemma.

Ordinarily a court would have no difficulty balancing the equities – the right to a fair trial, a man's life – against property interests. But here, Gilcrest is a man from Mars in a field of law that is foreign, and the property interests at issue could be worth hundreds of millions if not billions of dollars. Wearing black robes does not immunize a person from worry. The judge has to wonder. If Havlitz and his lawyers are correct and the court makes the wrong decision, if as a result a competitor takes trade secrets and uses them to crush Isotenics, there is no appeal to a higher court that can undo the damage. Sam Gilcrest may be defense oriented, but he is not oblivious to the fact that Isotenics is one of the largest employers in the county and a huge corporate taxpayer.

For the moment I would rather defer a decision than get a bad one on tactics that go to the heart of our case.

'Your Honor, perhaps there's some middle ground,' I say.

Gilcrest looks up at me over the top of the decision he is still reading at the bench. 'I'd be thankful for any suggestions,' he says.

Sims cuts me off before I can negotiate. 'Your Honor, if Mr Madriani is finished with the witness, I have one more before the court makes its ruling.'

'Mr Madriani, do you have any more questions of this witness?'

'No, Your Honor.' Not knowing what other trip wires and grenades lie hidden in the pile of papers in front of Sims, I don't dare ask about other documents they have declined to turn over. All I need is another mind-bending appellate opinion for Gilcrest to get lost forever in the dark forests of business law.

'Call your other witness.' The judge is still busy turning pages, trying to glean the exact dimension of trade secrets from between the printed lines. He motions to his bailiff to let Havlitz out and to buttonhole the other witness outside on the bench.

I am turned in my chair toward the doors at the back of the courtroom when she enters. Karen Rogan's eyes fall on me for an instant before she fixes her gaze down at the floor. She purses her lips in a kind of pained expression of nervousness. Clutching a small handbag to her side, she looks at me again, but only for a fleeting second after she is sworn and seated on the stand.

'State your name for the record,' says Sims.

'Karen Rogan.' Her voice cracks as she spells her last name for the court reporter.

'You work at Isotenics, is that correct?'

'Yes.'

'For how long?'

'Twe-twelve years,' she says.

'And what position do you hold?'

'My title is executive assistant.'

'And so that we can save the court some time, you worked as personal assistant to Madelyn Chapman, the victim in this case, isn't that true?'

'Yes.'

'And you've met Mr Ruiz, the defendant.' Sims points to Emiliano at the table.

'Yes, we've met. When he was working, providing security at Isotenics.'

It is clear that Rogan doesn't want to be here. Unless I miss my guess, this is not just the usual nervous witness. Even with Sims moving between us at the podium, cutting off my view of the stand from time to time, the obvious avoidance of eye contact by Rogan makes it clear that she is being used to drop a rock on us.

'Would it be safe to assume that in that capacity you would have been privy to a good deal of confidential information that passed through you to Ms Chapman and that some of that information would have included what are described as company trade secrets owned by your employer, Isotenics, Incorporated?'

'Objection, Your Honor. The term *trade secret* as used by Mr Sims is a legal term of art. I'm not sure that Ms Rogan is qualified to answer the question.'

'I withdraw the question,' says Sims. 'Isn't it true, Ms Rogan, that a good deal of the information that passed through your hands on its way to Ms Chapman was confidential?'

'I suppose.'

'So confidential, in fact, that some of this information regarding defense contracts is considered highly classified by the Department of Defense, is it not?'

'Yes.'

'And in that regard, isn't it a fact that you were required to undergo a background check in order to obtain a security clearance from the government in order to be employed in your position?'

'Yes.'

'Did you prepare written correspondence for Ms Chapman as part of your job?'

'Sometimes.'

'Did you open her mail and deliver it to her?'

'Yes.'

'From time to time, did you look at e-mail that was posted to her on the computer in her office, in order to respond to it on her behalf?'

'Yes. When I was asked to.'

'And did you place phone calls for her and receive incoming calls that were directed to Ms Chapman as part of your job?'

'Yes.'

'So, to the extent that information coming to Ms Chapman in any of these forms might have included confidential company information, that information would have passed through your hands, isn't that correct?'

'Usually. Not always. There were some matters that Ms Chapman handled personally.'

'But for the most part the information would have come through you, isn't that correct?'

'Probably. Yes.'

Karen Rogan, the woman who saw Ruiz and Chapman on the office couch doing heavy crunches – the redhead who became Harold Klepp's guardian angel – is, as I suspected, keeper of the company secrets.

'Now let me ask you' – Sims turns a little sideways at the podium so that suddenly there is a clear line of sight between the witness and where I am sitting – 'can you see the gentleman sitting at the defense table behind me, just to the right of Mr Ruiz?'

She nods.

'You'll have to respond audibly so that the court reporter can hear you.'

'Yes.'

'Do you know that man?'

She clears her throat. 'Mr Madriani, I believe.'

'That's correct.'

'And have you met Mr Madriani previously?'

She nods.

'Speak up.'

'Yes.'

'How many times have you met him?'

'Twice.'

'Can you tell the court when and where you met him?'

'The first time was several months ago, at the office at Isotenics, in the conference room. You remember? You were present,' she says.

'And the second time? Where was that?'

'At a bar. A club about a mile from the office. A place called Crash 'N' Burn.'

'What were you doing there?'

'I'd gone to meet some friends to have a drink after work.'

'Did you know that Mr Madriani was going to be there at this club?'

'No.'

'But you saw him there.'

'Yes.'

'Was he with anyone?'

For the first time Karen Rogan looks at me and doesn't look away, a pained expression. 'Yes.'

'Who?'

'A gentleman I didn't know. I've never seen him before.'

'And who else?'

A long sigh and a lot of angst as she looks around for something to say other than the truth. 'Harold Klepp.'

'And who is Harold Klepp?'

'He's the director of research and development for Isotenics.'

'An executive with the company, is that correct?'

'Yes.'

'Someone who, like you, is privy to a great many pieces of information regarding confidential business matters – information that no doubt includes sensitive trade secrets belonging to your employer?'

'I don't think he was engaged in corporate espionage, if that's what you mean,' says Rogan.

Sims ignores her and pushes on. 'In fact, isn't it true that Mr Klepp, being the head of research and development, would have access to information concerning the very core of the business of Isotenics: the design and programming of computer software?'

'I suppose.' She would like to tell the court that Klepp was on the ropes, outside the loop of knowledge and about to be fired – not that Sims doesn't already know this – but it wouldn't do any good and she knows it. My guess is that the only reason

Havlitz hasn't canned Klepp already is the fear that once he lets him go, the R and D man might feel free to talk. From what I am seeing, Rogan may now have her own head on the block.

How they found out about my meeting in the bar that night is anybody's guess. Given that Sims has had to drag it out of her on the stand, it is clear that Rogan was not the source.

'So, from what you saw, Mr Madriani may have already been at work trying to uncover confidential information regarding the company?'

'I told you before that I have no idea what they were talking about. I couldn't hear them.'

'So, for all you know, proprietary information may have already changed hands.'

'I don't know.'

'But you did talk to Mr Klepp afterward.'

'I did.'

'And did he tell you what they talked about?'

'Objection: hearsay.'

'Sustained.'

'Did Mr Klepp tell you that he had planned to meet with Mr Madriani at the bar that evening?'

'No.'

'According to what Mr Klepp told you, did he know that Mr Madriani was going to be at the bar that night?'

'He said he didn't have any idea that Mr Madriani was going to be there.'

'So for all intents and purposes Mr Klepp was ambushed by Mr Madriani while relaxing and having a drink after work. Is that your understanding?'

She nods almost sheepishly, the bobbed red hair dangling across her face, covering one eye. 'I suppose.'

'Your witness,' says Sims.

'I have no questions, Your Honor.'

'I can understand why,' says Sims. 'The defense has been caught red-handed delving into areas that they know are protected by commercial law.'

'Your Honor, we were investigating the case on behalf of our client. We not only have a right to do so, but a legal obligation. It's Mr Sims that wants to assert commercial interests in an effort to prevent the defendant from obtaining a fair trial. I doubt that I have to shine much light on the subject for the court to make out the shadowed hand of the DA's office behind all of this.'

'I object, Your Honor.' Templeton is sitting in his chair with his hand raised like a second-grader. 'We are not a party to this motion, Your Honor, and I resent any inference by Mr Madriani to the contrary.'

'You may not be a party, but you're driving the train,' I tell him.

'Enough,' says Gilcrest.

'Your Honor, we would demand a restraining order against Mr Madriani, his associates and agents, so that this kind of thing does not happen again.' Sims is back at it. 'At least not without notice and court supervision,' he says.

'Fine, we'll give notice so that we can depose critical witnesses here in court, Your Honor.'

'We would object to that, Your Honor.' Templeton, in one swift movement, is now standing on the seat of the chair so that the judge can see him better. 'There is no procedure in the law for that kind of a process, especially this late in the game. We're on the eve of trial,' he says.

'And who was it who sandbagged us with a last-minute motion to quash?' I ask.

'Not me,' says Templeton.

'I've heard enough.' Gilcrest slaps his hand on the bench. 'I'm taking the matter under submission. If Mr Madriani wants to offer written points and authorities in opposition to the motion, he will have until five o'clock this evening to file them. This being Friday, I'll make my decision Monday morning. Now, that's it. We're adjourned.'

Before another word can be said, Gilcrest grabs the papers in front of him, sweeps off the bench, and disappears down the corridor into chambers.

One of the guards already has his hand on Emiliano's shoulder. 'Let's go.'

As Karen Rogan comes down off the witness stand, she finds herself trapped inside the railing by the exiting lawyers, Sims and his cohorts. Standing there, she glances down at Ruiz. In that instant, with the guard's hand on Emiliano's shoulder, their eyes seem to meet. She shakes her head. And then, in a voice that is nearly inaudible, she mouths the words 'I'm sorry. Are you okay?'

He nods.

'Take care of yourself.' She bites her lower lip as she says it.

Emiliano smiles at her.

Then Rogan slips through the gate behind the lawyers, down the aisle, and out of the courtroom.

'Looks like you have at least one supporter out at Isotenics,' I whisper to Ruiz as I load papers into my briefcase.

He ignores the remark. 'So what happens now?' he asks. For the first time there is concern written in Ruiz's eyes, an air of disquiet in the tone of his voice.

'It'll be okay,' I tell him. 'Harry and I'll go to work on it the minute we get back to the office. Find some cases on point. The state can't just stash the evidence in a safe, turn the key, and lock us out. And they can't use Isotenics to do it for them.'

'But you forget,' he says.

'Forget what?'

'You're not dealing with the state or Isotenics,' he says. 'You're dealing with the federal government. They can do whatever they want.'

I shake my head. 'No, Emiliano. They can't.'

I told him once before that unless we can come up with the evidence, going to trial against the prosecution's case could end up being a game played only by fools or those who are desperate. As they chain Emiliano up to lead him away, I can tell by the expression on his face that he is beginning to wonder into which one of these two camps he has fallen.

CHAPTER
EIGHTEEN

L ike so many disputes in the law, the cases on
trade secrets all seem to fall between the
cracks. There are boatloads of appellate opinions
dealing with civil lawsuits and even a few in which
the theft of such secrets have been the subject of
hefty criminal prosecutions, but nothing that
seems to help our cause.

Harry and I scoured the casebooks until just
before five, when a courier delivered what little
we could find to Judge Gilcrest's courtroom. We
have been unable to locate a single decision
addressing the question whether, in a murder
case, access to trade secrets belonging to a third
party are available as evidence. We are now
dabbling in the dark, our defense teetering on an
issue of first impression for which the court has
no guidance.

Left to his own devices, Gilcrest has had to play
Solomon, giving a little bit to both sides. The result
is that Harry and I, as well as any agents in our
employ, including Herman, are now under a
temporary restraining order, at least until the
court can sort it all out. We are barred from talking

to anyone at Isotenics without first obtaining court approval by giving notice, thereby giving Isotenics the opportunity to block our investigation in court.

For our part, Gilcrest ordered Sims and the company to turn over all of the subpoenaed documents to the court for review. Not that the judge has staff sufficient to examine these – or that it even matters, since Sims has filed an appeal to the district court. Until this is resolved, nothing will be delivered. An eleventh-hour motion by Harry for a continuance to delay the start of trial has been denied. In short, all of this has the makings of an early disaster.

The court may be leaning over backward to accommodate Isotenics and their claim of trade secrets, but Gilcrest is a fox with a lot of hunts behind him. I sense that he knows that Templeton is behind this.

As if we need more bad news, our attempts to subpoena General Satz have failed one more time. When the process servers couldn't find him, Harry directed a letter to the legal office at the Pentagon in an effort to have them accept it on behalf of the general. This morning we received their written reply notifying us that, since the general is retired from the military and is a civilian appointee of the Department of Defense, his attendance at trial is a personal matter not involving the Pentagon or Satz's official position. Therefore they have refused to accept the subpoena and have returned it to us in the envelope.

'If we can't get Satz, we don't have squat,' says Harry.

'Maybe even if we do get him, we don't have squat,' I tell him. 'From what I've read, he's not likely to lie down and roll over – not if his performance in front of Congress ten years ago is any measure.'

'I remember.'

I have put Satz on our witness list, but without solid documentary or other evidence to nail his feet to the floor, I would be a fool to put him on the stand. Given his tenacity in front of a panel of crusty politicians who didn't even have to contend with the rules of evidence, Satz is likely to do a tap dance on us.

We are now deep into jury selection, eight days in court huddled at the table with our jury consultant, trying to mind-meld with strangers whose names have been churned out from computerized voter lists and drivers' license records at DMV.

In view of the fact that Templeton has never lost a death case in eighteen outings, a jury consultant with a track record on him does not exist. In two other cases that Templeton has tried, defense lawyers brought in one of the crackerjacks in the field, a psychologist from Berkeley with a résumé to shame the gods. Both times Templeton dealt them black queens by way of a verdict, and the death penalty to go along with it.

'What we need is a giant flyswatter so we can grind the little fucker into the carpet the next time he moves,' says Harry.

'You find one, I'll give it to the judge,' I tell him. 'At this point I think Gilcrest might use it. It was the last thing he needed. This is probably Gilcrest's final big case before retirement. And I doubt that he was hoping for a hundred-page treatise and a seminar on business law and the fine points on the exacting science of trade secrets.'

'Then why didn't he just tube Sims? Deny his motion to quash?' says Harry.

'Because if he was wrong, the downside was too steep. Don't forget, we asked for a pile of technical data in our last request.'

A second set of subpoenas sent out after my meeting with Havlitz at Isotenics demanded information on the IFS software. Jim Kaprosky helped us draft it. After listening to his history and researching his background, I am convinced there is no one in the world more qualified. After slamming his head against a wall for twelve years with the government over the issue, if anyone would know how to press this particular balloon without popping it, it is Kaprosky.

Harry chews on this for a moment.

'Besides,' I tell him, 'we can criticize Templeton but we can't stop him from talking to the jury, and we can't object because he's managed to turn physical disability into an advantage. He bonds with juries like he was welded to them. I'm afraid we're going to have to live with him.'

The problem with Templeton is compounded by the fact that he seems to have a rare gift for reading crowd dynamics, as if he can anticipate juror response before they do. This is no shell game. I'm convinced that the man has a sixth sense.

'And he has one big advantage over vaudeville.'

'What's that?' asks Harry.

'Most comedians can't evict members of the audience with a preemptory challenge.'

'True, but he's already burned more than half of his preemptories. Pretty soon he's going to be shooting blanks,' says Harry.

'Yes, but he's also softened his tune to harmonize with the audience he already has. The man's adaptable. He knows where he is, never loses his place. He knows exactly how many challenges he has left and what he has to do when he starts running dry. Unless I miss my bet, by the time he's finished, *our* jury's going to be in *his* pocket.'

'Well, I'm glad to see we're on top of things. So how do you propose to deal with him?'

Through the half-open blinds at the window nearest the door, I see Janice, my secretary, coming this way. She wouldn't bother us unless it was something important.

'If we're lucky, maybe we won't have to.'

'What are you talking about?'

I get up out of the chair and head toward the door.

'If you have a plan to push Templeton out of the case, I'd like to know what it is,' says Harry.

'Not exactly. Bear with me.' I give him a wink, then open the door before Janice can knock.

'There's somebody here to see you,' she says. 'I wouldn't have bothered you, but I didn't know if you'd want to see him. Says he's an old friend.' She hands me a business card.

I rub my thumb over the embossed gold seal to see if it is still hot from the press. *Representative, 42nd Congressional District*. Leave it to Nathan Kwan to have his congressional cards printed before the election results have hit the wire services in the southern part of the state.

As I enter the office half a beat behind my secretary, Nathan is sitting on the couch. He greets me with a big smile as I come through the door.

'Hey, buddy. Hope I didn't catch you at a bad time.' He's up off the couch, leaving the newspaper he was reading behind him on one of the sofa cushions.

'No, no. There's never a bad time to see an old friend. Especially an important one.'

'What can I say? Cream always rises to the top.' We both laugh. 'Along with bullshit.' We shake hands. It was a saying we had when Nathan and I shared space in the Capital County DA's Office more than twenty years ago now, a way of laughing at the overlords who shuttled us around, giving us case assignments and bragging about their brilliance in court when they used to try cases.

'I know you're up to your ass in the trial of the century. I was just reading about it in the newspaper,' he says. 'So I'll make the visit short. I guess we're both famous. Or should I say infamous.'

'More like it,' I tell him.

Nathan always has a warm smile, one of his best features, and a good sense of humor. His quest for power has never left him without a laugh and healthy appreciation for self-deprecation.

'I guess congratulations are in order!' I'm holding up his business card, reading it. 'Impressive.'

'Yep, gold seal and all,' he says. 'Pretty soon I'll have congressional cuff links. I'm told that if I can survive one term and get re-elected, they'll give me the decoder ring.'

Nathan has won the special election for the open seat in Congress created by the death of the incumbent. The last time I saw him he was nibbling at the edges. Two weeks later he jumped into the campaign with both feet. According to tidbits in the papers, he had been leaning toward the race quietly for some time, apparently sizing up the man's office in DC with a measuring tape right after he died.

'It was an opportunity, so I seized it.' He pauses a second. 'Okay, don't tell anybody, but I carpet-bagged.' Nathan's comic timing has always been pretty good. This has been all over the news up in Capital City for months. I've seen his opponent's charges in the headlines on the Internet. Nathan moved his residence into the district, large portions of which seemed to neatly coincide with his old Senate seat in the legislature.

'I'd like to say I planned it. The fact is, it was a godsend. I think I told you the last time we met I was about to tap out in the Senate. Term limits.'

'I remember.'

'Under the circumstances it pains me to say I got lucky. Did you ever meet Troy Olders, the congressman who passed away?'

'I don't think I ever did.'

'He was a very nice guy. Died of Hodgkin's. It was a long illness.' The way Nathan says it, I get the sense maybe it was a little too long. 'He was a friend. He told me when he was dying that if he could pick anybody to succeed him in Congress, it would be me. I cried. Can you believe it?'

With Nathan I can believe it. For a man steeped in the cynical world of politics, who has come a long way from a hardscrabble beginning, his emotions run to the sentimental side. Before law school he had been a cop for a few years on the Capital City force. This was after a stint in the Army. Nathan is a man with a million former lives. I am told he dug deep into his pockets on more than one occasion to help people in trouble. To Nathan, old-world liberalism is real, a kind of religion: Christian charity imposed through the ballot box. The product of an Asian father and an Irish mother, he is a man with dreams that, for the most part, he has realized – though if I had to guess, based on the card in my hand, he is not quite finished whipping that horse.

'I really didn't mean to interrupt, but it may be the last chance I have to get down here for a long time – my last trip south before I resign from the State Senate – so I wanted to stop by. I have something for you.' He has a big grin on his face.

I glance at Janice. This is why she interrupted to bring me his card.

Nathan turns around and reaches under the newspaper on the couch behind him. He comes out with a package. It is gift-wrapped in striped foil with a wide red ribbon tied in a bow. He hands it to me.

It is flat and heavy. I'm guessing maybe a coffee-table book.

'Open it,' he says.

I peel the ribbon off of one corner and let it drop, then tear the foil paper. Janice and the receptionist are looking on, smiling, trying to get a glimpse.

'What is it?' With Nathan I can never be sure. Whatever it is, it's boxed in cardboard under the paper. I split the cellophane tape holding the fold closed on one end of the box.

'Be careful.' Nathan puts a hand down to make sure it doesn't slide out onto the floor. Heavy wood and glass, the picture frame is upside down as I flip the empty box onto the couch. When I turn it over, I am startled to see myself under glass, a younger face and twenty pounds lighter. In the photo I am standing in the kitchen of our old home in Capital City. Standing next to me behind the center island is Nikki, my wife who has been dead nearly ten years now. She is holding our daughter, Sarah, in her arms.

'Sarah was only eighteen months old when I took that,' he says. 'I remember because you told me. You were a proud papa,' he says.

I have a lump in my throat. My eyes are watering. It is perhaps the best picture of the three of us I have ever seen, and one of the few I have left from that period of my life.

'Remember the old Olympus thirty-five millimeter? I used to carry it in my pocket. That's what I shot it with. Look at the detail. That was a good camera. Wish I still had it,' he says.

'I remember,' I tell him. 'You used to take pictures of everything in sight.'

'That's my Asian half,' he says.

I do the only thing I can think to do at this moment: I reach out and hug him, holding the picture tight in one hand as we stand in the center of my reception area, two guys, arms around each other, choking back sniffles. Nathan pats my back with one hand and holds the coffee cup away with the other so that it doesn't slosh on my shirt.

'Tell me it doesn't bring back memories,' he says.

'It brings back memories. Good ones,' I tell him.

'The best,' he says. 'I found the print in an old album. I had a negative made. I thought you'd want it.'

'It's beautiful,' I tell him. 'And to think you came all the way down here to deliver it personally.' We let go of each other. I'm wiping my eyes.

'I'd like to say that was it, but the fact is, I was tying up loose ends on committee business out at Isotenics.' He can tell by my look that I perk up with the mention of the company name. 'Do you have time for lunch? For old times' sake,' he says.

I look at my watch: eleven-twenty. It's a little early, but what the hell. I hand the framed photo to Janice for safekeeping. 'Would you tell Harry we'll pick it up again this afternoon? I should be back by one.'

We slip out of the courtyard through a service entrance in Miguel's Cantina, skirting the handful of reporters out on Orange Grove in front of the office. Nathan and I dodge a few cars and hoof it across the street to the Del Coronado. Within minutes we are cloistered in one of the corner booths in the restaurant on the hotel's main floor, out of sight, nursing drinks.

'You never told me what brings you down here.'

'Oh, that,' he says. 'That's nothing. Senate Committee on Reapportionment.' He touches the side of his nose with his finger. 'A lotta BS. I'll be glad to be rid of it. Pain in the butt, all the members constantly crying on my shoulder about their districts and where they want the lines drawn for the next election so they can do in all the competition.' Nathan talks as if he's never done this himself.

Politics is its own form of insanity. In California, beds in this asylum are assigned in the state legislature and Congress every ten years, with district boundary lines redrawn based on the last federal census. Ever since term limits were imposed on the legislature by voters, political panic in the order of a hotel fire has raged through the state capitol, with members of both parties eating their own in an effort to survive. The hallowed ground is Congress, where term limits don't apply.

'You remember. I used to tell you about the games played. Somebody running their district boundaries thirty miles along a railroad track so they could circle a university or capture some

281

ethnic ghetto while they registered all the hobos
along the way.'

'You must have done that one and forgot to tell
me about it.'

'Well, those were the good old days. Back when
Machiavelli was writing the legislative ethics rules.
When every vote cast in an election had an actual
voter behind it.'

To listen to Nathan, the state legislature is now
the third ring of hell. He can't wait to get out.

'But that's not the reason I wanted to talk to
you. I've been following the trial in the papers,'
he says. 'Your Ruiz case. I don't know the details,
but I heard something you should know. I was
out at Isotenics. They crunch numbers for us, do
the district maps. And I heard some comments
about this IFS thing. It came up in connection
with the trial. IFS has been in the papers.' Nathan
tells me this as if I'm from Mars. 'I know some
members,' he says, 'people in Congress who are
very upset about it. As they should be. I don't
know how you feel about personal privacy. You
know that I've always felt very strongly about it.
Computers. High tech. It's eroding any sense of
civil liberties. Pretty soon corporations and the
government are going to know more about us than
we know about ourselves.'

Nathan is now cutting to the chase. I can smell
him trying to get a jump start to some committee
in the House of Representatives. He is probably
telling them that he has an inside track with the
lawyer trying the case and that if they can pump
enough heat and fire up my skirt, they can use the
illumination to expose the White House. It's what
you love about Nathan: he never quits.

'Check out the nurse over there. I think I need

more medicine,' he says. Nathan's talking about the cocktail waitress.

'When did this meeting occur?'

'Hmm?'

'Out at Isotenics?'

'Oh, yeah,' he says. 'Couple of days ago. We were meeting with these two execs out there. One of them was midlevel type. I've been dealing with this guy for a couple of years. You know the kind: makes the company go. Jack lives in the corporate synapse, between executive decisions and action, if you know what I mean. Kinda fella who puts the spark in the gap that usually makes things happen.' He pauses. 'Good ideas man, and he usually knows what's going on. The other guy I didn't know. Never met him before. Jack's boss.'

I nod knowingly as I listen. Nathan has a way of making a short story long.

'Anyway, there were several of us at the meeting: two members of the Assembly, myself, and some congressional staff sent out to cover their interests. The two executives knew I'd just been elected to the house. They were overflowing with congratulations. Isotenics can use all the friends they can get in Washington right now, as I'm sure you're aware. If there was a fire hose long enough, they'd be pumping water from the Pacific to try and reduce the heat on themselves.'

I nod again and take a sip from my glass.

'I suppose they were trying to impress me, so you can probably take it with a grain of salt, for what it's worth,' he says. 'But one of them, the boss, gets a phone call during the meeting. We were in a rush to finish up since the assemblymen had to catch a plane.

'So this guy decides to take the call on the

extension in the conference room where we're gathered. All I can hear is half the conversation, but he's talking about the case. Ruiz's name comes up, so of course I'm all ears. Something about when the case is over they can ramp up again, but not until, he says. He's talking under his breath and I guess whoever's on the other end can't hear him, because this guy keeps saying he can't talk any louder, he's in a meeting. Fortunately I had my back to him, sitting right in front of the side table where he was talking. If I'd leaned back any further I'd have been on the phone with him,' says Nathan.

'Then he says – the guy on our end – he says something . . .' Nathan's reaching with the fingers of one hand as if he's trying to pluck the precise words from the air over our table. 'He says something: they're understaffed, that DOD is all pissed off, something to that effect. That if she had left it alone, everything would have been fine. But now that she's dead somebody's going to have to go pick up the pieces because she wouldn't leave it alone.' He looks at me to see if this is producing any revelations. 'I don't know if you're thinking what I'm thinking, but if you are, I'm thinking the dead person they're talking about has to be Madelyn Chapman, and the project DOD is involved in has to be IFS. Does it make any sense to you?' he asks.

'I don't know. It's possible.'

'It sounded to me like maybe they are caught in a whirlpool of shit at the moment and they can't get out of it until your case is over. That when that happens they're back in business. Doing something. God knows what,' he says. 'I may stick around and watch the trial. I have nothing going on up in Capital City. And it sounds like all the fireworks may be happening down here.'

'Do you have names? The two executives at your meeting?'

'Yeah. Jack Hansen is the guy I've been meeting with for years. The other guy, the guy on the phone, I'd never met him before. His name was Harold Klepp. Head of research and development.'

CHAPTER NINETEEN

This morning when I arrive, the hallway outside the courtroom is jammed, standing room only. I'm pushing my way through when I run face-to-face into Nathan.

'What are you doing here?'

He's drinking a Diet Coke from a can and laughing at me. 'You got more press here than the White House,' he says. 'I figure I'm resigning from the state senate next week, so I may as well be where the action is. I got nothing to do up in Capital City,' he says.

This is Nathan, the ultimate groupie. By next week he'll be trading secrets in Washington, the inside dirt on the trial, what it really means for IFS.

'I thought I'd come and see how you do. Besides, I haven't been in a courtroom in years. Thank God,' he says, and takes another swig from the can of Coke.

Several reporters, notepads in hand, cruise in my direction through the crowd.

'We'll have to continue this later,' I tell him.

Inside, the courtroom is already filling up. By

the time we convene, every seat will be taken. There is a line downstairs in front of the main door to the courthouse. I would estimate more than two hundred people are waiting to get in, hoping someone will leave and offer up their seat. Two bailiffs, one upstairs and one down, communicate by walkie-talkie, allowing one person into the courthouse at a time as seats are surrendered. It is a test for concrete kidneys and iron bowels. Get up to go to the john and you lose your seat.

The crowd is here to listen to Larry Templeton deliver his opening statement in the trial of *People v. Ruiz*.

For nearly two weeks now the cable news stations have been playing this up, leading hourly with speculation and hype as to the way the prosecutor will build his case. So many lawyers have now offered their televised guesses as to precisely how Templeton will play it and what kind of magic will be necessary for the defense to counter the state's evidence that it hardly seems necessary to try the case before the jury. Vicarious courtroom thrills have replaced the soap opera on daytime television. Without scripts or actors, production costs are cheap, since every lawyer in America for an hour of face time in the form of free advertising will offer their guesses and commentary for nothing, which is generally what they are worth.

I have heard my last name mispronounced at least five times on three different stations in the last two days. As I head down the aisle toward the swinging gate in the railing, I hear it whispered in a few places floating on the ether in the courtroom, and notice fingers pointing and a few heads turning. The Middle Ages may have been dark, but if having your every word explored and your image and each gesture exploited on the nightly news is the ultimate reward for life in the age of celebrity, society might do well if we were to regress to more primitive forms of communication. One wonders if the media cynics aren't right, whether the term *free society* has become nothing but an excuse for profiteers to transform life into a dissolute electronic fishbowl.

Halfway toward the front of the courtroom I see a head of gray hair as she turns. I am surprised to see Jean Kaprosky seated on the aisle about six rows back. I tap her on the shoulder from behind. She looks up and sees me. 'Oh, hi,' Jean says. She grabs my hand and smiles. 'I was hoping I might have a chance to talk to you. At least say hello.'

'Where is Jim?' I ask.

'He's not feeling well. He's been in and out of the hospital the last several weeks,' she explains.

'I didn't know.'

'He doesn't *want* anybody to know. His health has been slipping lately.' The tone of her voice has a certain finality to it. 'He has a hard time getting out and about. I take him to the doctor and that's pretty much it. My sister is staying with us for a while, so she's at home with him right now. He wanted me to come and see what was happening here and report back. I told him that I was sure that your case had nothing to do with what happened to us,' she says. 'But in Jim's mind, it's all connected. You understand.' She gives me an expression as if to say the mind is slipping along with the body. 'I don't know what to say to him anymore, so here I am.'

'Tell him . . . well, tell him for me that I hope he's feeling better soon.'

'I'll tell him, but I know what he'd like more than that: he'd love to see you, talk to you one more time. Here. Let me give you our address.' Before I can shake loose, she takes a scrap of paper and a pen from her purse and starts to scribble as she talks.

I have known for months that I could not use James Kaprosky as my computer software expert at trial. He was both conflicted in terms of his interests in the case and too ill. If we come to that – if Harry and I are able to get to the evidence surrounding Satz and Chapman, what was going on with the Primis software and whether it could have been a motive for murder – I have already retained another expert.

'Jim told me that he enjoyed the meeting at your office so much,' she says. 'He's mentioned it several times. He said that you and Mr Hinds were the first two people in years to take him seriously, to listen to the details of what happened. I hope you can read this.' She is scribbling her address, her hands a little palsied. 'Jim has lived with all of the misery regarding the litigation for so long it seems the only thing he can still relate to. He still gets phone calls from one of his lawyers every once in a while, but they all sort of drifted away. I think they felt so bad because of the result. And I suppose because we had such hope. The meeting in your office, while it dredged up a lot of bad stuff, was in its own way therapy for him. I suppose you could call it closure,' she adds.

'I wish there was something more I could do. It's an awful situation. The loss of your business, his health.'

'No. No. Don't feel bad. Come and see him.' She presses the note with their home address into my hand. 'I'll tell him that we talked, that I saw you.'

I wish her well. 'Say hello to him for me.' Then I head toward the counsel table.

Harry is already there waiting for me. At the table next to him is a young intern we have hired to operate the laptop, the computer that will be connected to the overhead visualizer aimed at a large projection screen for presentation of evidence to the jury as the case progresses. Jamie Carson is a UC law graduate waiting for his bar results, and is a possible addition to the firm. Harry has been working with him for months to gin up the computer, scanning in copies of police reports, crime-scene photographs, all of the documentary details that are likely to come in by way of evidence.

As I swing through the gate, past the railing, I notice that Harry's earlier fears have been realized. Two custom-made boxes, the one at this end with a step leading up to it, are spanned by wooden planks, each twelve feet long and two inches thick, arranged on top of them. In the center there is a third box to keep the spans from bouncing like a diving board. This entire affair has been set out in front of the jury box in preparation for Templeton's opening statement.

The prosecutors are not yet here. My guess is they are huddled backstage somewhere, probably in a room near the holding cells, putting the final touches on their opening and coordinating the visuals that have already been approved by the court for presentation at this point. Most of these are neutral, arrived at by stipulation: photographs of the outside of Chapman's house on the beach and of the rocky outcrop overlooking the ocean behind it, and a large aerial of the house taken from a police helicopter. There is a close-up of the murder weapon, a .45 caliber automatic, just as the cops found it in the flower bed near the seawall at the back of the yard, and another shot of the screen that was pried off the window and left propped against the side of the house where the killer gained entry. None of these present much controversy. All of them would no doubt be admitted into evidence even if we were to object. To save time and avoid the appearance of foolish disputes in front of the jury, we have stipulated to their use.

In the front row, just beyond the rail behind the prosecution table, is an elderly woman. It is Madelyn Chapman's mother. Sitting next to her is the victim's younger sister. They put the visual hex on me as I assemble the documents from my briefcase on the table.

Two rows behind them, Nathan sidles toward one of the center seats as some young kid gets up to give him his chair. The kid heads for the door. Nathan is using a legislative intern to hold his seat. Knowing Nathan, he'll probably have them sleeping outside on the sidewalk tonight, holding his place in line for tomorrow.

I take my seat and open the folder with a fresh notepad inside. Trying a case can be an exercise in writer's cramp as you catch all the details so that you don't miss anything on cross-examination.

Harry leans away from Jamie and the computer and across the open chair that has been left vacant between us for Emiliano.

'As you can see, they've already started constructing the gallows,' says Harry. He nods toward the planks spanning the space in front of the jury box.

I give him a resigned look. 'It's what we expected.'

'Yeah, but it's not nearly as menacing when it's just a mental image in your mind.'

A second later the door leading to the holding cells opens and the prosecution team enters the courtroom. They are led by Mike Argust, the lead homicide detective in Chapman's case. Argust is a twenty-eight-year veteran assigned to the case the night of the murder. Unless Ruiz testifies, Argust, who is the state's representative in the case, is the only other witness allowed inside the courtroom during the trial unless they are on the stand. Witnesses on both the prosecution and defense lists have been excluded by the judge following a stipulation by Templeton and myself. Potential witnesses have been instructed not to discuss their testimony with anyone except the lawyers and representatives for the prosecution and defense, and then only if the witnesses choose to talk with them. We are still awaiting a decision from the court on Sims's appeal concerning Gilcrest's ruling on evidence from Isotenics. No doubt, whatever happens, if Sims loses he will take the appeal to the state supreme court, if for no other reason than to stall for more time.

I tried to coax an affidavit out of Nathan Kwan regarding the telephone conversation between Klepp and whoever was on the other end of the line during Nathan's meeting out at Isotenics. A declaration under penalty of perjury might be enough to convince the judge to allow me to question Klepp more thoroughly. But Nathan declined. He said he couldn't get publicly involved, especially now, being new to Congress. It could blow up in his face. I understood. Bringing informa-

tion and delivering it to me was one thing. Getting
his name in the press and involved in the case on
the wrong side is another.

Argust takes the seat in the middle at the
prosecution table, counterpart to Ruiz. The
computer tech, an expert who performs visualiza-
tion duties in most of their heavier cases, is at the
far end. Templeton takes the chair nearest me and
climbs onto the box that is already assembled on
top of the seat waiting for him.

A few moments later a burly guard from the
sheriff's jail unit opens the holding cell door once
more. He is followed by a second guard. They take
their time, checking the courtroom, making eye
contact with each of the guards stationed at the
back of the courtroom and along the side aisles.
When they are satisfied, one of them turns and
offers the come-hither sign, the signal for the
guards inside to bring him out. Emiliano walks
through the open door followed by two more
guards. Harry and I both stand as they usher him
toward our table. The choreography here is like a
polka. Ruiz could turn in any direction and
instantly be dancing with a uniformed guard. They
surround him. I have demanded on several
occasions that none of this be played out in front of
the jury and that the guards melt into the walls
before they bring the jury panel in. If they fail in
any way, I will document each instance on the
record as grounds for appeal. A show of law
enforcement on this order can pollute a jury faster
than anything said at trial. It sends a less-than-
subtle signal that, not only does the state view the
defendant as a stone-cold killer, but that an over-
whelming show of force is needed to prevent him
from escaping and killing again, and to protect the

jury itself. If jurors begin to fear for their own safety, your case is over.

Ruiz is clean shaven; his hair, a little longer than when we first met, is neatly combed. He is dressed in a blue suit, white shirt, and solid burgundy tie. The suit is a bit baggy on his body since he could not be fitted for it. Janice, my secretary, selected Emiliano's attire off the rack from a men's shop a few blocks from the office. The shoes, buffed-up cordovans, are stiff as boards, right out of the box, making Ruiz's stride as he enters the courtroom a little stilted. They have to steady him to keep him from stepping on the feet of the guards.

Ruiz seems surprised, somewhat taken back by the size of the crowd in the courtroom, even though Harry and I have told him to expect this. He is looking out at them over the railing with an expression approaching mystification as they lead him toward the table. The guards wait until he finds his seat and takes it, hovering over him for a few seconds, checking things out before they back off. They finally leave us and take up positions at the sides and back of the courtroom. Two of the guards station themselves down the darkened corridor along the side of the raised bench leading to the judge's chambers in the back.

None of the guards or bailiffs carry firearms, only pepper spray and collapsible metal batons that, if used with enough force, can shatter a clavicle or fracture a skull. Whether the judge will be packing when he takes the bench, no one knows. In this state there have been enough violent confrontations in courtrooms – including a judge in Marin County who was taken hostage, then shot and killed outside the courthouse – that some judges have been known to carry loaded, concealed handguns under their robes.

Ruiz leans toward me and speaks almost without moving his lips: 'Quite a crowd.' He is breathing heavily. I suspect it is the largest group of people he has ever seen assembled in one place for any event in which he was the center of attention. Fighting a battle and staying alive is one thing; dealing with a crowd where everyone in the courtroom is looking at him as if he is some caged beast is another.

A few seconds later I hear Gilcrest whisper 'Excuse me,' down the darkened corridor. The judge is telling the guards to get out of his way so he can clear the hallway and mount the bench.

'All rise,' says the bailiff in a booming voice, and instantly everyone in the courtroom is on their feet. The judge quickly climbs the three steps and takes his seat. He opens the file in front of him on the bench. 'You may be seated,' he says. It takes a couple of seconds for the noise of shuffling feet and cushioned behinds to die down. 'The clerk will call the case.'

'*People of the State of California versus Emiliano Ruiz*. Case number . . .'

We have already waived a reading of the charges, so, with the preliminaries done, Gilcrest cuts to the chase. He looks out at the audience, a squinting stare that could freeze ice. 'Before we get started, I'm going to lay down some ground rules for the people in the audience,' he says. 'I don't want to hear any talking, shouting, hooting, clapping, or laughing from anybody out there. I don't want to see anybody reading newspapers or books in my courtroom. You want to do that, you go to the library. I don't want to hear any comments or see any signs being held up for the jury or anybody else to read. If I see any of this, you will be removed from the courtroom. No if's, and's, or but's.

'I don't want to hear any cell phones going off,' he goes on. 'I don't want to see anybody talking on a cell phone. In fact, I don't want to see any cell phones at all. All electronic devices should have been checked at the door. They are not allowed in the courtroom. If anybody has an electronic device, including any camera, recorder, or cell phone, now is the time to hold it up and announce it.' He waits for a moment and scans the courtroom with his eyes to see if any hands go up. 'Because if one of the guards or one of my bailiffs sees you with any kind of electronic device from this point on, they will seize it, and you with it. You will be detained,' he says. 'And trust me, you will not enjoy the reception or the accommodation in the county jail.

'I don't want to hear any audio recordings of the proceedings in my courtroom being played on the six o'clock news or any other news, and if I do, there will be a very select audience admitted to this courtroom for the next day's proceedings and from that point on.' This last is aimed at the first three rows of reporters seated directly behind us. 'I hope I make myself clear.'

You can almost hear the nodding of heads and bobbing of Adam's apples in the chairs behind us.

'If anybody gets up and leaves, they lose their seat. That goes for reporters as well as the public. There are no favorites in my courtroom,' he says. 'Now, if there are any questions, this is all posted on the board outside the courtroom as well as online, so that you can read it on your computers at home at night if you want.

course of your lifetime will ever
formidable duty as this. To decide
er human being is not something
us can ever take lightly. It is the
siness we are ever likely to attend
here for many days listening to
ving physical evidence.'

s being optimistic. Given the
m our perspective, the lack of it –
Ruiz is straightforward. It will
o more than a week, possibly ten
eir case, and – unless I can come
ng solid from Isotenics – another
to fall on my sword. Ruiz may get

says Templeton, 'you will be
applicable law by the judge and
sent to that room' – he points
oom to another door opposite the
he holding cells – 'to make the
decision of your lives: to decide
ndant, Emiliano Ruiz' – he turns
ts toward our table – 'murdered
an, and whether he did so with
d malice aforethought after lying
o return home from her job, her
, Incorporated, Software City. We
purpose of deciding the fate of

for a moment, then plunges his
is pocket, turns, and takes a few
away from the bench toward
le he allows the jury to consider

eyes now focus on Ruiz, studying
onse to the charge, whether his

'Mr Templeton, are you ready to proceed?'
'I am, Your Honor.'
'Mr Madriani?'
'We are, Your Honor.'
'Then we'll bring in the jury,' says Gilcrest.

A minute later, with one of the bailiffs leading the way, they file in, five men and seven women: a schoolteacher; an architect; two college students; an employee of one of the local telephone companies; a store clerk at Robinson's; a retired college history professor, one of our two picks who survived only because Templeton ran out of preemptory challenges; a bus driver for the local transit district; a housewife; a guy who installs fire suppression systems for a construction company; a waitress at one of the local Coco's; and a short-order cook who looks as if he's been eating too much of his own food. A cross section of modern America.

In addition there are six alternates seated in chairs just outside the jury box at the judge's end of the courtroom.

Fortunately for us, Templeton had to steer away from retired military personnel. With a naval base, Miramar, and Camp Pendleton all within a stone's throw, retired military make up a sizable chunk of the local population and are usually well represented on local juries. Ordinarily they are a good bet for a foundation around which a prosecutor can build a hanging jury, especially retired military officers. But with Ruiz – himself a retired career soldier – in the dock, Templeton can't be sure exactly how we will play this card. It could backfire on him. He has been cautious. One wrong pick – if the person has the sand to stand up against the mob and you have a hung jury – no verdict. If one is to listen to Harry, this is the best we can hope for.

My partner is laying most of his wagers on our history professor. According to Harry, the man is no doubt a liberal. He would have to be to have kept his job at a state university. He would be used to lecturing others and not likely to be cowed when people disagree with him. Harry is hoping that with any luck, if we can shape the evidence to conform to what we suspect may have happened, his history professor will vote to cut Ruiz free or, if not, that he will at least vote against death. It is the latter that is Harry's principal burden as counsel to Ruiz in the penalty phase, should we arrive at that point.

The jurors settle into their chairs. The judge welcomes them. He has already laid down the ground rules for the operations of the jury: what is to be considered evidence and what is not. Templeton's opening statement is not evidence; it is supposed to be an oral outline of what the state intends to prove by way of evidence. The evidence itself will come later, introduced during the course of the trial.

During Templeton's opening, jurors who are smart will take detailed notes of his promises so that they can determine later in the jury room when the trial is over whether he has delivered. For those who fail to take notes, it is my job to remind them of promises and failures. For this I will save two shots, deferring my opening statement until after the prosecution rests its case. At the end of the trial I will have one final opportunity, my closing argument, to reinforce this.

'Mr Templeton, are you ready to present your opening statement?'

expression at this moment is that of a cold-blooded killer.

Templeton may have just answered one of the more nettlesome questions that has plagued us for months. 'Lying in wait' is the single special circumstance charged by the state in their criminal complaint that allows them to seek the death penalty against Ruiz. They are apparently prepared to argue that he entered Chapman's house and either stalked her from room to room, seeking to kill her, or waited for her to come home from work and simply shot her as she came into the entry hall.

Harry and I have wondered for weeks whether Templeton would try to amend the state's complaint to add the charges of murder for financial gain or murder during the course of robbery or burglary, either of which would carry additional special circumstances to justify the death penalty. The key in all of this, of course, is the *Orb at the Edge*, the half-million-dollar piece of glass art that went missing from Chapman's house after the murder. It would appear that Templeton and the cops have no more idea what has happened to this piece of art than we do. If they had the *Orb* or knew where it was, and if they could connect it to Ruiz, there is now no question but that they would have brought the additional charges.

I glance over at Harry, who is making a note. This fact has not gone unnoticed by my partner.

'Yes, it is an awesome responsibility,' says Templeton, 'and one that an ordered and just society must place upon the shoulders of ordinary citizens, because an ordered and just society has no emperors, it has no kings, it has no spokesmen who speak to the gods. It has only ordinary citizens, whose judgment and reason it respects and whose decisions by long history and proud tradition are the legal fabric holding that society together.'

He veers into the evidence, nibbling first at the edges. He may not know what happened to the glass artwork, but for every deficiency Templeton highlights five or six points so that his case overflows like a horn of plenty. Most prosecutors might shy away from issues involving Chapman's wealth for fear that we would seize it and turn it against them in an orgy of class warfare. But not Templeton. The state's computer technician flashes images on the large screen on the wall of the courtroom across from the jury box, pictures of Chapman's home on the beach, her corporate jets, and the quarter-million-dollar Ferrari parked in her garage.

Templeton turns and walks slowly toward the other end of the scaffold once again, all the while talking as if he's conversing casually in a room filled with friends. At one point he nods toward the computer tech at his table, and suddenly a full head-and-shoulder shot of Madelyn Chapman, her face beaming with a smile, flashes up on the large screen. In the photograph Chapman appears youthful, vital, full of life, a measure of what was taken from her when she was killed.

He talks about Ruiz and his time in the military, the fact that he is a divorced father of two who took a job working for a security firm, and that the fates placed the defendant, a retired Army sergeant with nothing more than a high school education and a few units of community college, in close contact with one of the wealthiest women in the world.

Templeton starts to catch a rhythm, stopping at places along the top of the boards to face the jury straight on, bending at the waist, using his tiny hands, fingers extended, palms out, to emphasize important elements. At one point he strikes a pose like a magician about to throw flash powder into a fire.

'You will hear testimony that, during his employment providing security for Madelyn Chapman, Mr Ruiz was able to indulge in travel in the form of luxurious international flights on board corporate jets to exotic locations. There he was able to observe at first hand and up close the good life which he had never experienced before, certainly not in the military and certainly not before that time.'

He has taken the sword of Chapman's wealth from our hands and blunted it, and now proceeds to club us about the head and shoulders with it. He goes on.

For a moment Templeton dabbles at the edge of the ice. He would like to argue overtly that Ruiz could not bear to pass up this opportunity of a lifetime to gold-dig his way to wealth and comfort. This is the state's theory of the motive for murder. But Templeton saves himself, avoiding an objection to a conclusion that his evidence would never be able to prove. Almost leaning off the edge of the boards into the jury box, he pulls himself back and instead stays with the facts.

'You will hear testimony from witnesses,' he says, 'that there was a sexual relationship between the defendant and Madelyn Chapman and that, following her decision to end the security detail, Mr Ruiz was removed from the assignment and instructed by his employer to have no further contact with the victim. You will also hear testimony that he failed to comply with those instructions and that Emiliano Ruiz proceeded to stalk the victim and was observed on more than one occasion following Madelyn Chapman as she was engaged in private activities.'

Damaging evidence of this has been withheld from us until the last possible moment under the rubric of confidential personnel matters. It was the excuse Max Rufus used the day I spoke to him in his office.

Templeton looks to our table and smiles as he realizes the impact that all of this is having on the jury.

It is deadly. I can read it in their eyes, and Templeton hasn't even arrived at the meat of his case: the weapon and the wounds.

'Finally you will see documents and hear evidence from medical and ballistics experts and qualified crime-scene technicians that the two shots that killed Madelyn Chapman, the bullets that fractured her skull and destroyed her brain' – Templeton motions toward the smiling photograph on the screen behind him – 'were fired from a pistol that had once been in the possession of the defendant, issued to Emiliano Ruiz while he was in the military and which the defendant failed to surrender to military officials as was the proper procedure when he left the Army. We will prove not only that this handgun was used to murder Madelyn Chapman but that the two shots that killed her required expert marksmanship, and that the defendant Emiliano Ruiz was once considered one of the top pistol marksmen in the United States Army.'

The links may all be circumstantial, but as

Templeton lays them out for the jury, each one snaps in place with the sound of case-hardened steel. I can feel Emiliano flinch in the chair next to mine, overwhelmed by the desire to stand and tell the court everything, to vomit what he knows over the courtroom floor, to burst the bubble of inferences linking him to the murder, to place it all in the light of truth: that the gun was there because she had asked him to bring it, that she had fired it herself, that the only reason he was following her was because Chapman had asked him to, because she was scared, frightened of someone else. I can see his fists as they clench on the counsel table, and I place a hand on his forearm. He looks at me with a stark expression.

'Relax. It's their opening shot.'

Templeton is now on a roll, hitting his pitch. While I try to quell the rising panic in Ruiz, in my own mind I can feel and fully understand the reason for it.

'Ladies and gentlemen, the state will prove beyond a reasonable doubt that Emiliano Ruiz murdered Madelyn Chapman: that he did so in cold blood with malice aforethought and clear premeditation. We will prove that Emiliano Ruiz lay in wait for Madelyn Chapman inside her home, and that when she arrived he executed her with two closely grouped shots to the head fired from a distance of nearly thirty feet. We will prove that the shots that killed Madelyn Chapman required expertise in marksmanship of a kind possessed by very few people, a small and select number of shooters, and that Emiliano Ruiz was one of them. We will show by proof beyond a reasonable doubt that the application of the two closely grouped shots that killed Madelyn Chapman was a well-practiced routine in select circles of military marksmanship – a practiced routine that had only one purpose: to terminate a target with lethal and certain force; to put an enemy down and to make sure that they were dead. We will prove that Emiliano Ruiz was one of the foremost experts in the world in the use of this technique: a targeting routine known as the "double tap." '

CHAPTER TWENTY

There are ways in which Emiliano and Evo demonstrate stark differences that could not mark them more distinctly. From all appearances Ruiz was able to deal with and cope in a world of violence that destroyed my uncle. Whether they experienced the same things in combat, I will never know.

But it is the similarities between the two men that drew me to the case initially and that keeps me burning the oil late into the night, searching for ways to keep Ruiz out of prison and away from the clutches of the executioner.

For such a large and seemingly fearsome specimen of the species, my uncle suffered a near-total inability to defend himself verbally or to explain at times what was happening in the dark convolutions of his brain. In this regard, Ruiz is his brother.

Emiliano may be able to face down live fire from incoming incendiary rounds and shrug off lacerating shards from an exploding grenade, but the verbal arrows flung by Templeton in his opening statement have wounded him deeply. The unanswered charges have him left confounded, in a state of mental stammering, suffering from a seemingly fatal bout of frustration that I have in all my life only witnessed in Evo.

Standing hip deep in a marsh of unrequited accusations, Emiliano's faltering gaze – and the knowledge that he has finally confronted a field of conflict in which he is powerless to defend himself – is eating at his insides like acid etching steel. Each day on this battlefield he seems more the mirror image of the scarred soul that was my uncle.

To my knowledge, even in his darkest days of depression, Evo never became violent. Though there were times when he was so troubled that, because of his size and brooding appearance, he could seem menacing, in those years when I was old enough to realize what was happening, I have no recollection of him ever laying a hand on another living soul.

Repeatedly he would fall into the pit of silent despair. When this happened, my grandmother was unable to bring herself to make the tough decisions that at the time seemed right. Inevitably my father would have to swallow the pain of consigning his younger brother to the VA hospital, to the untold horrors of what in those days passed for treatment of mental disorders associated with 'battle fatigue.' Strapped to a metal table, Evo would be subjected to repeated sessions of massive electroshock therapy and given doses of early psychotropic drugs that, at best, as even the doctors admitted, were experimental.

When Evo was discharged from the VA, the only thing he could remember was the pain, the repeated sessions of agony that he lacked the words to describe. To the fertile imagination of a child, even these limited accounts conjured hair-raising visions on the order of the Inquisition. He pleaded with my father never to be sent back. I remember the expression of horror that welled up in his eyes as he begged that he never again have to go back for treatment. I was seven years old. The expression of fright on Evo's face and the cloying pleas, the tears running down the cheeks of a man the size of a mountain, scared the bejesus out of me.

Within months, sometimes weeks, my uncle would slide once more beyond the horizon of human contact to that cosmos in the mind where he could not be reached. My father would be compelled to return him to the VA. It was a cycle that would repeat itself over the years and from which we all sought refuge in our own way, to put it from our minds, to escape its painful reality: that Evo had become a dead man in the shell of a living body.

Decades later I came to realize that these acts of mental commitment took years from my father's life. There were times when I looked into his eyes that I knew he would rather have committed himself to this agony than to have sent his younger brother.

Even with all of this, in moments of despair when Evo lingered at the edge of oblivion, often it was my father who was the only one who could perform the magic of communication. A man who dropped out of high school to go to work during the Depression could do what doctors and psychiatrists could not. For some reason, in the depths of his psychosis, Evo's brain seemed to cycle back to the days of his childhood, when the protective hand of his older brother held sway. Over all the anger and angst, the raging storms of paranoia and fear, he could still hear the soothing tones of my father's voice.

My uncle spent much of his adult life in and out of mental institutions, on and off Thorazine and its progeny of mind-numbing drugs.

During this period there is one event that stands out in my mind. I will remember it until the day I die. It was late, a winter afternoon. My mother was making dinner and my father had just gotten home from work. It was nearing dusk when we heard a noise downstairs in the basement, a voice, then what sounded like pounding on the wall. We heard the screen door's squeaky hinge down below, and the slam as the coil spring pulled it closed. Someone had just left the basement. We looked out the window. I saw the unmistakable silhouette of Evo standing there in the middle of our yard. He had been rooting around in our basement, looking for something. My father went down to see what he wanted.

We listened at the window, my mother, my sister, and I. When we heard the word *guns* come out of Evo's mouth, it put a shudder through us all. Evo wanted his firearms, a hunting rifle and shotgun that my father had taken from his mother's house and locked away in a cabinet in our basement for safekeeping. Everybody had forgotten about them. Everyone but Evo.

I remember the two of them, my father and my uncle, standing in the yard talking for a long time as my mother paced the floor nervously, picking up the receiver on the phone and putting it down again, wondering aloud whether she should call the cops. Her brother was on the force.

I heard my uncle talk about hunting. My father

told him the gaming seasons were closed, pheasant was over and deer wouldn't start until summer. There was plenty of time. They could talk about it then. And the silent hope that I knew was in my father's mind: that by then Evo might forget.

Even in the gathering darkness you could almost see the furrowing eyebrows as my uncle struggled to do a mental check on the calendar, but he couldn't figure out what month it was. He gave up on hunting. Maybe he could just go shooting like they used to when he was a kid, some clay pigeons or tin cans.

'Where you gonna go?' asked my father.

Evo thought about this for a moment, his last memory. 'How about up at the ranch. Remember? We used to go shooting up there all the time.'

My father smiled and shook his head. 'No. They don't allow it anymore.'

'No?'

'No.'

The 'they' my father spoke of was himself, and Evo knew it. My father ran the ranch. Still, Evo never questioned him. Instead they both stood there, their bodies motionless, shaking their heads as if this, the banning of shooting on the ranch, was one more of the great tragedies of the changing times.

Then, watching from the window, I saw my father reach up and put a hand on his brother's shoulder. I remember how Evo, that hulking and scary guy, an immense shadow six inches taller than my father, suddenly sagged, his shoulders slumping. Whatever enthusiasm he had left for life at that moment seemed to escape from his body like a vapor into the fading light.

I listened as my father turned the conversation

to happier thoughts, recollections of their youth.
Maybe they could go fishing again, he said, though
even I knew it would never happen. I watched as
the two of them walked toward the old stone
fishpond in the center of our yard, and I listened to
the base hum of their voices as darkness devoured
their shapes. A few minutes later I heard them
both laughing. It was the first time I recall hearing
my uncle laugh out loud. It was musical. It tore my
heart out.

They talked for a long time out in the yard that
night. It seemed like hours, though I'm sure it was
not. At some point Evo, no longer remembering
why he had come, happy for the conversation and
the memories, walked toward our car parked at
the side of the house, and my father drove him
home.

This scene of my father and uncle through the
dim light of dust in the old backyard of our family
home is engraved in my memory, and will remain
so.

CHAPTER
TWENTY-ONE

Dr Robert Rubin is a board-certified forensic pathologist employed by the medical examiner, the coroner of San Diego County. Rubin is tall, blond, and thirty-one years old. He has been with the coroner's office just under two years, a whiz kid with a medical degree from George Washington University. This morning Templeton has him up on the stand going over the grisly details of Madelyn Chapman's murder.

'Can you tell the jury a little about your experience as a forensic pathologist? How many gunshot wounds have you had occasion to examine or to treat during your medical career, approximately?' asks Templeton.

'Somewhere between four and five hundred.'

'That many?'

'Yes.'

'You don't look old enough to have that much experience,' says Templeton.

'I was a physician and surgeon in the Navy assigned to duty with the Marine Corps prior to my residency in forensic pathology. So I had occasion to see a good number of gunshot wounds.'

'I see. How many years with the military?'

'Four.'

Templeton stands at the podium in the center aisle just below the bench as he examines the witness. He is held aloft on a step stool that slides under the podium, out of the way, when he is not using it.

'Four years with the Marines?'

'Yes.'

'And what was your assignment?'

'I was a field trauma surgeon. In theater.'

'In combat? A combat field hospital?' Templeton looks toward the jury for emphasis as he asks the question.

'That's correct.'

'And where did you serve? What geographic locations?'

'The Middle East, Central America; toward the end of my tour I was assigned for a short period to Bethesda Naval Hospital in Maryland.'

'So before you went on for your training in forensic pathology, you had an opportunity to observe, as you say, hundreds of gunshot wounds in this capacity with the military?'

'That's correct.'

'And since that time, since you became board certified in forensic pathology, how many gunshot wounds have you had an opportunity to observe as a qualified medical examiner?'

'I would say maybe sixty or seventy.'

'Isn't it a fact, Doctor, that among the qualified pathologists on the medical examiner's staff, you are considered to be one of the more qualified experts – if not the most qualified – in that office on gunshot wounds?'

'Perhaps. I've seen a lot of gunshot wounds.'

'Don't be modest, Doctor. The jury has a right to know your credentials.'

'It's fair to say there are two or three of us who have extensive experience in this area.'

'Isn't it a fact that your services have been loaned out to other counties and other states in connection with cases involving gunshot wounds?'

'That's true.'

'Fine, then let's turn our attention to the gunshot wounds suffered by Madelyn Chapman, the victim in this case. She was shot, was she not?'

'Oh, yes.'

'And did you have occasion to examine the body of Ms Chapman at the scene where it was discovered as well as to perform the autopsy on the victim?'

'I did.'

Under question by Templeton, Rubin provides the date of the autopsy and the fact that he was assigned to attend the body at the scene, at Chapman's home, that night and that he was the one who signed the death certificate following the autopsy. This is all carefully rehearsed, done well, in the way of all good rehearsals, so that to the untrained eye it does not appear to be practiced.

'Let's start with the evening in question, at the victim's home,' says Templeton. 'Did you have occasion to have photographs of the victim taken at that time, before the body was removed to the coroner's office for more detailed examination?'

'I did.'

Templeton stays on his stool as the homicide detective Argust paws through the box of evidence until he finds the photographs, one set for the judge, one for the witness, and one for us. From the stand, Rubin identifies the photos one at a time as pictures taken by police photographers at Rubin's direction on the night of the murder. As the witness does this, Templeton has them marked for identification, and when he is finished he moves the entire series into evidence.

'No objection.' I don't even look up as the photographs begin to flash on the screen for the jury, which now sees them for the first time. Some of the reporters in the front row try to lean forward to gain a glimpse of the screen, which is set at a slight angle toward the judge so members of the audience can't see it.

The series contains seven photographs that have been culled from among more than thirty taken by police at the scene that night. These come into evidence by stipulation, the judge having leaned on Templeton to drop some of the more hideous close-ups of what was left of Chapman's head. Most of the shots that survive are sufficiently distant from the body to provide at least some insulation from the grotesque details, blood and brain matter that sprayed the wall behind Chapman as the two bullets slammed into her skull. Strange as it seems, the worst of the lot is a full-body photo showing the high heel that twisted from Chapman's foot and remained standing upright on the floor as the impact of the rounds spun her in place as she went down. Like a freeze-action shot, it gives the jury dimension, some scale against which to measure the violence inflicted on the victim in the instant just before her death. As this picture goes up on the screen I hear some quiet sighs from the jury box. Even though I am not looking, I can feel twelve sets of eyes as they suddenly take a sharper look at my client.

'Let me ask you, Doctor. You said earlier that

you were able to examine the body at the scene, at the victim's house that night, is that correct?'

'Yes.'

'And can you tell the jury approximately what time that was when you first examined the body?'

'If I could refer to my notes . . .'

'Just a rough approximation,' says Templeton.

'As I recall, I believe it was a little before one a.m. I arrived at the scene about twelve thirty-five a.m. and some of the forensic technicians were still working around the body. So I had to wait just a few minutes before they cleared the area.'

Templeton slows the pace here, thinks for a moment, and allows the photographs of the murder scene now fixed on the screen to do some of his work for him.

'Let me ask you, Doctor, was it obvious to you when you arrived that the victim was already dead?'

'Oh, yes. The initial responding officers didn't even call the paramedics. As soon as they were able to open the front door, which they had to force, it was apparent to the two officers that Ms Chapman was dead.'

'And from your own observations before you had an opportunity to examine the body closely, were there any telltale signs that made it obvious that the victim was dead?'

'Yes. There was severe loss of blood and massive head trauma that was plainly obvious from some distance.'

'Are those indications displayed in any of the photographs posted on the visualizer screen for the jury?'

'Yes. You can see them pretty well in shots three, five, and seven.' The witness points to the screen with a small handheld laser displaying a bright green arrow aimed at the tangle of blood-matted hair and the dark pool of blood fanning out from under Chapman's head as she lies prostrate on the floor of the entryway to her home.

'Also the fact that the blood has a watery quality to it. You can see that here.' Rubin points again with the laser to one of the photographs. 'This is indicative of the loss of the cerebrospinal fluid that cushions the brain against impact within the skull. It would indicate that the cerebral cavity of the skull has been compromised in a manner that would result in rapid and catastrophic loss of blood pressure to the brain. Even if the brain itself had not been damaged by gunshot wounds, this loss of blood and cerebral fluid would certainly lead to death within a very short period of time. Three, perhaps four minutes at most.'

'As a result of your initial examination of the body or your subsequent and more complete autopsy, were you able to determine the cause of death?'

'After I conducted a thorough postmortem examination, yes.'

'And what was that cause?'

'Madelyn Chapman died of gunshot wounds resulting in massive trauma to the brain involving both the frontal and parietal lobes. The wounds inflicted resulted in irreversible destruction to major portions of the brain necessary to support life-sustaining functions.'

'You say wounds: how many gunshot wounds are we talking about?'

'Two.'

'Two. You're certain of that?' says Templeton.

'Yes.'

'And can you give us some idea how long it would have taken for the victim to die as a result of these wounds, in your opinion?' asks Templeton.

'Oh. That depends how you define *death*. If you're talking brain-wave activity – what you might measure on an EEG, an electroencephalogram – I would say that death was virtually instantaneous. If you're talking heart function, it could have taken anywhere from say two to four minutes. It's hard to tell. As regards heart function, it would depend on how rapidly blood drained from the body and how long it took for the trauma to the brain to interrupt or curtail the electromuscular impulses, the autonomic nervous system that regulates the heart. The sympathetic and parasympathetic nervous systems.'

'Whoa!' Templeton has his hands up. 'Let's not get too technical, Doctor. Let's keep it in the realm of the reasonable for those of us who flunked out of medical school and had to become lawyers.'

Jurors and members of the audience laugh – even Ruiz, until I step on his foot. It wouldn't do for jurors who are laughing to see the defendant joining in, especially in light of the ghastly photos still up on the screen. As the chuckles subside I can hear Harry growling under his breath at the other end of our counsel table.

'Doctor, can you tell the jury what evidence you found during the course of your examination of the victim, both at the scene as well as during your postmortem autopsy, to substantiate your findings as to the cause of death?'

'Upon examination of the victim's cranial cavity I discovered both a bullet and bullet fragments, all contained within the soft tissue of the victim's brain.'

Any residual smiles quickly dissipate inside the jury box.

'As a result of your examination of the victim, were you able to determine whether there were wounds other than the two bullet wounds that you have already identified found on the victim's body following death?'

'I was, and there were no wounds other than the two bullet wounds previously stated.'

'Other than the two bullet wounds to the victim's head?'

'That's correct.'

According to the witness, there were no gunpowder burns or stippling around the two wounds in question, eliminating the possibility of close-contact wounds with the muzzle of the pistol placed close to Chapman's head. According to the witness, given the size of the firearm in question, the shots would have had to have been fired from at least eight to ten feet to avoid the discharge of hot powder and gases onto the victim's hair and scalp. Also, the trajectory of the wounds would have been awkward for a close-in shot, as the weapon would have had to have been held above Chapman's head.

Rubin makes these points as they bring in more pictures, this time from the autopsy. Again these have been carefully vetted by the court to exclude shots that are likely to cause jurors to lose their breakfasts. Included among the photographs are two macro shots, one of a clearly recognizable lead bullet and the other of shards and fragments, flattened pieces of a dark substance with irregular shapes and edges, all laid out on white cloth with a ruler across the bottom for scale.

'One of the bullets was largely intact,' says

Rubin. 'It was sheared on one side, probably when it struck bone, and was somewhat deformed. It would be my opinion that it mushroomed under impact with the victim's head, both the bone of the skull and the soft tissue inside, as it radically reduced speed and lodged in the brain matter. The transfer of kinetic energy, the pressure caused by the entry of this bullet to the inner skull, caused a sizable portion of the skull at the posterior base of the victim's head to be blown out.'

The graphic description by the witness, along with the autopsy pictures offered up on the screen by Templeton's master of the computer, has the desired effect. Templeton looks toward the jury box to make sure that they have absorbed all of the grisly detail.

'I found this bullet lodged just inside the cerebellum of the victim's brain at the base of the neck.' The witness reaches around with his hand to the back of his neck as if to indicate location for the jury, and the judge describes this for the record.

'The other bullet was somewhat different, probably the second round that was fired. This bullet was of a different composition and it fragmented into multiple pieces inside the victim's skull. This was found during my postmortem examination lodged in several places, all of them contained within the skull, and had to be debrided from the brain tissue.'

'In layman's terms, Doctor?' Templeton wants him to define *debrided*.

'The bullet fragments had to be removed by scalpel and forceps from the brain tissue in which they had become lodged,' says the witness.

When I glance over at the jury, two of the women have their hands to their mouths, their gaze recoiling from the autopsy shots as Templeton's tech causes the pictures to linger on the screen.

'Doctor, from your treatment of bullet wounds as well as from your experience as a medical examiner, are you familiar with what are called jacketed bullets?'

'I am.'

'Can you describe for the jury what a jacketed bullet is?'

'The term *jacketed* refers to a metal lining that coats the outside of a bullet. A jacketed round is usually either a total metal jacket – what is known as a TMJ – or a partial jacket of some kind. That is, the softer lead component of the bullet is either completely covered by a harder metal material or partially covered. Copper is a common material for bullet jackets.'

'Thank you. Now, during the course of your examination of the victim's body, did you find any evidence that the two bullets that struck Madelyn Chapman had any kind of metal jacket?'

'I did not.'

'So the bullet fragments that you found were not part of a metal jacket that dislodged from either bullet in your opinion?'

'No, they were not.'

I look at Harry, who glances back with a quizzical stare. Neither of us can tell where he is headed. The pathology report indicated that the two bullets were unjacketed rounds but the significance of this is unclear.

'Did you weigh the two bullets in question? The largely intact bullet and the fragments of the other bullet?' Templeton asks.

'I did.'

'And what did you find their weights to be?'

'May I look at my notes?'

Templeton turns and directs his gaze toward me.

'Mr Madriani, any objection?' says the judge.

'No objection, Your Honor.'

Rubin opens the file sitting in his lap. 'With regard to the partially deformed bullet, we found the weight to be two hundred and twenty-seven point two grains. With regard to the fragments from the other bullet, the total grain weight was one hundred and ninety-seven point six grains. It is possible that I was unable to locate every fragment of this second bullet. The fragments did not respond to X-ray.'

Nor was this in the witness's written report.

'Do you have any idea what the calibers of these two particular bullets were? What size barrel or firearm they may have been fired from?' says Templeton.

I could object on grounds that the question exceeds the expertise of the witness, but there is no real point, and it's entirely possible, given the doctor's background with ballistic wounds, that Gilcrest would overrule the objection in any event.

'With regard to the partially deformed bullet it appears to be either forty-four or forty-five caliber. With regard to the fragments, there is no way to tell other than by grain weight, which would place the bullet resulting in those fragments within the same range, forty-four or forty-five caliber.'

'But the grain weights of the two bullets differ significantly, Doctor. How could they be the same caliber?' says Templeton. From the smile on his face it is obvious that he already knows the answer.

'The two bullets were made of different materials,' says Rubin. 'The first bullet was a lead alloy, a common manufacture, capable of being purchased in retail stores that stock ammunition. The second bullet was made of different materials—'

'Your Honor, I'm going to object.'

'On what grounds?' says Gilcrest.

'The question of bullet composition is well beyond the expertise of the witness, Your Honor.'

'I would remind the court that the witness has attended to patients with hundreds of bullet wounds,' says Templeton. He would press the outer edge of the envelope until it ripped.

'And if he has a degree in metallurgy from an accredited university, I'd be happy to let you go on,' I tell him.

Gilcrest looks down at the witness from his perch on the bench. 'Doctor, you don't have a degree in metallurgy, do you?'

'No, Your Honor.'

'Objection sustained,' says the judge.

Templeton doesn't lose a beat. 'Well, let me ask you this, then: during all of your years treating patients with bullet wounds and during your time as a medical examiner, have you ever had occasion to observe bullets or bullet fragments similar in appearance and apparent composition to the bullet and bullet fragments removed from the victim in this case, Madelyn Chapman?'

'Objection, Your Honor, to the use of the term *apparent composition*,' I say.

'Overruled,' says Gilcrest. 'The witness can answer the question.

'Twice,' says the witness.

'You've seen these before?'

'Two times,' says Rubin.

'And where was that?'

'During my service with the Marines.'

'Can you describe the situation in which you observed bullets or bullet wounds with characteristics similar to those found in the victim, Madelyn Chapman?'

It is now becoming clear why Rubin's background is so essential to Templeton's case.

'One was a training accident in which a Marine was killed. The other involved a foreign combatant who was delivered to our field hospital for examination and identification after he had been killed in battle.'

'Where did these incidents occur?'

'Both took place during active duty in the Middle East.'

Templeton doesn't push any further than this for specifics as to location. He leaves it open for me to possibly step on a land mine during cross. I make a note.

'Can you describe for the jury the similarities between the bullets or bullet fragments you removed from the victim, Madelyn Chapman, and the bullets or bullet fragments you removed from the victims in these other two incidents that you observed?'

'Objection, Your Honor. As to relevance.' If nothing else, I will force Templeton to give us a road map of where he is trying to go with this.

'Your Honor, if we could approach the bench . . .' Templeton wants a sidebar.

'Very well.' Gilcrest motions us forward. He flips a button on the bench and the courtroom fills with white noise. A special sidebar microphone connects with the court reporter so that she won't have to move. Neither the jury, the witness, nor members

325

of the audience can hear a thing in the area around the bench.

We assemble at the side near the stairs leading down to the judge's chambers, with Gilcrest standing on the bottom step, leaning over to converse with Templeton. We are virtually out of sight.

'Your Honor, I will tie it all together,' says Templeton. 'The witness has extensive experience with bullet wounds, particularly in the military. The weapon used in this case is a military-issue handgun. We have another witness later who will testify that at least one of the bullets used to kill Madelyn Chapman was a military-issue round, and highly sophisticated. This witness and the following witness will testify to the fact that these were special rounds, a composite alloy designed for their lethal effect and to avoid penetration through the target in certain situations. They were largely available only to police agencies and the military.'

'That doesn't mean my client fired them, Your Honor.'

'That's for the jury to decide,' says Templeton.

'None of this was in the witness's pathology report, Your Honor. Mr Templeton has hidden the ball on us one more time,' I tell Gilcrest.

'Not so,' says Templeton. 'The defense had every opportunity to examine the bullet fragments and to bring in their own experts.'

'Not when the fragments are called just that in the medical examiner's report,' I say. It is clear what they have done: led us to believe that the bullet fragments in question were simply parts of the second bullet. The report offers no number or size of individual fragments, just their aggregate weight.

'What is clear,' says Templeton, 'is that Mr Ruiz

was in the military. We know that, Your Honor. That's where he got the gun. And, according to our witnesses, probably where he got the ammunition used in the murder.'

' "Probably" is not evidence,' I tell Gilcrest.

'The bullets were frangible rounds,' says Templeton. 'A special manufacture for certain military weapons. In this case the forty-five automatic. That's what my witness will testify to.'

It's like playing lawyer's dozen. It takes a full round of objections and argument at the bench, but I finally smoke Templeton out.

The judge has heard enough. He puts his hands up. 'I'm going to allow the witness to answer the question,' he says.

I whisper to Harry as we head back to the table, 'You know anything about this?'

'There was nothing in the pathology report,' says Harry. Now it is clear why Templeton's expert in ballistics who is outside in the hall, waiting to be called, has reduced nothing to writing by way of a report. He is getting ready to slip a second sword into us.

Back on his step-stool stump, Templeton has his medical witness put a lance in our side by noting the similarity of the bullets used to kill Chapman to others he has seen during his time in the military. It is what he calls a composite bullet, frangible ammunition composed of polymers and a special bonding agent designed to fragment on contact with harder substances such as bone. According to the witness, this is why the second round disintegrated just after it penetrated Chapman's skull and why the entry hole is somewhat larger than the entry wound from the first lead bullet.

When Templeton tries to venture further into bullet design, I object. The judge sustains the objection, putting an end to it. 'Let's move on, Mr Templeton, it's getting late.'

'Just a few more questions of this witness, Your Honor. Let's concentrate on this second bullet for the moment,' he says. 'Were you able to determine the point of entry of this bullet into the victim's skull?'

'I was.'

'And what was that location?'

'The second round fired penetrated the skull just to the left of the anterior midline of the skull, approximately eight centimeters above the victim's left eye.'

'Here in the left forehead?' Templeton points with the forefinger of his left hand to his own head.

'That's correct.'

'Let the record reflect that the witness has confirmed the location of this entry wound consistent with an area just above the prosecutor's left eye,' says Gilcrest. 'And, Mr Templeton, if you don't want this court to shoot you, please allow the witness to provide the gestures as to physical description.'

'Sorry, Your Honor.' Templeton is right back to the witness. 'Can you tell us approximately how far the entry wound from this second shot was to the entry wound from the first bullet?'

'The second bullet . . .'

'Let's be clear for the jury. This is the frangible bullet you're talking about? The second bullet?'

'That's correct. That bullet made a somewhat larger hole, approximately sixteen point three millimeters from center point of contact of the first bullet. The bullet that I described as largely intact and composed of a lead alloy.'

'Could you give that to us in inches for the jury,' says Templeton, 'so that they can have some point of reference?'

'The two entry wounds to the victim's head were a little more than six tenths of an inch apart in terms of distance,' says Rubin.

'That's close as bullet wounds go, I take it?'

'That's very close, particularly when you consider that the impact of the first bullet proceeded to spin the victim around as it hit her.'

'You know this to be the case?'

'Yes.' As if on cue, the shoeless photo is back up on the screen. Rubin points to the photograph of the high heel standing upright on the floor in the entry, its toe pointing away from the body lying on the floor, as conclusive evidence of this. 'Upon impact the first bullet would have jerked the mass of the head in a twisting motion to the right. The body of the victim would have followed.'

'So, based on this evidence that the second round struck the victim before she could fall or be spun around, would it be safe to assume that the two shots in question were fired in very rapid succession?' Templeton asks.

The witness is already nodding his head. 'The two shots would have had to have been fired within a millisecond of each other. As fast as a healthy human hand and index finger could pull the trigger two times.'

'Thank you, Doctor.'

By the time Templeton is finished with the witness, there isn't much I can do to repair the damage. I go through the autopsy report item by item until I finally get to the point where I ask Rubin why he failed to include any mention of the frangible bullet in his written report.

He blushes a little and finally says, 'I guess at the time I didn't see it as particularly important.'

I could go after him on grounds that at some point he knew that the defendant who had been charged with the crime had a military background and that the murder weapon belonged to him. To do this, however, would merely reinforce Templeton's case. Instead I ask a different question.

'Dr Rubin, do you have any idea why the killer in this case, the person who murdered Madelyn Chapman – whoever it is – would choose to use two different kinds of bullets when shooting her?'

Rubin looks at me from the stand as if he has never really thought about this. He shakes his head. 'No. I'm afraid I can't answer that. I don't know.'

CHAPTER TWENTY-TWO

Templeton is shrewd. Timing is everything in a trial. He has knocked us off balance with the evidence of the frangible bullet.

The two clips from the murder weapon that were found inside Chapman's house were both empty. If they were originally loaded with frangible rounds, whoever shot Chapman took the time to discard all of the ammunition, making it impossible for us to be on the lookout for the distinctive bullets.

Ruiz has admitted to Harry and me that at one time he did have frangible rounds, issued by the Army for use in a special indoor military range. But he doesn't remember whether any of these remained in the clips that were packed away with the gun. According to Emiliano, he used spare clips when he and Chapman last used the Mark 23 pistol at the range, when he was showing Madelyn how to shoot. He left the bag with the two original clips at her house and never looked at them again.

Whoever set Ruiz up has done a masterful job, not only with the evidence, but anticipating the direction from which problems might come at trial. So far they have left us in the dark.

Templeton decides that, with the defense on its heels, this is the time to expose the weak underbelly of his case, to the extent that he has one, and get it behind him.

This morning they bring in the gun and its canvas case, along with the two empty clips and the silencer discovered on the rocks over the ocean.

Templeton has his principal evidence tech, Mitchell Perryman, up on the stand. Perryman is the man who headed up the team that marked, identified, and gathered all the physical evidence at the scene. He is a veteran, sixteen years with county law enforcement, and a student of endless courses in evidence gathering from the FBI as well as the state crime lab. But his department has had its problems in the last two years: first a scandal involving errors in the chains of custody in a string of felony cases in which one of Perryman's colleagues was caught falsifying internal records; then four months ago another of Perryman's associates was caught in misstatements under oath on the stand, which defense counsel called perjury and which is now on appeal in a major white-collar prosecution. All of this has left the people in Perryman's office feeling tainted, demoralized, and gun-shy on the stand.

'Let's start with the firearm,' says Templeton. 'The HK Mark Twenty-three forty-five-caliber semiautomatic pistol.' This has already been removed from its paper evidence bag and identified as the weapon found in Chapman's backyard the night of the murder.

'You supervised the photographing and collection of this weapon, did you not?'

'I did,' says Perryman. The witness has already identified an array of photographs, and they now appear up on the visualizer in order for the jury to see.

The gun itself is photographed lying on its side on top of a small mound of what appears to be dark potting soil heaped up like a soft mesa around the base of a rosebush. A ruler for scale appears just beyond the edge of the lawn along the bottom of the photo.

'Did you find the firearm yourself at the location photographed?'

'No. One of the first officers on the scene checked the yard to make sure that no one was there. He observed the firearm at that time but did not touch it or approach it. He kept it under visual observation until evidence technicians from our office arrived on the scene. That's when I first observed it.'

'And was it still in the position and as we see it here in the photograph when you first observed it?'

'Yes, it was.'

'What about the silencer?' says Templeton. 'Where was that found?'

The silencer, manufactured by a company in Vero Beach, Florida, that specializes in sound suppression for firearms, is a cylindrical tube about eight inches long. Its exterior is made of dull blued gunmetal with small round dimples lining the outside.

'That was discovered by one of the evidence technicians outside the rear seawall of the victim's residence on the rocks overlooking the beach,' says Perryman.

'And you observed this before it was touched by any of the attending officers or your own staff?'

'I did.'

'And did you have it photographed?'

'Yes.' Perryman identifies the photograph, a picture of the silencer lying on its side on the rocks perhaps ten feet from the edge where they drop off into the surf. Both the firearm and the silencer are neatly laid out on a small table in front of the jury box where jurors can observe them without touching them.

'Did you or your staff find any loaded cartridges at the scene: unfired bullets either of the caliber of the subject weapon or any other firearm?'

'No, we did not.'

'No loaded cartridges either inside or outside the house?'

'None that we found. And we looked thoroughly, including the use of metal detectors and the use of dogs trained to detect the odor of accelerants, including gunpowder.'

'Were there any fired or spent cartridges either inside or outside of the victim's house?'

'None that we found,' says Perryman. 'Again, we checked using canines attached to the bomb-detection unit.'

This is a mystery: why, with only two rounds fired, the police found two empty pistol clips belonging to the handgun and no spent cartridge casings.

'And the police and canine units came up with nothing?'

'Not exactly,' says Perryman. 'They found no spent cartridges. They did detect traces of expended accelerants along the railing on the second-floor landing above the entry area of the house and on top of one of the glass display cabinets just beneath that area.'

'When you say *expended accelerants*, could

you explain for the jury what you mean?' says Templeton.

'One of the dogs found traces of a substance including particulates of nitrate that were probably dislodged from the inside of a spent cartridge casing when it bounced on the top of the cabinet beneath the railing. Swabs were taken which later tested positive for concentrations of nitrates, both burned and unburned. These were found to be consistent with the discharge of smokeless gunpowder.'

'I see,' says Templeton. 'Did you form any conclusions as to what had happened at those locations as a result of these findings?'

'I did.'

'And what were those conclusions?'

'That a firearm was most likely discharged in the area along the railing at the second-floor landing and that the nitrates discharged by this action settled along the railing and top of the display cabinet beneath it.'

'I see. Were you able to determine whether the shots that killed Madelyn Chapman were fired from that location?'

'It is my opinion that they were. We checked all other areas in the house that would have a clear and unimpeded line of fire to the location where the body was found in the entry hall. None of those locations came up positive for traces of nitrates.'

'So by process of elimination you concluded that the shots that killed Madelyn Chapman were fired from the area of the second-floor landing above the entry?'

'That's correct.'

Templeton has the witness identify photographs of this area, several shots looking up from the vicinity around the front door as well as three photos, one with the crosshairs of a sight superimposed on the lens, aimed down at the floor of the entry hall in the area where Chapman's body was found. A chalk outline of her body drawn on the floor is still visible in the three pictures. These go up on the visualizer for the jury.

'Now let me ask you,' says Templeton, 'did you measure the distance from the railing in the area where you detected traces of nitrates to the location where the victim's body was found, on the floor of the entry?'

'I did.'

'And what did you determine that distance to be?'

Perryman doesn't even bother to refer to his notes. He has memorized this, one of the key elements of their case along with the rapidity of the two shots, the distance to the target.

'Twenty-one feet four inches, if you take into account the height of the victim when she was standing and the fact that the gun would most likely have been held at arm's length in a two-handed firing stance and slightly out over the railing.'

'Over twenty feet?' says Templeton.

'That's correct.'

'Two shots, both of which according to evidence already introduced were tightly grouped within slightly more than half an inch, and both of which struck the victim in the head?'

'As I understand it,' says Perryman.

'That's some shooting,' says Templeton.

'Objection.'

'Sustained. Mr Templeton, let's allow the witnesses to testify. Keep your comments to yourself. The jury will disregard the statement made by the prosecutor.'

'Sorry, Your Honor.' Templeton gives the judge one of his harmless smiles, open palms out and extended like a miniature Jolson.

He then moves on to defuse one of the problem areas of his case. Templeton covers the *Orb at the Edge*, that's still missing. 'Did you find any remnants of this, the glass art object that we know the victim purchased the day that she was killed?'

'No. But we did find the cardboard box and pieces of tape and packing materials. It appears that she had just finished unpacking this in the kitchen, a short time before she was killed.'

An earlier witness has already identified these materials. The merchant who sold her the art glass told the jury that the materials were gathered from the storeroom at the back of his shop and used to pack the glass before it was loaded into the front seat of Chapman's car.

'So the killer could have taken the item?' says Templeton.

'I don't know. All I can say is that we didn't find it at the scene.'

'And I assume that anyone who took it would probably want to dispose of it as quickly as possible.'

'Objection. Calls for speculation.'

'Mr Templeton. Please,' says Gilcrest.

'Allow me to rephrase it, Your Honor.' Having made his point, Templeton proceeds to make it again. 'Let me ask you, have you seen pictures of the art object in question, what are called catalog photos?'

'I have,' says Perryman.

'Was it your understanding, based solely on your

investigation, that the glass art item known as the *Orb at the Edge* was unique, a one-of-a-kind item?'

'Objection. Calls for speculation. The witness is not an art expert.'

Gilcrest weighs this for a moment. 'I'll allow the witness to answer based solely on his under-standing of what he discovered during the course of his investigation.'

'From everything I learned during the course of the investigation,' the witness says, treading carefully, 'it was unique. A one-of-a-kind item, as you say, and expensive.'

'So, based on this, if this item – once owned by the victim Madelyn Chapman and in her possession on the day that she was murdered – were suddenly to be found in the possession of another person, as an expert witness in the field of criminalistics and forensic evidence, I assume you would consider this to be incriminating evidence?'

'You bet. Absolutely.'

'And let me ask you this, based solely on your expertise and your experience in the field of evidence: Have you ever seen situations in which an accused criminal perpetrator or a suspect was motivated to dispose of physical evidence when that evidence might link them to a crime?'

'Yes, I have seen such situations,' says Perryman.

With a crayon, Templeton draws a picture of the obvious for the jury.

'Even an item of evidence that might have substantial monetary value?' Templeton asks.

'Yes. I have seen and am familiar with cases in which expensive evidence has been disposed of because it might link a suspect to a crime.'

Obvious as it may be, it is nonetheless effective.

In closing, he can now argue that theft of the *Orb* was never the motive for the murder: that Ruiz took it no doubt to throw the cops off his scent to make it look like Chapman's murder was a killing during the course of robbery. The state will argue that after the murder Ruiz had to get rid of it, since the art glass would have linked him beyond question to the homicide.

'During the course of your investigation, you were inside the victim's house for a considerable period of time, were you not?' says Templeton.

'That's correct.'

'And during that time, did you have an opportunity to observe and to inventory all of the items of expensive artwork that were present there?'

'I did.'

'During the course of your investigation, did you determine whether any other items of glass art were missing from the victim's residence besides the item known as the *Orb at the Edge*?'

'We were able to determine that there were no other missing items. The victim maintained a very active and up-to-date schedule of insurance on the items displayed in her home. She had a separate schedule for the items at her office. All of the items listed were still present following her death.'

'Except for the *Orb at the Edge*,' says Templeton.

'Correct.'

'Was that insured?'

'No. We knew about that only because we found the bill of sale and the merchant who sold it to her.'

Templeton makes the point: if the purpose was burglary or robbery, why didn't the killer take any of the other objects of glass? Even in haste he would have grabbed one or two of the more expensive-looking items to go along with the *Orb*. But he didn't.

Harry and I blow through lunch at Mac's.

'Whoever did it was either awfully lucky or had some insights,' says Harry. He is talking with his mouth full of barbecue beef, one corner of a large paper napkin tucked over the knot of his tie. Harry is hunkered over his plate, allowing the excess to drip down onto the plate.

'If I had to guess' – I poke around at my salad as I'm thinking – 'somebody who's spent enough time in court or has enough knowledge of investigative techniques to make everything point in the wrong direction,' I tell him.

Harry stops chewing just long enough to look up at me. 'You have a candidate in mind?'

'I don't know. I'm thinking about it.'

In the afternoon I get my shot at Perryman on cross.

'You say you found no spent cartridges at the scene, is that correct?'

'That's right.'

'That would mean that the killer must have taken the time to pick them up?'

'I don't know,' says Perryman. 'I can't answer that question.'

'We are talking about a semiautomatic handgun here, are we not? The pistol you say police found in Madelyn Chapman's backyard?'

'Yes. It's semiautomatic.'

'That means each time it fires a separate shot, it ejects the empty cartridge from the gun, does it not?'

'Objection,' says Templeton. 'The witness is not qualified as a firearms expert.'

'But he has found firearms at the scenes of numerous homicides, along with expended cartridge cases,' I say.

'I'll allow the witness to answer the question if he knows the answer,' says Gilcrest.

'A semiautomatic handgun would normally eject an expended cartridge each time it's fired,' says Perryman.

'Thank you. That means, assuming the state's evidence is correct, you would expect to find at least two expended cartridges at the scene, is that right?'

'I suppose.'

'But you didn't.'

'No.'

'So someone must have taken them.'

'I presume so.'

'Why would someone who had just murdered a woman – shot her twice with a handgun – stop to pick up expended cartridge cases?'

'Maybe they didn't want us to be able to trace the cartridges back to the handgun,' says Perryman. 'Tool marks,' he adds.

'But they left the handgun for you to find. Does that make sense?'

'That's not true,' says Perryman. 'From what we were able to deduce, the killer tried to throw the handgun over the wall in the backyard.'

'Ah. He tried to hit the ocean but he missed?'

This is their theory. Perryman doesn't like the way I've put the question, so he doesn't answer it. I ask it again.

'How could he – or she, for that matter – miss the ocean?'

'He didn't throw it hard enough,' says the witness. 'It probably hit the wall and bounced back into the yard.'

'Ah. I see. Your Honor, if I might . . .' I want Gilcrest to allow me to examine the firearm.

The judge nods.

This allows me a little freedom to move away from the podium and around the courtroom. I move to the table in front of the jury box and pick up the pistol. I smile at several of the jurors. Only one of them smiles back.

The slide of the pistol has been wired back, the chamber held open by a nylon cable tie so that it cannot be loaded without removing this: the standard safety precaution in most courtrooms and many private gun shops.

I turn toward the witness. 'It's heavy.'

He nods.

'Do you have any idea what it weighs?'

'If I could look at my notes . . .' he says.

'I have no objection.' I look at Templeton sitting on the box on his chair.

He shrugs a shoulder. 'No objection,' he says.

Perryman rifles through a few pages until he finds the one he's looking for. 'According to the manufacturer, the handgun without a loaded clip weighs two-point-four-two pounds.'

'So it would take a pretty good throw to make it to the ocean from the backyard of Ms Chapman's house.'

'My point exactly,' he says.

'Hmm. Can you show me where it hit?'

'Excuse me?' he says.

'Where this handgun hit the wall in the backyard. You say you believe that the killer threw the gun from the backyard but that it probably struck the wall and bounced back into the yard. That is what you just said. So, can you show me the marks on the gun where it hit the wall?'

Perryman is beginning to look a little uncomfortable in the witness box.

'That's just one possible theory,' he says.

'Yes. Well. If I hand you the gun, can you show me what part of it struck the wall? May I approach the witness, Your Honor?'

Gilcrest waves me on.

I hand Perryman the gun.

He takes it like it's some foreign object, not knowing which end is supposed to be up. He checks the handle first. It is pristine, as is the blued metal on the barrel, both sides, and the top of the slide.

'I can't say,' he says.

'You don't find any dents or scratches that might be consistent with the gun hitting the wall?'

He looks again. 'There's a little wear on the barrel near the crown. The bluing is off,' he says.

'But hitting the wall wouldn't cause wear, would it?'

'No. Probably not.'

'Do you see any major nicks or dents?' I ask.

'No.'

'Do you remember what the wall behind Madelyn Chapman's house is made of?' I ask.

He looks at me, not sure what to say or whether he should guess.

'What if I told you it was made of concrete cinder blocks covered with stucco? What would you say?'

'I don't know. I don't remember,' he says.

'Regardless of what it's made of, we know it's not made of goose feathers or foam rubber. So, wouldn't you expect a heavy object like the firearm in your hand, when thrown from some distance, to at least get scratched or dented somewhere when it strikes a solid object like a fence or a wall?'

'Not necessarily,' he says. 'It's possible it didn't hit the wall at all – that perhaps the perpetrator just didn't throw it far enough. It could have just landed in the flower bed.'

'Ahh. Theory number two,' I say. 'The feeble-armed killer.'

As I turn from the witness, a couple of jurors crack a smile.

I can tell by the look on Templeton's face he knows he's in trouble. He'd like to get the witness off the stand. If he had a hook, he'd use it now.

'How far would you say it is from the back edge of the patio at the victim's house to the point at the edge of the grass where the gun was found by the officer? Did you measure it?'

Perryman shakes his head.

'You have to speak up.'

'No. I didn't measure it.'

'I did. Would you be surprised if I told you it was thirty-two feet four inches?'

'I'll take your word for it,' he says.

'Maybe we could have the photograph back up on the visualizer.' I turn toward Templeton.

He looks at me like I'm a man from Mars.

'The state's photograph of the firearm in the rose bed,' I say.

'Ah.' He nods toward his computer assistant, and a second later the picture is back up on the visualizer.

'Can you see the picture?' I ask the witness.

'Yes.'

'Can you show me where this gun, the one in your hand, the one that weighs just a little under two and a half pounds, made an impression in the soil when it landed in the flower bed under the rosebush there?'

The look on Perryman's face is that of a deer in the headlights. He doesn't respond.

'You did say that no one touched the gun before it was photographed, is that correct?'

'Yeah. Yeah, that's right.'

'Well, where is the impression in the soil where it landed?' There is a small puddle of water just at the bottom left corner of the photo. The ground is wet.

Herman checked it. The sprinkler system at Chapman's house was on a rotating timer. It was set to water the entire yard, front and back, every day. The area around the bushes in the back had been soaked for over an hour just after three in the afternoon on the day of the murder. The killer dragged traces of soft peat from his shoes into the house near the window where he entered. The cops looked for shoe prints in the mud but found none. The killer was careful enough to stay mostly on the flat flagstones that formed a path through the garden to the back of the house.

I repeat the question: 'Do you see an impression in the soil when the gun landed?'

'Maybe it bounced on the lawn,' he says.

'Well, then, where's the skid mark in the mud? Wouldn't you expect that if something weighing almost two and a half pounds and made of case-hardened steel were thrown, say, thirty feet and bounced on the lawn and came to rest in the flower bed that it would disturb at least a little bit of the soil underneath the rosebush where it came to rest?'

'I don't know,' he says.

I can tell by looking that Templeton would like

to put his head in his hands at this point. But he resists the urge. At one time or another we have all been there.

'Let me ask you: Do you see any marks at all in the soil in that photograph?'

'I don't know,' he says. 'I can't tell.'

'Well, you and your staff took the photographs, didn't you?'

'Yeah.'

'I don't see any marks in the soil, and the photograph looks pretty clear to *me*.'

'Objection.'

'Sustained. The jury will disregard the comment by counsel.'

They may disregard it, but unless they are blind, they can't help but notice the undisturbed surface of the flower bed.

'Let me suggest another theory to you and ask you whether that theory is not in fact more plausible, given the physical evidence contained in your own photograph. Isn't it more likely, given what you can see up there on that screen, that whoever shot Madelyn Chapman didn't throw the gun at all but placed the gun – the one in your hand; the one weighing two and a half pounds – in the flower bed so that you could do exactly what you *did* do: find it there?'

If it were possible, Perryman would crawl out of the box at this moment on his belly, slither like a serpent out into the hall, and disappear. But he can't. Instead he offers up the answer of all witnesses who have hit into a sand trap on the stand. 'Anything is possible,' he says.

I take the pistol from his hand before he can run to a gun shop to buy a bullet. I head back toward the table.

'Can the witness be excused?' says Templeton. 'I'm not finished.'

I can almost hear Templeton groan as I say it. I put the gun down and pick up the silencer. The metal tube is only a fraction of the weight of the more solid handgun.

Perryman's gaze settles on the silencer like a child looking at a hypodermic needle. It is the problem when you already know what is going to happen and all you can do is bend over.

'Do you have any idea how far it is from the back of Madelyn Chapman's house – say, the edge of the back patio – to the rocks over the beach on the other side of the sea wall where this silencer was found?'

'No,' he says, shaking his head, then tries to get cute: 'But I'm sure you're going to tell us.'

'Would you believe me if I told you sixty-two feet, give or take a couple of inches?'

'Objection. There's no verification for this,' says Templeton.

'I can have our technician put the property plan map up on the visualizer if you like. It is drafted to scale, including the house. We've had each item of evidence marked on as to location where it was found.'

'That won't be necessary,' says Templeton. 'I withdraw the objection.'

I restate for the witness the distance of the supposed throw from the back of the house to the area where the silencer was found on the rocks: roughly sixty-two feet.

Perryman nods. 'I'll take your word for it.'

'Can we have the other photograph? The one showing the silencer on the rocks?' This time I'm looking directly at Templeton's computer wizard. I spare Templeton the task of assisting in the burial of his own witness.

The photo flashes up on the screen showing the abrasive surface of the sandstone with a few jagged outcroppings of more solid rock where the silencer came to rest.

'Perhaps you can show me on the blued gun-metal here where the dents and scratches are located where this silencer hit the sandstone after it was thrown that distance.'

Perryman takes the silencer, turns it over in his hands. He would swallow it whole if he could. 'Fine. So there's no scratches.'

'How is that possible? How is it that an object like this could be thrown roughly sixty feet, land on a surface of hard sandstone, hit rocks, and yet the bluing on the metal shows no indication of this? No scratches, no dents, nothing.'

'I don't know.'

'Could it be that somebody carefully laid it there?'

'As I said, anything's possible.'

'But if they walked all the way out there with the silencer in their hand, why wouldn't they just toss it into the surf? It can't be, what, more than ten feet to the edge of the rocks?'

'I don't know. I didn't measure it. But I'm sure you did.'

'Mr Perryman, nobody threw this silencer, did they?'

'I don't know.'

'They laid it on the rocks, didn't they? Just as they laid the gun under the rosebush, so that you and your staff could find both when you went looking for them. Didn't they?'

'I don't know.'

348

'The witness has answered the question,' says Templeton. Templeton wants it to end.

I head back toward the table with the silencer in my hand. 'I'm not quite done.'

This time I return with the bag, canvas camo, desert colors with pockets inside for the two clips and the silencer, a larger space for the handgun, and one more square-shaped pocket underneath it.

'Have you looked at this gun bag?' I ask Perryman.

'I have.'

'Do you know where it came from?'

'It's standard-issue military for that particular weapon. The HK Mark Twenty-three forty-five automatic,' he says.

'Ah, I see you've done your homework. Did you take the time to place all of the various components of this weapon in their proper pockets to see if they fit?'

'I did.'

'And what did you discover, if anything?'

'They all fit.'

'Yes, but was anything missing in this bag from the standard kit as it was issued by the military for the HK Mark Twenty-three?'

'Yes.'

'What?'

'A laser sight,' says the witness.

'Ah, yes. The missing laser sight. Did you find a laser sight anywhere at the victim's house or in her yard or on the rocks beyond the seawall?'

'No.'

'So you never found the laser sight.'

'No, we didn't.'

'And you never found any of the spent cartridges

or additional loaded rounds for the gun, either, did you?'

'No.'

'Did you have divers check the water, the area of the surf beneath the rocks, looking for any of this evidence?'

'We did. The tidal action was too rough for anything to be found.'

'So if someone threw the laser sight into the water, it would have disappeared, unrecoverable, correct?'

'Apparently,' says Perryman.

'Same with the bullets and any empty cartridges, right?'

'I suppose.'

'And yet, the killer didn't bother to toss the handgun itself into the water, or the silencer. Doesn't that strike you as curious?'

'Perhaps,' he says.

He has gone from 'I suppose' to 'Perhaps.'

'A few hours ago Mr Templeton asked you a question about your expertise in the collection of physical evidence at crime scenes. He asked you whether you had ever seen a situation in which the suspect or accused perpetrator in a crime would dispose of evidence that the suspect knew might link him to a crime, even evidence of substantial monetary value. Is that not what he asked you?'

'Yes.'

'And as I recall, you stated that you were aware of situations where suspects or accused perpetrators were in fact motivated to dispose of such evidence linking them to a crime, is that what you said?'

'Yes.'

'Then let me ask you a question: Assuming that

this firearm belonged to or was at one time known to be in the possession of the defendant Emiliano Ruiz' – I point to my own client at the counsel table – 'and assuming that he committed the crime as the state charges, why would he lay the firearm that links him to that crime in the flower bed in the backyard of the victim's house? Why would he leave the silencer on the rocks beyond the seawall behind that house? Why? Why, when he could have dumped them both into the surf and, as you yourself testified, they would have been swallowed up by the sea?'

The witness glances quickly at Templeton, then shakes his head. He seems about to be saying he doesn't know, then catches himself. 'Perhaps he tried and in the dark he didn't realize,' he says.

'That's the best you can do?'

'Objection.' Templeton is now standing on the lip of his chair that extends beyond the front edge of the box on top of it. 'Move that counsel's comment be stricken.'

'Sustained,' says the judge.

'I have no more questions of this witness.' As I turn to walk toward the counsel table, I see Ruiz looking at me, the slight glimmer of hope on his face, the first I have seen in more than two months.

CHAPTER TWENTY-THREE

I was sitting on the state's evidence report, the lack of impressions left in the soil by the gun and absence of marks on the silencer, for almost six weeks. I hoped that Templeton would not pick up on the inevitable sonar waves pinging just beneath the surface of his case.

Whenever arguments came up in chambers over evidence I would chirp loudly on some other point and hop in a different direction if the issue veered close to the photographs of the gun or the silencer. Like a bird protecting its nest, I feigned a broken wing over some other issue. In the end I was lucky, I suspect in part because Templeton was distracted by the embarrassment of riches presented in his own case.

'You did good. Very good. You nailed his feet to the floor, Counselor.' Emiliano is smiling at me this morning inside the holding area, one of the small cubicles just off the courtroom. He is buoyed by my cross-examination of Mitchell Perryman on the stand yesterday afternoon.

Decked out in his suit, a freshly starched shirt, and a different-colored tie each day, Emiliano looks

more the banker than a defendant in a murder
trial. He has learned to do a Windsor knot with the
tie. With the half shadow of his dark beard clean
shaven, he could pass for one of the sullen-faced
Adonises of modeldom, Mr December on the
calendar *Men of Combat*. He cuts a good image.
Whether the jury will try to put him to death is
another question.

'You really got that guy . . . The evidence man,'
he calls him.

'Sometimes lawyers get lucky,' I tell him.

'You should learn to take a compliment,' he tells
me. Emiliano has gotten the routine down so that
he knows almost exactly, even without a watch,
how much time he has once Harry and I arrive
before they call us out into the courtroom. His
orange jail jumpsuit is in a pile on the floor in the
corner. Superman changing in a phone booth.

Ruiz looks as if he's had a good night's sleep,
the first one in several weeks. 'The little things
that life gives to you sometimes. If you're like me,
it doesn't happen very often,' he says. 'You should
be happy about it.'

'Oh, I am. It would be nice to be able to come
up with a repeat performance, but I'm afraid that
Mr Templeton is not going to allow that to
happen.'

'Don't get me wrong: I'm not getting cocky, not
even confident,' he says. 'I know they're probably
gonna hang me no matter what. Still, I'd like to
think we went down swinging. And the way you
stuck the guy yesterday, I don't mind saying,
made me feel that at least maybe – you know,
like, maybe – we made a statement. You know
what I mean?' He looks at me.

'Yes.'

'Maybe that's all we can do. But I think some of the jurors are listening. I think they're asking themselves who set me up.'

'Let's hope so.'

'No, I mean it. The lady at the end, I saw her taking lots of notes. Trust me,' he says. 'You got 'em thinking.'

It is the one thing in a capital case that a lawyer always worries about, besides conviction and a death sentence: creating expectations in the client's mind that cannot be met.

'I don't want to be the one to throw a damper on the party,' says Harry, 'but we still don't have a ruling from the court of appeal on the evidence from Isotenics.'

'No, we don't. I talked to the judge about it this morning. In chambers with Templeton.'

'What did he say?' Harry missed the meeting. He was pulling some materials together for the day's witnesses.

'What can he say? He told me that if we don't have a ruling from the court by the time the state rests its case, he is inclined to give us a brief continuance.'

'How long?' says Harry. 'How much time?'

'Three days.'

'Three days? Lotta good that's gonna do.' According to Harry, this is just enough time to have a good anxiety attack.

'Gilcrest said there wasn't much he could do,' I tell him. 'With the jury sequestered, locked away in a hotel with guards to usher them everywhere they go, there is a limit to how long he can hold them and keep the lid on the trial.'

'The state, through Isotenics, is sitting on a pile of evidence, thumbing their nose,' he says.

'We think they are.' I don't want to place too much hope in the unknown.

'You know they are. Otherwise, why hide the ball?' says Harry.

'They can do that? Wait until the trial is over and keep us from getting the stuff?' Ruiz asks.

'The appellate court,' Harry says. 'They can do whatever they want. They can sit on the appeal until the case is over and then decide that, while we had a right to the evidence, the failure to give it to us was not prejudicial – that the failure to deliver didn't affect the outcome of the trial.'

'I don't get it. They can make up the rules like that?' Ruiz, the soldier with scar tissue from nicks and wounds all over his body, looks surprised.

'Welcome to the Middle Ages, son,' says Harry. 'They hold the pencil and wear the robes, so they get to write any fairy tale they like. And unless another set of wizards in black with a bigger wand comes along to slap them around, their fable becomes law – that is, at least as far as you're concerned.'

What Harry means is that if the appellate court realizes it has made a bad decision, they are likely to refuse to certify it for publication. In that case it will apply only to Ruiz. Lawyers would not be allowed to cite the decision as authority in other cases, and because of the decision's limited effect, higher courts would not be likely to waste their time reviewing it – though, in a death case, review to the state supreme court would be automatic. It would be an interesting social survey to find out how many people currently sitting behind bars in penitentiaries in this country are the victims of bad procedural decisions by appellate courts, written opinions that were dropped into a black hole and never certified for publication and therefore skirted review by more reasoned minds.

'Are we ready?' I ask.

Ruiz checks himself in the mirror one last time and takes a deep breath.

Harry nods.

'I just got one question,' says Ruiz.

'Jeez, only one,' says Harry. 'You're lucky.'

'You know, you asked me the other day about the frangible rounds, the bullets,' says Ruiz. 'I couldn't remember whether there were any in the case or not. But I do remember that over the last couple of years I shot a lot of them at the range before I was discharged from the Army. It is possible they were in the clips that were inside the bag.' The way he says this makes me wonder if perhaps there is something else he isn't telling us.

'What I don't understand,' he says, 'is why whoever killed her would have mixed the rounds, used two different kinds of bullets.'

The guard taps on the little window in the door, the signal that the judge is ready to get started.

'I don't have time to explain right now. Stay tuned,' I tell him.

We head to the courtroom, a constellation of guards segregating Harry and me from Ruiz until we get to the counsel table and take our seats. Chapman's mother and sister are in the front row again. Nathan is in the cheap seats today toward the back of the courtroom. His intern must have overslept. It doesn't look as if Jean Kaprosky could make it.

Templeton and his minions are already assembled at their table. A few seconds later the judge takes the bench and instructs the bailiff to bring in the jury.

This morning Templeton does a quick tap dance on our bones. His first witness is the ballistics expert from the county's crime lab.

The witness quickly identifies lands and grooves on the partially deformed lead bullet that correspond with several test bullets fired in the lab through the HK Mark 23, Ruiz's gun.

'Then there is no question in your mind,' says Templeton, 'that the gun that fired at least one of the rounds that struck Madelyn Chapman is that firearm, the pistol identified as People's exhibit six, is that correct?'

'That's right.'

'Let's talk a little about the other round. The frangible round. The bullet that the medical examiner testified fragmented into pieces inside the victim's body. Are you familiar with frangible bullets?'

'I am.'

'Can you tell the jury the purpose behind the design of such a bullet?'

'There are several purposes and several different kinds of frangible bullets. Usually they are subsonic rounds: that is, the velocity of the bullet is designed and intended to remain below the speed of sound, roughly a thousand feet per second.'

'Did the frangible bullet that struck the victim, Madelyn Chapman, fall in this category?'

'Yes.'

'Go on, tell us the purposes of the round.'

'A forty-five-caliber automatic, such as the murder weapon in this case, is generally – unless it's a special manufacture – in the nine-hundred-foot-per-second range in terms of bullet velocity. It is considered a large-bore pistol. Frangible rounds are a perfect fit for such a weapon. They could be used for target shooting where, for reasons of safety because of protocols of close-in fire training, you want to avoid ricochet. They are also used by law enforcement in certain hostage rescue situations – on board airliners, for example. The frangible round is designed to fragment whenever it strikes something harder than itself, so it avoids overpenetration.'

'What is that? Overpenetration. Explain for the jury if you could.'

'In a hostage situation – say, where there are numerous innocent hostages – you would not want to shoot through your intended target, have your bullet pass through one of the hostage takers and hit an innocent victim. So a frangible round would be a good choice. The fragments would be absorbed, contained within the target. Also you wouldn't want to punch holes in an airliner, perhaps have a ricochet go into one of the engines or a fuel tank.'

'What else? Any other purpose for a frangible bullet?'

'They're also used for their lethality,' says the witness.

The way Templeton moves his hands and smiles makes it clear this is the one he is interested in. 'Can you tell the jury a little about the lethal effect of these so-called frangible rounds?'

'Most frangible bullets are used in pistol loads where the velocity is lower than would be the case in a rifle. There is a tremendous transfer of kinetic energy when a bullet hits an object such as bone or flesh – a human target, for example.'

'Go on,' says Templeton.

'If a solid projectile passes cleanly through a target and doesn't encounter any major resistance, much of the energy of the round is dissipated outside the target. This is what is referred to as overpenetration. In a frangible round of the type encountered in this case, overpenetration is eliminated.'

'How is that?' Templeton asks.

'Again, because the frangible bullet is designed to penetrate and to fracture or fragment into multiple small, often tiny pieces the instant it comes in contact with anything harder than itself. As I said earlier, when this happens, virtually all of the unexpended kinetic energy is transferred to the target.'

'Is this why it's more lethal?' says Templeton.

'Yes. The transfer of that much kinetic energy generally produces shock. Most doctors will tell you that it isn't the bullet that kills in many cases, especially if it doesn't hit a vital organ. It's the fact that the victim goes into shock.'

'So the use of a frangible bullet would be particularly lethal?'

'I would say so, yes.'

'Would you say that someone using a frangible bullet fired at another human being was trying to wound them?'

'No.' The witness smiles. 'That's highly unlikely.'

'Would you say that their intention was clearly to kill the person being shot at?'

'Most likely, yes. Even if you struck the person in an area of the body that might otherwise be considered nonlethal, the transfer of kinetic energy would probably send that person into immediate shock. Unless the victim received very prompt medical attention, they would most likely die.'

'So is it your opinion that the person who fired a frangible bullet into the victim, in this case

Madelyn Chapman, would, by the use of that bullet, have indicated a fairly clear intention to kill Madelyn Chapman?'

'Assuming they know what they were doing, I would say so, yes.'

'Let's talk about that: whether the shooter in this case knew what he was doing. You are aware that there were two bullets fired into the victim in this case?'

'Yes.'

'And only one of which was frangible?'

'That's correct.'

'Why would someone, in your opinion, use two different types of bullets fired through the same gun?'

'Objection. Assumes a fact not in evidence,' I say.

Templeton turns and looks at me as if he is mystified.

'We don't know that the frangible round was fired from that weapon,' I say. 'There is no ballistics to confirm that. For all we know, there could have been two weapons fired.'

Templeton moves quickly to dispel the impression that two separate shooters may have acted in concert to kill Chapman. This could present a problem for him. 'We know from the trace evidence of the nitrates,' he says, 'that there was only one firing position, from the railing over the entry.'

'I'll sustain the objection,' says the judge. 'Reframe the question.'

'Assuming that one person, a single shooter, used the same handgun to fire both rounds, in your opinion, why might that shooter choose to load that weapon with two different kinds of rounds, one frangible and one solid?' Templeton asks.

'Probably for reasons of certainty,' says the witness.

'Could you explain?' says Templeton.

'Frangible rounds, while they are lethal and have their purpose, have been known to fail. In some cases they can fragment before impacting the target. The inclusion of a solid round would provide the assurance that the shooter may have wanted that at least one of the rounds would reach the target.'

'So, by including both types of bullets, the perpetrator – the person who killed Madelyn Chapman – would have had lethality, the deadly effect of the frangible round, and certainty, the reliability of the solid round. Is that correct?'

'In my opinion, yes.'

This is neatly done. Without this theory, Templeton faced the prospect that I might be able to argue with some plausibility that two shooters might have been involved. He has now shut that door nicely.

Templeton now starts to work a different angle. He gets the witness to confirm that he examined the fragments of the frangible round under a microscope and subjected several of the small pieces to examination by gas chromatograph and mass spectrometry. In essence this is a chamber in which the minute bullet fragments were burned at a high temperature and the gas emitted passed through a beam of intense light. The machine is able to identify the chemical composition of the particles. The chromatograph once married to the mass spectrometer, in which high-energy electrons bombard the molecules of the item being tested, producing what is in essence a chemical finger-print, no two of which are precisely alike. According to the witness, this allowed the ballistics lab to identify not only the manufacturer of the frangible bullet but the customer who bought it.

'Can you tell the jury,' says Templeton, 'if frangible ammunition of the type found here – the frangible fragments taken from the body of the victim Madelyn Chapman – is generally available to the shooting public, to the average citizen over the counter in a gun shop?'

'No.'

'Well, then, who is the customer, the end user, of this kind of ammunition?'

'Generally there are two: law enforcement and the military.'

'And can you tell us, do you know where this particular bullet, the frangible round used to kill Madelyn Chapman, came from?'

'Yes. The Lake City Army Ammunition Plant in Independence, Missouri. A small-arms ammunition manufacturer for the federal government.'

'And do you know who the intended end user, the ultimate consumer of this particular round, was? Which particular agency of the federal government?'

'It was shipped to the United States Army, Quartermaster Corps.'

'Thank you. Your witness.' Templeton comes down and pushes the stool underneath the rostrum.

I wait a second for him to clear the aisle before I take the podium.

'You say you fired several test rounds through the Mark Twenty-three pistol, the one identified as People's exhibit six, is that correct?'

362

'Yes. In order to acquire sample bullets against which to compare the one surviving bullet recovered during the autopsy.'

'And did *you* fire those test rounds, or did someone else fire them?'

'No. *I* fired them.'

'Let me ask you: When you fired these test rounds, did you mount the silencer, the noise suppressor that was found along with the weapon at the scene, on the firearm, or did you fire the test shots without it?'

'Both,' says the witness. 'With the suppressor and without.'

'Why did you do that? Can you tell the jury?'

'Because we wanted to see if there were variations in the ballistics, the microscopic marks that were left on the test rounds.'

'Were there?'

'No.'

'Do you know why there were none?'

'If the suppressor is functioning properly, there shouldn't be any variations. The bullet should pass cleanly through the bore of the suppressor without making physical contact so that it would leave no detectible striations on the bullet other than those imparted by the lands and grooves inside the barrel of the firearm itself.'

'And that was the case in this instance?'

'Yes.'

'When you fired these test rounds, did you notice any difference or variation in the recoil of the firearm when the silencer, the suppressor, was on the weapon as opposed to when it was not?'

The witness smiles from the stand.

'Your Honor, I'm going to object,' says Templeton. 'Exceeds the scope of direct.'

'Your Honor, the state opened the issue of test shots in the lab to confirm ballistics. I think we have a right to explore the area.'

'I'm going to allow the question. You can answer,' says Gilcrest.

'Yes. There was a marked difference in the recoil with the suppressor on the weapon as opposed to not having it on.'

'Perhaps you can explain to the jury what recoil is,' I say.

'It's the rebounding effect of a firearm as it is discharged. Law of physics: for every action there is an equal and opposite reaction.'

'Is this commonly known by people who shoot as "kick"? That when they shoot a pistol or a rifle, they might say it "kicks"?'

'Yes.'

'Can you tell the jury how much kick, how much recoil, the forty-five automatic, that gun on the table, People's exhibit six, produced when you fired the test shots.'

'I didn't measure recoil,' he says.

'But, since you had a chance to shoot the firearm both with the suppressor, the silencer, mounted on the weapon as well as without it, which way produced the most recoil?'

'Without the suppressor.'

'So there was more kick without the suppressor than there was when the silencer was mounted on the gun?'

'That's correct.'

'Can you give us an approximation as to how much less?'

'It was noticeable,' he says.

'Isn't it a fact that there is literature, data, to support the proposition that recoil is reduced by as much as thirty percent through the use of a silencer on a handgun?'

'That sounds about right.'

'Is it true that the silencer, especially on a large handgun, acts as a muzzle brake?'

'Yes.'

'Can you tell the jury what a muzzle brake is?'

'It's a device that can be applied, attached, to both pistols and rifles that serves to dispel some of the physical forces that produce recoil.'

'Usually attached to the end of the barrel, right?'

'Not always. Sometimes,' he says.

'But in this case the attachment of that silencer to that pistol' – I point to the table where both items are on display in front of the jury – 'served not only to suppress the sound of the shots fired but also to reduce recoil, right?'

'Yes.'

'Would the reduction of recoil generally produce more accuracy—'

'Not necessarily.'

'Let me finish my question.'

'Sorry.'

'Would the reduction of recoil generally produce or permit more accuracy in the firing of a second shot that is fired within close proximity to an initial or first shot – say, where the shots are fired within a millisecond of each other?'

He looks at me, thinks about this. 'Ah. Yes. That would probably be the case.'

'And it wouldn't matter whether the shooter was an expert marksman or a novice: the application of that silencer to that weapon by the reduction of recoil would serve to steady and make more accurate the second shot regardless, would it not?'

The question seems to produce a little nervous

tic in the witness's left eye; the lid flickers a couple of times. 'Yes. I suppose that's true.'

'Let me ask you about the two different types of bullets used in this case: the solid lead bullet and the frangible bullet. Were you able to determine that the frangible bullet was actually fired from that gun, the one in evidence, the Mark Twenty-three?' I point toward the table.

'No.'

'So the only bullet that allowed you to make a definitive identification as to the firearm used was the solid lead bullet?'

'That's correct.'

'And if, as in this case, the killer, the shooter or shooters—'

'Objection: assumes a fact not in evidence.'

'Overruled.' Gilcrest splits the hair and comes down on my side.

'If, as in this case, the perpetrator took the time to collect the spent brass and take it with him or dispose of it so that the police couldn't find it, as was done here – and if, just assuming, two frangible bullets had been fired instead of a frangible and a solid bullet – it would have been impossible to trace the bullets that killed Madelyn Chapman to that particular weapon, wouldn't it?'

The witness mulls this over, offers an expression of concession, nodding his head slightly. 'That's . . . that's true.'

'So, by using a solid round, the killer made sure that your laboratory would be able to trace the bullet that killed Madelyn Chapman to that weapon, isn't that true?'

'No. He took the chance that we would be able to trace the round to that firearm. It was always possible that the lead bullet could have been sufficiently damaged in firing that it would have been unusable for ballistics comparison.'

'Yes, but if he'd used a frangible round instead of the solid round, he would have made sure it couldn't be connected to that handgun, isn't that true?'

Grudgingly he nods. 'Yes.'

'That's all I have, thank you.'

'Redirect.' Templeton is off his chair and on his feet. He scrambles to the stool, pulls it out from under the rostrum, and mounts it almost in a single motion.

'Is there any evidence, any ballistic evidence, that the silencer was used during the commission of the murder of Madelyn Chapman?'

'No. Not that I'm aware of.'

'So it's entirely possible that the handgun in question was used for the commission of this crime without that silencer attached, is that not correct?'

'Yes. That's possible.'

Templeton has a problem: the noise of the two shots that killed Chapman. If any of the neighbors heard them, the cops would have a more definitive fix on the time of death. They don't. He goes to work on this.

'Can you tell the jury, how loud is that handgun?' He points to the pistol on the table.

'Suppressed or unsuppressed?'

'Objection: the witness is not a sound and noise expert.'

'I'm not asking for scientific measures,' says Templeton, 'only as to within his common experience, having fired the weapon.'

'I'll allow it,' says Gilcrest.

'Without the silencer, is that handgun, in your opinion, loud?'

'It's quite loud.'

'Did you have to wear ear protection when you conducted the test firing of the weapon?'

'I did.'

'Do you know – can you tell the jury – in your opinion, would it be possible for shots fired from that pistol inside of a house on the ocean, perhaps with the noise of the surf in the background, to be heard in adjoining houses or on the street?'

'I don't know.'

'Objection: calls for a conclusion beyond the expertise of this witness.'

'Sustained.'

Templeton fumes, then tries again.

'Assuming the shots were fired in rapid succession,' says Templeton, 'two of them: would they be distinct as gunshots to someone, say, situated inside another house perhaps a hundred feet away, with several walls in between?'

'Same objection, Your Honor.'

'Your Honor, the witness has fired thousands of test rounds; he has years of experience firing handguns, all kinds of firearms. He knows what they sound like inside of a building and out and whether two shots fired in rapid succession are likely to be recognized as that: two distinct gunshots. That's all I'm asking.' Templeton makes it sound like a plea.

'I'll allow the witness to answer that narrow question,' says the judge. 'Would two shots fired in quick succession be distinguishable as gunshots outside a house under the conditions specified by counsel?' Gilcrest has a finger shaking at the witness.

'In my opinion – in my experience – it's possible

that they would not. They would probably sound like muffled pops.'

'Is there a reason for that, within the realm of ballistics?' says Templeton.

'Yes. The fact that the forty-five automatic pistol is subsonic has a dampening effect on the sound. There are two factors affecting noise as regards gunfire, one being muzzle blast and the other the supersonic crack of the bullet as it breaks the sound barrier. The second factor is not present with a forty-five automatic.'

'Thank you,' says Templeton.

'Mr Madriani,' says Gilcrest. 'Anything more?'

'Very briefly, Your Honor.' I take the rostrum.

'Did you examine the bore of the sound suppressor, the silencer, in evidence in this case before you fired your test rounds through it?' I ask the witness.

'I did.'

'And did you find any gunpowder residue inside the bore of the suppressor when you examined it, before you fired it?'

'Yes, I did. There was residue in the bore of the suppressor.'

'Wouldn't that indicate that it had been used?'

'Yes. But there was no way to tell when it was used. It's possible that it was used the day of the murder. It's also possible that it was used on some prior occasion and put back in the bag without being cleaned. There was no way to determine how much residue was present or how long it had been there.'

The witness takes back a sizable portion of what he has given.

'Was there any rust in the bore?'

'No. Not that I could see.'

'Wouldn't there be some signs of rust inside the bore if the gunshot residue had been left inside the bore for any length of time?'

'Not necessarily. It would depend on the conditions of storage.'

'One final question. If the handgun, that handgun, was used with the silencer attached during the commission of this crime, would anyone outside of the Chapman residence, in your opinion, have been able to hear the two shots that killed her?'

He swallows a little, then looks up at me. 'No.'

'Where did you learn about recoil and suppressors as a muzzle brake?' Ruiz chews on a sandwich from the vending machine, the plastic wrapper on the table under his hand as we talk across the small stainless-steel table in the holding cell.

'I read a lot,' I tell him. 'I've been educated by other lawyers who have laid waste to me because they knew more than I did. And on occasion I've learned the hard way: by clients who have lied to me. Just as you have.'

He stops chewing and looks up at me directly in the eyes.

'What are you saying?'

'That you didn't tell us the truth about the rounds in the case. You knew they were frangible, didn't you?'

'I told you this morning: I forgot they were there.'

'No, you knew they were there. Where did they come from? Tell me. It's too late to play games. Who gave them to you?'

'Like I said, they were issued in the Army.'

'Not to just anybody, they weren't. Where did

you get them? Why were they issued to you?'

'For training,' he says. 'I told you it's what I did. I trained other soldiers. We did a lot of shooting in shooting houses.'

'What's that supposed to mean?'

'Situational stuff,' he says. 'Listen, trust me, you don't need to know. It doesn't have anything to do with this, with Chapman or Isotenics or any of this.'

'It does now. Templeton is bearing down on you. He's established that the rounds were purchased by the Army.'

'That's true.'

'He's going to prove that you were in the Army and that the gun in question was issued to you.'

'So it would make sense that the bullets would be in the bag with the gun, right? You made the point,' he says. 'Answered my question, the one I asked this morning. I think the jury is starting to understand what's happening here.'

'Good. Then they're a leg up on me,' I tell him.

'Listen, you gotta believe me. I didn't kill her. I had no reason to kill her.'

'Templeton hasn't gotten to that yet, but you can believe that he's working his way there.'

'The reason the killer used the solid round,' he says, 'is because he needed to tie that bullet to my gun. It's the frame-up. You made the point in court. Crystal clear,' he says. 'The jury is getting the picture. I know they are.'

'Listen, if you start trying to mind-meld with a jury, guessing what's going on behind twelve sets of eyes, you're likely to get the shock of your life when they come back with a verdict. What they heard today is that that bullet, the one that exploded inside Chapman's head, was purchased for use by the Army. Before he's finished, Larry Templeton is going to take that fractured bullet and sprinkle bread crumbs all the way from the tiniest piece right to your doorstep unless you tell me what's going on.'

'Nothing,' he says. 'Nothing's going on. I've told you everything I know about Chapman. I don't know who killed her or why. All I know is she was scared.'

CHAPTER
TWENTY-FOUR

With Sims holding us at bay at Isotenics, Templeton would like to wrap up the case before damaging evidence has a chance to erupt from that quarter. Harry may be gloomy concerning a decision from the court of appeal, but at this point Templeton is in the dark as much as we are. If there is anything explosive sitting in Chapman's files or on her computer, that dam could burst at any moment.

Templeton doesn't waste any time. In the afternoon he does what I have expected: he keeps it linear and goes for the jugular.

Major Hammon Ellis is an officer assigned to the Pentagon in Washington. Part of his duties involve custody of military records for small arms as well as firearms training at several military posts. One of these is Fort Bragg, North Carolina, Emiliano's last assigned duty post.

Ellis sits bolt upright in the witness chair. He is decked out in his dress uniform, gold oak leaves on the epaulets of his jacket. He is working from a manila folder in his lap, shuffling papers and identifying forms maintained by DOD to keep track

373

of government small arms, pistols, rifles, and automatic weapons and to identify the soldiers to whom they are assigned.

Templeton makes quick work of the chain of possession on the murder weapon.

'Heckler and Koch Mark Twenty-three forty-five-caliber semiautomatic.' The witness is looking at a folder with several sheets of paper. 'Yes, our records show that model with the serial number as stated was shipped to Fort Bragg, North Carolina, on the date indicated on the form.'

Copies of this have been handed to us, and Templeton moves the form into evidence. Without objection he nods toward his computer tech and suddenly the form in question appears on the screen for the jury to view.

'Your Honor, I would ask the court to take notice that the serial number on the weapon as set forth on this form is the same as that serial number on the handgun identified and marked as People's exhibit six. The Heckler and Koch, Mark Twenty-three forty-five-caliber semiautomatic pistol. In order to save time and avoid confusion, with the court's permission we will refer to the exhibit number with regard to the other forms rather than the serial number.' Templeton wants no mistake in the minds of jurors on this point. The firearm the witness is talking about is the murder weapon.

'Any objection, Mr Madriani?'

'No, Your Honor.'

Templeton turns back to the witness. 'Then let me ask you, is that an accurate copy of the original form in your file?'

'Yes, it is.'

'Can you tell the jury what that form represents? What it shows?'

'That the firearm in question, what you have identified as People's exhibit six, was shipped from Picatinny Arsenal in New Jersey to Fort Bragg on the date set forth on the form.'

Templeton directs the tech to leave the form on the visualizer while he has the witness identify another piece of paper from DOD, this one with a date and signature clearly visible. He moves it into evidence and it goes up on the visualizer next to the first form.

'Can you tell the jury what this form represents?'

'This is the document used by the Department of Defense for military standard requisitioning and issue procedures for small arms. When a weapon owned by the government, in this case the Department of Defense, is issued to anyone in the military, they are required to sign the form evidencing their receipt and possession of the weapon.'

'And does the firearm in question become their personal weapon, so to speak, for military purposes at that point?'

'It does.'

'So they don't have to check it in and out every day?'

'In some cases. For example, in basic training that may be required. But they only have to sign for it once, when the weapon is assigned to them, and then again on the required form when it is formally surrendered or returned to government stores, sometimes upon reassignment to a new post, or when the person is discharged from the military.'

'And in this case, is the form on the screen an accurate copy of the original in your folder?'

'It is.'

'And can you identify for us the weapon that this document relates to?'

'It's the same as People's exhibit six. You can see the serial number as well as the description, make, and model of the firearm on the line just above the signature.'

'And can you make out the signature? Can you tell us whose name that is?'

'The name in the signature block on the form is Emiliano Michael Ruiz.'

'So the form in question' – Templeton points at its DOD number and date up on the screen – 'would indicate that the firearm in question, what we have identified as People's exhibit six, was issued to Emiliano Ruiz on the date set forth, is that correct?'

'Yes.'

Templeton nods. 'Can you tell us, are you acquainted with Mr Ruiz?'

'Not personally, no.'

'Would you know him if you saw him?'

'Yes.'

'And how would you know what he looked like?'

'From military records,' says the witness. 'I had occasion to examine his Army records – including photographs, his military ID number – which also contained documents bearing his signature.'

'Is Mr Ruiz in the courtroom today?'

'Yes, he is.'

'Could you identify him for the jury.'

Before the witness can point, Ruiz stands up at our table. We have been prepared for this and decided that it would be best that Emiliano not be caught sitting or slouching at the table as if skulking from the jury.

'That's him,' says the witness.

'May the record reflect that the witness has

identified the defendant, Emiliano Ruiz,' says Templeton. 'Now, let me ask you, does your office or your department have any records evidencing the transfer of this weapon to anyone else?'

'No.'

'Does your office or your department have any records evidencing the surrender or return of this firearm by Mr Ruiz back to the military or to the Department of Defense upon his discharge from the military three years ago?'

'No, we do not.'

'Was Mr Ruiz required by law to return this weapon to the military – to turn it in at the time of his discharge?'

'He was.'

'But he failed to do so, is that correct?'

'Apparently,' says the witness.

With each question, the noose tightens.

'So the weapon in question, that handgun' – Templeton points to the evidence table – 'People's exhibit six, is actually property belonging to the United States government, is that right?'

'It is.'

Templeton has the witness testify as to Ruiz's skill with a handgun: the fact that he was at one time, according to records, on the Army pistol team and that his last assignment was as a range instructor at Fort Bragg. He offers no specifics. After some tugging and word twisting, Templeton gets the major to agree that Ruiz could be considered a 'world-class' shooter. I object on grounds that the term is vague, and the judge strikes it from the record and instructs the jury to disregard it. As if he can unring the gong.

Templeton then slows the beat a bit. He casts

about in the stack of papers on the podium until he finds what he wants.

'Let me ask you, Major, do you also serve as liaison in the Pentagon for small-arms training at certain military bases, including Fort Bragg in North Carolina?'

'I do.'

'In this capacity, are you familiar with small-arms training techniques?'

'I'm not an instructor but I am familiar with techniques and training regimen.'

'Are you familiar with firearms training techniques that are involved in what is called CQBs, otherwise known as close-quarters battles?'

'I am.'

'Can you explain to the jury what is involved in close-quarters-battle training?'

'It depends on the unit involved, but for the most part it focuses on small-group team techniques. The coordination used in a close-quarters assault. It's designed to teach techniques that might be used for the assault on a building to capture it, or possibly for hostage rescue or to take prisoners. The training would emphasize selective fire so that only intended targets are shot: shooting on the move, engaging multiple targets, how to sweep an area with the muzzle of a firearm to avoid friendly-fire accidents. It would also include procedures and practices for entry so as to provide covering fire for members of the team.'

'Would this involve training with live fire? Weapons that are actually loaded with live ammunition?'

'Oh, yes. Again, depending on the unit, it could be anything from hundreds to thousands of hours.

It would involve intensive live-fire training in realistic situations so that the techniques that are imparted become instinctive, instilled,' Ellis says.

'By *instinctive* you mean second nature?'

'Yes.'

'Do these techniques take a long time to learn?'

'To learn them well, so that they can be performed reliably in actual armed confrontations, yes. In almost any situation it always comes back to training,' says the witness. 'Studies show that what you learn at the instinctive level is what you will do when it comes time to perform, especially under stress.'

'Now let me ask you, with reference to that particular firearm' – Templeton motions toward the table where the Mark 23 is laid out – 'People's exhibit six. To your knowledge, was that model of weapon designed for any specific purpose?'

'Yes. It was designed under contract for the military, Special Operations Command, for use principally in specified situations including close-quarters battle.'

Most of this is included with the literature on the handgun from the manufacturer and in online articles, but the fact that Templeton has someone in uniform on the stand reciting it gives it more credence as it is delivered to the jury.

'Is that why the kit included with the gun contains a silencer – the suppressor?'

'Yes.'

'Oh, by the way, while I'm at it, do you know whether the possession of a silencer, a suppressor, by a private citizen, not a member of the active military, is a violation of law?'

'Objection as to relevance, Your Honor. There is no charge as to that issue.'

Templeton tries to slip one in under the belt.

'Sustained. Move on, Mr Templeton.'

'Just a few more questions, Your Honor.' He regroups. 'So the weapon, People's exhibit six, was specifically designed for applications involved in close-quarters battle?'

'Yes. It could be used in other situations as well.'

Templeton draws the witness back before he can wander too far: 'But it was designed with that in mind, is that right?'

'That's correct. The United States military ceased use of the forty-five automatic as the standard-issue sidearm some years ago. They went to a nine-millimeter pistol manufactured by Beretta at that time.'

'That's a smaller caliber, is that correct? Smaller than the forty-five?'

'That's right.'

'So what was the military trying to achieve by returning to the forty-five automatic in the form of that particular handgun? Again, I'm talking about People's exhibit number six.'

'Lethality,' says the witness.

Templeton turns to look at the jury wide-eyed, as if to say, *Where have we heard that term before?* Templeton's physical gestures and timing are worth the price of admission: his diminutive stature seems to magnify their effect.

'The forty-five automatic has more stopping power.' Ellis continues testifying right through Templeton's pantomime.

'One final point. You stated earlier that this model of firearm, People's exhibit six, was designed in part for close-quarters combat. With regard to training in that area, have you ever heard the term *double tap* used?'

'Yes.'

'Can you tell the jury what the term means within the realm of military training?'

'A double tap is a technique for firing two shots in quick succession into a single target.'

'And can you tell the jury the purpose of the double tap – what it's intended to accomplish?'

'To make sure that a target that goes down does not get up again,' says the witness.

'To make sure that the target has been killed, in other words?'

The witness nods. 'In a word, yes.'

'And would this technique, the use of the double tap, be instinctively instilled by training through close-quarters-battle techniques in those who underwent such training?'

'If the training was done properly, yes.'

'So that it might become second nature?'

'I would say so, yes.'

'Do you know whether the defendant Emiliano Michael Ruiz was schooled in these techniques, methods of close-quarters battle, and specifically the application of the double tap?'

'Yes. He was.'

Templeton turns on his stool toward me. 'Your witness,' he says.

Early Saturday morning, in the middle of a trial, I am camped out at the office, going over damage assessments.

The testimony by Major Ellis put some sizable holes in us. But this morning I am thinking that it could have been worse. During his testimony I had one of those moments of sudden revelation, as when the finger of the grim reaper brushes your shoulder. There was the definite sensation that

Templeton had dropped something in my path that he wanted me to touch.

Unless I am wrong, Hammon Ellis was the evidentiary equivalent of live ordnance, high explosives attached to a trembler switch just waiting for me to touch him the wrong way.

Templeton set the fuse when he had Ellis testify that he, the witness, had access to Ruiz's personnel files and used it to compare signatures. At that moment I realized that the prosecution knew more about my client's background than I did. Templeton is no doubt being fed information by the feds, who would like to wrap the case up and make it go away as quickly as possible. The fact that Templeton can get willing cooperation out of the Pentagon in the form of witnesses is an indication of their position.

Other than the broad field of training with firearms, Templeton never asked Ellis for specifics regarding what it was that Ruiz had done in the military. He left this dangling in front of me for a reason. He wanted me to tug on it. That way he could have picked the pieces of what was left of me off the courtroom walls after the answer.

Without knowing exactly what Ellis would say in front of the jury, I had to steer clear. But I am convinced that any question regarding Ruiz's background would have gone off in my face. The fact that Templeton would set this trap causes me to think that Emiliano's repeated assurances that none of this is relevant are wrong.

On cross, all I could do with Ellis was to get the witness to acknowledge that the original military kit containing the murder weapon also included a 'laser-light-aiming module,' the missing laser sight. The witness went so far as to admit that if this sight had been mounted on the pistol the evening of the murder, it would have made targeting easier. The question is, for whom?

There is something Ruiz is not telling us. While his skill with a handgun is clear, the details of what he did in the Army, besides range training, is a looming mystery that now has my stomach producing acid around the clock.

Efforts to plumb this with subpoenas served on the personnel office at Fort Bragg as well as the Pentagon have netted nothing beyond copies of the records already in our files, the ones with a seven-year hole in them. Phone calls by Herman along with a three-day trip to North Carolina turned up nothing. When Herman told them what he was looking for, he was even denied admission onto the base at Fort Bragg. With the publicity surrounding the trial, and with the political heat turned up under the IFS program, the screws have been tightened by the brass at the Pentagon, so that any information bearing on our case is now *verboten*.

As I'm sitting in my chair, weighing all of this, I feel a vibration on my belt. A second later the familiar chime on my cell phone rings. I take it out of the holster and check the incoming number. It's Harry's home phone. I flip open the phone and hit the talk button.

'Hello.'

'Where the hell are you? I called your house, there's no answer.'

'Sarah is off for the weekend with some friends. I'm at the office.'

'Guess what. I've got some news for you. Remember the name you were looking for?' asks Harry.

'What name?'

'The day we were going over the evidence. You wanted to know the name of the person who called Chapman's house from the restaurant the evening she was killed – who it was who called the cops.'

'Yeah.'

'You'll never guess.'

'Keep me in suspense,' I say.

'Maxwell Rufus. As in Karr, Rufus, and Associates. Ruiz's employer,' says Harry. 'And there's more.'

To pick up the slack, Harry hired another investigator, one of the larger firms downtown. Their report came by fax to his house late last night.

'They must work all hours,' he says. 'I found it on the floor in front of the machine in my study when I got up this morning. And the thing ran out of paper, so there may be more. Karr, Rufus is in trouble. According to the information in the report, the firm is facing serious financial problems, a settlement in a class-action death case, that could push them into bankruptcy.'

Rufus is one of Templeton's witnesses who is probably nearing the on-deck circle. We are guessing that he is likely to be up on the stand Monday or Tuesday.

'Are you sure of the information?'

'The report has an awful lot of detail, including a court-case number. It was filed in Texas eighteen months ago. They're on the brink,' says Harry.

According to the information, five years ago, while expanding their empire into the state of Texas, Karr, Rufus swallowed up a poorly operated competitor in Houston. Two years into the deal, one of their uniformed security guards apparently started stalking a female employee of one of the

large accounting agencies in a high-rise in
Houston's tony financial district. Karr, Rufus had
the contract to provide security in the building.

To makes things worse, the guard in question,
who was armed under the terms of the contract,
had a prior felony conviction for assault and
domestic violence in another state, something
Karr, Rufus claimed they didn't know anything
about.

'The problem is,' says Harry, 'according to the
FBI, which did a routine criminal background
check on the man when he was hired – part of the
normal background check required by the state for
licensing of security guards – Karr, Rufus was
notified in writing of the guy's felony conviction
almost a year earlier. How it slipped through the
cracks, nobody knows. The employee had lied to
the company when he applied for the job, checking
the box on the application that said *no prior
criminal record.*

'It hit the fan on August eighteenth three years
ago,' Harry goes on. 'The guard walked into the
accounting firm's main office on the twenty-second
floor armed with two semiautomatic nine-
millimeter Glocks and started shooting employees.
When the melee was over, seven people were dead,
including the guard, who shot himself along with
the woman who was the object of his affections.
The civil complaint was for seventy-five million
dollars and change,' says Harry. 'Karr, Rufus
settled out of court under terms of a confidential
settlement. But they had to borrow money because
the settlement was in excess of their insurance
coverage. The firm's headquarters in La Jolla was
used as security on the note, which is due in ninety
days. According to the information in the report,

unless they can refinance the note – and so far they haven't been able to – Karr, Rufus is insolvent. The bank will land on everything they have, including the building in La Jolla. Rufus won't be able to make payroll,' says Harry.

CHAPTER TWENTY-FIVE

This morning Larry Templeton positions himself to lay one more stone on top of the platform that is beginning to crush Emiliano Ruiz.

Gilcrest's earlier ruling that the state may not use the security tape of Chapman and Ruiz on the couch in her office because of its prejudicial effect has forced Templeton to do the next best thing. He calls Karen Rogan to the stand.

Rogan is the only firsthand witness who saw any part of the events shown on the tape, even though from the film it appears that she was in the room only briefly.

Templeton has already had a chance to evaluate Rogan during Sims's motion to quash the evidence that is still bottled up out at Isotenics. Rogan was not entirely cooperative during that outing, and Templeton knows it. He seems tentative in his approach with her.

'What is your position at Isotenics?'

'Personal assistant.'

He is looking down at the podium, checking to make sure he has all the items covered in his notes.

'To whom?' He looks up and realizes that the

question isn't clear to the witness. 'For whom did you provide these services?'

'At the present time, for Mr Havlitz,' she says.

'No. No. That's not what I mean. Before that. Before Mr Havlitz.'

'Who did I work for?'

'Yes.'

'Madelyn Chapman.'

'So you were Ms Chapman's personal assistant, is that correct?'

'Objection: leading the witness.' The objection is weak. The judge would probably overrule it, but he doesn't get the chance.

Templeton rephrases the statement into a question before Gilcrest can rule. 'What was your position in regards to Ms Chapman?'

The game here is one of control. With the objection, Rogan's eyes dart toward me. It doesn't take a palm reader to anticipate that Rogan might not be comfortable testifying about the events in Chapman's office that afternoon. I try to give her a signal: she has friends in court.

'I'm sorry, what was your question?' she says.

'Your position in regards to Ms Chapman: what did you do for her?' Templeton has to work to get her attention back on himself. His task is to control her as best he can.

'Oh. Personal assistant,' she says.

'I take it that that was a position of trust?' Templeton is back to his notes.

'I don't understand what you mean by *trust*,' she snaps at him a little, piercing green eyes from under the red hair.

When he looks up, Templeton seems flummoxed, flustered, suddenly overcome by a convulsion of awkward gestures.

'I didn't mean that you betrayed any trust.' Seen from behind, standing on the stool, his arms waving, he looks like half of a conductor whose orchestra is out of tune. 'What I meant . . . what I meant to say is, did you have ready access to her office, to the private space where Madelyn Chapman worked?'

'I suppose.'

Templeton's misstep in his choice of words has made her wary.

'I mean . . .' Templeton glances over his shoulder at me. He would like to ease into the subject delicately, lead her by the hand into the tulips of the frolic on the couch, but he knows this isn't going to happen.

'What I meant to say is, as Ms Chapman's personal assistant, did you have ready access to her office?'

'At times, yes.'

This isn't the answer Templeton wants.

'What I mean is, did you have to knock before you entered her office?' Templeton wants to show that Rogan caught them in the full bloom of the act because nobody thought to lock the door.

'Sometimes I would knock. It would depend.'

Templeton, who has started out on the wrong foot, now ends up in a hole.

Templeton takes a couple of seconds at the podium to regroup. He drops 'Mr Cute' and gives up trying to be nice. He draws the witness up sharply, bringing her attention to the date in question. 'Did you knock when you entered Madelyn Chapman's office that afternoon, about one o'clock?' he says.

'No, I didn't.'

'Was the door locked?'

'No.'

'So you were able to enter Ms Chapman's office?'

'Yes.'

'And as you entered, what did you see?'

'There was someone in the office with Ms Chapman.'

'And can you tell the jury who this other person was who was in the office?'

'It was Mr Ruiz.'

'Do you mean the defendant, Emiliano Ruiz?'

'Yes.'

Templeton gets into his stride. It seems the key to this witness is a firm hand.

'And what was Mr Ruiz doing as you entered the office?'

'He was seated on the couch next to Ms Chapman.'

'Seated?' Templeton's voice goes up a full octave as he says it. If Templeton was uncertain how far the witness would go in corroborating the contents of the videotape, he now has his answer.

'Did you say *seated*?'

'Yes. As I said, next to Ms Chapman.'

'Are you sure about that?'

'Objection: asked and answered,' I say.

'Sustained.'

Templeton tries to get a word picture of them at least semireclining: 'Where were they on the couch?'

'At the far end. As I recall, Mr Ruiz was at the end of the couch nearest the far wall. And Madelyn – Ms Chapman – was sitting close to him, nearest to me, as I walked in.'

The relative positions of Chapman and Ruiz as stated by her are consistent with the video, though *sitting* is not exactly how I would characterize most of the action on tape.

'Let me ask you, when you walked into the office that afternoon, did Mr Ruiz have his clothes on? Was he fully dressed?' Templeton asks.

'As I recall, to the best of my recollection, I think he was.'

'Was he or wasn't he fully clothed?' says Templeton.

'There was a lot of movement. It all happened so quickly. It's possible they were rearranging their clothing.'

'Rearranging?' says Templeton.

Rogan is bright. She gives him just enough so that Templeton can't have the judge jump on her to demand a straight answer.

At the other end of our table, Harry is leaning back in his chair, one elbow on the armrest with his hand up in front of his mouth, trying to shield the smile.

'What . . . how . . . how do you define *rearranging*?' asks Templeton.

'You know, straightening them. Sort of pulling things together,' she says.

A few of the jurors are now smiling. Before Templeton's eyes, Karen's testimony is transforming a heated happening on the couch, replete with scenes of pink flesh on tape, into a roguish fling in the hay.

'Were they putting their clothes on?'

'No. My recollection is that they were dressed. But as I said, it happened so quickly. As I recall, it's possible Mr Ruiz may have been closing a button on his shirt and Ms Chapman was straightening her skirt.'

From behind, Templeton looks dazed. He thinks about what he's going to say next. 'I'm sure this is very difficult for you . . .'

I suspect it's harder on him.

'. . . but I want you to think very clearly,' he says, 'about the details of what you saw that day.'

She nods innocently from the witness box.

'You say that Mr Ruiz' – he points back with a hand, not looking in the direction of Emiliano – 'was closing a button on his shirt?'

'As I said, it happened very quickly.'

'I understand that. But I want you to be clear.' There is a menacing tone in Templeton's voice as he says this, one notch from cautioning the witness about perjury.

'This movement that you saw: you said you saw movement when you came through the door?' says Templeton. 'Where was this movement? Where did it take place?'

'On the couch.'

'So they were both on the couch?'

'Yes. I think that's what I said. I was only there for an instant and then I left.'

'I understand. How long? No, strike that,' he says. Templeton seems flustered, not sure which way to go. He tries to go back and start over. 'When you opened the door, did you actually enter the room?'

'Yes. I went in a few steps. At least, that's how I remember it.'

'How far is a "few steps"?'

'I don't know. I didn't measure it.'

'Just an estimate?' says Templeton. 'Two feet? Six feet?'

'Maybe three or four feet.'

'So you opened the door and you walked in, maybe three or four feet, and you were looking right at them, correct?'

'No. Actually, as I remember it, I was looking at

some papers in my hand. So I didn't look up right away. That's why I was surprised.'

'Surprised by what?' Templeton thinks he has a hair of the donkey's tail.

'By the rapid movement on the couch.' The hair breaks off. 'That's why I went into the office in the first place,' she says. 'I had some letters for Madelyn – for Ms Chapman – to sign.'

'How long were you there, inside the office?' says Templeton.

'Two, maybe three seconds. It was an awkward moment.'

'I'll bet,' says Templeton.

'Objection.'

'Sustained. The jury will disregard,' says the judge.

If Templeton was hoping for a broad-ranging narrative with color commentary from the witness of the action on the couch, the director's cut of the videotape, he has come up empty.

'So while you were in the room for these two or three seconds, how close would you say Mr Ruiz was to Ms Chapman?'

'Oh, they were quite close.'

'How close?'

'They were up against one another.'

'Up against one another, their bodies touching?'

'Yes.'

'And what were they doing?'

'I'm not sure.'

'Were they touching one another with their hands?'

'As I said, when I looked up, there was a lot of movement. It seemed pretty obvious that they heard me open the door before I looked up and saw them.'

'So there was a lot of furtive movement?' says Templeton.

'I'm sorry. I don't know what that means,' says Rogan.

'Moving around as if they were trying to conceal what was happening?'

'Yes. I would say so. When I looked up, it appeared obvious that there was ... I'm not sure how to put it.'

'Use your own words to describe it.' Templeton is desperate for anything now.

'Well, some physical attraction between them,' says Rogan.

'What do mean by *physical attraction*?'

'Well, it looked as if perhaps they might have been engaged in an embrace when I opened the door,' she says. 'As I said, at that moment, when I came in, I wasn't looking up. So I can't be sure. But I got the sense that I might have interrupted a kiss.'

'A kiss,' he says. 'That's what you saw?'

'As I said, I didn't actually see it.'

'Your Honor, may we approach?' Templeton's had enough. He wants a conference at the side of the bench.

The judge waves us on. Harry and I both head up. Templeton scampers down from the stool and has to run to stay ahead of us. Gilcrest hits the white-noise button on the bench.

'Your Honor, this is absurd. It's ridiculous,' Templeton is sputtering before he gets to the stairs leading to the judge's platform. 'The witness's testimony is utterly inconsistent with what's on the tape. Your Honor, you saw the contents of the videotape. Does the witness's testimony sound like an accurate description of what happened? No.'

'Your Honor, she's testifying as to what she saw, her recollections,' I say. 'Besides, it's clear that Mr Templeton would use the videotape to poison the mind of the jury, to create the impression that a fling on the couch constitutes evidence of a long-term affair – that the defendant was starstruck, infatuated with Madelyn Chapman – when there is no evidence of this at all.'

'He was.' Templeton says it with big eyes, his hands extended on his short arms. 'There's evidence he was stalking her.'

'Your interpretation,' I tell him.

'We'll see what the jury thinks,' says Templeton.

'Gentlemen, enough.' Gilcrest wants to bring it back to arguments directed to the court.

'Your Honor, I demand the right to treat this witness as hostile and to use the videotape to impeach her. You saw the tape, Your Honor. She makes it sound as if they were holding hands,' says Templeton.

'That's not what I heard,' I tell the judge. 'She said she saw them rearranging their clothing. And that it was obvious that there was some physical attraction between the two of them.'

'That's what I heard,' says Gilcrest.

' "Physical attraction," ' says Templeton. 'Describing what's on that tape as "some physical attraction" is like calling hell a mild warming trend. Your Honor, that videotape has got to come in. Without it the jury has no sense of what was happening here. Certainly not from this witness.' For Templeton the pictures are worth a million words. He wants to show the sweat of passion on the couch so that the jury can get the full measure of motive on which to hang the ornaments of his evidence.

'I think they got the point,' says Gilcrest. 'And you can certainly argue it to them on closing,' he tells Templeton.

'Argue what?' says Templeton.

'That there was evidence of physical attraction,' says the judge.

'Yeah, that and a kiss,' says Harry.

'Your Honor . . .' Templeton tries, but the judge waves us away from the bench. He has made his ruling: the tape will not come in. Given the choice between warm desire and superheated lust that will poison the jury against the defendant, Gilcrest figures that warm is good enough.

As we leave the bench, the white noise is still on. Harry leans down into Templeton's ear with his hand cupped but loud enough for me to hear it. 'If it makes you feel any better, Larry, we all know that wasn't his hand she was holding.'

Having gotten the crap kicked out of us for a week, Harry can't resist rubbing a little salt in the wound.

From my recollection of the security video in Chapman's office, there was only a momentary glimpse of Karen Rogan in the fish-eye lens as she entered the room, then disappeared. Most of the action was on the couch, where it occurred at speeds approaching that of light, of Chapman and Ruiz pulling their clothes together.

Whether by instinct or intuition, given the understatement that is Rogan's testimony, I can only assume that she is not buying into the argument that Ruiz killed her boss. Call it good taste, but with Chapman dead and her mother and sister in the courtroom, I suspect that Karen Rogan saw little to be gained by offering up the sordid details of an afternoon long ago.

I pass on cross-examination of the witness. The lesson you learn is to leave well enough alone. But I ask the court to keep her available. With the desperate strategy that is shaping up in my mind, it may be necessary to call Rogan in my case in chief, whatever defense we can muster.

CHAPTER
TWENTY-SIX

Having been stung in the morning, Templeton is back with a vengeance in the afternoon. He calls Max Rufus to the stand.

The pieces surrounding Rufus are like a Chinese puzzle. Desperately in need of money and concealing an association with Madelyn Chapman that stretches back more than six years, he might be my top pick for the 'Some-other-dude-did-it'-of-the-Year award, except for one thing: none of the pieces seem to fit.

Harry and I have pounded sand all weekend trying to find a motive as to why Rufus might have killed Chapman. The sorry fact is, unless we've missed something, he had nothing to gain from her death – and much more to lose, given that Ruiz, one of Rufus's own employees, is now in the dock for the murder.

Harry and I have even tallied the missing art glass into the equation. But peddling the *Orb*, even at an inflated price, wouldn't begin to bail Karr, Rufus from their current financial problems.

There is some evidence that Rufus harbored his own passions and may have had his own romantic designs on the victim. But here again there is a problem. It is part of the reason I never bought into the theory that the killing was done by a jilted lover, Ruiz or anyone else.

From what I can see, the murder of Madelyn Chapman is not a crime of passion. It has none of the earmarks, no heated act of rage prompted by a moment of provocation, an argument or rejection. There is no sign of a struggle; even the broken bottle of cleaning fluid on the garage floor appears to have been dropped by Chapman herself when she left her purse there while presumably wrestling to get the box with the *Orb* into the kitchen. The fact that she had to do this alone indicates that there was no one with her in the car, or at the house, who offered to help. Even the cops have figured this one.

The only initial evidence of haste in disposing of evidence is the gun and the silencer. The fact that these were placed in their resting spots to be found later by investigators could be more apparent only if the killer had surrounded them with reflectors and flashing lights. At the same time he disposed of the laser sight, mixed the cartridges, and then got rid of the empties and the rest of the loaded rounds when the deed was done. Why?

I have thought about this long and hard. The only conclusion I can come to is that all of this was done for the same reason that a magician amplifies his movement and uses his hands in exaggerated gestures when performing a trick: in order to produce distraction.

Confronted with a seeming array of items that didn't make sense, and feeling the heat to solve a high-profile murder, prosecutors focused on the gun and the fact that Ruiz had been given his

walking papers when it was learned that he'd
become too familiar with the victim. The illusion
worked, but the fact remains that whoever
murdered Madelyn Chapman did it with precision
and planned it carefully. And unless I'm wrong, it
wasn't done for reasons of lost love.

This morning Rufus is accompanied by another
man. I assume this is his lawyer, probably assigned
by the firm's insurance carrier, trying to head off
any civil claims that might result from Ruiz's
conviction. The lawyer takes a seat inside the
railing behind the prosecution table.

Rufus is sworn and takes the stand. He is
dressed for the occasion, a blue pin-striped power
suit and a solid burgundy silk tie. His shoes are
shined brightly, sleek Italian loafers. The gold-
framed glasses and gray hair exude a kind of
austere, authoritative presence that I am sure
Rufus was going for this morning when he selected
his wardrobe.

A few preliminaries for introduction and identification and Templeton takes him quickly to the point.

'So, you are the managing partner of Karr,
Rufus, and Associates, is that right?'

'Yes.'

'And as such, do you reserve the right to make
final decisions on the hiring and firing of key
employees?'

'I do.'

'Did you consider the defendant, Emiliano Ruiz,
to be a key employee of the firm?'

'Yes. He was hired because of his experience
and his skills acquired in the military. Most of our
top employees have backgrounds either in law
enforcement, the military, or both.'

'And when you say *top employees*,' says

Templeton, 'how would you characterize the duties and responsibilities of these employees when they come to work for you?'

'Usually they would be in supervisory positions, heading up particular security details. We're not talking uniformed night watchmen or regular security guards here,' he says. 'Executive protection, both in the United States and abroad, is a large part of what we do. The employees we hire to perform these duties would be the crème de la crème of the industry,' he says. 'People who are already well trained, seasoned, and prepared to hit the ground running. Generally they would require a minimum of training, mostly in company procedures and coordination.'

'And in your opinion the defendant, Mr Ruiz, was such a man?'

'I thought he was.' Rufus glances toward our table with noticeable disdain as he says it. The key for Rufus is to distance himself from Ruiz and to show that he did everything a responsible employer could in supervising his employees; that the moment he discovered there was a problem, he dealt with it and did so decisively.

'But when you hired him you believed that he had the skills to perform the job?'

'I did. Yes.'

'When did it first come to your attention that there was a problem with Mr Ruiz?'

'It would have been about eighteen months ago. I was notified by one of our clients that there was a problem involving Mr Ruiz.'

'And who was that client?'

'Isotenics, Incorporated.'

'The company operated by the victim, Madelyn Chapman?'

'That's correct.'

'In his job, to your knowledge, did Mr Ruiz have contact with Ms Chapman on a regular basis?'

'He did. He headed up her personal security detail. He provided executive protection for Ms Chapman at home and when she was traveling.'

'In that capacity, did the defendant have access to Ms Chapman's home?'

'Yes. He was assigned to sleep in a separate room in the house on occasion in order to provide twenty-four-hour protection.'

'Did he have a key to Ms Chapman's house?'

'He did.'

'Before we leave that question, the question of the key, at some point in time, was Mr Ruiz removed from Ms Chapman's personal security detail by your firm?'

'He was.'

'And to your knowledge were the locks changed at Ms Chapman's house shortly after he was relieved of these duties?'

'Yes, they were.'

Templeton does this neatly, answering the question why someone with a key would have to break into Chapman's house through a window in order to kill her. At the same time he showers Emiliano with the damaging innuendo that the locks were changed because he was perceived as a threat. According to Ruiz, the locks were changed at his suggestion after Chapman approached him for some extra security, off the books, after the detail was dropped. Because of the elaborate security system, Chapman called Rufus's firm to oversee the work on the new locks. This is the only reason Rufus knows the locks were changed.

'In that regard, would Mr Ruiz have been familiar with the security system installed in the victim's home?'

'Yes, he would.'

'Would he know how to determine whether that system was on or off at any given time?'

'Yes.'

'And would he be familiar with the layout of the house?'

'Certainly, from having stayed there. Overnight.' Rufus tries to put emphasis on the last word, hinting to the jury in an effort to fill in the blanks missing from Karen Rogan's earlier testimony. There is little question that Templeton would have prepped him on this.

'You stated earlier that at some point it became necessary to remove Mr Ruiz from the personal security detail, the assignment involving executive protection for the victim, Madelyn Chapman. Is that correct?'

'Yes, there was a problem, as I said.'

Templeton nails down the time frame when this occurred and then steps out onto the ice. 'And what was the nature of that problem?'

'I was told that Mr Ruiz had engaged in some unprofessional—'

'Objection: hearsay.'

'Sustained,' says Gilcrest.

'At some point were you shown the contents of a security videotape involving Ms Chapman and Emiliano—'

'Objection.' I'm on my feet.

'Sustained. Mr Templeton!' Gilcrest gives him a stern look. 'The jury is to disregard the question. Mr Templeton, any more of this and I will see you in chambers,' he says. 'Now proceed.' If Templeton were closer, the judge would rap him with the gavel.

'What was your understanding of what had happened regarding Mr Ruiz at Isotenics?'

'Objection: hearsay, calls for speculation.'

'Sustained.' The judge is now looking down at the Death Dwarf with a cold stare.

Templeton is having trouble getting at it. He stops for a moment, shuffling the papers on the podium in front of him until he finds the note he's looking for.

'On May twenty-fifth last year, did you receive a telephone call from Madelyn Chapman?'

'I did.'

Templeton nods. Back on track. 'And during the course of that telephone call, what did Ms Chapman tell you?'

'She demanded that I terminate her personal security detail and specifically requested that Mr Ruiz be removed from that detail immediately.'

'Why? Did she say why she wanted this done?'

'She said that Mr Ruiz had become too familiar and that he had made inappropriate advances toward her, or words to that effect. I can't recall exactly how she phrased it.'

'And did you ask for details from Ms Chapman during this telephone conversation?'

'I did.'

'And what did she say?'

'She said that if I wanted details, I should look at the contents of a security videotape that was taken in her office the day before.'

Templeton would go back to the videotape and ask Rufus what he saw on it, but he knows the judge would come off the bench and beat him to death with the gavel.

'And did you remove Mr Ruiz from the security detail?'

'I did. Immediately,' he says. 'I assigned him to other duties.'

'Executive protection duties?' says Templeton.

'No. Standard watch duties. Night watchman,' says Rufus. 'While we conducted an investigation of Mr Ruiz's conduct.'

'Did you participate in that investigation yourself?'

'I did.'

'And did you give any instructions to Mr Ruiz at the time that you removed him from the security detail? I'm specifically referring to instructions regarding Ms Chapman.'

'Yes. I told him that he was not to go near her. He was to remain away from and off of the campus at Isotenics; he was not to go near her house, or to have any contact with her personally, in writing or by phone.'

'And did you consider these instructions to Mr Ruiz concerning the victim, Ms Chapman, to be conditions of his continued employment with your firm? That any violation would lead to his immediate job termination?'

'Yes, I did.'

There is a lot of back-scratching going on here, questions that I suspect have been inserted by the insurance carrier as a condition of cooperation by Rufus with the prosecution.

'Did you tell Mr Ruiz that his refraining from any contact with Ms Chapman was a strict condition of his continued employment?'

'I did.'

'Let me ask you a question. After Mr Ruiz was removed from the Chapman security detail, did you have occasion, during the course of this investigation, to observe his activities both on and off duty, and did you take videotape recordings of some of that activity?'

'Yes, I did.'

'And why did you do that?'

'I had reason to believe that, notwithstanding the fact that I had specifically instructed Mr Ruiz to avoid any contact with Ms Chapman, he was in fact following and observing her at different times. Again, after I had instructed him to stay away.'

'And where did this information come from?'

'An employee at Isotenics, Incorporated.'

'Can you tell the jury the name of that employee?'

'Victor Havlitz.'

'And who is Victor Havlitz?'

'He is currently the acting CEO of Isotenics, Incorporated. At the time he was vice president in charge of marketing.'

'So, based on information that Mr Havlitz had seen Mr Ruiz observing Ms Chapman, you conducted surveillance of Mr Ruiz. Is that correct?'

'Yes.'

'And what did you observe during this surveillance?'

'That in fact Mr Ruiz, the defendant, was following Madelyn Chapman and watching her. That from what I could see and observe, he was stalking her.'

'Objection, Your Honor! This is nothing but pure speculation on the part of the witness.'

'Your Honor, the witness is testifying as to what he saw.'

'I'll allow it. Mr Madriani, you'll have your chance to cross-examine the witness.'

I take my seat.

'And did you take videotape and photographs of this activity involving Mr Ruiz following and, as you say, stalking Madelyn Chapman?' Having been allowed through the tollgate, Templeton jumps on the stalking charge and tries to ride it like a hobbyhorse.

'I did.'

Templeton has his detective rummage through the evidence box on their table and comes up with a small digital videotape and three sets of photographs. The photographic prints are selected frames from the video as well as still shots. One of these goes to the judge, one to us, and the third to the witness on the stand.

'Do you recognize the photographs that have just been handed to you?'

Rufus flips through them, six pages in all.

'I do.'

'Can you tell the court what these photographs depict?'

'They are frames of the videotapes that I took along with some still photographs.'

'Were these taken during the course of your investigation of Mr Ruiz?'

'They were.'

Five of the frames show Ruiz standing, looking at Chapman in the distance, one of them while she is shopping at a boutique in the Village in La Jolla. Another shot, one of the more damaging pictures, shows him parked outside of her house half a block from the murder scene. He is sitting in his car, smoking a cigarette, as he watches the house.

'Do you recognize the video cassette?' This has been handed to the witness.

'Yes. The label shows my initials and the dates that it was recorded.'

'Did you alter the contents of the videotape in anyway?'

'I did not.'

'No editing?'

'No.'

'And was that tape in your possession the entire time before it was turned over to the police?'

'It was.'

'Your Honor, I would move the still shots of the individual frames and the photos as well as the videotape be entered into evidence and request that the videotape be played for the jury at this time.' Templeton wants to end the day on a high point so that the jury, having slept on it, will remember this well when it comes to deliberations. This puts me at a disadvantage, since I will have to wait until morning for my cross-examination of Rufus and an attempt to at least take some of the edge off of the stalking charge.

'Any objection to the photographs and the video coming in, Mr Madriani?' The judge is looking at me.

'No, Your Honor.'

Of course this has all been hammered out in chambers in pretrial motions. Harry and I tried a dozen ways to keep the tape out, all of them swatted down by the court. We have known for more than two months now that this tape would come in. We have viewed it repeatedly for hours in the conference room as well as on DVD on a laptop computer at the jail with Emiliano, trying to figure ways to defense it. The problem is that, without putting Ruiz on the stand, there is no way to explain his reason for following Madelyn Chapman or the fact that he was observed watching her house on three separate occasions, caught on film during two of them and shot with a long, low-light lens in the other.

As one of the bailiffs inserts the cassette into the player, a checkerboard pattern of pixels flashes on the screen. A second later a clear picture of Emiliano, his hands stuffed into the pockets of a leather flight jacket, appears on the screen. In the background, slightly out of focus but easily recognizable, is a shot of Chapman talking to some people on the street in the Village. She is smiling, vital, and animated.

Templeton has Rufus narrate the video as he works through the frames, going back and freezing them periodically to point out locations and clarify dates.

As the video continues, there is the sound of sniffling from the front row. I take a quick glance, but I already know what is happening. Madelyn Chapman's mother is crying; her only surviving daughter, who is wiping tears from her own eyes with Kleenex, attempts to comfort her.

At one point Templeton freezes the video, adjusts it just a little for clarity, and leaves it up on the screen. In the shot Ruiz is clearly visible standing on the sandstone shelf over the Pacific, his back to the ocean and the view. He is looking south, toward the rear of Chapman's house, through a pair of binoculars. In the distance is a blond figure. It is Chapman in the yard. She is stooping, clipping flowers or picking them. Behind her, no more than two feet away, is the screened window through which the killer entered her house.

CHAPTER
TWENTY-SEVEN

James Kaprosky is dying. He sits in an armchair next to the fireplace. This evening I visit him at his home out near Escondido.

He has been reading about the trial in the papers and watching all the talk on the cable stations, the kibitzing by lawyers, almost all of them now taking bets that after the verdict Ruiz is going down. The emphasis is on whether or not the jury will give him the death penalty.

'It's got to be more painful to watch these idiots talk to themselves than the trial,' says Kaprosky. He is hooked up to an oxygen bottle and is sitting in a recliner in front of the fireplace, a blanket over his legs. 'If I could get up out of this chair,' he says, 'I would come down there. At least give moral support.' With each phrase he struggles to regain his breath.

'No. No. You get better,' I tell him as I sit across from him on the couch, as though Kaprosky's recovery were a possibility.

He shakes his head. Kaprosky knows he hasn't got much time.

Jean is in the other room sewing, taking the

time to get some chores done while I'm visiting. She has brought coffee and a tray of cookies. I offer to pour some coffee for Jim but he says no.

At times he seems to ramble as his mind wanders through the legal hell that has been his life for the last decade or more.

'I don't know if you remember,' he says, 'a few years ago. Chapman and her company. They were sued for antitrust.' He smiles a little. 'One of the few . . . I wasn't . . . wasn't involved in.'

I laugh.

'Foolishness. Wasted years.'

'I don't think I remember the antitrust suit,' I tell him.

'Two private companies,' he says. He coughs. 'Tried to trim her wings. Competitors with Isotenics. After government contracts. My program,' he says. 'What they took and gave to Chapman. What she called Primis. It was unique,' he says.

'I know.'

'No. No. That's not what I mean,' he says. 'My software was its own operating platform. Didn't require any . . .' He stops to catch his breath. 'No underlying software to operate,' he says.

'I understand.'

The small tank at the side of his chair away from the fireplace is feeding oxygen through a tube under his nose.

'These other companies . . . had special applications . . . designed to run on top of mine. I shared the source code.' He smiles again. 'They were small start-ups. A niche market. Here and overseas. I didn't care. It was specialty software. I thought every little bit . . . adds something of use.' Then he shakes his head. 'But Chapman crushed them.' He sits breathing heavily for a moment as he thinks. 'She had to control everything. Dominated the market. She kept changing Primis. Every year. Tweaking it. Called it "updates."' He looks at the ceiling and smiles cynically now. 'She was busy . . . developing applications to take over . . . crush them.'

It is painful to listen to him struggle for breath, but it seems that I can't stop him from talking.

'She hid the changes . . . to Primis. Called them "trade secrets."' He looks at me. He's been reading the newspapers about Sims and his motion to quash.

'Cunning woman. Gave away upgrades, free,' he says. 'No cost. But when you booted . . . when you booted the new one . . . the old piggyback application . . .'

'Her competitor's software?'

He nods. 'Didn't work. Guess who had the only software replacements?'

'Isotenics.'

As I say the word he is nodding. 'She crippled the industry. Brought it to its knees. Stifled innovation. Made unneeded changes. Primis is a digital Tower of Babel.'

'You mean it's unstable?'

He smiles and nods as if this thought at least provides a little satisfaction. 'Sold it to governments. All over the world,' he says. 'All over the world.'

'Maybe I should go. Let me get Jean.'

'No.' He raises a palsied hand in a feeble gesture to stop me from leaving. 'Stay.'

'Just a few more minutes. I think you need to rest.'

'Plenty of time. I'll get a long rest. Your case . . . any chance?' he says.

I take a deep breath, offer up a long sigh. 'The truth? It doesn't look good.' Somehow divulging a confidence to a dead man doesn't seem to be an ethical violation.

His face is drawn. There are dark hollows and lines etched like canyons under his eyes. The loose flesh drooping from his chin and neck are a measure of the weight he has lost since just our last meeting in the office. I look at James sitting in his chair near the fireplace, with the hiss of the gas logs, a plaid wool blanket to keep him warm, and I know that I will not see him again.

'What happened to the antitrust suit?' I ask.

'Hmm?' Another tired smile crosses his face. 'Government stepped in.'

'Ah, of course. National security,' I say.

He shakes his head slowly. 'Brought their own suit,' he says. 'Took it over.'

He means the antitrust suit. 'The government stepped in and took it over?'

He nods. 'Convinced the companies.' He is talking about the two competitors. 'Wouldn't be in their interest . . . to continue,' he says. 'Year later it was settled. Out of court. The next year . . . Isotenics killed . . . three more companies. Same tactics.' There is a struggling rhythm of death in his words now as he fights for breath.

'I think you should rest,' I tell him.

'No. Need to talk to you. I think I know . . . how they're doing it.'

'What?'

'Feeding Primis,' he says.

He is talking about the raw data, the input of massive volumes of personal information needed to keep Primis and the supercomputers in Washington humming with private intelligence.

'How?'

'Looking glass,' he says. 'Mirror software.'

'I don't understand.'

'Spyware,' he says. Until this moment I might have thought he was hallucinating. He swallows hard and tries to sit up in his chair.

'No, Jim, sit back. Relax.'

As he tries to lean forward, he stretches the clear plastic tube leading to his nose. I'm afraid he's going to pull it free, or topple the small oxygen bottle on the floor.

He settles up in his chair. 'Man I know' – he tries to catch his breath – 'says NSA . . . wrote the stuff. Two years ago. Invisible,' he says. 'No way to see it. Plants itself on your machine. Spyware.'

Kaprosky is talking about NSA, the National Security Agency.

'No way to detect it,' he says.

'I don't understand.'

'What?' Kaprosky looks at me, breathless.

'How would they get it onto your computer?'

He nods and smiles, arches his eyebrows, relieved that I'm at least tracking what he is saying. He laughs to himself. As much breath as he can spare. 'Online. Government forms. Spyware. Check it . . . online,' he says. 'Mirror software. Called "looking glass." '

CHAPTER
TWENTY-EIGHT

In the morning Max Rufus is back on the stand. The judge reminds him that he is already under oath, and Rufus takes his seat.

I offer him a greeting: 'Good morning.'

He smiles and nods but doesn't say anything.

Today Rufus is fitted out in a charcoal pin-striped suit, starched white linen shirt with French cuffs, and gold cuff links. He's wearing a blue tie with tiny gold stars covering it to pick up the accents.

He leans back in the witness chair and crosses one leg over the other, his right ankle resting on his left knee. His elbows are on the armrests of the chair, the fingers of his hands steepled together just under his chin, the fingertips drumming together nervously.

I stand at the podium looking at him for several seconds as the last few coughs are muffled and people in the audience settle in their seats. Then I start.

'Mr Rufus, let me ask you ... Yesterday you indicated that Mr Ruiz headed up the security detail assigned to provide executive protection to Madelyn Chapman.'

'That's correct.'

'Can you tell the jury why Ms Chapman or, for that matter, other personnel at Isotenics found it necessary to retain executive security to protect Ms Chapman?'

He looks at me, a puzzled expression. 'I don't recall if there was a specific incident that prompted it,' he says. 'She had a high public profile because of the company and her responsibilities. It's not uncommon for people in her position to utilize personal security.'

'Do you know whether prior to or during the time that your company provided executive protection to Ms Chapman she received any threats, either verbal or written? Threats regarding her personal safety, I mean.'

'Oh, the usual crank letters, I suppose. Many of the people who we provide protection for receive any number of strange pieces of mail. With regard to Ms Chapman, as I recall, there were no what you would call credible threats.' He smiles at me.

It's obvious that the witness has gone over this with Templeton in order to prevent us from pumping up the poison pen mail into evidence of a risk from some other quarter.

'Yesterday I believe that you testified that you received a phone call from Madelyn Chapman at one point and that during that phone call she demanded that the executive protection detail assigned to her be terminated and that she – and I believe these are the words that you used – "specifically requested that Mr Ruiz be removed from the detail immediately." Is that correct?'

'That's right.'

'And I believe you went on to testify that when

you asked her why she wanted this done, she told you, and I quote' – I look down at my notes – ' "She said that Mr Ruiz had become too familiar and that he made inappropriate advances toward her." Is that accurate?'

'Well, words to that effect. I can't recall exactly how she said it, but that's the gist of it.'

'Is that a fact?'

He looks at me but doesn't respond.

'Isn't it true, Mr Rufus, that part of the reason Ms Chapman called you that day is not because she was angry with Mr Ruiz but rather she was angry with your firm?'

'No.'

'Isn't it a fact that Madelyn Chapman called you to complain not about Mr Ruiz but about the fact that your company had screwed up and placed a security video camera in her office without her knowledge?'

'Well, she . . . It's true. She did mention that.'

'Isn't it a fact that Madelyn Chapman screamed at you over the phone, not because of anything that Mr Ruiz had done, but because she had been compromised by the installation of a security camera in her own office when she was out of town traveling, and that no one had taken the time to tell her about it, so that when she came back, she was surprised to find herself on film?'

'Your Honor, I'm going to object to this.' Templeton is sitting on his box on the chair and raising a hand. 'The court refused to allow me to get into that videotape. And now Mr Madriani—'

'I'm not talking about the contents of the video-tape, Your Honor. I'm talking about the existence of a camera the size of a pencil eraser installed in the victim's office without her knowledge.'

'The witness can answer the question,' says Gilcrest.

'It was a mistake. We blew it,' says Rufus.

'That doesn't answer my question. Did she or did she not yell at you over the phone because of the installation of that camera in her office without her knowledge?'

'She ... she ... she was angry. I will concede that she was upset. I apologized. I told her that if I had known that no one had checked with her beforehand, the camera would never have been installed.'

'So she was operating on the good-faith belief that she had privacy in her own office, when in fact she did not?'

Rufus uncrosses his legs. He offers a dozen expressions on the stand, none of them happy. 'It's true she didn't know it was there. And she was upset about it, but she also demanded that the security detail be terminated and that Mr Ruiz be removed.'

'Well, let me ask you a question, Mr Rufus: If you had hired a company to provide security at your place of business and they came in and installed a camera in your office without your knowledge, and that camera caught you doing something in what you thought was a moment of privacy, would you not be moved in anger – I say in rage – to remove that firm and all of its employees from your presence?'

Right between the eyes. Rufus, sitting on the stand as if he has been poleaxed, is looking at me wide-eyed. He swallows hard. 'I don't know. I suppose.' It's the only thing he can say. Nothing else would sound reasonable, and anyone who knew Chapman and the fits of imperious anger that could overtake her knows it.

'Let me ask you, isn't it a fact that Ms Chapman fired the head of security at Isotenics immediately after her conversation with you on the telephone that day?'

'I'm not sure of the details,' he says.

'Did she or did she not fire the man?'

'He was discharged.'

'And on that very day, is that not correct?'

'I believe so.'

'And was he not terminated because of his failure to notify Ms Chapman of the existence of that camera in her office?'

'I'm not sure.'

'Would you like me to show you the declaration, signed under penalty of perjury, obtained from the gentleman in question?' This Herman was able to obtain because Chapman's former head of security no longer works for the company. He is not covered by Sims's motion to quash and the restraining order compelling us to stay clear of Isotenics and its employees.

'I'll take your word for it,' says Rufus.

'I'm not the one testifying,' I tell him, 'you are. Now, do you want me to repeat the question, or would you like to answer it?'

'I believe he was fired because of the camera.'

I take a deep breath, slow the pace a little, and cast an eye through my notes on the rostrum to make sure I'm not missing anything.

When I look up, Rufus is sweating, beads of perspiration running down his forehead. He mops it with a handkerchief from the inside pocket of his jacket, then wipes his upper lip with the other side.

'Can you tell the jury why Ms Chapman called you personally to complain about what had happened regarding the camera in her office?'

He looks puzzled, as if he's trying to locate the hook in the question. 'I don't know. I suppose because I was the head of the firm.'

'Isn't it true that you were a personal friend of Ms Chapman's?'

'I see what you mean. Yes, we were acquainted,' he says.

'Can you tell the jury how long you had known the victim?' I go from *Chapman* to *victim* for the implications it conjures.

'I don't know. A few years.'

'A shade more than six, to be exact? Would that be about right?'

'I suppose. What difference does it make?'

'Did you know her well?'

'We were social acquaintances. We did business together.'

'Other than providing security services for Isotenics and executive protection for Ms Chapman, did you have any other business relations with her?'

He shakes his head. 'No. That was it.'

'Did you ever travel with Ms Chapman personally?' I ask.

'I was wondering when that was going to come up,' he says. 'Yes, we traveled together once. One time.'

'And when was that?'

'About three years ago. And the press engaged in a lot of gossip that wasn't true,' he says.

'Where did the two of you go?'

'The two of us didn't *go* anywhere,' he says. 'The fact of the matter is that she was generous enough to allow me to hitch a ride on her company plane because it just so happened that she was vacationing in Italy at the same time that I had a security conference in Rome. When we landed in Italy, we went our separate ways. We ended up spending one day together relaxing just before returning home and the paparazzi with their cameras got a hold of it and made a huge deal out of it. She told me that they hounded her the entire time she was there. Wouldn't leave her alone. "The billionaire software queen." '

In the piles of documents in the box on the floor at Harry's feet are old news articles and photographs we have been collecting, mostly items out of the local society section. Several of these show Chapman over the last several years attending galas and charity functions accompanied by a number of different male friends. Several of the photos show her on the arm of Rufus.

Their difference in age and economic and social status causes me to suspect that this was nothing more than a matter of convenience for Chapman. No doubt she would have considered Rufus a safe escort for a high-profile outing in terms of gossip and speculation. That all changed when she spent ten days in a guarded villa near the town of Lucca in Tuscany. With an international software mogul staying in the neighborhood, Roman reporters descended on the place. One of the photos taken with a 900mm lens from bushes on the hillside above the villa, a grainy shot, shows Chapman sunning herself on a chaise near the pool. Next to her, decked out in swim trunks and reading the newspaper, is an austere, dapper-looking gentleman later identified as Maxwell Rufus. The picture set tongues wagging in the local San Diego press, speculation that a match was in the making. Whether it was business or pleasure was never clear. What is certain is that if there was something bubbling, it never brewed. After that, the only times the two of them were ever seen together were in groups with other people – outings similar to the dinner party that Chapman never made the night she was murdered.

I slip copies of the grainy photograph from the Italian press from under a stack of papers on the podium and have the bailiff deliver one to the judge and one to Rufus on the stand. I hand another to Templeton at his table.

I ask Rufus: 'Do you recognize this photograph?'

'Yes.' He barely glances it at, then dumps it contemptuously onto the railing along the side of the witness stand.

'Is that Ms Chapman and yourself in the photograph?'

'Yes.' Rufus isn't even looking at me now but glancing up at the ceiling instead.

'You say the press came to the wrong conclusions based on that photograph?'

'Yes.'

'That they engaged in a lot of wild speculation that wasn't true?'

'Absolutely.'

'Your Honor, can I have People's exhibit twenty-six up on the screen?' This is a copy of the frozen frame from the video taken by Rufus, the picture that Templeton left lingering up on the screen for the jury at the close of the state's direct examination of Rufus. Harry has had this single frame prepared for mounting on the visualizer so that it leaves enough room for another shot to be placed right next to it – a kind of split screen.

Gilcrest points his gavel at Templeton's computer wizard, and a second later one of the photographs taken by Rufus during his surveillance of my client pops up on the visualizer, the shot showing Ruiz watching Chapman on the street in La Jolla, where she is talking with friends.

'Isn't it a fact, Mr Rufus, that people – that perhaps this jury – looking at the load of photographs that you took of Emiliano Ruiz during your so-called investigation of his activities could jump to similarly erroneous conclusions as the press did with you and the victim while you were vacationing in Italy?'

Suddenly Rufus realizes that I'm not headed where he thought I was going: implications of an affair between him and Chapman. Whether the jury will land there or not is up to them.

'I don't think so,' he says.

'Your Honor, I ask that the photograph resting on the railing next to Mr Rufus's arm be marked defendant's exhibit next in order and that it be introduced into evidence.'

'Any objection, Mr Templeton?'

'No, Your Honor.'

I have the Italian newspaper photo put up on the visualizer for the jury to see; the other half of my split screen, a demonstration of how people can jump to the wrong conclusion by looking at pictures.

I turn back to the witness. 'Did you bother to talk to Mr Ruiz, to ask him what he was doing when he was watching Madelyn Chapman during the course of your investigation?'

'It wasn't necessary. I had directed him to stay away from her.' The way Rufus says it makes him sound like a jealous suitor.

'I see. You were conducting an investigation to find out what he was doing, but it wasn't necessary to talk to him about it? To find out what the real purpose of his activities were?'

'I knew what the purpose of his activities were. He was infatuated,' says Rufus.

'That's pure speculation on your part. Your Honor, I move that the witness's answer be stricken from the record and that the jury be instructed to disregard it.'

'So ordered,' says Gilcrest. 'The jury will disregard the witness's last statement and the witness will confine his testimony to what he knows. Do I make myself clear?' he asks.

Rufus nods.

Gilcrest verbally pulls Rufus up by the tie: 'I want to hear an answer when I give a direction.'

'Yes, Your Honor.'

'You may proceed.' The judge waves me on.

'Isn't it a fact, Mr Rufus, that to this day you don't have any idea what Mr Ruiz was actually doing when you were photographing him watching Madelyn Chapman?'

'The pictures speak for themselves,' he says.

'I suppose they would have to since you can't, even though you took them.'

'Objection,' says Templeton.

'The jury will disregard counsel's comment,' says Gilcrest. The judge is having to earn his supper. 'Confine yourself to questions, Mr Madriani.'

'Sorry, Your Honor.

'Is it not possible, Mr Rufus, given your lack of verifiable information concerning the activities of Mr Ruiz in those photographs and in that video-tape, that the photographs you took are just as deceptive, just as erroneous, and just as misleading—'

'No,' he says.

'Let me finish.' He allows me to repeat the entire

question while the jury considers his self-righteous stance.

'Is it not possible, sir, given your lack of verifiable information and your preconceived notions,' I add, 'that your photographs and that video of Mr Ruiz taken during what you call an investigation are just as deceptive, just as erroneous, and just as misleading as you claim that news photograph is of you and the victim in Italy?'

'No.'

'And how do you know that?'

He sits on the stand, silent, unable to come up with an answer that isn't the product of conjecture and assumption. Rufus is a regimented soul. All that mattered to him was that Ruiz had violated his instructions to stay away from Madelyn Chapman. He never bothered to confront Ruiz and ask him what he was doing. In the end the police arrested Emiliano, seized the tape and the photographs, and used them to jump to conclusions.

'I have no further use for this witness.' I turn and leave him sitting on the stand.

CHAPTER
TWENTY-NINE

I have no illusions: my performance with Rufus on cross-examination may have looked good to the audience, but it is likely to have produced more flash than effect when the jury finally locks itself behind closed doors for deliberations.

There is no discounting the fact that the video and photos taken of Ruiz by Rufus were compiled over a period of nearly two weeks. They show a pattern of conduct on the part of the defendant that is entirely consistent with the state's theory of the case. No matter the tune or the dance as regards mistaken impressions, the contents of the video – the fact that Ruiz was seen surveilling the victim with a pair of field glasses – will not be lost on the jury, especially after this is hammered home by Templeton in his closing argument.

The indisputable fact is that without putting Ruiz on the stand, there is no way that we can explain what he was doing watching Madelyn Chapman. And putting Ruiz on the stand would be like lighting a torch to find your way through a dark powder magazine. Even assuming that the jury would believe him, without knowing what secrets lurk in his background, putting Emiliano up for Templeton to take a shot at is not something I would choose to do. Though the final decision as to whether to testify rests with the defendant, it is not something I can recommend to him. I am fearful that Templeton would take him apart on the stand, especially given Emiliano's death wish in lieu of life without parole.

Tonight I am huddled over the keyboard of the desktop in my study, doing a Google search online to learn how my computer works.

I am taking Jim Kaprosky's advice, checking out the nature of spyware and looking for the two items that he mentioned during my visit to his house last night. When I got to the car I scrawled the words *mirror software* and *looking glass* on the back of one of my business cards. Tonight the note is sitting on my desk next to the keyboard.

When Harold Klepp mentioned the word *spyware* that night at the bar, I thought he was using shorthand to describe Chapman's Primis package, high-level security software intended to allow government to plumb the depths of personal information. I was wrong. Klepp may have been out of the loop at Isotenics, but he was hearing things from someone closer to the center of the action.

Chapman had been overheard using the term *spyware* during her argument on the phone with Gerald Satz. Klepp got the word right but, like me, he didn't understand the context, the fact that the word was being used in the technical sense: as a term of art, not to describe Primis, but something else.

According to the articles online, *adware* is a

computer term used to describe small bits of what is known as 'execution programming.' These are used by commercial firms to track information whenever a computer user goes online and visits certain sites. Shop for a pair of running shoes online, and the next thing you know you'll be getting pop-up screens trying to peddle everything for the foot, from sneakers to slippers. Chances are one or more of the sites you have visited has just attached bits of adware to the hard drive of your computer.

If you have a pop-up blocker – unless you run one or more scanning programs to search out and remove the adware – you'll never know it is happening, except that over time your machine will slow down as it loads up on the small bits and pieces. Most of it is harmless, though some can transmit viruses, worms, and other odious items that can kill your computer.

From the digital handshake of surfing the Web, you can also pick up the insidious little devil known as spyware. Generally this is a more sophisticated version of looking-over-your-shoulder as you shop. Spyware usually sends more detailed information to the vendor who planted it online. It is designed to track your shopping habits. According to the information, some of it is so sufficiently sophisticated that it can hunt out your mailing address and fill your mailbox with junk mail.

I do a search for the terms *mirror software* and *looking glass*. I score pages of hits, including a firm that produces medical software and a project by a large commercial software manufacturer. But none of these are what I am looking for.

Unless I misunderstood him, Jim Kaprosky

was not talking about proprietary software manufactured by a private company. He was talking about the software equivalent of aviation's spy-style Skunk Works, an operation buried in the dark tunnels of government that somehow has crafted a way to tap into home and office computers, anything online, and gather private data so that it can be processed through Primis.

If this is true, it would allow government to monitor patterns of conduct and individual activity at a depth and in detail that is mind-numbing.

Given the ever-increasing grasp of central governments around the world, the threat of mischief or worse posed by such technology is daunting. True, it could be used to thwart terrorism. But, unchecked and unseen, it could just as easily give rise to tyranny. Private information on a global scale could be used to chill political speech at a monumental level. In the hands of the unscrupulous, it could be harnessed to extort any number of favors from individuals in public office or those who control the economic throttle and pull the levers that make the world go around.

If information is power, access to personal digitized data in a form that is raw and unrestricted – coupled with processing software allowing oceans of it to be mined at the speed of light – is an open and engraved invitation to despotism.

Sitting in the blue haze emitted from the monitor in my darkened study, I am scrolling down the screen when my eye catches something. It's a tagline near the bottom of the page, a single news item from one of the wire services. In the second line of the description is the abbreviation *NSA*. I pull it up.

The article is brief and two years old. According to the wire-service story, a spokesman for the National Security Agency has denied reports that his agency has pioneered a computer bug known as 'looking glass,' software designed to track and transmit large volumes of digital data in highly compressed microbursts. According to the initial reports, which have now been denied, the software was believed to be intended for use in foreign intelligence gathering and engineered in a form that would be virtually invisible except to the most sophisticated scanning devices.

I print the article out and scroll on. There are two more articles. When I try to pull them up, I find that both have either expired or been removed from the Internet.

Piecing together what Kaprosky told me and from the information on adware and how it works, if the government is using looking glass as a form of spyware at some or all of its online sites, this has ominous implications for anything remotely approaching a free society.

Businesses or individuals going to their computers for tax forms or electronic filing, some of which is now required by law, would have no way of avoiding the attachment of virtually invisible spyware to their computers. Everyone from farmers reporting agricultural production, to banks dealing with the Federal Reserve, to doctors and hospitals using computer uplinks to communicate with government regulatory agencies, could be having their confidential data files scanned at the speed of light with no oversight or restriction on how it is used.

Those possessing the keys to this kingdom would be the ultimate inside dealers. They would know the details of every business transaction before it occurred, like playing Monopoly with loaded dice.

In the area of privacy, everything from patient medical records to supposedly confidential financial data, from the content of e-mail to personal notes and records maintained on home computers, could be scanned.

If this is true, and if the system is in full bloom, any computer that has ever surfed to a government site is probably already infected. In this case, its data and anything networked to it is being scooped up without notice or benefit of a search warrant. If Kaprosky is right, all of it at this moment could be running through high-speed lines in compressed microbursts to computers running Primis in the basement of the Pentagon.

CHAPTER THIRTY

Our mystery man, retired general Gerald Satz, has now disappeared. Two days ago a relentless process server, a friend of Herman's working out of Washington, DC, finally gained access to Satz's outer office in the Pentagon, only to be told that Satz was gone.

According to the information, the general is out of the country on government business. They will not say when he left, when he will be back, or where he is. According to his staff, Satz's location and his itinerary are confidential for reasons of security. What is clear is that Satz will not be available for the trial. The government is sealing off the last small fissures in the cover that might shed light on what happened between Madelyn Chapman and the Pentagon in the days before she died.

Friday afternoon, the end of the week, and Templeton is sitting at the cusp, right at the edge of the state's case in chief. He is a master of timing, and the feeling is palpable as he climbs the stool to take the podium. You can almost smell it, like ozone in the air after a jolt of lightning: the packed courtroom seems to crackle with a psychic charge.

Like a pint-size philharmonic conductor, Templeton would like to end his case on a crescendo, some high note that he can leave ringing in the minds of jurors, for them to ponder as they kill time, sequestered in their hotel rooms over the weekend, waiting for the defense to begin its case.

'Mr Templeton, do you have any more witnesses to call?' Gilcrest looks up only briefly as he makes a note on the blotter in front of him. The jury is in the box.

'One final witness, Your Honor.'

'Very well, let's do it,' says the judge.

'People call Jensen Quinn to the stand.'

I glance over at Harry, who has already leaned forward in his chair, his elbows on the table as he turns to look at me. His face is an expressive question mark, a shrug of the shoulders. He has no clue.

Harry fingers through the separate piles of paper on the table in front of him until he finds a copy of the state's witness list. This is nearly eighteen pages in length, names single-spaced and numbered along the left-hand margin. There are hundreds of names here, people Templeton thought he might want to call, long shots that in a pitched battle over some minute point could come in handy, others that would be called only if the factual sands underlying the case shifted beneath his feet. I suspect many of the names were grabbed out of phone books in the library and dropped on his list like chaff among the wheat to distract us, so that we would waste time checking them out.

I lean into Emiliano. 'Do you recognize the name?'

He shakes his head. He is turned now, looking

toward the back of the courtroom, toward the double doors where the bailiff has announced the name out in the hallway.

A second later I hear the whoosh of one of the swinging double doors at the rear of the courtroom as it opens and closes. Before I can turn to look behind me, I notice that Emiliano's face has gone ashen. There is something in his fixed gaze that I have not seen before. It is the focused appearance of fear. A second later, when he snaps around to the front, his breathing is heavy, his eyes darting.

I turn to look behind me. At the back of the courtroom there is a man talking to the bailiff, who is directing him up the main aisle toward the front of the courtroom. He is of medium height with dark, wavy hair. He's wearing a tan jacket, slacks, and a polo shirt. As he heads up the aisle I get a better look. His eyes are directed straight ahead, as if he is consciously avoiding any eye contact with the people at either table and instead is staring off into the ether.

I look over toward Harry. He has slid the state's witness list toward the center of the table in front of Ruiz where we can all see it. Harry's finger is on the page next to the name *Jensen Quinn*.

I cup a hand and whisper to Ruiz, 'Do you know him?'

He nods quickly, twice, a kind of muted gesture. 'I knew him as Jack. It's what he went by in the military,' he whispers back.

'What's he going to say?' I ask.

A little shake of his head, a shrug of his shoulders. Ruiz is telling us he doesn't know.

'What is he going to say on the stand?' Harry is whispering through clenched teeth from the other side. He has picked up the same signal of panic from Ruiz that I have.

Emiliano falls silent, his eyes on the witness, who is now raising his hand to be sworn in by the clerk.

'Do you swear to tell the truth, the whole truth, and nothing but the truth?'

'Ah do.'

'Take a seat and state your name for the record.'

He sits in the witness chair. 'Jensen Jonathan Quinn.'

He has a distinct accent. If I had to guess, I would say the southeast hill country, maybe the western Carolinas or Tennessee.

'Mr Quinn, my name is Lawrence Templeton. I'm a deputy district attorney with the county of San Diego. We have met and talked to one another on one earlier occasion, have we not?'

'Yes, sir.'

'Are you sometimes known to your friends as Jack Quinn?'

'Yes, sir.'

'You don't have to call me *sir*. Just relax. All you have to do is answer the questions truthfully and we'll get you out of here as quickly as we can.'

'Yes, sir. Sorry,' he says.

Several of the jurors are smiling.

'That's okay, we all understand. It's natural to be a little bit nervous. Let me ask you, Mr Quinn, are you a member of the United States military?'

The witness shakes his head. 'Not at the present time. No, sir.'

'But were you at one time a member of the United States Army?'

'Yes, sir.' The witness blushes, shrugs his shoulders.

'That's all right. Old habits are hard to break,'

says Templeton. 'If it makes it any easier for you, you can just go ahead and keep on pretending I'm a sir.'

The jury laughs.

'Mr Quinn, can you tell the jury what type of work you did when you were in the Army?'

'I was in the infantry, Army Rangers.'

'And where were you stationed?'

'Fort Bragg, North Carolina.'

'You're currently out of the Army, is that right?'

'Yes, sir.'

'How long have you been out?'

'Let's see.' He thinks for a moment. 'Fourteen, almost fifteen months now.'

'And you were honorably discharged, is that correct?'

'Yes, sir.'

'How long were you in the Army?'

'Eight years.'

'And during all that time, were you stationed at Fort Bragg?'

'Except for the times when mah unit was overseas, yes, sir.'

'Did you see any combat during this period of time?'

'Yes, sir. In the Middle East. Twice,' he says.

'And both times that you were in combat, were you a member of an Army Ranger unit?'

'Ah was, yes, sir.'

'And can you tell the jury, are the Army Rangers considered to be what is known as an elite unit within the military?'

'Yes, sir. They are.'

'And what was your rank or grade when you left the Army?'

'Ah was a staff sergeant.'

436

'Would members of the Army, enlisted service-men or women, have to go through special training to become an Army Ranger?'

'Yes, sir, they would.'

'And can you tell the jury what kind of training would be involved in order to qualify to become a Ranger?'

'Well, besides basic training and advanced individual training, to get your MOS—'

'Excuse me. What is an MOS? Can you explain for the jury?'

'Oh. Yeah, sorry. *MOS* is short for "military occupational specialty." Mine was advanced infantry.'

'Thank you. Go ahead. What else is required to become a Ranger?'

'Besides that, you have to graduate from airborne school.'

'Become a paratrooper, is that right?'

'Yes, sir.'

'And what else?'

'You have to complete RIP,' he says.

'What is RIP, Mr Quinn?'

'Ranger Indoctrination Program.'

'Is that it?'

'Yes, sir.'

'Would we be safe in assuming that all of this – the basic training, the advanced training, the airborne school, the RIP program – all of it involves fairly rigorous physical aptitude on the part of the recruit, the person trying to become an Army Ranger?'

'Yes, sir.'

'Your Honor' – I interrupt Templeton's flow – 'I have to object. I'm sure all of this is very interesting, but it's irrelevant.'

437

'Mr Templeton, I'm beginning to wonder the same thing,' says Gilcrest.

'Your Honor, if you'll just give me a couple more minutes, I think you'll begin to see the relevance.'

'Very well, get to the point,' says the judge.

'Mr Quinn, at one point after you became an Army Ranger, did you consider making the Army a career?'

'Ah did.'

'And what changed your mind?'

'I was passed over,' he says.

'You mean to say you were passed over for a promotion?'

'No, sir. Ah was turned down on assignment to another unit.'

'And what was that unit?'

'First Special Forces Operational Detachment. First SFOD, sir.'

'And is there another name that that unit is more commonly known by?'

'Yes, sir.'

'And what is that name?'

'Delta Force.'

'And where is Delta Force located? Where is their headquarters?'

'You mean officially?' asks the witness.

'Yes.'

'Nowhere. According to the Army, they don't exist.'

A few people in the audience laugh. They've seen the film or read the book, the bloody battle on the streets of Mogadishu. Delta is like Area Fifty-four out in the desert. Everybody knows it exists, but the government won't admit it.

'Why is that? Why won't the Army acknowledge Delta's existence?'

'Because it's classified. Everything about the Delta is off limits.'

'Where do they exist, unofficially?' says Templeton.

'At Fort Bragg, North Carolina.'

'The same place you were stationed when you were in the Rangers?'

'Yes, sir.'

'And can you tell the jury why you were turned down, disapproved for assignment to Delta Force?'

I'm getting a sick feeling, the kind of sensation you feel just as Vesuvius erupts up the esophagus.

'Because someone said . . . because I was found not to be qualified for certain live-fire exercises with small arms.'

'And can you tell the jury who made that determination? Who said you weren't qualified?'

'He did.' The witness nearly comes up off his seat, reaching out to point toward Ruiz. Emiliano is just sitting there, his back against the chair, looking at the witness with a blank stare.

'And when you said "He did," who are you talking about? Can you identify this person by name?'

'Yes, sir. Sergeant Emiliano Ruiz,' he says.

'You're talking about the defendant?'

'Yes, sir.'

'And at the time that Sergeant Ruiz found you not to be qualified, was Sergeant Ruiz a member of the Army Rangers?'

'No, sir. He was a member of Delta Force.'

There is stirring out in the audience, the hum of voices. The judge cracks the gavel on the hard oak surface of the bench, and suddenly there is silence.

'Can you tell us a little bit more about Delta Force? What exactly does that unit do?'

'Counterterrorism, hostage rescue . . . They're the tip of the spear,' says the witness.

'What does that mean, "the tip of the spear"?'

'They're elite, sir. Top of the heap.'

'I'm going to ask you to take a look at . . .' Templeton nods toward the detective at his table, who gets up as if on cue and retrieves the murder weapon, Ruiz's handgun, from the evidence table. 'I'd like to ask you to take a look at this firearm.'

The detective hands the pistol to the witness.

'Do you recognize it?' asks Templeton.

'Yes, sir.'

'Can you tell the jury what the letters *USSOCOM* engraved on the side of that firearm, near the barrel, what those letters stand for?'

'They stand for United States Special Operations Command.'

'And what is the Special Operations Command?'

'They're the command unit over Special Forces, Green Berets, Rangers, all of the elite units in the Army.'

'Would that include Delta Force?'

'Yes, sir. Especially Delta Force.'

It's clear why Templeton didn't use the army officer, Major Ellis, his firearms training expert, to make the point. Ellis would have disclaimed any knowledge of Delta. He probably would have suffered terminal memory loss if Templeton had even whispered the name. Harry and I now know the answer to the mystery, why Ruiz had dropped off the edge of the earth for seven years, according to his military records. He had entered the shadow world of Delta.

Templeton slows down, checks his notes. He wants to carefully map out the final approach in his head. At this point, impact, vivid contact on all the high peaks for the jury, and the order in which they are touched is everything.

'Have you seen that pistol or one like it before?'

'Yes, sir.'

'Where did you see it?'

'In training at Fort Bragg. The Delta Force training base,' he says.

'Can you tell us what was happening with the pistol when you saw it for the first time?'

'It was being fired.'

'Can you describe the circumstances in which it was being fired?'

'It was being used for a training demonstration in one of the shooting houses.'

'Can you tell the jury what a shooting house is?'

'It's an indoor enclosure used for training. Live-fire exercises. Simulation training for insertions and hostage rescue.'

'And is there another name for a shooting house? Something else that soldiers sometimes call it?'

The witness nods. 'Sometimes they're called killing houses.'

The impact of the two words on the jury is almost palpable. I watch as at least four of them make a note of it on paper.

'And when you observed this demonstration, who was firing the pistol in question, the Mark Twenty-three forty-five automatic?'

'It was Sergeant Ruiz.'

'And do you recall, was he demonstrating anything in particular that day, the day you saw him with a pistol similar to the one in your hand?'

'Yes, sir.'

'Can you tell the jury precisely what it was that he was teaching that day?'

'We were all inside the killing house,' says Quinn. 'Sergeant Ruiz was showing us the proper procedure for target selection with the pistol.'

'The Mark Twenty-three?'

'Yes, sir.'

'Go on.'

'He was showing us how to sweep each target so that we could hit it twice, so that we could put it down – what is known as a "double tap."'

At this moment Harry would drop his head onto the table except that half of the jury is watching us. The other half is taking notes.

Templeton now has the detective deliver a photograph to our table. It's an eight-by-ten glossy, black-and-white, a picture of a group of soldiers, none of them looking particularly spit-shined, some of them with mustaches and longer hair. Most of the soldiers in the group look like they are older, some of them in their early thirties. Sitting on the ground in the front row is Emiliano. In his hand, unmistakable with the long silencer attached and what appears to be a square block of metal under the barrel, the laser sight, is the Mark 23.

'Your Honor, I object. We've never seen this photograph before.'

'I only got a copy this morning,' says Templeton.

Gilcrest waves us forward to the bench and hits the white-noise button.

'It was delivered to me by the witness during the noon break,' says Templeton. 'Outside in the hallway. He only found it last night among some old papers in his files. He had copies made this morning.'

'Your Honor—'

Gilcrest holds up a hand, palm out, to silence

442

me as he studies his copy of the photo, delivered to him by the bailiff.

'Are you offering the photograph to show that the firearm depicted in the picture is the murder weapon?' asks the judge.

'No, Your Honor. Only to show that the defendant was familiar with and skilled in the use of the model of that handgun.'

'Your Honor—'

'I'll allow it for that purpose,' says the judge. 'And I'll instruct the jury accordingly.'

'I object, Your Honor.'

'Mr Madriani, a witness has already linked the murder weapon to your client. It's been established that it was issued to him in the Army. I can't see any harm in showing the jury a picture of him holding a similar firearm.'

A picture being worth a thousand words, I could split hairs with him all afternoon, but he slaps me down, and we step back to the tables.

Templeton has the witness identify the photograph, and less than a minute later it's up on the visualizer in front of the jury. The judge can instruct them until hell freezes. The picture of the murder weapon in Emiliano's hand, projected onto a screen the size of that in a small movie theater, has a transforming effect inside the jury box. If the weight of evidence means anything – if Harry, Ruiz, and I were sitting on a balancing scale at this moment – our heads would be jammed up against the courtroom ceiling.

CHAPTER
THIRTY-ONE

H arry and I are alone with Ruiz in the holding area off of the courtroom.

Emiliano is overflowing with apologies. 'I'm sorry, but I couldn't tell you. We were sworn to maintain the secret. There is a presidential decision directive.' He cites to us the number, what is known as PDD-25.

'What does it say?' I ask.

'Gave us immunity from the law, as long as we didn't tell anybody what we did. That was the condition,' he says.

I look at Harry. 'If there's a presidential directive barring public disclosure as to Delta, and if it has the weight of law,' I say, 'we might be able to use it.'

Harry thinks about this. 'Ask the judge to strike Quinn's testimony? Instruct them to disregard the photo? They've already seen it,' says Harry. 'He's already ruled that the photo can come in.'

'He didn't know about the directive and neither did we. We ask for a mistrial.' I turn to Ruiz. 'Do you have a copy of the directive?'

He shakes his head. 'It's classified. I only saw a summary.'

'What did the summary say?'

'Nothing about Delta. But the people who saw the document, who had clearance to see the whole thing, they said it excused us from the law. Total exemption, they said, everything, as long as we didn't talk, even *posse comitatus*.'

'Delta was operating in the US?' says Harry.

Ruiz nods.

Posse comitatus is federal law adopted after the Civil War to rein in US troops and to prevent them from being used against their own citizens, except in federally declared emergencies.

I had seen claims in the press about Delta's activities inside the United States. But until now I had always discounted them.

'Don't ask me where, 'cuz I can't tell you,' he says. 'That's why I couldn't say anything when you asked me what I did. The seven years,' he says.

'You've never seen the actual document?' says Harry. 'The directive?'

'Just the summary. None of the troops in Delta saw the real thing. But we were told that we were excused from the law. Everybody under Joint Special Operations Command was.'

'Remember I asked you whether you'd ever been to Special Operations Command, and you said no?' I look him straight in the eye.

'That was the truth,' he says. 'They're located at MacDill Air Force Base, in Tampa. I've never been there.'

'You knew what I was talking about.'

'Yes.' He looks at me, then down at the floor, and nods. Emiliano stands in the corner of the room, his hands stuffed into the pockets of his suit pants, looking like a chastened schoolboy. His jacket lies on the floor where he took it off and threw it when he came in.

'I know you're angry,' he says. 'You have a right to be. But what was I supposed to do?'

'For starters, come clean with your lawyers,' says Harry.

'And if I told you about Delta, what would you have done? You would have had to find some way to tell the jury about it. Then Templeton would have been all over it.'

'But we could have brought it out,' says Harry. 'Now it looks like we're hiding it. And the picture, the one with the gun in your hand . . .'

'I don't carry a gun anymore. That's the fact,' he says. 'I haven't carried a gun since I left the Army. You know what I use for protection?'

Harry shakes his head as if he could care less.

'A water pistol,' says Ruiz. 'You don't believe me? Ask the cops,' he says. 'Sure, they didn't put it in their report. They put it under "personal items" when they booked me. But that's all they found when they arrested me.'

'Why the hell would you carry a water pistol?' says Harry.

'Pretty handy,' says Ruiz. 'You fill it with ammonia, it's better than pepper spray, and you don't need a license to carry it. You hit somebody in the eyes or the nose, believe me, they ain't gonna bother you no more.'

'And you can do that at a distance with a water pistol?' says Harry.

Ruiz just looks at him and nods slowly, as if to say if he had his water pistol he'd show him right now.

'Let's not let the jury in on that little secret,' says Harry. 'When it comes to target shooting, I don't think we'd need to give them any more credentials. All the same, you shoulda told us about Delta.'

'Why? So you could put me on the stand and ask me questions I couldn't answer? I took an oath, a vow,' he says, 'never to reveal what we did in the unit. I don't care how it comes out, you mention Delta and Templeton's gonna squat all over it. Besides, my time in Delta had nothing to do with Chapman's murder.'

'How do we know you're out?' Harry is reading my mind.

'What do you mean?'

'How do we know you weren't working for Delta when you were out at Isotenics? According to everything we're hearing, they were having a lot of problems with the Pentagon,' says Harry. 'The brass might like somebody on the inside providing information as to what Chapman was doing.'

'This is bullshit,' says Ruiz. 'You saw my discharge papers. You think they would let me sit here and rot if I was part of Delta; working for them?' He shakes his head. 'They would have had somebody else arrested by now. The government may have killed her, but I didn't do it. That's why I'm the patsy.

'This was a setup from day one,' he tells us. 'It wouldn't matter how it came in. The minute anybody used the word in that courtroom, Templeton would have pointed at me and said, "The murderer from Delta." Hell, they're already saying it.'

He looks at Harry. 'You read the newspapers. You see what they're saying. How we're all highly tuned killers. How they train us to murder and then don't give us therapy,' says Ruiz. 'How we're all trigger-happy, wired-on-the-edge macho men trained to slap everybody around the minute we don't get what we want.

'But they don't talk about that when some asshole sets off a bomb on a bus or flies an airplane into a building. No. Then they just want it taken care of, and they want it done so it's clean, sanitary,' he says. 'They want their own professional killers. They want us to be the best in the world. They want us ready to go when things happen, but they want us to be nice when we're sitting on the shelf. To shoot the enemy in a humane way, which means they don't have to watch it,' he says. 'They want to be told that all the bad guys are dead, and if not, why not. And when you slow down to reload, they want to draw a line in the dirt and say, "That's it, you can stop now," while the fuckers who shot us are sitting over there, just the other side of the line.'

He stands there looking at Harry, fire in his eyes. 'You want to know why I didn't tell you? That's why. Because the lawyers who do their cases in court, and the reporters who report it, don't live in the same world I do. They live in a fantasy world where you can eat hot food, and drink clean water, sit on a clean toilet seat, and turn everything on and off whenever you want, like a light switch. So you can forget about Delta. The only question now is, where do we go from here?'

'You finished?' says Harry.

'Yeah, I'm finished.'

'I'd love to forget about Delta,' says Harry. 'Now, if you can just tell us how to get the jury to do it . . .'

'It had nothing to do with Chapman's murder. I told you, I didn't kill her. Everything else I said was true. I don't know who shot her or why. She was afraid. She called me and asked me to keep an eye. That's what happened, and that's what I told you.'

Without putting Ruiz on the stand, we have no way of even asserting any of this, much less proving it. Confronted with the videotape and photos of Emiliano 'stalking' the victim, his story that she asked him to provide security without telling anyone else, and that she was afraid of some mystery assailant, appear both self-serving and highly convenient to the point of being contrived. To put Ruiz on the stand to testify to this would be judicial suicide. Templeton would shred him on cross.

'Son, let me tell you,' says Harry, 'so that you know exactly where you stand at this moment. And I'm not telling you this to make you feel any worse than you already do. Larry Templeton is going to ride that photograph, the shot with the gun in your hand. He's gonna whip it like a stallion right through his closing argument. I can tell you right now, with absolute certainty, that picture will be the last thing lingering up on the visualizer when the lights come up and the show is over. When that happens, if I were a betting man, and I am, I'd be placing all my money on the prosecutor.'

'Thank you for your honesty,' says Emiliano. He looks at me. 'How 'bout you, Counselor?'

'I don't like to gamble. If I had my choice, I'd start over.'

'That would be a neat trick,' Ruiz says.

There's a rap on the door. It's Gilcrest's bailiff. He has one of the guards open it from the outside with his key.

'Judge wants to see all the lawyers in chambers,' he says.

The guards take Emiliano. Harry and I head out into the empty courtroom. We round the bench and go down the side hall toward the back. Gilcrest's office door is open when we get there. Templeton is waiting for us in the outer area.

'What's this about?' I ask.

Larry shrugs. 'Your guess is as good as mine.' He follows Harry and me through the door.

The judge looks up from his desk. 'Gentlemen, I hope you don't have any plans for the weekend, seeing as mine were just trashed. I've received a phone call from the clerk at the Court of Appeals,' he says.

'They made a decision on the evidence,' says Harry.

'No,' says the judge. 'It seems Mr Sims has decided to withdraw his appeal.'

Harry and I look at each other.

'Well. Looks like you're finally going to get your evidence,' says Templeton.

On the way out of the courthouse Harry is hitting numbers on his cell phone, calling the office, telling the staff to cancel their weekend plans. We separate near the bank of elevators. I tell Harry I'll see him at the office in the morning, and I take the stairs. One floor down, I step out of the stairwell and head for one of the pay phones.

I don't use my cell phone; I don't want to call from the office or the house. It may not even be a technical violation of the judge's gag order, but I don't want to find out. The phone rings twice. I'm hoping that he's there. On the third ring he picks up.

'AP, Saentz here.'

'Hello, Tim.'

'Who is this?'

'Deep Throat,' I say.

He recognizes my voice.

'I just want to give you a heads up, nothing about the trial,' I tell him. 'But you might want to call the Court of Appeals to find out if anything happened today.'

'Really?'

'Really.' Then I hang up.

I head for the stairs. On the way, I walk right in front of the door with the sign on it. The one that reads: Courthouse Press Room.

Saturday morning and Gilcrest's irritation is surpassed only by his wife's. The judge has had to tell her that their weekend anniversary trip to Santa Barbara is off. Today he is camped at his office in the courthouse as we use Herman to act as courier, shuttling boxes of documents across the bridge, reams of paper from Isotenics, as quickly as Gilcrest can review them.

The judge promised us a three-day continuance if the evidence was released. True to his word, he has given the jury Monday off as we pore through piles of paper.

We have researched the presidential decision directive. PDD-25 is classified. All that exists is a summary online. It deals with joint military operations between the United States, the UN, and NATO. Ruiz is right: the summary says nothing about Delta Force or the Joint Special Operations Command. Harry and I made a desperate pitch for more time from the judge, but Gilcrest said no.

Under the circumstances he doesn't have much

451

choice. With the jury sequestered, locked up in a hotel downtown with bailiffs and sheriff's deputies to act as chaperones, the court is caught between a rock and a hard place. Gilcrest can't allow them to go home, not with the state's evidence now rooted firmly in their brains. There is no telling who they would talk to, what news programs they might watch, or what newspapers they could read.

If he were to keep them camped in a hotel for days while he delayed the trial to give us more time, he would likely have a mob on his hands when they returned. The fallout of their displeasure would splash all over the defendant, since he's the only one the jury can punish. Either way, the court is likely to run headlong into a mistrial or end up on the rocks following an appeal.

'Next time I see Templeton, I'm gonna stuff the little shit in a shoe box and ship him to Mongolia bulk mail.' Harry is bent over one of the boxes, rifling through paper, sniffing for anything that smells as if it might be useable in our case.

This morning we have pulled in the entire staff: both secretaries, the receptionist, and two clerks, including Jamie, our law grad-cum-computer tech, to sift through reams of paper. The chances of us even touching every page, much less reading them all, are remote.

Harry and I are under no illusion. The last-minute timing on the evidence drop from Isotenics was arranged courtesy of the prosecution. Templeton knows that if the evidence from Isotenics were withheld from us entirely, there is a good chance that any conviction or death sentence would be overturned on appeal. If that were to happen, the courts would remand Ruiz for a new trial. Templeton wants to take that arrow out of our quiver. As usual, his timing is impeccable. Having rested his own case on a mountain peak on Friday afternoon, he has buried us in a paper blizzard over the weekend before we open our own case for the defense.

'I think they call this marshaling the evidence,' says Harry. 'If this is organization, I'd hate to see what chaos looks like.'

The only silver seam in this dark cloud is on the front page of today's paper. Next to the three-column headline announcing DOUBLE TAP DEFENDANT, MEMBER OF DELTA FORCE is a boxed sidebar. The story has a wire service by-line reporting that an appeal filed by the victim's company, Isotenics, Inc., which had managed to bottle up evidence being sought by the defense, was withdrawn late yesterday afternoon. Attorneys for the company would not say why. According to the story, as a consequence, at least fifty-eight boxes of documents, enough to fill a small moving van, were expected to be released to the trial court within hours.

Given the fact that the court had not made a decision delivering an opinion, I knew that it would not issue a press release. It would take two or three days before somebody in the press stumbled over the news that Sims had withdrawn his appeal. By then it would be too late. If I am correct, my audience for this story will be up all night, burning the midnight oil in the lamps at the Pentagon and the offices of the Justice Department in downtown DC.

I put the newspaper down and go to work. We are looking for anything that sheds light on Chapman's dealings with the Pentagon: printouts of e-mails between her and Satz, internal memos, letters, and copies of telephone messages and phone logs. Anything addressed to Defense or the Pentagon is being organized in separate stacks on the table in the conference room under the watchful eye of Janice, my secretary.

One thing that I know with certainty at this point: if the case goes to the jury for a verdict, Ruiz is dead.

I finish a box of documents, check it with a red marker and write my initials, and set it in a separate stack outside in the hallway of the office. Out in reception there are boxes stacked halfway up the wall and three deep against it, a new delivery by Herman, who has gone back to the courthouse for more. I paw through them, turning a few of the cardboard transfer boxes to check for labels or notations.

'Think I found something.' It's Jamie, working at one of the secretaries' desks behind me.

'What is it?' I'm still feeling my way around the cubes of cardboard.

'The box I picked up. There's a note on the side. Says *M. Chapman – desk* on it.'

'Let me see it.'

The note on the side is in black marker and dated. Jamie lifts the lid.

Inside are copies of the contents from Chapman's desk the day she died. Most of these are materials we already have from noticed motions served on the cops. There are handwritten notes, copies of telephone slips, full-page copies of single yellow stickers that were stuck to the glass surface of her desk. A reduction from a computer spreadsheet on letter-size paper, the words *42nd Cong* in pencil on the front. These are the dizzying numbers Harold Klepp told me about that night at the bar, the ones Chapman took from him and threw in her inbasket before she told him to get out. Klepp was right: she never got to it. I have seen all of this before. It was scooped up by the homicide investigators who descended on Chapman's office that night, before Havlitz and Isotenics could get their lawyers to lock the doors in order to filter the stuff that was leaving.

I'm nearing the bottom of the box when I see something that catches my eye. It's a gray-toned black-and-white copy of a telephone message slip. I pluck it out. On the lines under the boxes, on the one marked *Please call*, is the neatly penned note *Needs to talk about 'Looking Glass.'* On the *From* line the name *Gerald Satz* is written elegantly in the same hand, and a phone number with a 703 area code. The note is directed to *MC*, Madelyn Chapman, and initialed at the bottom by the message taker, *KR* – Karen Rogan.

CHAPTER THIRTY-TWO

Tuesday morning. I am snarled in traffic on the Coronado Bridge heading to court to make my opening statement in *People v. Ruiz*. The cell phone on my belt rings. It is Janice, calling from the office.

'I just got a phone call,' she says. 'I thought you'd want to know. Jim Kaprosky died last night. His wife called. She said to thank you for coming by, and that he went quietly in his sleep.'

I don't remember the rest of the trip. It's as if I am on autopilot. I end up in the quiet car, in the parking lot a block from the courthouse, the engine off, not knowing how I got there, my mind deep in thought.

I have seen much of death, of both friends and family. The fact that a man I spoke with barely three nights ago now rests in that place, beyond reach, seems to affect me in ways I had not expected.

It seems I have reached that point in life, much nearer to the end than the beginning, so that of late I have been thinking a great deal about what lies beyond the arc of this life. Will we find friends there, those we have loved and lost? In that moment, does some part of our being, unhampered by brain or body, slip from this form into an infinite realm unaffected by the limits of time or physics? These are questions that cannot be answered by tasting fruit from the tree of knowledge. It is the lasting lesson, the ultimate unknowable, man's legacy from Adam's fall. It is a bridge to be crossed only by belief, the intimate and secluded secret that lies between us and our maker.

As I lock the car and head for the courthouse, I hope and pray and choose to believe that one day we will find the light and love of a transcendent God. And that if peace may be had, that Jim Kaprosky, having finally been freed from the furies of this world, is there now.

When I arrive, the courtroom is filling fast. The hallway outside is a scene out of *Gandhi*, a sea of heads swimming on shoulders, all of them moving, trying to get through the bottleneck of the open double doors to their seats inside. Nathan is here again today, moving his way up in terms of seniority. Today he has worked his way up to the middle of the courtroom.

Harry is already set up at the table, Jamie with the laptop, though we have precious little to put in it at this point.

Emiliano has not been brought in yet. The guards won't do that until the crowd is seated and the doors at the rear are closed and guarded, inside and out.

Templeton is at the table with the detective Mike Argust and his computer tech. He is introducing Argust to three other men, all inside the railing. I have not seen them before. Two of them are younger, I would say in their early thirties; the other is older, his gray hair finely groomed. In pinstripes, all carrying bell-shaped leather briefcases, they have the look of government about them. Over the hum of voices in the room I can't hear what Templeton is saying to them.

The two younger guys are smiling; the older one has a more serious expression. His suit is a bit wrinkled and he looks tired, as if he's been on an airplane all night.

As I approach the bar railing at the main aisle, Templeton nods in my direction but doesn't look at me as he continues talking to them. The older man turns and looks at me, the kind of expression you might get from a hired gun who is sizing you up. Even with the wrinkles and tired eyes, he is dapper and fit, in the prime of litigation life. I am guessing that he has a fairly high GS rating, as if Justice probably saves him for Sundays and going-to-trial-use only.

The other two are gofers. One of them looks like he might be military by the way the civilian suit fits him, as if he hasn't had it on in a while.

As I lay my briefcase on the table and sit, Harry comes over and says into my ear, 'I think you got their attention.'

'We'll know shortly,' I tell him.

A minute later they lock up the back doors, one sheriff's guard posted inside and one out. By now they have it down to a routine. Two minutes later, almost on the dot, the holding-cell door opens and they bring in Emiliano. As he traverses the area in front of the prosecution table, the lawyer from Washington gives him a hard look. He watches Ruiz as he walks the distance to our table flanked by guards. The lawyer doesn't look away until he notices me watching him.

Emiliano sits down in the chair and leans toward me. 'Who the hell are they?' Like a dog sniffing for dominance, Ruiz can smell them.

'I think they work for your former masters,' I tell him.

'What do they want?'

'That's what we're hoping to find out.'

Gilcrest comes in, takes the bench, and slaps the gavel down. The bailiff intones, 'Court is in session. The Right Honorable Samuel Gilcrest presiding.'

'Be seated,' says Gilcrest. This happens before the lawyers and some in the audience can get halfway out of their chairs.

The judge arranges some papers on the blotter up on the bench, then looks over and sees the mob sitting in the chairs inside the railing, behind the prosecution table. 'Who do we have here, Mr Templeton?'

The gray-haired man starts to rise from his chair, the fingers of one hand gently touching the closed center button on his jacket, all the gestures of a Renaissance courtier.

'Just visiting counsel, Your Honor.' Templeton doesn't offer any introductions beyond that.

'Very well, take your seats, gentlemen.'

The gray hair sits down.

'Any motions or documents?' says the Judge.

'Yes, Your Honor.' Harry is on his feet.

'We would move at this time for a directed verdict, and move that the court dismiss the case against Emiliano Ruiz in as much as the state has failed to meet its burden of establishing evidence beyond a reasonable doubt. I have points and authorities, Your Honor.'

'You can have the bailiff bring them forward,' says Gilcrest.

'Your Honor, if I might . . .' Templeton has his hand up. He would like to go to the podium and get up on the stool to argue the matter.

'That won't be necessary,' says the judge. 'I'm going to take the motion under submission at this time and allow the defense to put on its case — unless, of course, the defendant wishes to have me make a ruling on the motion at this time.'

The motion for a directed verdict is a mere formality. It must be made at the close of the state's case or else it is deemed waived. If Gilcrest had granted it and cut Ruiz free, both Harry and I would have needed cardiac shock therapy to bring us back. As it is, we don't require that the judge embarrass us in front of the audience. We allow him to sit on the motion until the end of the trial, when he can use it to make confetti.

'Mr Madriani, are you ready to proceed?' he says.

'I am, Your Honor.'

'You can bring in the jury,' says Gilcrest.

A few seconds later they begin to file in. They take their seats in the box. The alternates march around to the front and take the six chairs in the corner of the courtroom up front. Several of the jurors are looking toward Templeton's table. They've noticed that there are extras here today. Lawyering must be slow.

The judge greets them and gives them a moment to settle in, then looks at me. 'Mr Madriani, you may begin.'

I stand, walk over, and take up position directly in front of the jury box. 'Good morning, ladies and gentlemen.'

A few of them smile. Most, having been here long

enough by now, are no longer charmed by the social pleasantries. They have seen too many pictures of brain matter and blood, watered down with spinal fluid, to be entertained by a smile and a greeting.

It is common practice for the defense in a criminal case to reserve its opening statement until after the prosecution has laid out all of its evidence for the jury. That way you have a chance to tailor your response and see where you stand.

The fact that we have been pushed off a cliff leaves me floating in air, and while I'm squarely in front of the jury box, I will be making my statement to a different audience, and for an entirely different purpose.

I begin slowly, deliberately. 'Your Honor, ladies and gentlemen of the jury.' I acknowledge the presence of Madelyn Chapman's mother and sister sitting in the front row. I gesture toward them but I don't look. I know that this would only bring expressions of rebuke, which I would rather avoid.

Using their names, I tell the jury, 'They have suffered greatly. They have a right to our respect as well as our sympathy. But most of all' – I bring my voice up in volume, so that several of the jurors look startled – 'they deserve to have the real killer, the person who perpetrated this crime – the person who actually murdered their daughter, their sister – caught, convicted, and punished. What greater travesty could occur not only to the defendant but to those who loved Madelyn Chapman than to convict the wrong person?' I ask. 'In this, the state is failing them miserably. For whoever commissioned the murder of Madelyn Chapman and whoever carried out that crime is not in this courtroom today.'

Templeton begins to stir in his chair, about to

jump on me for making an argument during my opening.

'Ladies and gentlemen, while the defendant, Emiliano Ruiz, has absolutely no duty, no obligation, no burden, to prove his innocence, and while the state bears the highest burden to prove his guilt, proof beyond a reasonable doubt, the defense will produce evidence to establish beyond any question that Emiliano Ruiz is innocent of this crime.

'In determining who killed Madelyn Chapman, the most critical issue, the most vexing question, is, why was she killed?' I look over at Templeton in his chair, and the three lawyers sitting behind him, a dramatic pause, as if to say the state has failed this question.

I turn back to the jury. 'We will produce evidence that Madelyn Chapman was killed because of something she discovered.'

It has been clear from the beginning that, rather than attack Chapman and accuse her of playing sly games with the government over the use of her software, the better approach is to cast her in the role of heroine, the doer of good deeds, who paid with her life for trying to undo evil.

'So why was she killed? What was it that Madelyn Chapman discovered that caused her death?' I pause for a second or two. 'Ladies and gentlemen' – I drop my voice a half octave so that some jurors lean forward in their seats to hear – 'the defense will produce evidence to prove that the victim, Madelyn Chapman, discovered a scandal of immense proportions. We will produce a document showing, beyond any question or doubt, that the computer software produced by Isotenics, Incorporated, the company run by the

victim, Madelyn Chapman – the computer program
known as Primis, the key component to IFS, the
government's Information for Security Program . . .' When I turn to look toward Templeton's
table, the gray hair in the suit is all eyes and they
are directed at me like a laser '. . . the software
designed to run IFS, the project that is under
review by the Congress of the United States at
this very moment – was in fact transformed before
the victim's own eyes and was being used by
elements within our own government to spy on the
American public.'

There is a hum of voices in the audience. The
guy with the gray hair is out of his chair, leaning
over, whispering into Templeton's ear.

As I turn I can see Templeton out of the corner
of my eye trying to quell a mini-rebellion behind
him. Turned partway around on top of the chair,
he is whispering and gesturing with his hands.

Gilcrest slaps the gavel. 'I'll have it quiet or I'll
clear the courtroom. Mr Templeton, please. Excuse
me, Mr Madriani.' The judge apologizes for the
interruption.

I offer a smile, a shake of the head, and gesture
as if to say, 'No problem. Please feel free to kick
the crap out of the prosecutor at any time.'

'Mr Templeton, have your guest take his seat.'
They are still whispering and doing pantomime
with their hands as the judge breaks it up.

'Sorry, Your Honor,' Templeton apologizes, and
the guy in the suit sits down.

'Please, go ahead, Mr Madriani.'

The problem with most of this is that I have no
evidence. The gulf between what I am promising
and what I can prove would swallow the Aswan
Dam.

'As for the defendant, Mr Ruiz,' I tell them, 'our evidence will show that he was simply in the wrong place at the wrong time, a convenient scapegoat whose firearm from his earlier military service was discovered and used to commit this crime. The evidence has already shown that there was no serious effort to dispose of this weapon after the crime was committed, but that instead the killer laid the gun in the garden, where the police would trip over it, and placed the silencer on the rocks, where it would be found. The evidence will show that this is not the rational conduct of a man who knows that the firearm in question will be traced back to him. So you must ask yourself once again: Why was this done?'

Templeton objects, claiming that this last bit is argument. He asks the judge to strike it from the record.

'So ordered,' says Gilcrest. 'The jury will disregard the last question posed by counsel.'

Time to light the coals at Templeton's table again.

'We will show beyond any question or shadow of a doubt that Primis, the software developed by Madelyn Chapman and sold by her company, Isotenics, Incorporated, to the federal government, had been transformed by sinister forces and used to spy on the very citizens it was intended to protect.'

This time it's a gang bang. All three of the government lawyers are out of their chairs, huddled at Templeton's shoulders, pumping protest into his ears. The judge slaps his gavel. I look at the bench, and by the time I turn around again, the scene at Templeton's table looks like part of the refectory wall from Leonardo da Vinci's

Last Supper, everybody jumping on Judas and the paint peeling off the wall.

This time I don't let it stop me.

'We will produce a witness who will sit on that stand' – I point to the witness box – 'and will testify under oath that Madelyn Chapman was killed after she discovered that her software had already been harnessed to millions of personal computers and industry networks. That it was being used daily to read and copy massive volumes of private information, everything from personal medical records to financial information and personal correspondence. That anything and everything being processed, stored, or sent by computer was being read and copied by super computers in Washington, DC, without your knowledge or your consent.'

When I glance back toward Templeton's table, the expression on the lead lawyer's face looks as if he's had a stroke.

'We will show by witness testimony that Madelyn Chapman complained bitterly *and loudly* when she discovered this fact. And that she was murdered in order to prevent her from revealing the existence of this *spyware.*'

With the emphasis on the last word, there is an uproar in the courtroom. The judge bangs the gavel, but at least a half dozen reporters in the front row bolt for the door.

'Silence!' Gilcrest shouts in a booming voice, so that even Templeton is jerked a little in his chair. 'Those people, the ones who just ran out' – he points with his gavel – 'they do not get back in. Do I make myself clear?'

'Yes, Your Honor.' One of the bailiffs heads out to get names and descriptions so he can enforce the banishment.

'Fill their chairs with members of the public,' says Gilcrest. 'Somebody's gonna get ringside seats.'

As people start moving to fill the vacant chairs, Nathan Kwan seems to hurdle forward four rows like an Olympic athlete and ends up in the center of the front row.

It takes the judge five minutes to restore order. I take my seat at the table. The entire time Templeton is arguing with the government lawyers, giving me the evil eye whenever he can spare the time. The three lawyers are angry. I would be, too, if Templeton had manipulated the release of tons of paper from a defense contractor without giving me the courtesy of a phone call or the opportunity to review the information. God only knows what it is that we have back at the office because, given the limited time frame, Harry and I sure as hell don't.

Templeton could have no way of knowing that he was putting his case in jeopardy, because Templeton had never met Jim Kaprosky or been briefed on the shoals and pitfalls of national security. When he had Sims open the floodgates on the documents from Isotenics, Templeton put himself up to his hips in muddy water. Now the crocodiles are stirring on the beach. The only question is, can I get them to snap?

CHAPTER
THIRTY-THREE

Templeton is talking with both hands, eyes like saucers, a broad smile on his face, his most sincere expressions of assurance. He now turns the other way so I can no longer see his lips moving. But I can read his mind. He is trying to convince the three government lawyers that Harry and I have a briefcase full of nothing but air.

'Mr Madriani, you want to call your first witness?' says Gilcrest.

If Templeton's guests don't do something soon, the judge is going to force me to open it. And then everybody in the courtroom will know that, not only is the briefcase empty, but Harry, Emiliano, and I are all sitting here at the table naked.

'Your Honor, the defense calls Karen Rogan.'

'Karen Rogan.' I hear the name repeated by one of the bailiffs out in the hallway.

Templeton manages to get the three lawyers to sit down again, but the older one is shaking his head. He seems no longer to be asking Templeton: he is telling him. It may only be wishful thinking, but my sense is that the prosecution is now on a short tether.

467

Rogan enters the courtroom through the main doors in the back. As she walks up the aisle toward the bench and the witness chair, every head in the audience turns. The three government lawyers take a bead on her. Then they confer. Puzzled expressions, and then one of the younger ones gets up and heads for the door.

The judge doesn't stop him: the privileges of sitting inside the bar's railing.

Rogan steps up to the platform. The judge reminds her that she's already sworn in. She takes the seat and repeats her name for the record, then spells it.

'Good morning.'

She nods at me and smiles politely.

'Ms Rogan, as I recall from your earlier testimony, you are employed at Isotenics, Incorporated.'

'That's right.'

'And that prior to her death you worked as executive assistant to Madelyn Chapman, is that correct?'

'Yes.'

'Can you tell the jury where your office is located at Isotenics?'

'I work on the second level of the headquarters building on campus, the executive level, in an open area.'

I pick through the pile of papers on the lectern in front of me and pull out a schematic of the Isotenics headquarters, the wedding cake with a dome out in the hills above La Jolla. The bailiff delivers a copy to the witness and the judge, and one is dropped on Templeton's table.

The witness identifies the location, marked with an X on the drawing where her desk is located on the second floor. The floor plan is printed to scale.

I have the drawing marked defense exhibit next in order and moved into evidence. There is no objection from Templeton, and a second later the drawing appears up on the visualizer. Now the jury and the two government lawyers who are still sitting there can play along.

'And the two double doors directly across from where your desk appears in the drawing' – I hit the desk and then the doors on the screen with a laser pointer in my hand – 'where do those doors lead?'

'That's the CEO's office.'

'By *CEO*, do you mean the chief executive officer of Isotenics, the head of the company?'

'That's right.'

'And during her time, before she was killed, did Madelyn Chapman occupy that office?'

'She did.'

'How far would you say it is from your desk to those doors?'

'I don't know. Maybe ten feet.'

'If I told you that, according to the scale on this floor plan, which was obtained with documents that we received from Isotenics, the distance is almost exactly eight feet, would you question that?'

'No. That's probably right.'

'And inside the CEO's office, do you see another area with a small rectangle, marked with an X?'

'Yes.'

'Can you tell the jury what that represents?'

'I suspect it's the location of the desk. Ms Chapman's desk.'

'Does it look as if it's in the right place in the drawing? Is that about where Ms Chapman's desk was located?'

We play a little tongue tag and she finally agrees that the desk was no more than ten feet inside the double doors. While Chapman's office was immense, one of the interior walls was lined with shelves containing art glass and other collectibles. She had her desk turned toward the two walls of windows that looked out toward the Pacific so that when she sat behind it, her back was to the double doors.

'I know it's a strange arrangement,' says Rogan, 'but it's what she liked. She wanted the view. She loved looking at the ocean.'

'So while her desk was, say, ten feet away from the doors to her office, by the time she sat in her chair, she was probably less than eight feet from those doors, is that right?'

The witness is nodding. 'Yes, I said that's about right.'

'And if she pushed back from the desk, perhaps leaned back in her chair – say, to talk on the phone – she might be only seven or eight feet away from the door to her office.'

Rogan nods.

'You have to speak up for the reporter.'

'Yes. That's right.'

'So the total distance from your desk to where Madelyn Chapman sat at her desk was no more than sixteen to eighteen feet.'

'Yes.'

'Do you know what the doors to Ms Chapman's office were made of?'

'They were wood panel. I think they were probably pine. They were a little different than the other office doors on that level: Colonial. They had been put in by a decorator hired by Ms Chapman.'

'What were the acoustics like?' I zero in: 'Was it possible to hear what was being said inside Ms Chapman's office if the doors were closed? From your desk, I mean.'

'The walls were thin,' she says. 'The building was designed to look old, but it wasn't. I told her once that her office needed some soundproofing.'

'You told Madelyn Chapman?'

'Yes.'

'And did she have that done?'

'No.'

Until this moment I couldn't be sure. Now I am. Karen Rogan is signaling me to pop the question. I stop nibbling and put my fork in the enchilada.

'In your capacity as executive assistant to Ms Chapman, did you place and receive phone calls on her behalf at Isotenics?'

'Yes.'

'Did you ever either place or receive a phone call to or from General Gerald Satz at the Pentagon in Washington, DC?'

With the mention of the name, there is a little buzz in the courtroom. The judge looks but lets it die down.

'Yes, many times.'

'Do you recall a telephone conversation between Ms Chapman and General Satz in which Ms Chapman's voice was raised in apparent anger.'

'Objection,' says Templeton. 'Vague as to the time period.'

'Sustained.'

'Within the last, say, three months before her death, do you recall a telephone conversation between Madelyn Chapman and General Satz in which the tone and level of Ms Chapman's voice became elevated in apparent anger?'

'Yes.'

'Objection,' says Templeton. 'How can the witness possibly know who the victim was talking to unless she was listening on the other line.'

'Why don't we ask her, Your Honor?'

'Do it,' says the judge.

'During the time that you heard this conversation, were you listening on the other line?'

'No.'

'Then how did you know that Madelyn Chapman was talking to General Satz?'

'Because Ms Chapman had asked me to place the phone call and I transferred the general to her line.'

I turn to look at Templeton's table just as one of the doors at the rear of the courtroom opens. It's the government lawyer who left, coming back. He hustles up the aisle. This time he is carrying some papers in his hand. He moves quietly through the gate in the railing, hands the papers to the older lawyer, and takes his seat again.

'And when you transferred the call to Ms Chapman, you hung up after that?'

'Yes.'

'But you say you still heard part of the conversation?'

'I heard Ms Chapman's voice.'

'And what was she saying?'

'She was angry. She was shouting.'

'Was there anyone else in the office with her at the time?'

'No.'

'Do you ever remember her shouting like that before?'

'She could get angry, lose her temper. But I'd never heard her like that before.'

'What did she say? Do you remember the words?'

'She said something to the effect that "You lied to me. You set me up. You're using spyware and you didn't tell me."'

There's the stir of voices out in the audience.

'You're certain about that? That those are the words she used?'

'Yes.' She nods. There is no hesitation.

I turn to look at Templeton's table. The three lawyers are huddled. Templeton turns to try to head off another revolt.

'Ms Rogan,' I say, 'do you know what the term *spyware* means?'

'Objection.' Templeton spins around on his box, trying to put out fires on both fronts now. 'The witness is not a software expert.'

'Your Honor, I'm not asking for an expert opinion. I'm asking the witness what her understanding of the term was at the time she overheard this conversation – that is, if she had any understanding.'

'I'll allow it for that purpose,' says Gilcrest.

The older lawyer with the gray hair is on his feet now, standing near his chair and looking but saying nothing. Boring holes into the witness.

'At the time you overheard the conversation, what was your understanding of the term *spyware*?'

'As I understand it, it is special software designed to attach to people's computers in order to mine data, collect information from their hard drives.'

'So you had heard the term before?'

'Yes.'

'From whom?'

'Engineers. Software-design engineers at Isotenics.'

'And, to your knowledge, did Isotenics make spyware?'

'No, not that I'm aware of.'

I reach into the pile of papers in front of me on the rostrum. Moment of truth. I slip out the copy of the telephone message from the box of documents collected from Madelyn Chapman's desk the day she died. The bailiff delivers a copy of this to the witness and the judge. Harry drops one on the table in front of Templeton.

The government lawyer leans over his shoulder. When he sees the words *looking glass* penned in an elegant hand in the middle of the slip, he puts a hand on Templeton's shoulder, and for a moment it looks as if he's going to strangle him from behind. He has his face down at Templeton's ear. Templeton is shaking his head. He doesn't want to hear it.

'Ms Rogan, is that your handwriting on the form that is copied on that sheet of paper?'

'Yes.'

'Did you write that note?'

'Yes, I did.'

'Can you tell the court what it is?'

'It's a telephone message slip, taken by me and directed to Ms Chapman.'

'And what's the date on that slip?'

'March twenty-third.'

'This last year?'

'Yes.'

'Three days before Madelyn Chapman was murdered?'

'Yes.'

'And who was this phone call from?'

'General Satz.'

'Did you take the call personally on behalf of Ms Chapman?'

474

'I did.'

'So you talked to the general on the phone?'

'Yes.'

'And can you tell the jury what he wanted?'

'Your Honor.' I hear the voice from Templeton's table, but it's not Templeton. 'Excuse me, Your Honor. My name is Edmund Yost.'

Gilcrest looks confused, not sure that he is actually hearing some stranger interrupting proceedings in his courtroom. 'I am senior counsel at the Department of Justice, representing the Department of Defense, Office of Intelligence.' He reaches behind him without even looking.

One of the other lawyers hands him a stapled sheaf of papers.

'I have an order in my hand issued earlier this morning staying these proceedings indefinitely, signed by the senior judge of the Foreign Intelligence Surveillance Court of Review in Washington, DC.'

'Let me see that.' Gilcrest holds out his hand.

The lawyer hands the papers to the bailiff, who takes them to the judge. Gilcrest looks at them, flips a page, and reads. The document appears to be only a few pages long.

'Mr Templeton, did you know about this?'

'Your Honor, I just found out,' he says. 'I haven't seen that document. In answer to your question, no, I didn't know. Not until just now.'

'It appears to be in order,' says Gilcrest. 'I don't see any date for the lifting of the stay.'

'There is none, Your Honor.' This from the gray-headed counsel from DC.

'This court has no authority to supersede a federal court order. By the same terms, the defendant is entitled to his day in court. I cannot hold the jury indefinitely. What do you propose I do?' Gilcrest puts this to the government lawyer.

'I'm sorry, Your Honor. The United States government takes no position regarding the outcome of this trial.'

'Other than to stay the proceedings of it indefinitely,' says the judge.

'Your Honor, perhaps a brief continuance until we can sort this out,' says Templeton.

'No,' says Gilcrest. 'I may have no authority to override a federal court order, but I surely have authority to control the proceedings in this court. Based on this order, which will become part of the record, this trial is now over. I'm declaring a mistrial. The jury is released. The defendant Emiliano Ruiz is discharged. This court is adjourned.'

There's an uproar in the courtroom.

I look over at Larry Templeton. It is the first time I have ever seen him at a loss for words.

Harry is sitting there looking at me, dumb-founded.

'You son of a bitch.' He is laughing, smiling at me. It has finally dawned on him exactly what I meant that day in our office when I told him that if we were lucky we might not have to deal with Templeton at all – or, for that matter the jury.

The judge is off the bench.

'You, of all people, shouldn't be surprised,' I tell him. 'You are the one who's been telling me all these years that I can always count on the federal government to screw things up.' Harry is up and grabbing me by the shoulders, giving me a hug.

'What else could I do?' I'm saying in Harry's ear. 'Instinct told us he didn't do it. This was the only sure way out.'

'I don't believe it. Sonofabitch.' This time it comes out as one word. Harry can't contain himself, slapping me on the back. He turns, pulls Ruiz up from his chair, and lays a hug on him.

Emiliano seems dazed, stunned by the speed of what has just happened. 'I'm free.' I can read his lips, but I can't hear the words over the mayhem in the courtroom. Reporters are leaning over the railing as the guards hold them back.

While the uninitiated might censure me for failing to establish Emiliano's innocence, to clear his good name, under the circumstances this would have been a fool's errand. Unfortunately the criminal law was never equipped to prove innocence. It was crafted to establish one thing only: guilt. In the eyes of the public, which holds the collateral to all of our reputations, the absence of guilt is seldom seen as the equivalent of innocence. In Emiliano's case, even a jury verdict of acquittal would leave half the world wondering if Ruiz didn't in fact murder Madelyn Chapman. Weighed against the possibility of a death sentence, only the feebleminded would have elected to go to a verdict as opposed to the certain result of a mistrial. But one thing is certain. The state will never try him again. They would face the same impediment: a federal government intent on protecting the mysteries of state under the rubric of national security.

In the confusion of the courtroom, I fail to notice that Rogan is leaving until I see her in the center aisle, merging with the audience heading for doors.

I go after her before she can disappear into the mob outside. Out in the hallway it's a madhouse, reporters with notebooks pushing and shoving. Within minutes they open the doors and allow them to clear their cameras through the security line downstairs. Crews are staking out space, setting up lights to get the doors leading to the courtroom with the department number on the wall next to them good as background shots.

I see Nathan holding forth with some of the reporters. The fledgling congressman from another city whose office in Washington, when it is finally assigned a week from now, is likely to be a coat closet a mile from the Capitol, is establishing his credentials as the resident political expert on IFS and what Congress will do now.

Several of the reporters are hanging on me, asking questions about IFS, what information we have. The flashes from cameras and the heat of the lights of the Minicams make me put my hand up in front of my eyes.

Templeton comes out of the door behind me, heading as fast as he can in the other direction. They chase him and Templeton starts running.

I finally catch up Karen in the crowd, take her by the arm. When she turns she seems surprised. 'I wanted to thank you. I couldn't earlier. The judge's gag order.'

'No need to thank me,' she says. 'I did what I was supposed to. Can they rearrest him?' she asks. She's talking about Emiliano.

'They could, but it won't do them any good. They'd run into the same wall that just fell on them. National security trumps all,' I say.

'If I ever get in trouble, I want you for a lawyer,' she says. 'What do you think he'll do now? Mr Ruiz, I mean.'

'Why don't you ask him?'

'You think he'd talk to me?'

'I'm sure he would.'

Suddenly she smiles. I have suspected for a while that Karen's testimony on the videotape may have been motivated by something more than her simple wish to maintain Chapman's name unsullied.

Nathan is finished with the press for the moment. He comes up and plants himself near us, listening as I talk to Karen. The way he is eyeing the pretty redhead, I can tell that Nathan is looking for an introduction.

The press follows him and suddenly it's a crowd. One of them tries to ask me a question.

'I have nothing to say.' I have told Tim Saentz, the AP reporter, that as soon as the trial is over, he has the exclusive on anything I can talk about.

The three government lawyers come out of the courtroom. The press abandons us and mobs them, leaving Karen and me to talk, Nathan hanging on the periphery.

Kwan suffers from the political equivalent of seasonal affective disorder. He would die if he could not bask in the reflected glory of the latest topical event.

'One last question, then I have to run. How's Mr Klepp doing?' I ask her.

'Harold?' She looks at me. 'You haven't heard?'

I shake my head.

'Harold was put on administrative leave, escorted off the Isotenics campus the day after you talked to him at the bar. He hasn't been back since. The only reason they didn't fire him was to keep him quiet. It seems I wasn't the only one at the bar that night.'

What she means is that someone else saw us and told Victor Havlitz.

Nathan spies the network logo on one of the

cameras. 'Be back in a minute,' he says. He sidles over toward the reporter with the microphone standing there, getting ready to do his lead-in for a spot on the nightly news. Kwan hands his newly minted congressional card to the cameraman. The guy is busy making adjustments to his tripod and lights. A second later the three of them, Nathan, the reporter, and the cameraman, are negotiating the news value of a little face time for the freshman congressman.

'I'm sorry to hear it. About Klepp, I mean.' My mind is wandering. Staying up three nights in a row going through boxes and prepping for trial has me exhausted.

'It's fine,' she says. 'Harold already has another job.'

My eyes are on Nathan in front of the camera as Karen talks. He is a perfect politician: glib, superficial, manipulative. He has a grand sense of self and a natural talent for a profession for which lying is usually listed at the top of the job description; in short, the clinical definition of your average sociopath.

I hear the words *Department of Defense* and my hobbled attention is drawn back to Karen. 'They offered him a job auditing software quality control for the Department of Defense, Office of Procurement.' She's talking about Klepp's new job. 'Can you believe it? I don't think Victor knows yet.' She smiles and winks. 'I'd like to be a fly on the wall when they tell him.'

Somehow I suspect that her ear may be connected to Victor's outer door when this happens. Karen Rogan, the keeper of company secrets. I will never know exactly how much she really knew about IFS and Satz, the information they were mining. But my guess is that I barely scratched the surface.

Harry comes out of the courtroom behind me, trailing some print reporters like flies. 'Ruiz wants to talk to you,' he says.

One of the reporters turns on me. 'Mr Madriani, what does this mean for IFS?'

'In a minute,' I tell him.

'See you later. I'm gonna call your office. I want his number.' Karen is talking about Ruiz. She turns and wanders off down the hall.

'They won't release him from the jail until one of us gets the judge to sign the discharge order,' says Harry.

'Why don't you take care of it.'

'He'd like to thank you,' says Harry.

'Right now I have something I have to do. Tell him I'll catch up with him in just a few minutes. Ask him if he can stick around.'

I turn to head down the hall.

'Where are you going?' says Harry.

'County law library,' I tell him.

'The library?' Harry looks baffled. He throws his hands in the air. 'Whatever.'

CHAPTER
THIRTY-FOUR

I take the elevator down to the main floor and go out the door and across the street.

Three minutes later I'm inside the county law library doing a Nexus search on two names.

It takes me less than a minute to find what I'm looking for. The two names, *Nathan Kwan* and *Isotenics, Inc.*, produce a brief news article more than three years old. The dateline is 'Capital City':

> The governor today signed into law SB 1478, the controversial state tax legislation authored by Senator Nathan Kwan (D-Capital City). The legislation is designed to give manufacturers of computer software in the state selling their products or providing services to government agencies sizable state tax incentives that would permit them to reduce their corporate federal income tax liability. The legislation became embroiled in controversy when it was discovered that a single company in Southern California was the exclusive beneficiary of the bill. According to estimates, under the terms of the

legislation, Isotenics, Inc., located in San
Diego County, stands to reap more than $200
million a year in corporate federal income tax
savings.

It is what I feared: the confirmation that Nathan
Kwan murdered Madelyn Chapman.

All the small parts of the puzzle had been in
front of me all the time. For some reason I couldn't
assemble them until Karen slapped me in the face
with the news that Harold Klepp had been
marched from the Isotenics campus the day after I
met with him at the bar. At that moment I knew
that Nathan had lied to me.

The day he came bearing a gift to my office, the
old picture of Nikki in the kitchen in Capital City,
Nathan told me about the telephone conversation
he had overheard while out at Isotenics. He told
me about the midlevel executive named Jack, and
his boss whom he'd never met before, Harold
Klepp, and how he'd overheard Klepp on the phone
talking about IFS and the Defense Department.
The only problem is, Nathan couldn't have heard
the conversation, because Klepp wasn't there. He
was already off the job, posted away from the
Isotenics campus, on administrative leave in a
holding pattern until the end of trial, when they
could fire him.

It's little wonder that Nathan went off to talk to
the reporter and do an interview when he heard
Karen mention Klepp's name and what had
happened to him. His heart must have gone
through the floor when he heard it, wondering if I
would put it together. Why would he bring me
such a lie?

Ordinarily, I might pass it off as a natural

'Kwanism,' Nathan trying to nose his way into the case for political dirt that he could trade in his new job once he got to Washington. But then I remembered that day when Janice handed me his new business card: the one with the embossed gold seal – the one that read *42nd Congressional District*. I had seen that number someplace before.

As I stood in the courthouse hallway, watching Karen Rogan walk away, it hit me. It was on the papers found in Madelyn Chapman's in-basket: the census data that Walter Eagan had scrambled so badly when he was dying, the papers that Chapman had grabbed from Klepp when he told her about the problem. The ones she'd told him to forget about. The ones on her desk the day she died.

There was good reason for her anxiety. She wasn't busy. She was scared. Eagan, Chapman's man Friday, had not made a mistake, he had cooked the numbers in the '42nd District.' Congressional redistricting is performed under federal law every ten years, following the new census. Drawing new boundary lines for congressional districts within each state is done by the state legislature in accordance with rules set forth by law.

In this case Isotenics had been hired by the legislature to create the software so that computers could lay out the new congressional boundary lines for the entire state. They would pump in the census tracking data and prepare a master plan by computer for new boundary lines, adding new congressional seats since the state's population was growing. Within the general guidelines of those projected boundaries, incumbents and ambitious candidates could haggle to cut a few corners, but the major boundaries would usually hold fairly firm. Generally, unless there was a reason, no one would bother to look behind the cut of the initial plan, figuring it was grounded on federal census data. The press would spend all of its time looking for scandals among the shavings where corners were cut and where dragon heads were added to gerrymandered districts.

But Nathan Kwan had mastered a whole new scam. He had captured the process at an earlier stage. He had cooked the numbers at a level deep enough that no one except software experts would ever check. Eagan had arranged the initial software so that the Forty-second District would become a mirror image of Nathan's old state senate seat where name recognition on the ballot would carry the day. Anyone wishing to run against Kwan would be dead on arrival at their campaign headquarters.

It was payback for the tax bill Nathan had carried three years earlier for Chapman and Isotenics. No doubt Eagan probably had to push the boundary lines out of shape on a dozen other districts to make it work.

The problems all started when Eagan died. Stuff fell through the cracks. Klepp saw the numbers. Because he was software-savvy, he was able to check the program. He realized that the tracking data for the original cut didn't add up. If the courts found out, they would order a whole plan, new software to be programmed. Nathan's dream district would end up scattered all over the map, flowing onto the turf of other political warlords who could run against him at election time and kick his ass. He wasn't the only politician hunting for a safe seat in Congress, facing term limits and politician annihilation. Members of the legislature were eating their own in the struggle to survive.

Add to this the fact that Chapman was already embroiled in the political firestorm of her life. Congress and the press were bearing down on the Primis project, Isotenics's crown jewel. She didn't have time for Nathan and his problems. She certainly didn't need the distraction and added strain of a budding scandal over redistricting. Ordinarily it is one of those subjects that tends to cause the eyes of wary citizens to glaze over. Learning that politicians are prone to engage in shady deals when feathering their own nests has all the jarring revelation of informing them that the ancient Greeks spoke Greek. Talk to the average voter about census-tracking data, and they will go to sleep. But tell them about a deal to carve a district in return for a new tax loophole involving bribery, a deal in which the name of a certain company, Isotenics, surfaces and you have a story with legs. Add to the fact that Isotenics is already on the working press's hit parade because of its intrigues with the Pentagon and its proclivity to produce software that allows government to snoop into John Q's e-mail, and you have a story that might just get up on those legs and trample your company.

Chapman's deal with Nathan suddenly took on risks she wasn't prepared to face. If Klepp talked about what he saw, it wouldn't take rocket science to connect the tax bill with the funny district boundary lines favoring Kwan.

Seeing the dangers, and considering Chapman's natural inclination to grow and to defend her empire, she would have cut right to chase. She probably told Kwan to go away. That the deal was off. After all, what could Kwan do? He couldn't go running to the police or the press and complain that Chapman had reneged on a deal to bribe him: a cushy tax break in return for a seat in Congress.

My guess is that when she told him to get out, Nathan must have gone ballistic, Caligula on his worst day. It must have put a shudder through her. This was probably the reason she asked Ruiz to help her out, to keep an eye on her for security's sake, off the books. Chapman couldn't go back to her board of directors and ask for security again, not after making a scene over the video in her office and canning the executive protection detail. The board would want to know why. What could she tell them: that she'd gotten a good deal on bargain day and bought a legislator to boost the bottom line? Corporate directors might appreciate the results, but they wouldn't want to know the details if it might mean an invitation to a courthouse party by way of a felony indictment. Any hint of a scandal and they would push her out the door.

The stage was set for a bloody collision. Unless he wanted to go out, hang a shingle, and go broke practicing law, Nathan had to get rid of her before she could reprogram the redistricting software and scatter his dreams of Congress.

Nathan – the former prosecutor, the former Capital City cop, the ex-Marine – would know a good handgun when he saw one. How he found out about it and knew where it was is anyone's guess. But, knowing Nathan, where there was a will, there was a way.

With the laser sight to zero his shots, the silencer to dampen the recoil, and the railing on the balcony to steady the piece, putting two shots into Chapman's head from upstairs as she stood in

the entry below was probably one of the easier
things he had to accomplish that day. On the others
he didn't do as well.

In the brief time that he was a prosecutor, the
analysis of evidence was not high among Nathan's
gifts and talents. The closest Nathan ever got to a
crime scene as a cop was setting up barricades at
the perimeter and driving by in a squad car.
Putting the silencer on the rocks and setting the
pistol in the flower bed as if it were made of crystal
– I'm sure that never dawned on him as an issue.

Nathan's burning need to know where the case
was going, and to steer it in any direction except
the one that might take it back to his own front
door to roost, was the reason Kwan attached
himself to me and why he has been camped in the
courthouse for the last two weeks. Nathan wasn't
there to glad-hand the press: he was trying to make
sure that all the diversion he engaged in that day
at Chapman's house continued to lead us all in the
wrong direction.

I print out a copy of the story on Kwan's tax bill
and walk toward the elevator. If we had our cell
phones I would call Harry at the courthouse and give
him a heads-up. As it is, they are locked in our cars
out in the parking lot.

In the empty elevator I ride to the main floor.
It's already getting dark outside. I hustle out the
front door, right into his arms.

'I was wondering what you were doing, going to
the library. What do we have here?' Nathan plucks
the folded paper from my hand before I can fold it
further and lose it in a pocket.

He opens it and reads. 'That's what I thought.'
At this moment Nathan seems filled with regret,
his face a portrait of lament. He shakes his head,

but doesn't say anything, as if he can't speak. 'I never wanted it to come to this,' he finally says.

When I look down, he is holding a small automatic, blued gunmetal, the slide on top slick with oil glistening in the light from the street lamp overhead. It's almost lost in his hand, which is tucked under his open suit coat. Anyone looking at him, even up close, might think he has his thumb tucked over the top edge of his belt, talking to me western style.

A block down, on Broadway, the street is teeming with people, all heading home at rush hour. But on the side street along the courthouse, the sidewalk is empty.

The gun looks like a .380. Deadly. Gang-bangers use them all the time because they are easy to hide.

'Nathan, you don't want to do this.'

'You're right, I don't.' He shakes his head.

I can't imagine the panic and confusion going on inside his brain at this moment.

'Why couldn't you just leave it alone?' he says. 'You won your case. Your man is free. Why did you have to go poking your nose in? I love you, but you're a . . .'

A woman comes out the door of the library, shoots us a quick glance, and keeps going.

'You're a pain in the ass,' he finishes the thought.

I start to walk past him, like I'm going to follow the woman toward the courthouse across the street. Kwan moves in front of me and blocks the way, his little pistol almost in my stomach.

'Don't. I want to talk,' he says. 'I want you to understand.'

'Nathan, listen to yourself. Do you hear what you're saying?' At the moment I have to wonder if I'm talking to Jekyll or Hyde.

His eyes dart toward the entrance of the library, where the lights have just flickered. Closing time. He knows we can't stand here.

'Let's go this way.' He follows up the suggestion by nudging me with his free hand, turning me away from the courthouse.

I turn and start to walk, slowly.

'Nathan, listen to me.'

I start to raise my hands—he says, 'Put 'em down.'

'Nathan.'

'Don't . . . don't talk right now, just walk.'

He is right behind me, the pistol in his outside coat pocket. Nathan knows this is a risky area. The jail is just down the street ahead of us, the courthouse behind us.

When someone has a gun in your back, there is a natural inclination to cooperate. But reason tells me that, given what I now know, if he gets me out of this area, I'm a dead man.

He comes up next to me like we're two friends strolling down the sidewalk, with me on the inside. He now has both hands stuffed into the pockets of his suit jacket so that it looks more natural. End-of-the-day working stiff just stretching the pockets of his coat.

If I try to run he is going to put a bullet in me. Maybe more than one, considering the speed with which a .380 can fire.

In the distance I see a figure, a lone man wearing jeans and a light tan jacket as he steps from the main entrance of the county jail a block away. He turns and walks up the street toward us on the other side. In the dim light just after dusk I cannot make out any features, though he appears to be looking this way. For an instant I think about calling out. Nathan reads my mind.

'Let's take a short cut.' He takes his left hand out of his pocket, turns to me, and guides me toward an alley that divides the block.

'Keep going,' he says. He's looking around, at the sides of the building and the utility poles. My guess is Nathan is looking for cameras. He's not taking me for a ride. Whatever he's going to do, he intends to do it here.

Kwan is pushing me westward along the alley. This is not good. There is nothing ahead except littered service entrances and a few dumpsters. With muni buses a block away, revving their engines as they pull away from the bus stop at rush hour, if Nathan pushes me against the side of a building and gets up close, he could put a bullet in me and it's possible no one would even hear it.

We cross the street and we're halfway down the alley on the next block when he stops just beyond the end of a large green metal dumpster. 'This will do,' he says.

I turn and look at him. 'This is where you want to talk?'

He pushes me into the breach formed by the end of the metal bin and the concrete protrusion that is the rear service entrance to a building.

My back is against the wall.

'You wouldn't understand,' he says. 'You couldn't.' There's a sound like someone clearing his throat in the alley behind him.

As Nathan turns to look, there is a quick flash, a reflection off an arcing stream that disappears in the shadows of his face, his free hand reaching up toward his eyes. The stringent smell.

I hear him moan as I reach out and push the hand with the gun to the side and away.

'Excuse me.' Before I can even process what I

491

am seeing, Emiliano Ruiz closes the distance like an apparition. He is wearing jeans and a tan jacket, the figure I saw exiting the jail. In a fluid motion he takes the gun in one hand and the back of Nathan's head in the other. When he brings his knee up, Kwan's head sounds like a hollow melon hitting a boulder. Nathan's knees buckle, and he hits the asphalt like a sack of cement.

Stripping the clip from the .380, Emiliano pulls the slide and ejects the round from the chamber while he bares his teeth, holding a small red plastic squirt gun between them.

I'm leaning against the wall of the building, unable to stand upright with Kwan lying across my feet.

Ruiz takes the squirt gun from between his teeth, tosses the metal pistol into the dumpster, and crushes the clip under the heel of his shoe. Then he rolls Kwan off my feet so I can stand up.

Ruiz is wearing street clothes, the T-shirt, jacket, and jeans that I must assume he was wearing the night the cops arrested him. You would never recognize him in a crowd. The everyman, wiry and invisible.

'They took me back to the jail so I could change, get my stuff. I was heading back to the courthouse to look for you. You disappeared. Then I saw you coming this way, but you went down the alley. I thought I'd check it out. Didn't think you guys were ever gonna stop walking,' he says. 'And I didn't want to leave without saying good-bye.'

CHAPTER THIRTY-FIVE

Every so often my thoughts drift to Jim Kaprosky and the notion that at least someone benefited from his years of toil in legal hell. Emiliano Ruiz is a free man.

In all, he had spent more than a year behind bars, confined in county jail, awaiting trial. For twenty-three hours each day he had been held in an eight-by-twelve-foot cell, isolated from other inmates because of information, vague in its nature, communicated by the military to jail officials that Ruiz was skilled in the martial arts and that he should be considered an extreme risk as an inmate.

About six months ago I received a letter. It was from Emiliano. He now lives somewhere along the Deschutes River in the state of Oregon. He has gone to court in order to legally change his name in an effort to recover some of the peace and privacy that he had before his became branded in the public psyche as the 'Double Tap Killer.' Along with the letter was a picture of Emiliano standing in front of a small mobile home. Next to him was his new wife. She was holding their first child. Both were flaming redheads.

Nathan Kwan was arrested and prosecuted for the murder of Madelyn Chapman, attempted murder for his acts in the alley with me, as well as a number of felonies involving political corruption. Kwan's lawyers were able to cut a deal so that the former legislator and congressman is now serving a term of more than thirty years at Pelican Bay.

They might never have convicted Kwan in Chapman's murder except for one thing: the *Orb at the Edge*. The piece itself is now resting unceremoniously somewhere in a landfill. Nathan admitted that, had he known what it was worth, he might have been tempted to fence it. But, knowing Kwan, I doubt it. The risk that the cops might find it and trace it back to him were simply too great. Nathan placed it in a large plastic trash bag and smashed it into small shards before depositing all the sharp little pieces in a dumpster behind a grocery store in Chula Vista the night of the murder. The problem for Nathan was that some of the pieces didn't stay in the bag. Trace evidence found on a pair of slacks in Nathan's closet revealed small shards of blue glass along with traces of dust, a unique compound of lead and powered pigments known to have been specially mixed and used by the artist in crafting the blue *Orb*. It is the problem with a piece of art that is peerless: the materials used to make it are often one of a kind. Nathan's strong suit was never evidence.

As part of his plea bargain, Nathan also gave up information regarding the murder weapon and how he knew where to find it. It turns out this was a gift from Chapman's Mexican maid, the one who walked off the job one day and never came back.

Kwan, who had watched Chapman's house on

and off for more than a month, guessed that the maid was illegal. He followed her home, found out where she lived and where she hung out. She went to a local tavern at night. Nathan dressed down, struck up a conversation, and fed her drinks at the bar one evening. After she was mildly swacked, he made sure the word *Isotenics* came up so that the woman tried to impress him with the fact that she worked for Chapman, who owned the company. He picked up details about the size and the layout of the house, the fact that Chapman never turned on the security system. And then the clincher: the maid volunteered that she had stumbled over a very large pistol in a dresser drawer upstairs when she was putting things away one day. Apparently it frightened her. Nathan couldn't believe his good luck. As he told his interrogators, 'If you have to shoot somebody, it's always nice if you can get them to supply the gun.' Kwan wanted the cops to be looking in the wrong direction from the get-go. He knew the caliber of the gun from the description the maid gave him. She remembered enough of the letters engraved on the side that it took Nathan less than five minutes searching online before he found the Mark 23, a contract piece made for Special Operations Command that only came in forty-five caliber. As far as Nathan was concerned, he'd found the Grail. He brought his own bullets and then discovered he didn't need them. He swapped out rounds anyway, just to mix things up in an effort to confuse the cops further.

When he was finished fishing for information, Nathan drove the maid from Chapman's house with an anonymous call from a pay phone one afternoon. He identified himself as an angry neighbor and told her that Immigration was on their way out to pick her up. The woman left and never came back. This removed the final live-in obstacle to Chapman's house.

Kwan will not be eligible for parole until he is nearly seventy years old.

In the months since he was arrested, pled out, and sentenced, the media frenzy surrounding the name *Nathan Kwan* has transformed it into a synonym for corruption that makes it difficult for me to recall that there was ever a time, in another life, when Nathan was a friend, part of the social unit that was my world.

I have often wondered what part of the cancer that ate his soul resides, perhaps in a more benign state, within each of us: the need for approval, the appetite for adulation that comes from some ancient, subterranean part of our being.

Nathan could tell you about every good cause and social need, from education and protection of the environment to the banishment of poverty, and was willing to tax us to the nth degree to pay for them all. At times he could make you love him, as he did that day when he delivered the photograph to my office.

In the next breath he could sell his soul to some liquor lobbyist or gambling tycoon, carving a massive tax exemption in the law for their benefit, and he would see nothing wrong in any of this. He would laugh and tell you that consistency was 'the hobgoblin of little minds.' The next day he would climb back on the stump and rail against loopholes for the rich, and under Nathan's definitions of truth and commitment he would mean it.

I wonder if I knew him at all, or whether it is even possible to discern those forces that transform the human soul to commit an act so calculated and brutal as the murder of Madelyn Chapman.

As for Isotenics and the government's IFS program, or Information for Security: congressional committees, the Pentagon, and civil-liberty groups continue to battle in a ceaseless war of probes and investigations. With ever-emerging technologies and the explosion of classified projects within the government, it will probably never be known to what degree private information has been plundered. What is certain is the peril that such technologies present for the future. Given the mandate by governments that all shall participate in the advances of the electronic age, the pace, noise, and fury of the future carries with it immense risks for privacy and the inevitable destruction of those sheltered and quiet places where each of us can reside in peace.

EPILOGUE

A few years ago I found myself sitting in my study, tears running down my face. My aunt had called to tell me that my uncle, my father's little brother, Evo, had died. He had been diagnosed with throat cancer a few months earlier, the chimney that never stopped smoking, and was in the hospital for tests when his heart gave out. The death certificate read *myocardial infarction*. In a way it was merciful. My father had passed away two years earlier. Now they were both gone.

In later years Evo's mental state had improved enough so that he lived at least at the margins of normal life. New medications and therapy helped. While his moods could swing wildly and severe stress could put him in his chair to stare at the wall, he was able to drive again, though he never went far. He ran errands for my grandmother in the years before she died.

As my father grew older and his health failed, I found myself filling the void.

I once had to help Evo out of a scrap with the law. Pulled over in a routine traffic stop, you might think his first instinct would be to run, but it wasn't. Seeing the red light in his mirror, Evo crossed two lanes of traffic and slammed on his brakes so quickly that a man riding a ten speed along the shoulder plowed into the back of my uncle's car.

The fellow ended up on top of Evo's trunk, upside down but unhurt, and mad as hell. Weeks later my uncle could laugh about it, gapped teeth and all. But at the time it wasn't funny.

The initial stop for a bad brake light now produced an angry cyclist and a cop, who I am sure was beginning to wish he had never seen my uncle or his car. It was about to get worse.

Screaming at my uncle from behind the cop, the cyclist demanded that Evo be arrested. In the meantime my uncle was fumbling with his wallet.

Told to get his license out, Evo couldn't get the lumber that were his thumbs and fingers to function enough to slip the license from the plastic window in his wallet. He tried to give the wallet to the cop. The officer wouldn't touch it, only the license. Evo wasn't saying anything. He was trying to stay away from the cyclist, whose adrenaline rush was being enhanced by elevated testosterone levels, now that he realized this colossus driving the car wanted no part of him.

At some point, amid the shouting and chaos and with Evo backpeddling up the sidewalk, my uncle tried to pass the officer a twenty-dollar bill. The officer wasn't sure whether Evo was trying to pay the fine, bribe him, or simply purchase continuing protection against the cyclist.

With the cop in the middle, it must have looked like a comic maypole: a spindly, red-faced cyclist in tights, jumping up and down, shouting, trying to reach around to grab some shirt every few seconds, coming away instead with a few hairs the texture of fence wire from my uncle's arm. People driving by must have thought the guy was on drugs, chasing someone with ten inches of reach and a hundred pounds on him. If Evo had fallen on the guy, the man's injuries would have been fatal.

Unable to get his license out, with the cop in the middle and the cyclist pushing them up the street, Evo kept pulling the only thing he could get his fingers on from his wallet: currency from the large open pocket.

With a fistful of bills in his face and an agitated biker climbing up his back, demanding an arrest, the cop did the only thing he could. Evo found himself snagged in the gears of the law, sitting in the county jail, charged with a fix-it ticket for a bad brake light and bribery of a peace officer – a possible four-year stint in the joint, depending on the amount of cash in his hand at any given moment.

It took me an hour to get Evo out of jail with an order signed by a judge. It took me a few more days and a carload of medical records from the VA to convince a supervisor in the DA's office that he really didn't want to go to trial, bribery being a crime of specific intent. Evo had full mental disability, certified by the government with shrinks in attendance to testify; he was a man who'd had more voltage passed through his body than most cons strapped to 'Old Sparky'; who during periods of his life had difficulty forming the requisite intent to get out of his chair and walk to the kitchen – and when he did, he usually couldn't remember why he'd started the journey. It was not a case in which to sound the bugle and mount the charge for clean government.

After viewing the size of the box and feeling the

weight of the medical records inside, the prosecutor allowed my uncle to fix his brake light and go. And so we did.

But even in death it seems my uncle was fated. My aunt, his sister, was to endure one last losing battle, this one with the VA. I learned years later that my uncle's military records never properly reflected his first name. At induction, some clerk had typed in the name 'Elvo,' instead of 'Evo,' so that to this day it is the name 'Elvo' that marks his grave. Go online and you can find it – the name Elvo Angelo in the records of the Golden Gate National Cemetery. Like the tomb of the unknown, Evo rests for eternity, under another name.

The experience with my uncle taught me that not all men who die in wars are buried immediately. It also gave me an abiding respect for those who have experienced what most of us have not: the indescribable chaos and horror of battle, and the nightmare memories, images and visions that sear the soul.